Walking
on
Broken Glass

WALKING
ON
BROKEN GLASS

Christa Allan

Abingdon Press fiction
a novel approach to faith

Nashville, Tennessee

Walking on Broken Glass

Copyright © 2010 by Christa Allan

ISBN-13: 978-1-4267-0227-3

Published by Abingdon Press, P.O. Box 801, Nashville, TN 37202

www.abingdonpress.com

Published in association with WordServe Literary Group, Ltd.,
10152 S. Knoll Circle, Highlands Ranch, CO 80130

Cover design by Anderson Design Group, Nashville, TN

Library of Congress Cataloging-in-Publication Data

Allan, Christa.
    Walking on broken glass / Christa Allan.
      p. cm.
    ISBN 978-1-4267-0227-3
    1. African American women—Fiction. 2. Women alcoholics—Fiction.
I. Title.
    PS3601.L4125W35 2010
    813'.6—dc22

Printed in the United States of America

1 2 3 4 5 6 7 8 9 10 / 15 14 13 12 11 10

In memory of my precious grandson
Bailey Ramon Cadoree
who taught me how to live
April 23–May 24, 2000

Acknowledgments

You're holding my dream. Because of the thin threads God wove to connect people, places, and events, it became a reality—a reality that far outshone the one I'd always imagined. But then that's what makes God awesome.

Henry David Thoreau said, "If you have built castles in the air, your work need not be lost; that is where they should be. Now put the foundations under them." My castle has been built; now I'd like to introduce you to everyone responsible for its foundation.

To my five children:

Michael: purveyor of medical information and father of Emma and Hannah, my delightful grandgirls whose smiles remind me what's truly important.

Erin: my ever-patient Google-girl, formatter, critiquer, and finder of minutiae, who endured listening to me whine and fret, and still answered my calls. Bless you, Andrae, my generous son-in-law, for sacrificing your time with Erin so she could help me.

Shannon: without you, I wouldn't know Marc Jacobs from Mark Twain, and I certainly would be a fashion nightmare, as would my characters. I'm learning to walk in high heels, I promise. Your humor provided my stress-relief.

Sarah: you spent time with puzzles and books without complaining while Mommy wrote. You also learned how to fix my coffee; you're a trooper.

John: I've followed your Facebook rules, so now it's your turn to make good on your promise to marry Oprah so I can score a guest spot. Or, you can use your influence and book me on the Les Miles show. In the meantime, thanks for being you.

To my brother, Johnny Bassil, who loved me when I wasn't lovable; your support has been my anchor. To Carolyn Ekman, my mother-in-law, for your calls, your company, and your kindnesses.

To Carrie Randolph, who knew about this novel when it was a baby, and whose enthusiasm gave me the courage to keep typing. You've traveled so many roads with me; your friendship has been a generous gift. To Shelley Easterling Gay whose lesson-sharing saved me during my writing marathons and whose feedback I respected. You and Carrie put the brain in my storm. To Melissa Strata-Burger and Carole Jordan for readings on demand. To the GNO group for monthly sanity dinners and girl-talk.

Dennis and Rhonda Stelly and Linda Moffett: for harboring us after Hurricane Katrina.

To my Barbe High School students, for encouraging my dream. To my Fontainebleau High School extended family, for nurturing and celebrating it, and to Lakeshore High School's staff and students, for being a part of its arrival.

Thanks to: Cheryl Wyatt, my constant cheerleader when I first dared to write. Lisa Samson, whose critique of this novel in its early stages pushed me forward. Jessica Ferguson for insisting I attend an ACFW Conference, and to Mary DeMuth for reaching out and giving me hope.

A venti-sized thanks to Rachelle Gardner of WordServe Literary, my dynamic and industrious agent, who "got" Leah. Your phone call changed my life. You walk me off ledges, steer me back to writing, and teach me how to be a professional in this business.

7

To Barbara Scott, my fearless and tireless editor at Abingdon Press, who championed this novel: I admire your faith, appreciate your tenacity, and enjoy your friendship. You believed in Leah, and I will be forever grateful. Thank you for your expertise in bringing her story to life.

To Peggy Shearon, Fiction Publicist, and all those at Abingdon: thank you for all you do to bring our novels to readers.

To my husband, Ken: You played more golf, cooked more meals, and watched more movies so you could disappear during deadlines and I could focus on writing. Your confidence in me gave me courage. Your goofy jokes made me laugh when I wanted to cry. And when I didn't believe in myself, you did, and you let me lean on you until my belief could stand on its own. I'm so grateful for the ways you've blessed my life.

And to everyone who reads this novel, thank you for turning these pages.

Patient Discharge Statement

If I had known children break on the inside and the cracks don't surface until years later, I would have been more careful with my words.

If I had known some parents don't live to watch grandchildren grow, I would have taken more pictures and been more careful with my words.

If I had known couples can be fragile and want what they are unprepared to give or unwilling to take, I would have been more careful with my words.

If I had known teaching lasts a lifetime and students don't speak of their tragic lives, I would have been more careful with my words.

If I had known my muscles and organs and bones and skin are not lifetime guarantees, that when broken, snagged, unstitched, or unseemly, cannot be replaced, I would have been kinder to the shell that prevents my soul from leaking out.

If I had known I would live over half my life and have to look at photographs to remember my mother adjusting my birthday party hat so that my father could take the picture that sliced the moment out of time—if I had known, if I had known—I would have been more careful with my life.

Leah T.
August 4

1

Cruising the sparkling aisles of Catalano's Supermarket, I lost my sanity buying frozen apple juice.

Okay, so maybe it started several aisles before the refrigerated cases. Somewhere between the canned vegetables and cleaning supplies. I needed to kill the taste of that soy milk in my iced vanilla latte. Darn my friend Molly, the dairy Nazi. I blamed her for my detour to the liquor aisle. Decisions. Decisions. Decisions. What to pour in my Starbucks cup? Amaretto? Kahlua? Vodka? And the winner was . . . Amaretto. Perfect for an afternoon grocery event.

Ramping up the coffee seemed like a reasonable idea at the time. I'd left the end-of-the-year faculty party and thought I'd be a considerate wife and pick up dinner for Carl on the way home. He told me before he left for work that morning that he'd meet me at the party. Probably he had one too many meetings, which, since I'd probably had one too many beers, made us just about even. Don't know if we matched spin cycles in our brains, though. That was the point of the coffee. A rinse cycle of sorts.

I'd just avoided a game of bumper carts with the oncoming traffic in the organic food aisle when I remembered that I needed juice. On the way to the freezer section, I maneuvered a difficult curve around the quilted toilet tissue display. My coffee sloshed in the cup in tempo with my stomach. I braked too swiftly by the refrigerator case, and a wave of latte splotched my linen shorts and newly pedicured toes. Ick.

Rows of orange juice. Apple juice was on the third shelf down. I reached in and, like a one-armed robot, I selected and returned can after can of juice, perplexed by the dilemma of cost versus quality. *Okay, this one's four cents an ounce cheaper than this one. But this one's . . .*

My face would have reflected my growing agitation, but the stale icy air swirling out of the freezer numbed it. I held the door open with one hand, tried to sip my coffee with the other, and wondered how long it would take before full body paralysis set in. I stared at apple juice cans. They stared back. Something shifted, and my body broke free from a part of itself, and there I was—or there we were. I watched me watch the cans. The rational me separated from the wing-nut me, who still pondered the perplexities of juice costs. Rational me said, "Let's get her out of here before she topples head first into the freezer case and completely humiliates herself."

I abandoned my cart, a lone testament to my struggle and defeat, near the freezer cases and walked away. If I could fill my brain with alcohol like I filled my car with gas, it wouldn't have to run on empty. It wouldn't leave me high and dry in the middle of a grocery store aisle.

No, not dry this time. High. My brain is either high or dry, and it doesn't seem to function well either way.

So that was my epiphany for sobriety.

Apple juice.

2

Carl was late, too late to watch me as I weaved my way from garage to bedroom.

What was today?

Friday. Forgot.

Carl's poker night. Reprieve.

I opened my bedroom closet door and considered changing into my scrubs, but that would've meant negotiating a path to the laundry room to pull them out of the dryer. Since I'd submerged my internal GPS in an Amaretto bath, I doubted I'd make it. The T-shirt and shorts I wore would do just fine. I peeled away the layers of comforter and blankets on my side and let the sheets tug the weight of my weariness into bed.

Two bathroom visits later, I felt the mattress concede as Carl's body plowed onto his side of our bed. As usual, he reached his arm toward me, his right hand landing on my hip. As usual, I didn't move and waited for the morning.

I woke up a rumpled mess, still wearing my coffee-stained shorts and black tee. I didn't need a mirror to know my flat-ironed hair was smashed to my head, except for the twisted front bangs, which stood off my forehead in a lame salute. The sunlight from the bay window drilled through my eyelids. I slapped my face into the pillow but instantly regretted disturbing what could only be tiny thunderbolts in my brain. I needed to see a doctor. I woke up with far too many head throbs.

I felt the swaddled tightness as I rolled over. Carl always tucked in the sheet on his side of the bed as if to prevent me from rolling out. I turned toward the empty space on the other side of the bed to escape the sharpshooter sun.

I plucked the note left on his pillow. Thin, angular letters: "Golf at 8. Call Molly." At the bottom, smaller print but all caps: "LET YOU SLEEP. CAN'T WAIT FOR YOU TONIGHT." I shoved the note under his pillow and tried not to breathe in the whisper of his musky orange cologne.

Why did I remember what I wanted to forget, yet forget what I wanted to remember?

I stared at the ceiling, my eyes stung by my own thoughtlessness. Molly was probably geared up for major annoyance. Saturday mornings were reserved for our two-mile trek through the greenbelt trails of Brookforest. Late was not a time on her clock. I still wore my watch, and late ticked away: 9:00.

Molly Richardson and I met two years ago at the Christmas party for Morgan Management. Both of our husbands had recently joined the firm. She and I had barreled into the bathroom, about as much as one could barrel in ruffled silk chiffon and elastic-backed, three-inch spiked shoes. We crashed reaching for the door handle.

Molly grabbed the knob, steadied herself, scanned me, and said, "We have to stop meeting like this. People will talk."

A woman with a sense of humor and cool shoes in the midst of granite-faced consultants. Our friendship had expanded since then beyond the boundaries of business. We knew almost everything there was to know about each other. Almost everything.

I willed myself to vertical and plodded to the phone on Carl's side of the bed. One of our concessions after we moved into this house: blinding sun in my eyes; ringing phone in his ears.

I punched in Molly's number.

One ring. "You up?" she said.

"Meet you there in fifteen." I hung up knowing Molly would understand that fifteen meant twenty. I yanked on clean shorts and a sports bra, but kept the leftover T-shirt from yesterday. Yesterday. Apple juice. Was today the day I would practice not drinking? Did I pay for groceries? No bags on the kitchen counter. A half bagel waited on a plate.

I passed on breakfast and grabbed my keys from the top of the washing machine. Carl really needed to hang a key rack. I locked the leaded glass doors, unlocked the wrought-iron gate, and walked through a gauntlet of Tudor and French provincial houses. Molly and I always met at the cul-de-sac entrance to the trails at the end of my street.

Molly was in her ready zone. She alternated long, bouncing genuflects to stretch her legs.

"I'm always amazed that your calves are almost as long as my legs," I said and slid the fuzzy banana-yellow headband hanging around my neck to around my head to tame my disobedient hair.

"Save that for one of your hyperbole lessons." A tint of anger edged her words.

"Hey, Moll, I'm sorry. Carl forgot to wake me up when he left for golf this morning."

"It's his fault you're late?" I knew tone, and her tone definitely indicated she thought exactly the opposite. "Did he wake you up for school too?"

Sarcasm lesson. "Sometimes," I said.

She smiled.

I moved close to forgiveness. "Okay, almost always."

A laugh.

Suffering over.

"Let's get started before the sun sucks the life out of us," she said.

Only a silo-sized vacuum cleaner hose could suck the energy out of Molly. Twenty years younger and she'd be on meds for hyperactivity. Instead, she's on meds for infertility. She and Devin had been baby practicing for almost two years. Practice had not made perfect. Over a year ago, when I told her I was pregnant, I almost wanted to apologize. Carl and I hadn't planned to be parents. But we were. For six weeks. Then Alyssa died. I stopped feeling guilty around Molly. Mostly I stopped feeling.

I bent over, pretended to adjust my shoelace, and hoped Molly didn't see the grief floating in my eyes.

"I'm ready." I popped up. Perky trumps pity. "And wait till you hear what happened."

When I chronicled the latest school dramas, my body didn't feel so heavy as I pounded my way down the path. A paralegal for trial attorneys, Molly didn't share many details about work. We entertained ourselves some days imagining which kids in detention would become lawyers and which ones would need lawyers.

"So, get this, I'm handing out tests, and—"

Her power walk shifted down two gears. She held up her hand and said, "No, Leah. Stop." American manicure this week, I noticed.

I looked over my shoulders thinking some school person had materialized behind us and Molly had just rescued me from embarrassment and possible unemployment. No one.

"Safe. Trail clear of suspects." I rattled on.

Another shift down. We now strolled.

"I have to talk to you about something, and it has to be today." She tucked her shoulder-length cinnamon-shaded hair behind her ears, a habit I'd learned meant she was ready for serious.

I sidestepped a clump of strange goo. "What's up?"

Molly pointed to a bench where the path split to lead to the pool or school. That always struck me as an unfair choice for kids on their way to school in the mornings.

She sat. Scary news was sit-down talk. I paced.

"You drink too much."

My feet stopped, but my soul lurched. My ship of composure pitched suddenly on this wave of information. I willed myself to calmness, "Who are you, Molly? AA's new spokeswoman?" The ten-year-old inside of me rose to the surface. "Oops, gender bias. New spokesperson?"

"I'm serious. No more jokes. I've been praying about this for weeks, not knowing how to say this to you. After last night, I knew it couldn't wait."

"Oh, so God told you to talk to me. Got it." I scattered pinecones with the tip of my Nikes.

"I don't think you get it," Molly said. "God hasn't text messaged me about you." Her cool hand wrapped itself around my wrist. "Would you sit down, please?"

I wanted to walk away—run, really—but her words anchored my heart. I couldn't move. I waited. I waited to breathe again. Waited for the tornado of emotions to stop swirling in my chest. I sat.

"Yesterday, Carrie called to see if you'd made it home. She wanted to drive you, but you absolutely refused. When she asked about whether to call Carl to pick you up, you told her . . . well, that's not worth repeating."

"So I had a few too many. It was a party. People drank. I drank. I'll apologize to Carrie for whatever I said."

"You don't remember, do you? Do you remember that night we went to Rizzo's for the company dinner?" She paused while two tricycling kids and a set of parents meandered past us.

If my brain had a file cabinet of events, the drawers were stuck. Dinner at Rizzo's. Retirement. Somebody retired. I tugged at the memory and tried to coax it out.

"Of course I remember. That guy, what was his name? He retired." I leaned back and wished the wrought-iron bench slats were padded.

"And?" Not really a question.

"And, what? Since you already know the answer."

"Leah," she said and leaned toward me. I still couldn't look at her. "Dinner was late. You grabbed the wine bottle from the waiter, gave him your wine glass, and then told him you two were even. You said if we'd pound our silverware on the table, we'd be served faster. You almost dropped a full bowl of gumbo in your lap. You said it looked like something you'd thrown up the night before."

I wanted a button to zap a force field around me. I wanted silence. A piece of me had broken, and Molly had found it. If I talked too much, other pieces might shatter. I couldn't risk it. I couldn't risk turning inside out.

"You were out of control," she said, the words filed by her softness so the edges were smooth when they pushed into me.

Yes, and out of control was exactly what I'd planned.

I couldn't look at Molly yet. I couldn't admit to my best friend in the universe that Carl told me almost every night something was terribly wrong with me. I thought I'd managed to divide myself quite nicely: Leah in the bedroom and Leah outside of the bedroom.

"I want to disappear," I said to the grass blades mashed under my shoes.

"You are disappearing. That's the problem. You're my friend. I want you here." She slid next to me and placed her hand on my shoulder. "In the two years we've known each other, your drinking has gotten worse. I know you suffered after losing Alyssa. I know you still do. But you need help, or something awful is going to happen."

I wanted to hate her. But how could I hate a friend who loved me enough to save my life?

"I lost my sanity at the apple juice case," I repeated to Dolores, the intake clerk who scribbled information onto whatever form they used to admit the inebriated. She placed her pencil on the glass-topped desk, clasped her hands over the clipboard, and peered at me over her reading glasses.

"Were you buying it to mix drinks?" she asked quietly, as if afraid the question would hurt me.

I'm being admitted into rehab by a woman who clearly failed to understand that apple juice mixed with few, if any, hard liquors. My galloping knees knew *that* was something to be jittery about. Hadn't I explained the twelve-pack of beer in the grocery cart? Why would I be worried about mixing? Did rehab centers hire teetotalers so they'd never have to worry about employee discounts for services?

"Noooo. It just seemed too overwhelming to decide which brand to buy. You know, the whole cost per ounce thing."

No doubt Dolores knew I was ready for admission after that, but she persisted. She asked who referred me.

"This was all my friend Molly's idea. She even made the appointment for me. This morning after our walk. Before my husband's golf game ended." Good grief. My inner child needed a nap.

This information about Molly seemed both unsurprising and amusing to Dolores. "Yes, it often works that way. People see in us what we can't see in ourselves. Don't need mirrors here."

Thirty minutes later, Dolores and I agreed I would voluntarily admit myself the morning of July 4.

Leah Adair Thornton. Age 27. Middle-stage alcoholic.

3

Carl . . . I'm checking into Brookforest, the rehab clinic . . ."

Carl looked as if someone was approaching him with a rope and a fast horse.

Seeing his eyebrows almost meet in the middle of his face, I was relieved he'd chosen a table wedged in the corner instead of a booth in the middle of the restaurant.

The strategy Molly and I had concocted was for the night to conclude with my enlightened and sympathetic husband reassuring me all would be well. Already the plan required some tweaking. Maybe, before I blabbered on, I could guarantee background noise by paying a bus-person to strategically drop a tray of dishes.

"How is it that you've suddenly decided you drink too much? Maybe it's not the drinking. Maybe you're just having a nervous breakdown."

Carl had obviously not read the script I'd mentally prepared for him.

I should have planned this better. Having breakfast as dinner to tell my husband of five years I'm leaving him for a month was probably frowned on by Dolores and the admissions staff at rehab. But after tonight, it might be a new question on the screening test:

"Do you consider breakfast a more appropriate meal at which to reveal your addiction to a loved one?"

When I announced I thought I drank too much, I theorized it'd be best not to be drinking. Although breakfast could be counted technically on the list of acceptable meals for having drinks. On our last visit to New Orleans, we'd reserved a table in the Garden Room at Commander's Palace. I had gauzy memories of sipping mimosas and Bloody Marys, listening to jazz, and sleeping in the taxi on the way back to our hotel. But our local Eggs in a Basket in my little suburban oasis was as far a cry from Commander's as I was from being an angel in a Victoria's Secret commercial.

I managed to remain mute until waitress Tina finished jotting our orders and cruised off in the direction of the kitchen before I answered Carl.

"Right. A nervous breakdown. I'm having a nervous breakdown—in the summer when I'm not teaching." My drawling sarcasm shifted to rising frustration. "Besides, haven't those gone out of style? Really, does anyone even have a nervous breakdown in the twenty-first century? What is that anyway?"

Rhetorical question lesson.

"What do you want from me, Leah? I think I'm meeting you for dinner, and you slam me with this?" He slid his fingers into the top pocket of his shirt, reaching for his phantom cigarettes. He quit two years ago, but the gesture lingered.

Tina materialized from behind me and placed the coffee carafe on the table. She smiled at Carl, who'd started orchestrating his dining concerto. First, he slid the utensils from the faux-cloth napkin. Then, one by one, the knife, fork, and spoon pirouetted in one hand while he wiped them off with the napkin in his other hand. It was a ritual I expected at every meal away from home, but this was Tina's first show. She was mesmerized. Carl, however, was oblivious to his one-woman audience.

Still no coffee cups.

I leaned forward, as if on the brink of revealing tabloid information. "Tina," I whispered, "what's the likelihood of finding cups for the coffee?"

Her crimson lips puckered as if they'd just been pried off a lemon. She puffed her cheeks and sashayed off to what I hoped was the holy grail of lost coffee cups.

Carl was either studying his reflection in the spoon or analyzing a smidge of gunk. I watched him. In that silly moment, surrounded by strangers and noise, I glimpsed the Carl of my heart and heard fragments of delicious laughter. It swished by like those faces on the metro in Ezra Pound's poem, like petals on a wet, black bough. If only I could collect them to reassemble a relationship.

The high-chaired baby behind him leaned over, bombed the floor with scrambled egg, and applauded himself. I tried not to stare, but tides of longing swelled in the hollowness that should have been filled with Alyssa.

Carl waved his hand in front of me. "Come back. Food's here." I'd obviously underestimated Tina's stealth capacity. Again, she hovered. Her brown tray seesawed near my head. My head, not Carl's.

She transferred her cargo of blueberry blintzes, whole wheat pancakes, and, finally, coffee cups to our table. She wedged her tray on her left hip and plunged her free hand into her tassel of chocolate hair braids.

The young waitress produced a pencil with a flair David Copperfield would have applauded. "Anything else y'all need?"

Sure, place my order for love, joy, peace, patience, kindness, goodness, faithfulness, gentleness, and self-control. But Tina was in the business of feeding bodies, not souls. I just said, "No, thanks."

Carl's attention shifted to his plate. Each round, golden pancake was stabbed and lifted with one fork tine. He swirled his buttered knife between each one in figure-eight patterns so precise the Olympic committee would have awarded him a 9.7 score—at least if the judge from China cooperated.

I poured myself a cup of coffee and wondered again how to explain my drinking problem to the man who, oddly enough, always said I was never satisfied. If I told him about a fabulous house under construction nearby, he'd ask why the one we lived in wasn't good enough for me. I thought we had conversations; instead, he thought we had indictments.

"Pretend someone asked if you wanted to invest gobs of money in something that disappeared in minutes. Or asked you if he could smash your head with a baseball bat. Or asked if you wanted to vomit profusely."

"Why would I want to do such patently stupid things?" He talked to his lap while he smoothed out the wrinkles in his napkin.

"Exactly!" I punctured the air with my fork and knife on their way to dissecting my blintzes. "See, normal people would wonder if they were being interviewed for a reality show for the criminally insane."

Carl surveyed his options from the syrup carousel. His steel gray eyes scanned my face. "And?"

"And, well, alcoholics listen to this and think we're talking to someone we threw up on the night before. We'd offer him a drink. We'd hope he'd ask if we were ready for another round." I launched a chunk of blintz into my mouth and wondered if

I'd soon be attempting a serious conversation with a purple-stained tongue.

The aluminum carousel squeaked as he fidgeted between maple syrup and pecan praline. He stopped at maple and wiggled the little pitcher from its sticky neck hold.

"How do you come up with this stuff? Who told you all this?"

Where was a chalkboard when I needed one? I would've dragged my fingernails over it. Several times.

"Me. I told me this."

The food arrived at the next table. Bacon. The smell pulled me into Sunday morning breakfasts at my parents' house when I was still in college. When I was still single. When I was still in denial.

Carl sighed, one of those we've-been-here-before shallow breath sighs, and raked his fingers over his newly shaved head. Two months ago Carl decided he'd rather have no hair than curly hair. I'm grateful he's not of those lumpy-skulled men who look like they needed spackling to even out the shape.

"I think, Leah, you might be confusing fun at parties with flashback guilt from skipping church."

He intended the church bait to lure me into one of those dog-chasing-its-tail discussions—lots of activity, but nothing's ever resolved. He's selling church? I wasn't buying. Carl only appreciated organized religion because it provided a legitimate tax deduction. Church, or at least the building, was a place to be seen, not by God, but by the upwardly mobile faithful. As for me, well, God was on my "To Do" list. Somewhere between watching the grass grow and death.

"Carl, it's not just parties. I drink every day. Not just weekends. And we both know the church thing has nothing to do with alcohol. And I've tried to stop drinking . . ." My fingertips sketched squares on the table as I spoke. The last few words barely escaped my lips.

He floated his napkin over his leftover wedges of pancakes. My weight-conscious husband covered his food to stop himself from overeating. Covering up worked for too many things in his life lately. He'd once uncovered his world to me and to the possibility of a life less rigid, less predictable, less careful.

Our first Christmas morning as newlyweds, Carl brought me breakfast in bed and told me to close my eyes. He placed something on my head. I laughed and asked him if he had a tiara made for his princess.

"Not unless you're a rodent," he said. His voice smiled.

I opened my eyes, reached up, and my hands grazed a felt cap with ears. Mickey Mouse ears. He'd arranged for us to spend a week in Disney World: a week he scheduled to begin that very afternoon.

No more Magic Kingdom.

"Real alcoholics can't stop. You've stopped. So, how can you be," he coughed out, "an alcoholic?" He stacked his plate on top of my empty one. "I have a drink when I come home from work. So you get drunk occasionally. So what? You're creating a crisis. Plus, rehab? Drastic solution, wouldn't you say? Do fat people just give up food?"

Carl reached for the carafe. "Wait." He stopped pouring. "Is this what you and Molly drummed up on your walk this morning? I knew you couldn't have come up with this ridiculous idea on your own. You're so easily influenced by people, and you're so impulsive. Haven't we talked about this?"

No, we did not talk. He talked. I listened. Again and again and again. "This" translated to "you're supposed to discuss important issues with me before making a decision."

I looked past Carl at egg-bomber baby now shaking the contents of his bottle onto the highchair top. A bottle probably filled with the apple juice I left behind. I guess he has a mother who can get through the grocery store without marveling that both beer and diapers can be purchased in a twelve-pack.

"Did you hear what I said?"

I measured his irritation with the yardstick of voice deliberateness. Machine-gun delivery. Code Orange: high annoyance with flashes of impatience. If I persisted, I risked Code Red: anger with ranges from shout to rage. I could retreat. Retreat was as familiar as his rage cycle—a cycle I could both provoke and subdue.

"Of course I heard you."

"Leah." A familiar honeyed shift in his voice. Carl reached across the table and held out his hands, his invitation for me to place my hands in his.

"Besides, what's a few drinks? You know how free, how passionate you become when we're in bed. I think about those things you do . . ."

I yanked my hands out of his as if he'd scorched them.

Tina reappeared at the perfect psychological moment. She handed Carl the bill. "Y'all have a good night now, and hope you come back soon."

Carl rewarded her with a grin. He must think I'd backed away from him because Tina walked up. I forgave her the lost coffee cups at that moment.

After he calculated Tina's tip ("pre-tax" he always reminded me), then stacked the quarters as paperweights on the dollar bills, Carl said, "It's late. We're both tired. We don't have to make any decisions tonight."

I grabbed my purse off the floor. "You're right. We don't have to decide tonight." I stood and threaded my way out of the restaurant.

I hope I'm forgiven the lie.

It was not a "we" decision.

It was mine. All mine.

4

The ride home provided an abundant blessing of silence. The manna of quiet sustained us until we opened the back door. The brochures from the Brookforest Center interrupted, screaming for attention from where I'd left them, held down to anchored to the top of the washing machine by my keys.

"Is this the information you picked up today?" Carl handed me my keys with a dash of eyebrow admonition, slight lift accompanied by equally slight eye-widening.

I locked the door; he grabbed the papers.

"Can we talk about this tomorrow? It's late, remember?"

I dropped my purse on the cypress dining room table. Solid, unassuming, a natural scrubbed-clean-face beauty, aged and flawed, a table with character and style. We had found it in a Magazine Street antique shop in New Orleans when we visited my parents a few months before Alyssa was born. When we imagined Hallmark holiday and Rockwell painting reenactments at the Thornton home.

Sometimes, between the early evening beers and the after-dinner liqueur-laced lattes, I'd relax with a glass or two or three or four of wine in the dining room. Settled in a chair, I'd stretch my legs until my bare feet were propped on the edge of the table and feel a wee bit sad the table had more going for it than I did. But, as my mother always reminded me, "You have to suffer to be beautiful." That cypress beauty spent untold years in a swamp before it was dredged up, hauled away, milled, and created.

There'd be no table talk tonight.

"What's this?" Carl held up a paper as I walked past the sofa where he sat. Paperwork from Brookforest littered the coffee table.

I didn't have to look. I knew he'd found the admission form. My brain triggered an emergency alert system that must have included a tiny pyromaniac who darted around my insides and started little fires.

I wished real life took commercial breaks. *We interrupt this pending marital eruption to provide the wife time to delay, defer, distract—or will she signal defeat?*

"I'm not sure. I'll look at it in just a minute." My dishonesty and I turned around and headed to the kitchen.

"Where are you going?" I didn't know if he looked as confused as he sounded because my face was, once again, buried in a refrigerator. This time I pushed aside Coke Zero cans on the shelf and prayed I'd find a Miller Lite lurking behind one of them. A prayer for beer. I'm a spiritual reprobate.

Success. I'd drown my little internal fire starter and fuel my courage at the same time. I grabbed a beer, kicked off my sandals, and barefooted myself to the battlefront in my den.

Uh-oh. Once again, that Wild West look held Carl's face hostage. "What are you doing? Drinking a beer? Didn't you just tell me you're an alcoholic?"

"That's exactly why I'm drinking the beer." I sat on the sofa, set the can on the coffee table, tucked my hair behind my ears, and looked at Carl. "Okay, here's—"

"Get a coaster. You'll leave a ring on the table." He lifted the can and grabbed a tissue to wipe the faint sweaty circle.

I pulled the shiniest of the brochures over and pretended my tongue was numb for a nanosecond so I'd not blurt out a scathing comment. Carl hated my sarcasm when it was aimed at him.

"This'll work." I reached for the beer, drank more, tried again. "Carl, I talked to someone at the center. I need to do this. Maybe tonight my thinking I drink too much sounds like high drama to you. I just know I can't control my drinking. The admissions counselor—"

"Who gives a rip what some stranger told you? I don't. What made you think you could go off and do this—" he shook the paper at me "—without talking to me first?"

I curled my legs underneath me, stretched my denim skirt over my knees, and wondered if Carl realized two small bubbles of maple syrup had hitched a ride on his lightly starched, white cotton button-down shirt. He hated shopping. Had no idea which cleaners I used. What would he do with this shirt for a month?

"I don't know, really. I mean, of course I was going to talk to you. I guess I just didn't think—"

"Exactly. Once again, you just didn't think," he said, as if relieved I finally provided the answer he expected. "How many times do we need to have this conversation?"

And there it was.

The hill I was willing to die on for the compromise I wasn't willing to make.

I finished the beer, clasped my hands around my knees, and pulled my legs against my chest. I held on tightly. My heart flopped like the fish dad would pull off his line and toss on the pier. A few more beers and the words could ride out on the river of my waning inhibitions. But so could my conviction.

Deep breath. "I'm doing this. I have to or I won't get sober or stay sober. You may not understand right now, but it's what I need to do. I'm admitting myself on the fourth." Exhale.

I found the hill. Carl found the dam, and it exploded like a grenade filled with ball bearings. He shot up with such force I almost tumbled off the sofa.

"The fourth? You're going in on the fourth? Are you crazy? Did you forget about the weekend? Your dad's coming in. We're all supposed to meet my parents at the lake house." Angry desperation brewed a toxic combination.

"They'll understand. It'll work out. I don't know. Go without me." I pitched solutions, but the batter left the plate. "Isn't my sobriety more important than going to the lake?"

"Oh, right, I forgot. This is all about you. Your alcoholism," which he pronounced more like "al-co-hall-izim." He paced in front of the sofa. I tried to move past him. This would all go down so much easier with another beer. Or a glass of wine. He stopped in front of me, almost mashing my toes with his deck shoes. "Well, if you're a real alcoholic, then where are you stashing it? That's what real alcoholics do, right? Hide bottles?"

He scissored through the house from the family room to the kitchen to the study in an Academy Award performance. I followed him in the newly created Unsupporting Actress category.

Things were tossed, nudged, lifted. Merry Maids were going to be anything but when they arrived next week.

"Carl, I promise I don't hide bottles anywhere. I'm not that kind of alcoholic. I mostly drink Miller Lite," I said, though I'd left out "or anything else."

He shoved the bottom drawer of his desk closed. The handle clanged against the wood like metal teeth chattering in the cold. He paused on his way out of the study. Just a few paces behind him, I stopped and waited. But he didn't even turn around when he said, "Don't say another thing unless it's to tell me you give up this lunatic notion of yours." Each word from his mouth was a bullet intended to kill my determination.

I didn't want to provide the ammunition, but I fueled his search with the news I wouldn't abandon my "crazy idea" of going into rehab.

He pushed the guest room door open. The room had been the nursery. I begged him to stop. But he reached into the belly of the closet, shoved the pink gingham diaper bag he found into my chest, and dared me to unzip it.

"Why didn't you fill this with alcohol? Not like it'll ever be filled with anything else again." His voice throbbed with anger.

The closet floor and its contents drifted in a swelling carpeted sea. Tidal waves of the closet's barren dampness, Carl's exploding accusations, and the lingering scent of baby powder sweetness crashed over me. I rode them out until the floor finally settled itself underneath me.

"How dare you! How dare you!" I summoned a voice from places in my soul I'd buried a lifetime ago. My arms cradled the pink bag. I fell to my knees. I wanted to suffocate myself in the quilted softness. Its emptiness screamed of what was, what could have been.

If I could have truly prayed again, this would've been the time.

When Carl pushed past me, he left behind the rank bitterness steaming from his skin. I despised him at that moment. It was the strongest emotion I'd felt toward him in a long time.

I curled into a ball on the closet floor with the diaper bag as my pillow. I told myself I'd drink the pain away later. My going-away present to myself.

After I woke up from my closet sleep, I returned Alyssa's bag to the safety of the wicker hamper where we'd stored the too few belongings of her too brief life.

Another night of sleeping in my clothes. A sour slime coated the inside of my mouth and oozed its way to my stomach with each swallow. I ached to throw up, but my body wouldn't participate. Too far away from my bathroom to shove my finger down my throat, I sat on the floor, leaned against the wall, and willed my neck to support the weight of my head. The closet that cocooned me last night now folded in on me. Each breath mixed a cocktail of sadness, regret, disappointment, and anger.

I unwound myself and shuffled to the kitchen. I found Carl, asleep on the sofa, his head propped on the rolled arm. His legs tangled the crimson chenille throw I spent ten minutes a day arranging to look like it'd been carelessly tossed. Reassured by his crackling snores that he would stay asleep, I didn't disturb him on the way to my last rewards of orange juice and vodka.

5

Molly leaned against my closet doorframe and surveyed my options. She'd volunteered to help me skim my wardrobe for the appropriate alcoholic-in-recovery attire.

I didn't tell her about the emotional earthquake a few days ago. Carl and I didn't even mention it to one another. The energy of that night diluted itself in the tedium of the next day. Since that night, we occupied the same space, but we hovered in different orbits. It worked for now.

And now I'm cross-legged on the closet floor, surrounded by mismatched shoes and uneven stacks of wearables and not-on-your-lifes.

We spent hours coordinating, eliminating, and parading ourselves in one after another of my generally disastrous fashions. My mother-in-law had spirited my maternity clothes away a long time ago. All that remained were my before, during, and after weight loss sizes, ranging from oh-my-gosh to oh-I-just-wish.

"So the good news is you can wash clothes there. The bad news is you'll be the one doing the washing. Do you think they'll let you schlep around in your jammies? Not the boxers, of course, but . . ." Molly stopped mid-sentence, an incredibly annoying tendency, which usually signaled she was talking to herself.

"I doubt many of the patients have a devoted *Vogue* subscriber packing for them. I bet the suitcase of choice is a grocery bag or one of those nifty purple velvet pouches that make you feel better for overspending on Crown Royal."

I debated telling Molly about my stash of those bags. I'd shoved them into an empty Kotex box. I knew Carl would never have a reason to explore the contents of any box labeled maximum overnight protection, extra length with wings, and delicately scented. I just couldn't bring myself to ditch them; it seemed like such a waste. Especially with those gold-roped tassels. I decided not to tell Molly. Once I'm long-term sober, I might find some righteous use for those little bags.

We reviewed the list of contraband items. Not allowed at any time: aerosol cans, mouthwashes with alcohol, nail polish, nail polish remover, needles, tacks, pins, staplers, staples, food, matches, perfume bottles, razor blades, glue, metal cans.

I'll walk around an unshaved, unscented, halitosis-impaired, unpolished, and unmani/pedicured nightmare. How will we tolerate each other?

Also included on the list as not appropriate were weapons, illicit drugs, books with violent themes, and seductive clothing. Weren't these life-inappropriate, not just rehab off-limits? Who needed instructions to not bring drugs to rehab? Am I one of these people?

The upside of being in a treatment center? Molly reassured me it was a respite for the fashion-conscious. I could rest knowing not only would haute couture police not patrol, they won't even be allowed to carry weapons.

I eyed a stack of clothes that didn't make the rehab cut. "You think I could plop down there, wave my arms like a wild woman, and make one of those snow angels?"

"Is Carl thinking maybe you should be making snow devils?" Molly didn't even make eye contact. She just kept rolling my clothes and then arranged them in my suitcase like puffy, rainbow-colored sausages.

"Why? Has he talked to Devin?" The hope that hitched a ride on that question surprised me. I thought I'd suffocated it, left it for dead. But there it was—a gasp of promise. If Carl had said something to Devin, even an angry something, he was trying to make sense of this. And that would mean he wanted to understand.

Molly looked at me, and I read the disappointment in her eyes before she spoke. "No," she said softly as if wrapping a brick in cotton made it any less painful when it hit you. "I just guessed . . ."

I tossed her a pair of socks. "It's fine. You guessed right. I'm the one who guessed wrong."

———⦿———

A bag of mini-Snickers, a bunch of grapes, and a bowl of popcorn later, we declared ourselves finished, having experienced the delirium of the mentally exhausted. Mine, however, had been supplemented by vodka. Another of those "you're such a good girl for finishing this dreadful task, you deserve a reward." Clearly warped, but I'd had these conversations with myself for years. By now they seemed logical.

We wheeled my suitcases to the foyer and parked them near the stairs. I wanted to joke about waiting for the bus to pick me up for beer camp, but it didn't feel funny. Not then. Not standing there with Molly, who had risked our friendship. What did I know of real courage? Mine came from bottles.

"I'm so proud of you. I'm praying for both of you." She hugged me with a fierce tenderness, and before she let go, she whispered, "You'll make it through this. I promise."

I believed her.

I hoped it would be enough to start.

Journal 1

When I refused to sacrifice myself, I'd bear the consequences the next day. Carl would accuse me of being frigid, tell me I needed help.

In front of our friends, he'd say, "That little head of hers can't even balance a checkbook. It's a good thing she's so pretty; otherwise, I'd wonder why I married her." He'd tell them how he'd drag his hand across the antique foyer table to check it because my idea of clean was only one layer of dust.

In the bedroom, he would rage as if his anger could pierce my unwillingness. "A wife should want to make love to her husband," he'd sneer. Wasn't he generous? Didn't he provide for me? He'd remind me that I didn't have to work like some of my friends. I was the one who chose work anyway. Didn't that count for something? He tolerated my overspending. "When are you going to be a wife? A real wife? What's wrong with you? When are you going to fix this?" The void left by those unanswered questions became our battlefield.

I slogged through every day, dreading the inevitable night. Knowing it would come again and again and again and again. We'd wake the next morning, and it would be the unspoken war between us. Me the prisoner. Carl the occupying force.

He wouldn't relent. If he failed to capture my body, he would succeed in demanding my soul. Even when I won, I lost.

That morning, the one where I was going to have to walk myself into treatment, I heard the click of the door before I saw him stride into the bathroom. The thick glass of the sliding shower doors distorted his body—the body I once welcomed and invited to press against my own. Tender and careful and patient. I once longed for him. But not today. Not for many days after everything changed.

I watched, through the curtain of water that framed my face, as he reached for the white towel. It slithered off the bar on the shower door, caught between his two hands. He clutched it and leaned against the linen armoire.

Carl waited. Waited for me. Again.

The pelting drops couldn't dissolve the revulsion that snaked from my bare feet into my stomach and wound its way to my throat. I grasped the handle; the water stopped. Only heaviness of the inevitable separated us.

"If you're going to that place for a month, then you're taking care of me first." The edge in his voice ripped the stillness.

I accepted my defeat.

6

The drive from our house to the Brookforest Center the morning of July 4th was an eight-mile Jerry Springer episode. All bets were off once the suitcases landed in the car.

Carl opened the passenger door of the Range Rover for me, but the intensity of his closing it practically propelled me into the driver's seat. Before he slammed his own door, I grabbed the dashboard and braced myself for another carnival ride.

"You're determined to do this, aren't you?" He hit the brake pedal. "And you're leaving all the dirty work for me. I'm the one who has to call your dad. Call my parents. Did you do that? Of course not." A horn blew behind us, and Carl used primitive sign language to communicate with the driver.

He ranted from the red light to the green light and beyond. I didn't answer. I focused on collecting pictures. With every block we passed, I opened and closed my eyes like a camera lens. Click. The duck pond. Click. Starbucks. Click. Rows of crepe myrtles and pear trees. Click. Joggers. Click. Carl. His mouth opened and closed and opened and closed. Click. My reflection in the car window. A diluted Monet watercolor of auburn hair, olive skin, green eyes, rose-shaded lips.

Papa Hemingway was a part of all he met. I was reflected in all I passed.

"Are you even awake?"

Who wouldn't want to be the audience for a one-man performance of my wrongdoings and shortcomings?

One mile to go. One word. "Yes."

Minutes later, the car lurched into the parking area like a bulldozer had plowed into the back. My head almost separated from my neck. I thought my admission would change to the emergency room where I'd be treated for brain trauma. *So, Mrs. Thornton, were you an alcoholic before or after the dashboard permanently waffled your forehead?*

"Is it safe to open the door?" I'm poised to take off my seatbelt, but Carl still hadn't turned off the car. He looked like a figure in the Wax Museum: a splotchy red-faced unhappy one.

"You are coming in with me, aren't you?" I wondered if he intended a drive-by, and he'd reappear in thirty days. "Pretend you're dropping me off for summer camp." I slid forward to grab my purse off the floor where it had landed during one of Carl's Daytona speed-racing turns.

"You know," he shifted into park and turned the key, "you always do that."

Wax figures don't last very long in this heat. I wondered if he'd considered that. "What do I always do?"

"Make jokes when there's obviously nothing funny going on," he said.

"That's why I make jokes. Because there's nothing funny happening." I scooted out the door before he had time to restart the car and headed for the entrance.

We lived in one of those shiny ad-attractive, oil-corporation-planned, Stepford communities not yet gobbled up by the city of Houston. One could be born and die in Brookforest and never know an entire world waited beyond the front- and back-gated entrances. Schools, hospitals, entertainment, supermarkets, offices, gas stations, all demurely tucked into lush wooded spaces.

Careful zoning assured residents they wouldn't be unduly offended by the sight of golden arches rising from stately pine trees or flashing signs altering the moonlit, star-studded sky.

And, with what I came to appreciate as tremendous foresight on the part of these urban planners, accommodations had been made for a treatment center for the addicted and psychologically impaired residents. Of course, like any monument to the dark side of society, an innocuous sign only inches above the manicured landscaped parkway simply stated, "Brookforest Center." One had to then maneuver two winding miles edged with evenly spaced pink and purple azaleas to find the three-story, white-washed brick and glass building.

We managed to enter the lobby without injury to self or spouse. The receptionist led us to a waiting room—a meat-locker cold waiting room, which explained the butcher-wear of the staff. Shivering in my mint-blue polished cotton skirt and white linen blouse, I hoped I'd remember to ask Molly to bring my denim jacket or a hoodie.

Carl didn't speak. We sat like two strangers who stared at the wall, expecting the movie to begin anytime. I reached into my purse for my cell phone so I could send a quick text message to Molly. Before I could find it the Admissions Counselor walked over to escort us to her office. Ms. Antoinette Wattingly could have doubled as Oprah's sister, her taller sister. Right away, I'm impressed by a woman who can pull off a pair of Tory Burch leopard suede ballet flats. Well-paid staff, maybe? Fortunately, Carl's designer shoe radar was incapacitated. But not his suspicion radar. If he knew what those little cuties cost,

Ms. Wattingly and her leopard ballet flats would be dashing out the doors after us.

Once the intake process started, Carl stopped cooperating. He informed Ms. Wattingly that drinking every afternoon and on weekends couldn't be indicative of alcoholism or else half the civilized world would be lining up for treatment.

"Well, perhaps they should be, Mr. Thornton. Now if you'd look over and sign these papers." She slid the insurance release papers across her polished walnut desk. "Leah came to us. We do not solicit clients. Obviously, your wife thinks that her consumption of alcohol is problematic."

Carl signed the papers, then growled, "What's problematic is my wife being gone for thirty days, my life undergoing an upheaval, and my money funding this place."

The disgust in his voice injected itself into my spine. My body reacted with the familiar stillness that protected me most nights. Even Ms. Wattingly shifted. Both of us now sat straight-backed in the overstuffed chairs. She stared at Carl. I stared over Carl's head into my future.

"Your wife's been gone a lot longer than the thirty days she's about to be away from you. She's just realizing this and maybe you will, too, once you're coming to family sessions."

The industrial stapler jawed its way through the paperwork and cracked the immense silence that swallowed her office. I avoided eye contact with Carl. In fact, I wanted to avoid any contact with him. I cheered Ms. Wattingly on, relieved to allow her to be my voice.

"What family sessions? And how many of these am I supposed to attend?" Carl shot me that look that screamed, "Oh, one more surprise?"

I shrugged. I didn't ask for a syllabus. I just showed up for the course. But right now, my anxiety and I wanted a hall pass. Maybe they could keep Carl, and I could leave.

"Mr. Thornton, I realize this is difficult for you. You didn't want this, but here you are. Your wife is not running from a problem. In fact, she's running straight into it, by choice. Brookforest does not want repeat business. Without family support, Leah may not stay sober."

"So now it's my job to keep her sober?" Carl barked.

The "her" slapped my dignity in its face. I crossed my legs and turned to Carl, "Please don't talk about me as if I'm not even here."

His jaw jutted forward in that way it always did before he launched into one of his tirades.

Ms. Wattingly tapped her pen on the desk. I wondered if she wanted to tap Carl, hard, right on the top of his shaved head. "You know, maybe it's time for Leah to finish her intake on the floor with the nurse. In the meantime Mr. Thornton, I'll have our Family Services Coordinator give you an overview of your involvement for the next month."

She rolled her chair back and then stood behind her desk as she punched a button on her telephone. "If Leah's suitcases are out of the car, I can have someone from the night staff pick them up. Hand me your purse, Leah. We'll need that too."

I reached between the chairs where Carl and I sat facing the desk. Carl's hand wrapped itself around mine.

"I don't need help getting my own purse." The edginess in my voice startled even me.

"I forgot. You can make your own decisions, right?" Carl said.

Ms. Wattingly walked around her desk, reached for the only Marc Jacobs purse I've ever owned in my life, and handed it to the nurse at the office door. This must be what parents felt when they turned their kids over to a babysitter.

"Leah, you'll be going with Jan; she's the charge nurse today. Now's the time to tell Carl good-bye. He and I will finish talking later." She stepped out of her office and closed the wood-paneled door.

Carl stood and looked down at me. "Are you even going to stand up to tell me good-bye?"

I didn't bother with one of my usual snappy comebacks. I was too tired to engage in verbal volleyball. Besides, I couldn't afford any withdrawals from my almost depleted emotional reserves.

I unfolded myself from the chair and faced Carl. My five-foot-two-inch self never seemed as short as it did then. I lifted my face to meet his gaze.

"I know you don't understand. I know you're mad. I'm sorry. I'm really sorry."

I wasn't sorry, but I knew it's what he wanted to hear.

He wrapped his arms around my waist, tugged me toward him, squeezing so tightly his shirt buttons mashed into my cheekbone. He smelled like woods and oranges. I circled my arms around him, more to steady myself from falling into him, and closing what little space there was between us.

"I know. I'm sorry too," he said. "I don't want to be away from you. I'm going to miss you at night." He leaned over to kiss me, and his hands traveled under my blouse. Damp and clammy on my bare skin, they moved up my sides. His finger-tips grazed my bra.

"Don't. Not now." I jerked myself away from him and almost fell sideways into the chair.

He couldn't have known he'd just provided the strength I needed to place myself into the care of Nurse Jan.

Journal 2

Drinking wasn't a conscious solution at first. One night, after dinner with friends and too much wine, I lazily offered myself to him.

My reckless advances amazed us both. I could do and say things that otherwise would turn me inside out. I could give him what he wanted. I detached my soul from my body, and watched as my soul retreated to the safety of a hollow space in my heart. Then my body would comply with the orders I issued.

The day after, he'd be grateful, like a child released from a punishment. He'd repeat and replay the acts and conversations of the previous night.

I detested listening to him. I convinced myself someone else said and did those things. But I could see that sacrificing my body to him at night softened his anger and relaxed his frustration during the day. Made it all so much easier to deal with.

I started, then, to make drinking my salvation.

The performance required practice and careful timing. Too sober and I couldn't dissociate myself from the drama. Too drunk and I'd risk vomiting. I'd swing my leg over the side of the bed and hope one foot on the floor would stop the room from swimming. But too often, it didn't relieve the heaving, and I wobbled to the toilet to hang my head there. I consoled myself that I'd remember little of it the next day.

None of that mattered to Carl as long as I made sure I returned to bed. It became a complicit arrangement between us. He knew I drank so he could, as he said, finally be a husband. And I knew that he knew.

He didn't physically abuse me. He didn't drink too much. He didn't use drugs. He didn't gamble. He didn't have affairs with other women. But I wished he had given in to one of them.

I wished he'd give me a reason to leave. No, really, I wished he'd give the world a reason. Some visible, tangible, obvious reason. At times, I begged him to find relief outside of our bedroom.

He always refused. Not because he felt loyal or committed or even religious. He wouldn't because he knew it was what I wanted.

7

The interminiable admissions process made me wish I'd kicked off my morning with Grand Marnier in my coffee instead of a flavored creamer.

First, there was the tour. It all sounded like, "this is that, and that is this" to me. For most of it, I suspended my peripheral vision, dreading the sight of a familiar face. Then, I spent hours fluttering through papers requiring my signature and eternal promise to release everyone from responsibility for me. Except myself. Jan rescued me after the last round of signing. "Ready?"

"Probably not." If I'd waited for ready, I'd still be home.

Nurse Jan steered me through the brocade wallpapered halls, softened every six to eight feet with rivers of deep blue chintz curtains that puddled lavishly on buttercream tiled floors. When we reached the doors that separated the newly sober from the nearly drunk, she punched a series of numbers into the black-buttoned pad on the wall. The monster doors slowly obliged, opening their wide steel arms to my world for the next thirty days.

The fluorescent lights hummed overhead as we walked the short distance from the now-closed doors to what looked like a nurses' station. Two semi-adults perched on stools, flipping through charts. How embarrassing. I'm being held hostage by people who don't look much older than the ones I teach. They had already known we were on our way because of the closed-circuit cameras in the hallway. What a bizarre experience to stand there and watch myself watch me.

Chart Reader 1 stood, smiled, and extended a hand. "Hello. My name is Matthew. I'm one of the interns. Glad you're here."

He was tall, but he had one of those triangular builds that reflected hours of muscle building. An over-compensator, I figured. He had a firm, friendly grip. Not like one of those well-water handshakers, the ones who felt compelled to pump my arm like they expected water to spurt out of my mouth.

"Me too. Glad I'm here, I mean. Well, I'm not glad I have to be here, but that's another story, right?" I stared at his long blondish hair pulled back in a ponytail, wondering why white men bothered to let their hair grow long. I mean, they weren't going to braid it or corn row it or French twist it or pigtail it or ever want an up-do.

"Right," he said, a grin playing around his mouth. Matthew wore a white button-down collared Oxford, khaki pants, and deck shoes. And, I think, for someone who looked ready to step into an L. L. Bean catalog, he seemed a bit too happy to see me. I should ask later if they get paid per admission.

He relieved Nurse Jan of my suitcases and wheeled them into the belly of the center station. Chart Person 2 said, "Welcome," took a set of keys from Matthew, and headed off down the hallway.

"Jan and I need to review some last-minute paperwork. We'll finish going through your suitcases, return your purse, and then show you your room. There's a waiting area over there," Matthew said and pointed to the right, "where you can watch television while we do this." For the tiniest moment, I felt a swish of random panic. *I'm really here. I'm really alone.* Matthew must have seen that shadow dance across my face because he stopped the symphony of zippers as he opened my bag and whispered to Jan who moved to rescue me from myself.

"You might be more comfortable over here." Jan's voice thawed my frozen moment as she took my hand and guided me to a room on the other side of the one Matthew had pointed to. She flipped the nearby light switch. "This is the patients' rec room," she said, with a Vanna-like sweep of her arm.

Rows of ceiling lights crackled on, like bright kicks in a chorus line, revealing a new section of my house away from home. The lavish decorating never made its way past the monster doors and into this oyster white rectangle of a room. Tired olive green, square-cushioned, pseudo-leather sofas separated by bow-legged tables rested against three of the walls. Each table held an assortment of game boxes and magazines. The one coffee table in the room supported stacks of paperbacks and half a dozen ashtrays of various amoebic shapes. A television on an A-frame metal stand and a card table with four chairs took up space on the fourth wall. No creamy tiles here. Cigarette burns like pockmarks covered the stiff, grass-green layer of worn carpet.

The room, of course, opened to the center station, so we didn't have to go far. But now my panic had evolved into self-pity. I had to acclimate myself to this utilitarian space that begged for an HGTV makeover. Plus, the gray haze of stale cigarette smoke remained suspended in the room. I'd need an oxygen mask to sit in it for more than five minutes.

My feet parked themselves at the threshold and refused to move in the direction of Jan's outstretched arm. "Is there a no-smoking room? And where are the patients? Am I the token alcoholic for the month?" With each syllable my voice rose, despite Jan's reassuring pats on my shoulder.

A surge of craving. I wanted to go home. Not home, really, as in the two-story, blackmail-in-waiting Tudor, our wedding gift from Carl's parents, Landon and Gloria. Home was that place wine or gin could bring me to. The place where I didn't have to feel. Where I could be someplace without really ever leaving where I was. Numbness, the friend I relied on, wasn't invited to this place. Party's over.

I scratched the top of my left hand with my right so vigorously that snail-sized red welts formed. Carl hated when I did that. I did that a lot.

Jan's cool, tapered fingers softly pressed my hand. "Stop. You're about to draw blood." She reached around with her left arm and gently hugged me, all the while holding my hand still.

For the first time I noticed we were about the same height, but she seemed fragile and light. She probably bought shoes, maybe even her clothes, in the tween department. Short dark-brown layers framed her face—a cut not too many women since Audrey Hepburn could pull off, but Jan did and did it well. Without the black-framed oval glasses she wore, she'd look like a twelve-year-old.

Her brown eyes scanned me. Were they hooked up to a monitor somewhere?

She gestured in the direction of a sofa. "Let's sit. Are you hungry? I can order a tray for you or you can get ice cream. We keep it stocked here on the floor. What do you want?"

Given a choice between nutrition and ice cream? What a place: legitimate ice cream. It's not gin, but it qualified as comfort food. Two Nutty Buddy cones later, I learned I had arrived at the beginning of the month when most new patients checked in and old ones checked out. The ones in between were on weekend leave and due back in less than an hour. All of the patients on the floor smoked. I could ask for a time when the room could be a no-smoking place, an hour or so during the day, Jan told me, but I figured that would have been a quick trip to Nerdville and wouldn't win me the patient of the month award. Not a good way to start.

Matthew walked over. "You just earned your badge from the suitcase inspection department. Jan's going to show you to your room. We'll give you some time to settle in, then we'll go over the game plan for the next seventy-two hours, okay?"

We all understood my "okayness" didn't really matter. But I figured it would be dumb to be rude to the person who could be my ice cream supplier for the duration of my stay. Jan and I peeled ourselves off the couch, and she led the way to the room.

Welcome to drabness. Two twin beds with navy blue corded bedspreads separated by a white nightstand with a lamp. A standard, hospital-sized closet and a bathroom with question-able lighting. The one six-drawer dresser squatted across from the beds. A student-sized desk with a small lamp perched on its corner faced the only window.

My suitcases and purse waited on the bed—the one closest to the bathroom. One plus for early arrival.

"Your roommate's due to arrive tomorrow, so you'll have the space to yourself tonight. A few of the other patients will be coming back soon. Go ahead and unpack, settle in, and I'll be back later. Don't leave the room until I come back."

If Nurse Jan and her posse knew I was gloriously grateful for the freedom and securely comforted by the safety provided by two very large, very locked, and very bolted steel doors, they might have transferred me upstairs to the psych floor.

I'd grown up sharing a room with my grandmother to shar-ing a room with Carl. Finally, I was all by myself. The fact that I was placed on a twenty-four-hour watch stifled my tempta-tion to break into a happy dance, which for me would have been more of a herky-jerky happy dance (there was definitely a reason my mother didn't name me Grace). Jan would have charted that movement as the beginning of my DTs—delirium tremens.

I eased into my faded black sweatpants and my equally worn-out school T-shirt and purposely fell backward onto the twin bed, a bed I could roll around and over in. A pillow, well, actually rectangle-shaped foam parading as a pillow, but, no matter. I could smash it and bunch it and fold it relentlessly, recklessly. Even the milky-white institutional sheets, grainy like the finest of sandpapers, reassured me of the almost impossibility of slipping out of the bed.

The city's annual Independence Day display squelched my one-woman celebration of freedom. The night belched ribbons of emeralds, rubies, sapphires, and diamonds. Sizzling colors exploded—some whining and screeching in protest—then pulsated one last time before they surrendered themselves to the sky. I sandwiched the pathetic little pillow under my head and would have been content to enjoy my window view of the fireworks except that I started feeling like lit bottle rockets had thrust themselves into my brain through my ears. Were aspirins allowed in this place? Surely they didn't expect me to pull myself off every medication. I had no clue how to help myself.

Jan had closed the door almost an hour ago. Now, not only was my head cracking open, but the Nutty Buddy cones were trying to work their way back up. No telephone in the room. Not like I could call room service. Was I supposed to knock on the door to get *out*?

Between rocket bursts, I heard voices, then laughter. I knocked on the door. It was a pathetic, ninny knock, obviously attracting no one since the laughter continued. The thought occurred to me that they might be laughing and wondering why the blazes I just didn't open the door. The sour taste in my mouth competed for attention with the brain reverberations. I wanted to pound the door down with my fists, scream, and run.

I felt stupid for being so obedient. Always the good girl. And, wow, if my friends could see me now.

My knuckles vibrated from banging on the door. I paused and heard the measured swish of feet. The doorknob turned, and Jan called my name. She found me, a human lump kneeling on the floor, my butt on my feet, my arms wrapped around my waist, surrounded by vomit.

Journal 3

When I could step outside of my torture, I could see that Carl truly couldn't understand. That he thought giving myself to him shouldn't be an act of obligation or disgust, but one of gratitude and anticipation and joy.

Sometimes, I felt his confusion. Yet, as time drifted by, he seemed to care less and less about what I felt. I was willing to admit fault. I couldn't open my planner and point to a time, a day, a month, or even a year when I could say, "Here, this is the time it started to go badly. Here is the day, and this is what happened."

No. Even before our loss, it was something so undefined, so gradual, so vague—like a cancer—it metastasized undetected, but, at some point, its malignance made itself known.

To survive the daily dread, the knowing that every night would be a useless struggle with demons, I numbed myself. Over and over and over.

8

Retching up your insides was probably not high on the "Getting to Know You" guide for patient/staff relationships. My putrid mess shocked me, but it didn't surprise Jan; in fact, she expected it.

A cleaner version of me emerged from the bathroom and found Jan had already cleaned and somehow fumigated the room. Jan's eyes snapped to meet mine. She stared for an instant, but long enough to make me squirm. Was it my hair? Dried naturally, it frizzed and curled around my ears, like poodle hair on steroids. I'd scrubbed my body raw, removed every remnant of makeup, and slipped into a clean outfit.

"I'm so sorry," I said and looked around for some way to help. "I would've helped you clean up." Already I needed someone to clean up after me. Carl's voice saying, "can't take care of yourself," pulsated through my veins and adjusted to the rhythm of my heart. Every beat reminded me of my irresponsibility. What if he was right? "I'm really embarrassed," I said.

"Leah, most symptoms of alcohol withdrawal happen within seventy-two hours after that last drink. From what I've read on your intake chart, you were in mid-stage dependency.

For the next two or three days you'll probably feel shaky, tired, have killer headaches and nausea and vomiting," she said.

"Or you may not." Jan shrugged her shoulders, pulled the cord to close the laundry bag, and shoved it into a basket that she had brought in after finding me on the floor. "But it's not unusual for patients to not want to eat or sleep. Sometimes they feel a roller coaster of emotions from being really irritated to being really excited."

"I can't wait. And the good news is?" Pouty sarcasm tinged the question. I'm already wearing Day 2's outfit on Day 1. Molly and I definitely didn't factor in these unexpected wardrobe changes when we were busy figuring out the definition of "appropriate recreational clothing."

My whining yanked Jan to a standing position. "The good news? Let's start with you're alive. You're not having violent seizures. You're not in a coma, and you're not having to be sedated so you won't injure yourself or someone else. Have you ever watched someone experience delirium tremens? No, of course not. More good news. And—" She shifted forward, held the basket with one hand, and pointed at me with the other—"you're here. That's the best news of all."

She handed me a small book pulled from the pocket of her scrubs. "Here, this is yours. I was supposed to give it to you tomorrow, but I think you could use it now. Write your name in it and today's date so you don't forget tonight. Matthew will stop by when he's finished checking in everyone from their weekend passes. He'll talk to you about tomorrow. After that, it's lights out."

I sat cross-legged on the bed. Jan walked over and placed *The Promise of a New Day* on the nightstand. She gently patted my knee, "I'll see you in the morning. Remember, one day at a time."

She and the cart squeaked out of my room. I picked up the book of daily meditations. On the raspberry cover, a woman with long, flowing hair and outstretched arms faced a bright yellow sun the size of a half-dollar. Puffy white clouds separated the woman from the sun.

Seriously? Will I be doomed to cheesy as a sober person? But a book with melodrama-woman on the cover beat out no book. Sadly, it also trumped *Anna Karenina*. I'd dragged *Anna* along, all eight-hundred pages, because of a subconscious need to punish myself or to pose as a breezy intellectual. I remembered Molly lifted the novel and asked if it would be a doorstop.

I found a cheap plastic pen in the nightstand drawer: white with *The Brookforest Center* imprinted in black. I imagined not too many of those left the center. It would, though, be a great conversation piece. I could tell people the center provided free treatment, but their pen cost over fifty-thousand dollars. But then the only audience for that humor was probably already outside the door of my room.

Changing into my pink scruffy terrycloth robe, I wiggled under the covers, propped my marshmallow pillow against the headboard, and leaned back. I neatly printed my name and the date on the first page and stuck the pen back in the drawer. I opened to today's date, July 4, and read Judy Grahn's quote, *"She walks around all day quietly, but underneath it all she's electric angry energy inside a passive form. The common woman is as common as a thunderstorm."*

Matthew told me the next day that he had found me curled on my side, snoring, clutching the meditation book close to my chest.

Journal 4
I struggled to stay awake every night—read books, watched mindless television programs and movies so old they were monochromes,

drank mugs of coffee, waited until I could be sure he'd fallen asleep—
and then I could ghost myself into the bedroom.

I quietly switched off the lights in the den and hoped he had left
the bedroom door open. I always made an effort to avoid causing the
door hinges to moan or else the sound would stir him. After I softly
shuffled to the bed, I lifted the sheet and blanket ever so carefully.
Then, I lightly perched on the edge of the bed, testing, as my weight
shifted the balance.

Feeling no perceptible movement, I raised my bare feet from
the carpeted floor in an orchestrated, practiced ballet. Like minute hands on a clock, my feet quietly ticked their way to the bed.
I'd lie on my left side, facing empty space so my shallow breaths
wouldn't stir the dead air. My head barely grazed the pillow—no
sudden movements—everything achingly slow, but fluid. I waited,
still, corpse-like, waited for a stir, a shift in body weight. I dared not
allow myself the luxury of expansive breathing until his snoring was
rhythmic and offensively solid.

Some nights my protective and routine concert was successful.
I'd wake up in the same position I'd so carefully arranged myself in
during the darkness.

Many nights I failed.

9

A knock on the door woke me from a sleep interrupted by frequent trips to the bathroom. I didn't know if I should hang my head over the toilet or sit on it. Angry tidal waves of headaches crashed against the shore of my skull. I didn't remember reading about a wake-up service or midnight parties. My mind needed more time to rouse itself than my body. I opened and closed my eyes while my brain rummaged through its files for something recognizable. Home? No. Beach house? No. Uh-oh? Yes.

I untangled myself from the web of sheets, blanket, and bedspread that had crept up during the night and scarfed my body. I sat in bed, hugged my knees to my chest, and stared through the darkness.

How long had I slept? I smiled at the question, knowing my mother's response would have been, "Doesn't matter. God never sleeps." For most of my life, I imagined God suffered from eternal insomnia. No wonder He would, one day, stage Armageddon in an act of horrific vengeance. He'd been sleep-deprived by mothers for centuries.

No matter what earthly horror had been inflicted upon me, I depended on my mother's soothing pronouncement to wrap itself around my damaged ego. "God never sleeps" was my maternal shield against the worldly infidels, a no-nonsense ointment to heal my emotional bruises. It was a global warning for friends turned traitors, boys who never called, and employers who manipulated. I comforted myself with the promise of heavenly havoc when the offender reached God, assuming the possibility existed that would allow such a cruel person to reach that height.

I had no doubt my mother watched my life unfold or, maybe, unravel. She'd probably jab God in the stomach with that manicured hand of hers just in case, in a surprising spiritual snafu, He might nod off when her daughter needed Him.

Let the jabbing begin.

Another knock, this time accompanied by an unrecognizable female voice, "Breakfast in a half hour." I rubbed my right hand over my bare left wrist as if doing so could magically make my watch appear. Funny how you become so accustomed to the feel and weight of things on your body—the clunky stainless steel watch, the diamond and emerald tennis bracelet—like that phantom pain sensation amputees felt even after the limb had been removed. Not that jewelry deprivation was, on any level, comparable to a loss of limb. I'm rationalizing now, just in case, what? In case my thoughts were being zapped to a morality guard who would incarcerate my pettiness?

My rumbling belly signaled hunger or trouble. I figured I should at least cruise the breakfast options. After my two-step floss and brush, then my three-step skin care, I skipped the multi-stepped cosmetic routine. No one knew me here. We might as well each be assigned an alias since using a name outside of this hospital was almost a federal offense. Unless, of course, they admitted a celebrity in dire need of publicity.

Day 2. I wore white linen capris and a screaming orange sleeveless blouse scheduled for Day 3. The pants grabbed a bit too much when I bent over and reached for my new white canvas shoes. I spotted the meditation book on the floor near the bed. Sometime during the night, it must have fallen out of my hands. Probably on one of my bathroom trips. I placed it on the bed, finished tying my shoes, then opened it to July 5 and read, *"It is good to have an end to journey towards; but it is the journey that matters, in the end."* Okay, Ursula K. Le Guin, let's you and I journey to breakfast, and we'll take it from there.

Another knock.

"Five minutes," mystery voice called out.

Did anyone ever open a door around here? Did they not realize there's a hall of people in various stages of withdrawal and recovery, and knocking was not conducive to either one?

A deep breath later, I opened the door that separated me from what I am, and what I might become.

10

Voices rose and fell from the once empty patient rooms of the previous night. The ten-year-old inside me didn't want to walk into the room alone. Frankly, neither did the twenty-seven-year-old who housed her. I neared the center station but didn't see the familiar faces of Jan or Matthew.

Great. They deserted me too.

"Leah?" The voice of the knock approached. With the exception of wearing sneakers instead of deck shoes, she wore clothes identical to Matthew's from the night before—khakis and a white collared blouse. She, however, twisted her long hair into a loose chignon. I couldn't tell if the charcoal-shaded wisps and strands that surrounded her head and neck were purposeful or just the result of sloppy braiding. She didn't wear a drop of makeup, her eyes were the color of aquamarines, her skin was flawless, her legs rivaled Julia Roberts's—already I'm not liking this chick.

"You got her," I answered in my best perky voice.

"I'm Cathryn. I work days." She reached out to shake my hand.

"I guess I'll know I've been here awhile when I've stopped shaking hands. How many more of you are there?" Judging by

Cathryn's deadpan stare, not too many mornings kicked off with someone's skewed sense of humor.

"Not enough. Not nearly enough," she answered. With both hands, she tucked her bangs into the uneven mass of hair on the top of her head. "I'll introduce you to the group, then you and I will walk to the cafeteria together so I can catch you up on what you'll be doing today."

Bodies littered the drab room of yesterday. Two were lying on the sofas, hands cupped under their heads, eyes closed. One stood in the middle of the room and aimed the remote control at the television; stations flicked on the screen in measured beats. One sat in the back, legs crossed, and flipped through a magazine. Cathryn and I walked into the middle of the room. No one noticed, or they pretended not to notice.

Surely, this Tropicana orange blouse was a shocker to anyone's morning.

"Everyone, this is Leah. She arrived yesterday afternoon," Cathryn said. Magazine-flipper raised her head, glanced at me, and nodded. Station-flicker waved over his shoulder with his free hand and continued cycling through the cable offerings. Sleeper number one, I learned later, was Doug. He grunted without even bothering to open his eyes. Sleeper number two actually stood, swaggered over, and patted me on the back. He was young enough to be one of my students.

"I'm Vince. Welcome to Junkie Paradise. Even though you don't look like no junkie. Whatta ya' in for?"

"Thirty days," I answered, and he howled in laughter.

Cathryn waved him away, "Vince, be nice. Save it for group."

"Aw, Ms. Fitz, you know I'm nice. Just tryin' to make conversation," he said and turned to me. "Sorry if you thought I was laughin' at ya. I thought you was tryin' to be funny."

"No problem," I mumbled and wished I'd worn something in military camouflage so I could disappear into the surroundings. Go figure. When I thought I was funny, everyone looked at me like I'd just spit. I answered a question honestly, and I'm the last comic standing. This place was definitely off center. Sober people must operate in an alternate universe.

Cathryn flicked the overhead lights on and off, a move that stirred Doug enough to open his eyes and grunt twice.

"Stop flashing those lights in my face. I feel like I'm home with my old lady." Doug pushed himself up into a sitting position, but his body slouched into his lap as if his muscles were still asleep.

"Doug, if your old lady wanted you home, she wouldn't have stuck you in here. Again. Benny, hand that thing over; you don't have a license to speed through all those channels."

Benny pointed and clicked the remote directly at Doug. "Sober, drunk, sober, drunk, sober, drunk."

I shuffled behind Cathryn, wondering if she'd provide sufficient protection when Doug flew off the sofa to beat the blazes out of Benny. That familiar spool of anxiety unrolled in my gut, and its threads flew into my hands and knees. I rocked back and forth, heels to toes, heels to toes, stirring the nervousness as if I could somehow dilute it through the motion of my body. The body in the corner sighed hugely and, without even lifting her eyes to the scene playing out in front of her, continued to flip magazine pages. Vince disappeared into what I suspected was the bathroom.

Doug stood, dragged the back of his knobby hand over his wide mouth, then wiped it across his well-worn Levis, and wrestled the remote from Benny. But instead of this being the prelude to the battle I anticipated, both men laughed as Doug, now in control, pointed the remote at Benny, "Pot head, Coke Nose."

"Are you two kids finished now? You're about to be late for breakfast." Cathryn shook her head back and forth in the way harried mothers do after telling their precious Rambo-tots to stop eating bugs for the zillionth time.

Vince appeared from around the center station and pounced on the elevator button. When the doors opened, the men filed in. Vince straddled the space between floor and elevator. "So, Annie, ya' coming or what?"

Annie abandoned her page-flipping and strolled through the room to where I stood next to Cathryn.

"Y'all go ahead. I'm taking the stairs." Her Southern drawl suited her unhurried style. She pulled a purple hair clip out of denim overalls that must have fit looser three sizes ago, and clipped her streaked brown hair into a fat ponytail. Her eyes were the color of green signal lights, so unreal they looked like wet paint. Midnight-black eyeliner edged her lids, which were covered with moss-green eye shadow. Her lashes fanned out like they'd been dipped in wax. I made a mental note to discuss her foundation choice, a tan that made it seem as if she'd taken her face to Florida and left her body behind.

"After Theresa arrives, the women won't be outnumbered," Cathryn said, as she unlocked the stairwell door and held it open.

Annie looked me over like a statue she might have been deciding to buy, glanced at Cathryn, shrugged her meaty shoulders, and said, "Yeah, guess not," before she traipsed down the stairs.

Cathryn closed the door, stepped back over to the central station, and grabbed a clipboard hanging on the wall.

"Leah, open the door next to the one I just closed. We can talk in that office."

An acid pit sloshed against my stomach walls. Tiny creatures pounded bass drums against my temples. My hand started to itch again. I couldn't stay here. I didn't belong in this institution. I wasn't like these people, this subculture of misfits. Our mutual exclusion of one another proved that. Molly meant well, but she pushed me too far, too fast. Too enthusiastic. I should've waited. Clearly, I didn't fit the definition of a textbook alcoholic. I'd already proved I could give up alcohol for more than twenty-fours hours. I'd explain all this to Carl, who would explain it to whomever who would then arrange for my discharge.

"Is there a phone in there? I need to make a phone call. A private phone call." I hoped I'd used my best assertive voice, but the one I heard belonged to a child. *I just need to relax.* I mean, one phone conversation with Carl, and I'm headed to the beach house. Or Molly. I could call Molly. She'd understand once I told her about this bizarro world I'm locked in. I'm sure we can find a place for people more like me, people I'd feel comfortable with.

Cathryn walked around me to the office, and I thought I heard her say, "No phone calls" as she passed.

"Did you say, 'No phone' or 'No phone calls'?" I massaged my forehead where the temple drummers had relocated. Phone deprivation? What would the ACLU think of this? Surely this was a Civil Rights issue. No answer. Maybe she hadn't heard me.

I wandered into the office, a sparse, ugly room. Cathryn sat behind a submarine-gray steel desk, creating handwriting havoc in a chart. My body was as hesitant to move as my mouth was to open. "What did you say about the phone?"

The tidal waves in my stomach intensified. I wanted to sit, but I might constrict the pool of nausea. Besides, there was no phone in here. I'd have to go someplace else anyway.

She looked up at me. "No phone yet. Sit down, and I'll explain."

"I don't want to sit down. I want a phone. I know there are phones here. I've seen them. I've heard them ring. I want a telephone. I want to call my husband."

My words marched out of my mouth like good little soldiers, slowly and deliberately.

"No one has phone privileges for the first seventy-two hours. That's one of the things we need to discuss." She closed the folder, stood, and tilted her head toward me to make eye contact. "Let's talk. You can eat breakfast after that."

I sent the troops out to battle one more time. "I don't want breakfast. I want a phone."

"I know. In forty-eight hours you can use the phone. But, for now—" she slipped the clipboard under her arm, and pointed toward the door "—we're going to breakfast. Your face is as white as the paper I'm writing on."

I was clearly not winning this battle.

11

My trauma over the phone issue re-prioritized after I bolted out of the office in a desperate search for the nearest bathroom. This business of moving to sobriety wasn't much different than moving away from being drunk—they both involved throwing up. I didn't remember this being mentioned in the brochure, either.

Breakfast was a culinary disaster. Foods that ordinarily and happily co-mingled on a plate proved less appealing in stainless steel troughs guarded by hair-netted people wielding long slotted spoons. Whatever hope I held out for the coffee dissipated as soon as I spotted "de" in front of "caf."

Could I survive a month on Nutty Buddies? Maybe rehab was a blessing in disguise. Sobriety and weight loss. Double-teaming the addictions. A real two-for-one. Grams would be so proud I had scored such a deal.

I settled for two buttermilk biscuits with strawberry jelly, and warm orange juice with what I hoped was pulp clinging to the sides of the glass. Cathryn and I sat at a table for four in the corner of the cafeteria. Floor to ceiling panels of glass were evenly spaced between wide stucco columns. On one side of the room, diners could look beyond the glass into a wide semicircle of bushy purple azaleas. They surrounded a three-tiered pineapple-topped cement fountain flanked by black wrought-iron benches. On each side of the garden, red brick walkways wove through manicured sections of crepe myrtle trees, small magnolias, Mexican heather, and eager sunflowers. No evidence a frenzied world lurked beyond the landscaped perimeter.

"Finish eating. I'm going to ask Dr. Rizzuto to escort every-one upstairs," said Cathryn. She walked over to a wiry-haired man whose white lab coat hung from an inverse hourglass body. He scraped his leftovers into a deep plastic bin, gave her a thumbs-up, and ambled over to the group's table.

"Okay, folks. Make sure you don't leave anything behind. We'll head back up and have time for a smoke break." Maybe I should start smoking. Even the intense sun, soggy humidity, and suffocating cigarette smoke would have provided a wel-come break from the stale air inside.

I stared at the human mishmash as they shuffled plates and chairs on their way out of the cafeteria. They discarded me, a broken toy on their playground. I was either an untouchable or invisible.

"Don't you worry, honey," my mother consoled me from the heavens. "They may be ignoring you, but remember God's always awake."

Well, Mom, today was one of His narcoleptic days.

I shifted my attention to Cathryn, who had refilled her cof-fee cup. She slid into a chair and launched into my agenda items for the next two days, none of which included recess. At the end of the those forty-eight hours, we'd have another chat about my schedule of individual and group therapies, phone and visiting privileges, weekend releases, occupational ther-apy, and mandatory on- and off-site AA meeting attendance.

"So, how are you feeling? And spare me the 'I'm fine.' I know you're not." She sipped her coffee and waited.

"I'm not fine. I don't even know what fine means anymore." I knew what it used to be, long ago and far away. I checked Cathryn's hands. No engagement ring or wedding band. Maybe she won't even understand what comes next. "Some things, some parts of my life I'm, um, not missing at all."

Coffee cup down. Eyebrows up.

"Really, I mean that. It's hard to explain. Well, not hard to explain. I guess I never had to explain it. But, anyway, I'm scared to be here, but I'm scared not to be here. Then I have these gigantic headaches and a three-ring circus going on in my stomach." I took a break from talking and twisted my paper napkin around the empty orange juice glass. I had to be careful. I already sensed a trickle in the floodwall I had so carefully constructed. If I said too much, I couldn't contain the breach. It would unleash an uncontrollable emotional torrent.

I took a deep breath. "I feel bad for Carl. It's not like he asked for any of this. I just dumped all this stuff in his lap and ran here. He called my dad because I just couldn't do it. And what's he supposed to tell our friends and neighbors when they ask where I am? Like poor Mr. Rossner at the end of our block, who started a petition to ask the network for a Houston CSI. By the end of the month, he'll suspect Carl's buried me in the backyard." There. Good word play. End on a grin. I'd run out of dry napkins to twist, so I stacked the little gold tin jelly containers.

Cathryn slid her empty coffee cup to the side.

"Well, has he? Has Carl buried you?"

"Would I be here if he had?"

I stacked and restacked, knowing if I stopped I might get careless and vulnerable. I stayed focused by making sure I placed the grape jelly squarely on top of the boysenberry.

Cathryn gazed at the top of my head for quite some time. She'd probably already figured out I dyed my hair.

"Well, I don't know. Maybe that's a question you'll have to answer eventually . . . with someone else. I'm not a therapist. I'm sorry if I made you uncomfortable."

I scrinched my mouth to trap the wicked snicker behind my teeth. Her Pee Wee League definition of uncomfortable couldn't run on the same field with Carl's Professional Leaguers. I swallowed and mumbled, "Not at all."

I unstacked the jellies and arranged them in alphabetical order. Apple, boysenberry, grape, raspberry, strawberry. I'm far too entertained by these things. But how else was I supposed to distract myself? I didn't really want to talk, and I honestly didn't want to be talked to. I returned the little boxes to the basket and looked at Cathryn.

"Carl will figure out what to do," she said. "He was given some ideas last night after we brought you to the unit. You have to trust this is where you're supposed to be. The universe has a way of accommodating even our most unexpected plans."

"The universe accommodating me?" I asked. "It's about time. I've been accommodating the universe for most of my life. For somebody who isn't a therapist that sounds like a lot of psychobabble."

She laughed. "I guess you can't work here for five years and not pick up some babble," she said. "Universe later . . . you now. What do you need?"

"Today, I need to know that whatever I eat won't make an encore," I told her.

"And I want a drink. When am I going to not want a drink?"

Journal 5

I learned long ago to use compliance and submission to save myself. That to say no only postponed the inevitable. His demands, his accusations, or worse, his sickening pleas for solitary relief all led to revulsion.

I'd wake some nights, terrified by the crushing reality of the nightmare, by its unrelenting physical closeness. But sometimes it was not a nightmare. I'd awake to his weight pressing on me, his hands groping under my clothes, which I often slept in as an irrational defense. None of it mattered—clothes, no clothes. He would be on top of me, and his goal was not ever waking me up—awake, asleep—like the clothes, they weren't an issue. He wanted a body on which to press his own. I could feel even the mattress beneath me surrender to him.

There would be no stopping until he was spent. He never asked if I was awake. He didn't speak. He wanted what he wanted, when he wanted it, and how. I pleaded. He pushed. I cried.

I remembered how my cousins would ambush me in the pool, knowing I couldn't really swim. They would shove my head underwater and howl when I struggled. The harder I fought, the louder and deeper their laughter.

I used those lessons on those nights. I learned to perform—to act as if none of it mattered.

12

I spent the day like a human boomerang and traveled from one office back to the central station on the floor only to be sent out to yet another office. A seriously flawed system, it seemed, for psychological assessments.

While I schlepped around, subjected to everything from blood work to brain busters, I missed lunch. I headed back to the floor to alert Cathryn. I stepped off the elevator, but as I walked to the central station, I saw that I'd have to wait for her attention.

She and another woman, but one taller and wider, played tug-of-war over a backpack. The woman's hair looked like it had been caught in a blender. Wild strands poked out in every direction, some of them weighted down with colored beads woven on the ends. I definitely wouldn't want to tangle with her. I stopped and debated if I should hang out in my room until the quiet signaled the storm had blown over. But I'd experienced enough hurricanes in New Orleans to know the eye of the storm seduced people into a false sense of security. My empty stomach growled, so I'd have to tolerate the drama if I wanted food.

"Theresa, the information we sent detailed exactly what you couldn't bring here," said Cathryn.

"It did not say anything about laptops. No cell phone, no iPods. That's all. Nothing about laptops." Theresa wore enough rings, chains, and bracelets to stock a boutique jewelry store. Each back and forth tug between the two elicited a chorus of clinks and clanks on her wrists. Her well-ringed hands gripped one bag strap while Cathryn clenched the other. I wanted these women with me at Macy's One Day Sales.

I figured one or both of them would soon surrender, and I could resolve this hunger issue. My stomach now sounded like a small lawnmower. But I'd underestimated Theresa's persistence.

"Look, Miss, I know you have a job to do, but I don't see how this laptop's a problem. Like I said, the brochure didn't say I couldn't have one."

"It didn't say you could," said Cathryn. Her eyes bored tiny holes in Theresa's head.

"King Solomon had an answer for this," I said and realized, too late, the sounds I heard had spilled out of my own mouth.

Theresa turned to look at me, and, in that moment of surprise, Cathryn swooped in for the kill, pulled the bag toward her, and then shoved it under the counter.

A few seconds of incomprehensible language later, Theresa focused her attention on me.

"Or maybe not." I told her.

Now that we were face-to-face, Theresa's youth surprised me. And the Egyptian-like application of her black eyeliner mesmerized me. She pointed one of her cherry red fingernail daggers at my nose. Her bracelets provided background music, "Girl, who asked you to jam your way into my business? Huh? Does this concern you? No. It's your fault that lady got hold of my laptop." She showered the space between us with sprays of spit as she ranted.

As flattered as I may have been that Theresa thought I qualified as a girl, I realized I might need to stay clear of her for a few days. My hunger prevented me from being intimidated, but I knew my alter ego, Patty Peace at any Price, would have to find a way to smooth this over. Later.

I rocked back and forth, my heel-to-toe distress lullaby, and contemplated the next step. Cathryn chimed in and solved the problem for me.

"Leah, meet Theresa, your roommate. Theresa," Cathryn grinned with perverse delight. "Leah checked in yesterday. I'm sure she won't mind showing you to your room, right Leah?"

"Why do people here always ask me questions they either already know the answers to or don't care to know the answers to?"

Cathryn moved from behind the counter and took the file I held from my marathon of tests. Theresa stomped over to her, her hair beads bouncing like small marbles. A few beads almost swatted Cathryn in the face. "I can't believe I'm supposed to share a room with Miss Goody Two-Shoes here. She already got me ripped off once. What? You want she should spy on me? This some kind of joke?"

I knew Cathryn didn't have the capacity for this sort of humor. Theresa and I were doomed.

"I will chew chunks of sheetrock off this wall if I don't get something to eat soon. Can we postpone this fight until after lunch?" I looked at the clock. Lunch for everyone else ended two hours ago. I tried not to stare at Theresa, who struggled with a wedgie in her abundant stonewashed jeans.

"Yeah," said Theresa, "I didn't know them people downstairs wanted to talk so much. I never ate. Where's girly-girl here gonna eat? And don't give me no ice cream. I want real food."

So, Theresa already knew about the ice cream. Hmmm. But before I had time to contemplate Theresa's familiarity with rehab, the elevator thumped to the floor, and the morning crew streamed out the open doors and made their way to the rec room.

As the foursome passed us, Theresa yelped and plowed her way over to Doug. His back to her, he never saw her propel herself in his direction. She surrounded his scrawny waist with her spongy arms and squeezed. Any more enthusiasm in that maneuver, he could have belched out a whole chicken. Doug emitted a loud primal grunt and yelled, "What the—"

Theresa released him. "Doug, my man! It's the Mexican Mama! Can you believe this? Both of us back here. How many round trips this make for you, Alkie?"

Doug readjusted his pants, which Theresa had swiveled around his body. "You won't make too many more if you keep that up. How many of the family jewels you pawned this time?"

How touching. A reunion.

Could I dump food in my stomach now?

<hr />

Cathryn took Theresa and me to the cafeteria while everyone else attended group. Theresa lifted not one but two eyebrows when the server asked if she wanted her sandwich on whole wheat.

"Lady, if I cared about eating stuff good for me, I wouldn't look like this," she pointed to her hips. "Do you have fries? Chips just won't cut it."

We carried our trays to a table. Cathryn sat with us and drank her iced tea. I ate my turkey avocado wrap. We didn't have to squirm in awkward silence because Theresa's frantic food fest entertained us. Theresa didn't eat her food, she assaulted it. She surfaced for air long enough to shovel in fries between bites of her hefty club sandwich. It left her little time to verbally bombard us. No problem for me. I just wanted to eat without fear the meal would be a repeat performance.

Theresa swooped in on the few bacon crumbs on her plate, then leaned across the table and bared her teeth at us. Not a pretty sight.

"Got any leftovers?"

"Well, just a few," said Cathryn.

A few? I rolled my eyes. What a diplomat. An entire afternoon snack waited between her teeth.

"You can pick up a toothpick on our way out. I have to show Leah where to go for her next appointment, then you and I will go back to the floor."

"I don't need no toothpick." Theresa raked between her teeth with her thumbnail. "How's this?" She pushed her top lip up, and I dreaded to think of the extent to which Theresa could push the boundaries of acceptable behavior.

Bits of green still lingered in a few places, but Cathryn looked at her watch. "We need to get moving. You can finish cleaning up when you settle down in your room."

As I walked toward the place Cathryn directed me, I heard Theresa shout, "Catch you later, Miss Two Shoes."

I opened the door to find those predictable white walls again, platinum shag carpet, two semi-stuffed wingback chairs, and no windows. Anxiety rippled the skin on my back, perched itself on my chest. I'd seen these "we're so sorry to tell you" rooms in medical hospitals where doctors bring families to deliver tragedy.

Maybe no one would show up. Maybe Cathryn goofed and confused the rooms. Maybe I officially lost what brain cells I hadn't already destroyed.

What's the protocol for waiting in a nearly empty room? I sat in the chair closer to the door. The air-conditioner vents shivered when the thermostat kicked off; otherwise, the silence loitered in the room like an unwelcome guest. I made a deal with myself that if no one appeared after I counted all the ceiling tiles, then paced for two hundred steps, I'd leave.

Trey pounced in at ceiling tile number seventeen. I didn't yet know his name. I just knew he caused my first official almost heart attack.

13

Is the sky falling?"

Trey's resonant voice might have startled me. But his mere appearance had already pushed my short-circuited heart right through my open mouth. I popped up, as my quirky Aunt Joycie used to say, "faster than a pimple before prom." My grandmother, often appalled by her daughter's unpredictable perceptions, promised us she took the wrong baby home from the hospital.

I eased back into the chair. "No, but I think my heart rate might be." By then my eyes had bounced back into their sockets so I could survey this intruder. He wore a suit, definitely atypical attire from what I'd seen so far, and he wore it well. No tie, but a starched pinstriped shirt. His light brown hair was flattop military style. Instead of carrying a leather brief-case though, he had a navy blue backpack slung over his left shoulder.

He didn't smile. In fact his lips could have been carved into the space above his chin. He walked over to the other chair, turned it to face me, sat, unzipped his backpack, and with-drew a slim manila folder.

"So, Leah," the words rolled out of his mouth as he crossed his right leg so his ankle landed on top of his left knee. "My name is Trey. Today, I'm here to introduce myself and ask you a few questions. We'll be talking more in other sessions."

"Do people in this place ever have last names?"

He still hadn't made eye contact with me because he spoke into the now open folder perched on the crook of his leg. He coaxed reading glasses out of the inside pocket of his tailored suit, slipped them on, and continued to stare at the papers in front of him. "Is that important to you? To have a last name?"

"Well, it sure makes alphabetizing easier," I said. The room felt colder. I curled my feet in the chair and hoped the hospital also treated frostbite.

He glanced at me, reached into the backpack again, pulled out a black Mont Blanc fountain pen, and scribbled in the folder. He stopped writing, shoved the pen in his breast pocket, and scanned my face.

"Tell me why you're here," he said.

Again with the asking things they already knew the answers to. "It was a slow summer. I needed a change of pace." I yawned and didn't bother to hide it behind my hand. When was this going to end? A nap. That's what I needed. When were those scheduled? I stared at Trey, who examined the fingernails of his right hand.

He glanced up, still expressionless. "Do you always joke about serious issues in your life?"

I hated this guy. He had the personality of a bran flake, the warmth of an unlit match, and a lifetime supply of questions.

"Yes, but I'm very serious about the funny issues, so I figure it all balances out," I replied.

To say that he was void of expression may somehow suggest he was capable of one. I did not have evidence to that effect. Trey could have been a mannequin temporarily bestowed with the ability to breathe. His sea-green eyes provided the only splash of color in his barren face. He did not speak. I remembered playing those staring games with my friends. The person who looked away first lost. I bet Trey never lost.

"Are we finished now?" I hoped he would send me on my way. To my nap. And a Nutty Buddy. Maybe two.

"Finished? I don't think we've even started, do you?" He reached into his inside pocket again. Probably to fish out his pen to record my unwillingness to comply. No pen. Out came a Mickey Mouse Pez dispenser. With a swift click, he pinned back Mickey's ears. "Want one?"

Was this a new psychological profile? Would accepting or not accepting candy from a therapist offering a smiling Disney character provoke a Freudian response I might later regret?

"It's only a piece of candy, not a lifelong commitment. If you don't want it, just say so."

The apple juice syndrome. That intense confusion and struggle over something so trite and stupid had found me again. And I suspected, somehow, Trey could detect my ridiculous one-woman bargaining over a piece of candy.

"You just don't seem to be the Pez type. Or maybe it's just seeing Mickey decapitated. Anyway, thanks, but no." I pushed out my best saccharine smile and feigned a relaxed state, in a positive and expectant sort of way, to end this blather.

Mickey went back into the pocket, but this time out came the pen, poised over the still open folder. Trey peered at me over the reading glasses.

"So, let's try this again. Tell me how you came to be here. No jokes. No evasions."

"Miller Lite. I drank way too much of it, way too many times. And that's not a joke. I wish it was. But it's not. Besides, don't you know all this anyway? You have my chart." My weary voice fell on the floor like wet clay. My resolve to model Trey's stoic demeanor waned in the tedium of answering a question that no longer seemed a mystery. Counting the ceiling tiles again seemed a riveting alternative to this boring inquisition.

"Leah," Trey scratched the pen across the paper for a few lines, "we'll be working together in family group therapy. I've read the chart. I'm not interested in the person on this paper." He slid it into his backpack. "I want to hear your voice tell your story. I want you to hear you tell your story. Really, there aren't that many new stories anyway. They're all variations on a theme. It's the theme we're going for here. You're an English teacher. You'll catch on." He relinquished a crooked smile.

My Grams used to say babies weren't really smiling; they just were delighted to have passed their little gas bubble. I was Trey's little gas bubble.

He shrugged on his backpack. "We'll talk tomorrow afternoon during group. You should be on the schedule with everyone else." He looked at his watch. "Cathryn will be here in a few minutes to walk you back to the floor."

I didn't have to wait long. When Trey opened the door, she stood on the other side. They exchanged polite greetings yet jockeyed past one another in the doorway as if afraid one might magnetize the other. Trey nodded in Cathryn's direction and mumbled, "She's all yours." Then he sprinted around the corner. I watched as she watched him dash away. She didn't turn her attention to me until Trey's backpack disappeared.

I almost crashed into the wall after I catapulted out of the chair. I must have looked like the kid dropped off with the sitter whose mother had just appeared with the sweet promise of predictable normalcy.

"I am *so* glad to see you," I told Cathryn, and I meant it. We both laughed. Now that was frightening.

On the return trip to the floor, Cathryn told me Carl, my father, and Molly had all called for a progress report. I wasn't allowed phone privileges yet, but family and friends could call in for an update. Not having phone conversations proved to be a blessing rather than the curse I'd originally thought. I didn't have to regurgitate my every waking and sleeping moment. I didn't have to listen to the outpourings of sympathy, anger, or guilt from anyone else. Blameless. What a deal.

She summarized the calls, starting with Carl who wanted to know if I was medicated, sleeping, and/or anxious to see him. "A rousing chorus of 'No, no, and no,' on those," I told her and she didn't ask me to elaborate. Molly wanted me to know she was praying for me, for Carl, and for anyone who had anything to do with my successful sobriety. Even though I hadn't given much positive thought lately to God, I felt comforted knowing I had my personal prayer warrior going into battle for me. And I knew Molly was fierce. She'd be kicking evil butts all over the place on my behalf.

And then there was my father. Cathryn said she spoke to him the longest. I wasn't surprised. My dad didn't know a stranger. And he and Carl were the best of friends. He said Carl was the son he never had, a curious statement always made out of earshot of my brother. Dad loved football and food and family and friends. Together or separately. After my mother died, he added Johnny Walker Red and Chivas Regal to the list.

"Your dad said if you needed anything—food, money—just let him know. He'll get it to you." Cathryn paused. Her voice softened as the elevator whirred to the next floor. "And he said to tell you he loves you very much."

My shoes blurred as I stared at them through eyes brimming with tears. How deeply had I disappointed him? I hadn't allowed myself to think about him until now. After Mom died, he was like a man who'd spend days preparing a Thanksgiving meal only to watch it all rot because no one showed up. When he visited, he'd shamble around the house, following me from pantry to kitchen to laundry room to kitchen again. I learned not to stop too short or turn too quickly. He wanted so desperately to be needed.

"What can I do? Do you need to hang any pictures? I can do that for you. I've been looking at your garden. I could put more cypress mulch around the bedding plants in the front. How about a trellis?"

I'd tell Carl, "My dad's coming next week. Don't fix anything. In fact, break something if you can. Are any pipes leaking? Faucets dripping?"

I didn't think he'd call, at least not so soon. I didn't want to think about him, figuring out how to fix his daughter. I doubt if he'd talked to Peter. He and my brother heard life through separate radio channels.

Maybe it was better Dad didn't have to prepare my mother for this disgrace and failure in my life. I pictured him standing in his kitchen, surrounded by the new, fingerprint-proof, stainless steel appliances and emerald-green granite countertops my mother had selected only a few months before she died. He'd be talking on the cordless phone while he sat on a wicker stool near the raised bar. Neither one of them ever bought into the concept of cordless phone freedom. They'd hover near the phone base as if secured by an invisible line. My mother would tell me to "hold on" when she'd hear the microwave beep. She'd set the phone on the counter, ignore my screechings that she could carry me with her, and then return after she'd pulled out her cup of hot water for her tea. After several fruitless attempts to yank my parents into some degree of advanced technology, I surrendered. My father still ignored call waiting and usually erased messages on the answering machine in his attempts to listen to them.

By the time my phone restrictions ended, Dad would have had time to stir the news around, letting it dissolve like an Alka-Seltzer in water.

The elevator doors clanged open.

"How did he sound? My dad, I mean." I pushed my words over the dam in my throat that held back rivers of regret and guilt and shame.

"Kind," Cathryn said. "He sounded kind and caring and concerned, Leah. He told me all he wants is for you to be well. He said something along the lines of, 'You take care of my baby, now. You know, she's my only daughter.' No pressure, huh? Oh, I almost forgot." She smiled, pulled paper and a pen from the counter, and handed them to me. "He said to write what you want to eat on your first weekend home, and he'd be there to cook it for you. In fact, he promised to cook extras for the staff."

"My father believes any problem can be solved by raw oysters, a crawfish boil, and Blue Bell Natural Vanilla Bean ice cream slathered on hot apple pie," I said.

"Who am I to argue with that?" Cathryn chuckled. "Write on, girl."

───※───

That night my new dysfunctional family and I went to the cafeteria for dinner. I hadn't spent more than five minutes with anyone in the group since the time I met everyone in the communal playroom. And even though Theresa was admitted after me, the crew already welcomed her. She knew Doug, so that put her miles ahead of me on the rehab food chain. I watched her move around and envied how easily she laughed with the group, chatted with the staff. But was I supposed to want to be like the woman who felt comfortable checking in for round two? Something about that seemed skewed. So, did recognizing the lunacy of that logic mean I was better or worse?

I trailed Benny and Vince, who argued over who would serve first at the volleyball game that night. Funny how the more a person's world shrinks, the more otherwise insignificant acts grow. I suspected this wasn't the first time they had discussed this.

"Man, you suck at serving," Vince said. "Come on, you seen me slam that ball over the net so hard, old Doug wished he'd be on his way to another blackout."

"What? You think we're here for Olympic tryouts or somethin'?" Benny playfully shoved Vince into the elevator. "How much fun you think it was standing there watching you pound the ball at them? We wanna play volleyball, not watch you be hero-server boy."

Their banter continued as we walked through the cafeteria door. Annie brought a magazine with her. What a shocker. Guess she didn't plan to engage in a stimulating dinner conversation. Had to give it to her. The chick used those mags as her "no talking" signs. And it worked. Of course, Doug and Theresa yapped on, totally involved in their little festival of memories.

I'm an outcast among outcasts. How pathetic. But what was I going to talk to these people about? Symbolism in *The Scarlet Letter*? Not exactly a mystery as to what brought us all together. Besides, my life compared to theirs was beyond boring. It wasn't like we were going to have reunions after we left Brookforest. We couldn't find each other anyway; we didn't even know one another's last names.

"Hey, Miss, you gonna get a tray or what?" said Benny.

"Sure, I'm on it. Sorry," I said, embarrassed to be so mesmerized by my conversation with myself.

I wasn't sure if it was the sight of meat slabs soaking in juices the color of oil spills or the cacophony of pungent aromas that created a ruckus in my gut, but my tray didn't make it past the salads. A geyser of yesterday's meals came up from my stomach and crashed its way to the shore of my mouth. I bolted to the bathroom.

Benny's voice followed me, "Miss, you forgot your tray."

14

I was alone.

Well, about as alone as a recovering alcoholic can be in a treatment center. After my mad dash out of the dining room, I skipped dinner and headed upstairs.

Jan had already started her shift and met me as I stepped off the elevator.

"Whatever they're serving down there must be toxic. You look terrible," she said and steered me to the sofa.

"Happy to see you too," I told her and plopped on the cushions. Jan started to sit next to me, but I held up my hand to stop her. "If you're going to sit, please be gentle. My stomach is sloshy, but I need something. How's the stash of Diet Cokes and crackers?"

"That's not dinner. You haven't eaten well since you've been here. What about a sandwich? Or soup? Both?"

"None of the above. How about peanut butter and jelly? I can handle that."

"No problem. In fact, you're in luck. We already have peanut butter on the floor. It's Matthew's, but I'm sure he'll be a good boy about sharing. I'll send him down for some of those packs of jelly Cathryn told me you're so attached to." Jan patted my hand and walked down the hall to find the peanut butter.

By the time the crew returned from dinner and the ritual volleyball game, I'd retreated to my bed. The gaggle of voices in the hall reminded me my new roomie would be joining me tonight, and Jan would be calling "lights out" soon. My moment of decision.

I could: a) stay awake and attempt a mini-bonding experience with Theresa, or b) turn off the lamp, wiggle under the covers, face the wall, and let her think I was sleeping. The kicker was neither option was an honest one. I'd either be pretending to want to be friendly with Theresa or pretending to be asleep.

The door creaked open.

"Man, how does this little white bread chick expect me to see in this room?"

Theresa flipped on the overhead lights, and I flipped on the bed. I plowed my face in the pillow.

So much for any of the above.

"Hey, I wake you up?"

The next morning I woke up to an empty room. Theresa's bed was unmade, and her boxer shorts and T-shirt were on the floor. At least she wasn't the queen of neat. Not that, judging by her disorganized hair, I really expected her to be. But, obviously, I'd been wrong before about lots of things. Having to share a room with someone as bizarre as Theresa was enough to deal with. I certainly didn't need my mother's clean clone following me into therapy.

My mother had a place for everything, and everything had its place. Dad referred to their house as the museum. In the kitchen, the collection of four tin canisters on the left side of the cook top all faced large apples out. In the family room, the coffee table arrangement moved left to right: a stack of three books chosen because the hardcover shades coordinated with the room's harvest colors, a woven basket filled with large pine cones Dad merrily brought home from the golf course ("Aren't these remarkable, Lola? Can you believe the size of these things?"), and three inches up and two over, a fan of four magazines that were replaced monthly. I wouldn't dare move one of her knickknacks for fear some silent alarm would reverberate in my mother's clean control room.

One night, after too much ouzo at the Greek Festival, Dad zigzagged through the crowd to find Carl and me as we watched the Hellenic Dancers. "Quick, gotta tell you the new name I came up with for your mother. Sh." He looked around, spotted her, and waved as she stood in the bakery line for more baklava. "I'm . . . I'm getting Morrie over at the trophy shop to make a plaque for her. It's going to have her name and—" He slapped the table with giggling delight, "—a line that says, 'official rep for the FBI—Female Bathroom Inspectors,' and he's drawing a little toilet underneath." He must have changed his mind when the anise-flavored liquor worked its way out of his system, because he was still alive months later.

All those years of cleaning, dusting, polishing, vacuuming, swishing, and swashing had taken their toll. When I finally moved out of my parents' house, I became a creature of clutter. I surrounded myself with a happy jumble of books and papers and dishes, both clean and dirty. The disorder comforted me. Drove my mother crazy. She'd wince when she walked in. Probably itched to grab a roll of paper towels and a spray bottle of anything with the word "disinfectant" on the label. Clutter had a life of its own, but it gave me a chance to make order out of chaos. I'd experience a spiritual, Genesis-like satisfaction in seeing the gleam of an empty sink, the bareness of the polished pine desk.

So now I had a partner in grime. Maybe there was hope for us.

Oddly, no knocking on the door this morning to wake me. Maybe installing Theresa in my room was alarm enough. I showered and pulled on slouchy sweats Molly insisted I pack. "You have to wear something that lets you eat another bowl of ice cream." My butt-freeing sweats and I stood on my toes by the sink. I was trying to reach the mirror to determine how much time I had before my eyebrows formed a straight line when the bathroom door swung open.

Theresa's body filled the open space of the door frame. Her perfume—and that would be a kind description—occupied the rest of the space. "Girl, you gotta learn to lock this door if we gonna be sharing this room." She didn't move. She stared.

Was I supposed to speak? She didn't seem quite as threatening, but then I noticed she hadn't yet applied her war paint. And she definitely did not have mental telepathy or she surely would have swatted the blazes out of me by now.

"Okay." I glared back.

"So, you finished or what 'cuz I got some business to do in here, you know?" She pulled a pink plastic case out of the front pocket of her jeans and wiggled it as if I was capable of seeing only moving objects. "This ain't no pencil case." She waved the tampon container toward the door. "I'll let you know when I'm done."

Lucky for her, the universal rule of menstrual cycle sisterhood worked in her favor here. "Sure." I shrugged my shoulders and eased past her. I hoped the fumes of whatever perfume she wore wouldn't settle on me in the seconds I needed to escape.

I headed to the rec room to wait to be herded to breakfast. After last night's feast of peanut butter and jelly, I woke up ready to chew on the pillow.

The women were the only ones moving around. Annie was back in her corner with her ever-present magazine. I tossed a feeble "hello" in the direction of *Good Housekeeping*. It nodded back. Maybe I could dash across the room, yank the magazine out of her hands, and . . . and what, genius? Run away. Yep. That's probably what I'd do. A few seconds of brain-numbing ridiculous behavior followed by the awful recognition of my own stupidity. And then flight. Hmmm. Why does this feel so familiar?

"Hey, the bathroom's yours if you want it now. I even sprayed it all up for you." Theresa's burp punctuated her arrival in the rec room and her announcement. "Whoa! Watch out now." She laughed, slammed her fist into her chest, and then *umpfed* on the sofa next to me.

"Thanks, but I'm all done for now," I said, grateful to bypass the aromatic aftermath of Hurricane Theresa. Any other year, I'd be combating the aftermath of a weekend at the lake house. Morning Bloody Marys, margaritas for lunch on the pier, late afternoon sunset martinis, and wine with dinner. My 24-hour prescription for surviving the toxic dose of Carl's mother during the day and Carl at night.

"So, what's with book chick over there?" Theresa said, and nodded her happy curls in Annie's direction.

I pretended to be intrigued by the viewing guide scrolling on the television. She leaned closer and whispered, "She stuck-up or something?"

I glanced at Annie, who still hadn't moved. She had to have heard Theresa's question. I'm sure half the wing heard her. A Theresa whisper is on the level of ordinary conversation.

"I don't really know. Maybe you should ask her."

Theresa leaned back into the mushy sofa cushion, folded her arms behind her head, and eyed Annie like she was up for auction. Her feet alternately tapped the floor; the movements rippled up her body and jiggled her stomach to the beat. Even deep thinking was a physical activity for Theresa.

"Nah," she said, "I don't think I'm gonna need someone else to talk to. I got you, right?"

At that moment I wanted to bash Annie and her magazine-addicted self over the head.

15

On the way down to breakfast, Cathryn announced the day would start with a group session with Dr. Sanders.

"That ain't no good after breakfast," Benny grumbled.

"Yeah, so what meal is it good after, huh, kid?" We could always count on Doug for our reality check.

"Me, I don't care when it starts as long as I got time to go the bathroom," Theresa said.

I shifted to let Theresa out of the elevator and caught Annie either twitching or actually winking at me. The corners of her mouth seemed suspiciously turned skyward for a nanosecond. Her usual slather of green eye shadow had been replaced by an iridescent violet, meant, I think, to coordinate with the tie-dyed pink and purple blouse shoved into waist-cinching khaki shorts. Annie's clothes had not yet surrendered themselves to what must have been a new body shape.

"So, how are you and Theresa working out?" Annie didn't lift her eyes from the gray cafeteria tray she pulled from the stack. I looked over my shoulder, not even sure she was talking to me. We were the last two in line, so she really was breaking her vow of silence.

"I can tolerate anything for twenty-three more days," I said. "Even these scrambled eggs with bits of what I'm praying are bacon or some sort of meat substance."

Annie stopped to survey the bread options. "Yeah, but now you're doing it sober." She picked up two lumpy biscuits, stacked them onto her plate next to her mini-tower of sausage patties, picked up her tray, and walked toward an empty table at the far edge of the cafeteria.

So much for the beginning of that friendship.

How could Annie not like me? Most people at least liked me. Well, if I didn't count my mother-in-law, and I didn't. The thud of absolute loneliness that crashed into my gut echoed through the dining hall. How ridiculous! I'm a professional. I have a college degree. Plus graduate hours. I have friends. I have a husband. A house in the right zip code. I drive a Lexus. And not one person in this motley assortment of human beings talked to me.

I ate at a table for two near a window. At least I had a view if not a human companion. I swirled the syrup on my disorganized stack of pancakes. Not at all like Carl's. What was he thinking as he ate breakfast this morning? Probably not about dreading group therapy.

Dr. Frank Sanders already sat in the group room when we arrived. He stationed himself in a chair closest to the door. Was that to expedite his getaway or to prevent ours?

A circle of submarine gray folding chairs waited. The only seats not occupied were on either side of the doctor. Naturally. But my teacher-self realized the advantage of not being in eye-lock view of the man in charge. Peripheral vision tended to eliminate the possibility I'd have to be subjected to one of his squirm-inducing stares.

Everyone was quiet. Sanctuary quiet. Like any moment a priest or minister or rabbi or Dali Lama would start services quiet. Even Theresa was mute. She held her pudgy hands hostage under her thighs, which seemed to ooze off the seat, and stared at her kneecaps. Doug's long legs acted as ballasts as he teetered on the back chair legs, his neck barely holding up his head. His splotched hands, threaded together on his bloated stomach, were the shade of pancakes I barely ate for breakfast. The boy teens' U2 fire-red shirts were the only bolts of color in the otherwise naked room. The overhead lights were so white and punishing they could have been used for police interrogations. The unforgiven in an unforgiving room.

Dr. Sanders looked around, taking emotional temperatures as his eyes flicked from one of us to the other. He smelled fresh, like pine trees, like my brother. If I closed my eyes for just a moment, I could pretend Peter sat next to me, and we were in the movies waiting for the lights to fade into black. Only there's no black, no fading, no Peter.

"First day, first group. Let's start with an introduction. First names only and how you came to be here. I'll start." Dr. Frank, a psychiatrist, was in recovery from an addiction to Demerol and Dilaudid and other pain medications outside the realm of pronunciation.

I prayed we'd do the clockwise round because my tongue felt paralytic, and a Civil Defense air-raid siren drilled into my eardrums. I heard Vince's post-adolescent voice and stopped holding my breath.

"Hey. I'm Vince and, like, my mom, she told me I had to be here or else she'd, like, figure out a way for me to be in jail, ya know. She got all whacked when she found out I was skipping school. Well, I guess I'm addicted to pot, X, whatever gets me flying. I ain't old enough to buy alcohol." He shrugged his shoulders.

"Dude, that's funny." Benny gave him a fake punch in his arm. "You not being able to buy drinks or go to bars and you still ended up here."

No one else laughed, not even a stifled giggle. I wanted to award him bonus points for catching the irony of it all.

"Me? I'm Benny. My old lady, she liked that guy Elton John. Guess he's a guy. Anyway, she liked the song he wrote about Benny and his jets. So, I'm nineteen. I started using, but I told my old lady when I get here she the reason I'm here. I mean, look where she got my name."

I knew I should listen to Benny's story—there's probably a test later. But no matter how often I swallowed, the knot in my throat wouldn't dissolve. I had that first day of school shivering anticipation, only then I knew what I was going to say. I wished I had a script. If my contacts didn't make me want to rip my eyes out I wouldn't be forced to wear glasses, which at this moment slipped down my oily nose. At least the sweats camouflaged my lumpy legs, which had been acting as silos for the ice cream that had become one of my daily food groups.

"Leah?"

My child voice escaped before I had time to add years to it, "Oh, I'm sorry. I'm next?"

Dr. Sanders didn't answer. He just nodded and gripped his pen. An extra fine point. My favorite. I lusted after pens. I probably shouldn't share that today. Someone coughed. I focused on the outer rim of Theresa's hair.

"Well, my name is Leah. I'm married. My husband's name is Carl." Each word sounded like a stone carefully placed. I paused, knowing I'm supposed to share how I became a willing inmate. *I'm here, if you really want to know the truth, which if we did, none of us would be here, but the truth was I have to be drunk to have sex with my husband. So now I'm here, and I'm not only not drinking, I'm not having sex.*

"Umm. Well, I'm here because my friend Molly took me to lunch and said I needed to stop drinking. Not that I was drinking all that much. But, you know, I'm just mid-stage, and, well, I just mostly drink beer."

Doug snorted. "Girl, I've spilled more beer on my tie than you drank in your whole little life. I don't even know why you're here."

"Doug, shut it down. You don't need to be all over new chick, giving her a hard time and all." Wow. Theresa to the rescue?

"Seems to me like she got lost on her way to the country club or somethin'." Doug slapped his hands on his knees and leaned forward. I wasn't sure if he was going to throw up or stand up.

"Leah?" Once again, Mr. Doctor's voice. "Why are you smiling?"

"Why am I smiling?" I echoed, rotated my wedding band, and stared at the floor. This wasn't a question I was prepared to answer. I didn't read about a smiling probation period in the papers Ms. Wattingly had given me. Why did it matter? A test? Lady or the tiger? Sobriety behind one door. Insanity behind the other. Still the band spun around my finger. So much friction, my fingers would explode into flames. My hand on fire would put a stop to that smiling.

"I . . . I just smile. I don't think about it, really. I always smile. I mean not always, but mostly." I was a stammering adult, apologizing for a smile. This was why people drank. This and the fact that I now held a conversation with the floor.

"Uh-huh." Mr. Doctor's pen tap-danced on his clipboard.

I knew that response. I practiced it often in teaching, mostly at parent conferences or in discussions with school board personnel. Loosely translated, it meant, "I don't believe one syllable of what you're telling me, and I don't think you do, either, but we're just not going to go there now."

Finally, I suspended my psychic transference with the floor. When I lifted my head, the first face I saw was Annie's. Her eyes were dull, like unpolished silver. An invisible screen separated us. She focused on a movie playing itself out, one only she could see. I stopped smiling.

The pause allowed time for random body shifting. Even my well-padded posterior felt numb. It didn't help that the room could have doubled as a meat locker. The near-freezing temperature must have some effect on addictions. In that space of quiet, I allowed myself my first deep breath since the mini-interrogation.

Everyone else seemed comfortable with the stillness. Me? I waited for the other shoe to fall. Why?

Exactly.

Why did I have to gird myself for impending doom? If the bad thing hadn't already happened, it's sure enough going to happen, and it's just a matter of time, probably even closer than you think if something good's happened, so buck up, baby. Hold on. The breath out of everyone's mouth was a gale force wind.

A few coughs broke the stillness. Theresa sneezed and wiped her hands on her jeans. One of the U2 kids belched. They both laughed. Annie surfaced from her meditative state. Doug snored. Amazing. Minus the gravel he seemed to be processing through his nostrils, he could be mistaken for someone deeply prayerful.

"We'll shut down introductions for now. Let's review some ground rules for these group sessions. First," and this time Mr. Doctor smiled, "would someone mind elbowing Doug over there?"

Journal 6

"You need help."

Oh, yes, I thought, more than you could possibly imagine. But the words that danced from my mouth wore different clothes. "You're probably right."

He stopped counting the pairs of folded socks stacked in the corner of the suitcase to turn to me. I stood behind him. Out of arm's reach. "Probably? No, that's where you're mistaken. There's no probably."

The suitcase yawned on top of the tightly made bed covered with a cranberry silk quilt and a floral embroidered duvet. Carl's lips made an almost perfectly straight line between his nose and his chin.

"I'm going out of town for over a week. I told you last night I needed you. In fact, I told you even before I left for work yesterday I couldn't wait to get home. And you? You won't come to bed with me."

She flinched as the raw disgust in his voice crawled down her back.

"You watch some stupid shows on television, read. I never know what you're up to out there while I'm in here waiting. Waiting for you. When you finally get yourself in bed, you won't let me touch you. How's a husband supposed to survive like that?"

She stilled her body and waited. This would not be the end of the tirade. I knew he must punish me as he felt I'd punished him. At least this was familiar. I knew what to expect.

He walked over to me. His meaty hands filled the hollows of my shoulders. He leaned over. His mouth pressed against my right ear. I focused on the Miersdorf watercolor hanging on the wall. Painted with jazzy reds and inky blacks and sapphire blues, the piano grinned at the shadowy figure perched on the piano stool. I made myself tiny inside the shell of my body. His moist whispers coated my neck. The clammy wetness reminded me of the mulch in my father's backyard and how, when he'd turn it over, a manure-heavy steam would rise from the pile.

"I'll be home on Sunday. We can make up for all the lost time. I know you'll be ready then."

16

"Do you know what's worse than group with Dr. . . . ? Oh—I know. Nothing," I said to Jan, whose afternoon shift started while I suffered in the Little Shop of Therapy Horrors. Actually, I was talking at her since I didn't want or ask for a response. Judging by the lazy grin on Jan's face, I wasn't the first trauma victim suffering from post-group syndrome.

I power-walked around the nurses' station, grateful for the locked windows that kept me from leaping—of course, how much damage could I do to myself from the second floor—but also to outrun the cigarette smoke wafting from the rec room.

"There are no windows in that room. That's perverse. And it's freezing in there. Nobody told me I'd need a coat. Walking out of that place . . ."

"Hey, at least you didn't have to be carried out." Jan's smile betrayed her attempt at sounding serious. "Anyway, think about this," she said, scooting her desk chair over to reach the ringing telephone, "visiting starts on Sunday." She was laughing by the time she answered the call.

The weekend morphed into some never-ending story of impending doom. First, when we leave the group session we'll board a bus Friday evening for our first AA meeting away.

Then I'm pummeled with the thought of visitors. The army of ants that paraded through my stomach decided to pitch tents.

It's almost time for another meal. Here, meals have little or nothing to do with hunger. Maybe, before I'm totally sober and completely, certifiably ready to leave here, my stomach will adjust to this schedule. Not that it matters. I've already learned to eat on demand. When I'm hungry, I hope there're enough Nutty Buddies or Blue Bell mini ice cream sandwiches in the freezer to stuff into the empty rumbling cave.

Today, though, it seemed pointless to even try eating. I was sure some reverse gravitational law would kick in—and whatever I sent down would reappear. Already, I couldn't believe there was a time when I used to pray to not have to cook yet one more meal.

Mom always said to be careful what you pray for—you might just get it. "But," she'd be quick to warn, "it may not come wrapped in the package you're expecting. Remember that before you start asking God for all kinds of foolishness. Sometimes you're just borrowing trouble."

The yellow bus coughed its way out of the parking lot, entering Trace Street with just enough energy to squeeze into the snarling early evening traffic. This pumpkin was not the carriage I expected. But then, I wasn't headed to the ball either. Maybe school buses were used as part of the aversion therapy. Don't make us too comfortable, or else we may not want to leave.

We arranged ourselves like so many strangers, careful not to invade one another's space. The bus leveled the playing field. No one person had authority in this territory. Even Doug sagged a little less—which was Doug-ese for saying he was actually sitting straight. All eyes seemed focused on the shifting shapes of cars and glass buildings that, as the sun set, blazed like fingers of fire sprouting from restaurants and strip shops and gas stations. Each of us viewed the city through a window of our own. Protected from noise for so many days, hearing only the hum of florescent lighting, the drum roll of central air conditioning, the cafeteria clatter, and the thumping of doors as they opened and closed, the assault of traffic surprised us. We were so reverent we could have all been in silent contemplation for a spiritual retreat or holding a memorial service for a mutual dearly departed.

Myrtle, the bus driver, who could have been a not-so-distant relative of waitress Tina, was a burly, plum-faced woman. Her faded magenta hair poked straight out from the back of her head like a squirrel's tail. She was decked out in a sunflower yellow and blue plaid cotton housecoat snapped up the front, brown men's socks, and slippers. If this was the *attire de rigueur* for AA meetings, Molly and I had spent way too much time in my closet.

After a chorus of adolescent whining and begging Myrtle tuned into the rock station. Mick Jagger's static voice scratched and screamed through the radio. Benny and Vince started singing, Theresa chimed in, and their voices rose to meet Mick's.

I gripped the seat in front of me as the bus lurched and belly-flopped its way to its destination. I think the place was called Serenity. There's something bizarre about us having to be transported to serenity.

The kids and Theresa laughed as they joined Mick, and then I watched as, one by one, everybody in the bus picked up the tune. Even Doug choked his way through a lyric or two, his emphysemic rock-tumbler throat singing sounding like Keith Richards.

So, there I sat and wondered why I felt like an idiot. Why was participating in this song fest so difficult for me? I couldn't allow myself to act silly even when there would be no real or lasting consequences. Though in my impulsive, spontaneous moments of the past, I'd be loud or brassy, like when I started "Second Lining" at one of the company dinners. Carl had reminded me of the definition of low profile. But in three weeks, I'd never see these people again.

When I drank, I imagined myself like Julie Andrews singing on a mountain top, twirling and twirling, facing the heavens, arms outstretched. I could be delightful and deliriously goofy when I filled myself with enough beer or wine or vodka or whatever. The alcohol bashed the self-imposed emotional straitjacket the sober Leah would be terrified to remove. Drunk Leah felt light, almost ethereal. Eventually, I had the best of both worlds—a fun-filled Leah who, the next day, couldn't remember the havoc she wreaked or the embarrassing improprieties.

But no booze, no coping mechanism. I didn't know how to act like a truly sober person. And I didn't know I'd have to actually start feeling—feeling scared and angry and sad—and I'd have to start remembering.

Less than an hour ago, I had to be coaxed onto the bus. Jan's voice echoed Mom's when she had scrunched her body on the floor to peer under her bed, negotiating with Edison, our neurotic thunder-shy cat. Mom's fleecy-warm voice belied the verbal assault.

"Edison, if you don't crawl from under this bed in the next thirty seconds I'm going to shave all of your hair and pierce your ears."

Now Mom was gone, Edison was hundreds of miles away, probably looking over his shoulder for Mom, and I was the one who wanted to stay under the bed. All dressed up, my neatly creased khakis and my white button-down Gap almost starched blouse. My white canvas backless sneakers. And I couldn't, wouldn't, budge. My body froze. I didn't want to leave the center. I didn't want to walk through those doors. I wasn't afraid of going to the AA meeting. I wasn't afraid of getting on the bus. I wasn't even afraid of coming back. I simply couldn't leave what had come to mean security. I was safe here. No one could hurt me or force me to do anything.

The only other time I experienced this terror was when I woke up and found Alyssa, so still in her crib, so agonizingly still. They pulled her away from me, and she never returned. The overwhelming frightfulness of that moment gouged my soul—emptiness I tried to fill with Robert Mondavi and Johnny Walker and Miller Light.

When Jan said it was time to leave, my legs refused to transport me. I scratched the back of my hand, watching those familiar snail-like welts return. Maybe Carl felt tiny shifts in his universe with every motion of my fingernails urging the redness on.

"What will happen to me? How will I know I'm coming back? What if there's an accident? Please, please don't make me go. I want to stay. I'll stay in my room. Just don't make me go." Thankfully, everyone else had been escorted to the bus, missing my unscripted, irrational performance. How did she know to send everyone away? What had she seen in me? What part of myself had I unknowingly given away?

I pleaded with her. I grabbed her hand. She pried it loose, leaving the indentation of a halo pressed into my palm from her diamond ring.

I made her promise nothing bad would happen to me. That I would come back.

"Leah, breathe. You can do this. Just put one foot in front of the other." Jan pointed me in the direction of the bus. She walked so closely behind me that our bodies made one lumpy shadow.

I felt like I was in one of those recurring dreams where I'd end up in school without wearing my Peter Pan collared button-down shirt, or I'd be wearing the shirt but not have a navy blue knife-pleated skirt to tuck it into. I looked around the bus. No one pointed or laughed, so I must still be fully clothed.

Not one of them looked at me.

They sang in one loud voice now, knowing, of course, that Mick was absolutely right. What we wanted, we could not have. What we wanted was alcohol or sex or drugs or money or any combination of those. What we needed was sobriety. That search for sanity linked the construction worker, the physician, the loan officer, the high school students, the house-wife, the thief, and the waitress.

Mick's song became our anthem.

17

We arrived.

Cars littered the blacktop slab like grown-up Hot Wheels tossed from the sky by careless children of the gods. The bus nosed its way along a chain-link fence, separating the parking lot from the painted white brick church that hovered on the edge of the street.

Myrtle leaned over, tugged on the black handle, and the bus doors yawned opened. "Party's over. Time for me to grab a Subway before the meetin' ends." She stood and swiped her hands across the front of her housecoat, wiping off some invisible gunk from her lap. "Three twelve-inch subs only $11.99 tonight," she announced to the backs of the newly and begrudgingly sober riders who shuffled down the bus steps.

Theresa paused by my seat. "You coming with us or what?"

I chanted my silent mantra when the bus stopped: *I will lift myself off this seat. I will move my legs forward.* But my rebellious feet protested. *Sorry. No can do. We're happy right where we are.* I stared down at my sneaker-clad size sixes, hoping no one else heard them screaming at me. "You are being so disobedient and a little confused about who's in charge here," I sneered.

"Girl, who are you yapping at?" Theresa's voice reminded me I only felt alone.

I pushed myself off the seat and slid a foot forward. I could beg Myrtle to let me ride with her to Subway just this one time. We could get orders to go. Deliver them to the meeting. Were AA meetings catered? Probably not. But they could be. I could start a new business: The Thirteenth Step. *I came to believe in the value of proper nutrition and shared this . . .*

Myrtle cleared her throat. Twice. "I'm hungry, and the meetin's about to start."

I didn't see her face because I focused on convincing my feet to shove themselves out the door.

"She's on her way out, Miss Myrtle. Cinderella here's not going to be late for her first AA meeting," said Matthew. I'd forgotten he was even on the bus as the intern in charge of this wacko field trip. His pat on my shoulder was a gentle push in disguise.

The bus doors clamped shut as the yellow carriage growled away. "She's going to torture us with jalapeno breath, isn't she?" I asked Matthew.

"Nah. She'll eat enough white chocolate macadamia nut cookies to not have fire-breathing dragon mouth. Anyway, she's really harmless. Well, on a full stomach," he said. His scuffed deck shoes slowed to match the pace of my now not-so-white tennis shoes. Every man in Carl's extended family owned a pair of Sperry Rand deck shoes. They were a rite of passage—their totem symbol of manhood.

"Why don't women have deck shoes? Are we not supposed to be on the deck?"

Matthew stopped. "Are you talking to me?"

Once again, my brain failed to lower the guard gate before the thoughts escaped and expressed themselves in words.

"No. Your shoes remind me of my husband." Carl's shoes, though, would continue their brisk stride. "Ever since Carl, I associate deck shoes with sailing." I hoped Matthew didn't notice my lower lip trembling as memories hitched a ride on our conversation.

"I don't sail. They're just comfortable and easy to get on and off." He bent to tie one of the leather laces that had worked its way loose. I massaged the gravel with the bottom of my right foot, waited, and tried not to stare at his backside, which was just as cute as his front side.

"So—" he straightened and nodded toward the front of the building. "You ready?"

"Does it matter? I'm here."

Whatever this was, it was no longer a church. The building had been through some conversion of its own. It looked like one of those ranch-style houses built decades ago for families fleeing the inner cities. An unimpressive steeple clung to the roof. A whitewashed plaque had been nailed over a larger wooden sign near one of the paneled double doors. The word *Serenity* had been blow-torched on by someone with the generic cursive handwriting of a cake decorator.

If my friends could see me now.

College graduate.

Teacher of the Year.

Wife of a Corporate Vice-President.

Alcoholic.

The door swung open. Smoky cigarette ghosts beckoned from the alcove.

"'Bout time ya got here. The meeting ain't gonna wait for you, Miss Thing." Theresa's coif-of-the-day, a fountain of hair sprouting from the top of her head, waved me in.

No one warned me I might need a personal oxygen tank to survive my first AA meeting. I thought I'd follow Theresa into the room, but the smoke-heavy haze parted and swallowed her. I looked around for Matthew, but he had stopped to talk to some guy whose penny-colored dreadlocks formed a spongy curtain around his face.

Two long, brown tables surrounded by a jumble of folding chairs were end to end in the middle of the room. Against two of the walls were more folding chairs. No one was sitting. People were clumped around the room, but most of them hovered near the table that held three coffee pots. Frequently, a medley of voices and laughter would break through the surface. The faces were strangely familiar. How could I possibly know anyone here other than my little bizarre busload from rehab?

If I thought goofy-looking humans in varying stages of stupidity filled AA meetings, then I'd been reading the wrong books. These people weren't dressed in clothes snatched from the bottom of a Goodwill bag. They weren't gathered in corners sharing markers to write "I'll work for food" signs on torn pieces of refrigerator boxes. They didn't reek of stale gin and tonic, didn't stumble, wail, or gnash their teeth. A youngish woman with a Coach bag slung over her left shoulder carefully stirred her coffee and nodded slowly as a suited, square-faced man read to her from a paper he held. A group of women, some wearing J. Jill linen outfits, the others in designer jeans and polo blouses, laughed as a petite woman in their circle demonstrated what I hoped were dance moves.

Vince and Benny blended in with a swarm of teens who could have just walked over from a high school or college campus.

I'd expected to feel displaced. But I felt more relaxed than I did the first time I walked into the Flower Estates Country

Club to meet Carl's parents for dinner. I'd obsessed for days about what to wear and then finally dropped too much money on strappy black BCBG heels and an ocean blue raw silk bubble dress from Anthropologie. Until that night, the closest I'd been to the Holy Grail of private clubs that limited memberships to families with three-syllable names was billing them for plumbing supplies they ordered from my father's hardware store.

But that night at their club, my initiation into Thortons' inner circle was as comfortable as open shower stalls at summer camp. Judging by the clinical stares of some members dining in the clubhouse, I felt sure I must have dragged sheets of quilted bathroom tissue on my shoes as I walked to the table.

Later, Carl admonished me. He said I only imagined their disapproval. "Whatever it is you're feeling is more a reflection of what you think of yourself than what people here may think of you." Even so, I immediately excused myself to find refuge in the ladies' room where I checked my heels and readjusted my pantyhose. I wished I could have stayed in there, chatting with Peggy, the kind attendant who handed out paper towels so the ladies wouldn't have to exhaust themselves by pulling them out of the dispenser.

A few years later, as Mrs. Carl Thornton, I'd been granted the privilege of membership. One of the first club events Carl and I attended as a married couple was the wedding of a prominent somebody's daughter. Between the cake cutting and the bouquet tossing, I'd wobbled outside, handed Carl my quilted Chanel clutch, and vomited their exquisitely expensive hors d'oeuvres into the wading pool. Carl told me I collapsed on one of the pool lounge chairs and congratulated myself on my symbolic act of retaliation.

No bathroom attendants at AA meetings. Alcoholism was an equal opportunity disease with open enrollment in its discreet, sparsely decorated clubs.

How proud Gloria Hamilton Thornton would be to finally brag to her bridge club that her only daughter-in-law had been selected for membership in a club so exclusive she had to be driven for almost an hour in an unmarked school bus to find it. In all fairness, even my mother wouldn't have posted this news flash on her office bulletin board.

Mom never liked "who does she think she is" Gloria. She tolerated her for me. When Gloria entered the same orbit as my mother, strangers would have nominated Mom for the woman most likely to appear as if she's on Prozac award. She transformed into a one-dimensional version of herself, her expression a carefully constructed façade, crafted from years of pretending she enjoyed her secretarial job and cemented with the promise of her only daughter's future happiness. If Mom surrendered God's ear for just a moment and materialized in this room, what face would she have worn for me?

Theresa reappeared, a cup of black coffee in one hand and a small blue book in the other. "Hey, me and Annie's been lookin' around for you."

I choked out an "Oh," swallowed the pronoun lesson, and mentally strangled my thoughts before they had lives of their own. She handed her coffee and book to Annie, alternately tugged the straps of her denim overalls, then wiggled her entire body into some balance between comfort and modesty. The whole routine was somewhat fascinating, like watching one of those circus cars and wondering when the clowns would stop jumping out. She grabbed her coffee cup so quickly some of it splattered on the floor like swollen black raindrops. Annie hopped backward, saving her sandaled toes from a mild scalding.

"I'll go find some napkins," she said and handed Theresa the book before she plodded off in the direction of the long tables.

"Man, I hate when that happens. Now my tank may need a refill in the middle of the meetin'." Theresa's gauge must have worn out years ago.

She looked in Annie's direction. "She's an okay kid, you know. Just gotta give her a chance. She's had a real messed-up life, and she don't trust too many people, especially women, right away."

I wasn't sure what shocked me most. That Theresa was capable of whispering. That she knew enough scoop to be able to relay this information. Or that she supposed Annie's unfriendliness mattered to me. If Theresa defined Annie's life as "messed-up," what dysfunctional ruler was she using to measure her own life?

"Anyway," Theresa continued, indicating a response from me was not expected, "don't say nothing to her about what I told you." She handed me the book she'd been holding. "Matthew asked me to give you this. Said it's yours to keep."

More books? First, a book of daily devotions in the hospital and now this. The size of a chunky paperback, the book had a blue cover embossed with the words Alcoholics Anonymous. I thumbed through the five hundred or so pages. "So, when's the test? And why aren't there any pictures in this thing?"

"It's your Big Book. It's kind of like an AA Bible," Annie said. She handed her stash of napkins to Theresa, who tossed them on the floor, held them down with her foot, and proceeded to swipe the coffee spill.

Theresa stared at the wet glob of napkins.

"Just bend over and pick them up. You can't leave that mess there," said Annie, who strolled away to the tables.

"Man, I don't clean this much at my own place." Theresa grunted. She held the mess between her thumb and forefinger like biohazard waste and shoved it all in her coffee cup. The chatting pods of people broke apart and searched for seats. "We better find us a place to land. The meetin's about to start."

My first AA meeting. Hmmm. Where does one record this memorable event? The page of firsts in Alyssa's petal pink baby book flashed in front of me. "First smile, first car ride, first—" The empty page screamed my heart's loss. But no one had yet created an adult version. "First marriage, first baby, first baby lost, first marriage lost, first addiction, first recovery . . ." Maybe creating a grown-up's scrapbook of events could be my post-recovery contribution to capitalism. Documented, of course, under "first post-recovery entrepreneurial enterprise."

Mr. Suited Square Face called the meeting to order. Everyone gravitated to the long brown tables placed end to end and surrounded by a haphazard arrangement of folding chairs. A few worn loveseats provided second-row seating for the latecomers like Theresa and me.

A mushroom cloud of cigarette smoke billowed. I looked around for my little dysfunctional family. I dreaded the possibility that, if this was like some classroom experience, Theresa and I might have to engage in small group sharing. I considered relocating before this "function" officially started. Annie and Matthew sat next to each other at the table, but there were no empty chairs on either side of them. Doug and his sidekicks were clumped at the far end of the tables. I heard a distinct noise I suspected didn't originate from Theresa's mouth. "My bad," she giggled and waved her hand in front of her face. Her signature bracelets bounced against one another, a little background chorus that, unfortunately, didn't scare away the smell. But she kept waving.

"Yes, on the sofa," Mr. Square Face said, pointing in our direction. "Are you volunteering to start the Serenity Prayer?"

Theresa looked at her hand as if it had been a new appendage that suddenly sprouted from her wrist. I scooted back on the sofa and luxuriated in the smidgen of joy her squirming provided.

"Me? Oh, no. I was getting your attention for my friend here." Theresa reached back and wrapped her traitorous leg-of-lamb arm around my shoulder. "She wanted to do that."

18

My tongue stuck to the roof of my mouth when I heard Theresa volunteer me to lead a prayer I didn't even know. I coordinated my lips enough to mumble, "Uh, no, not tonight, but thanks."

I wanted to slap the braids right out of her electrified hair with that new Big Book. It was only my first AA meeting, but I was certain assaulting a fellow alcoholic wasn't one of those Twelve Steps. I was also sure that humiliating the newcomer wasn't either, but I supposed she evened the score between us. Theresa's embarrassing me was her payback for what she felt was my fault for Cathryn confiscating her laptop.

A voice from the back of the room said, "God, grant me the serenity to accept the things I cannot change . . ."

Serenity? They're kidding, right?

I'm supposed to accept watching my barely six-week-old daughter being lowered into the ground in the tiniest casket I never wanted to see? For weeks I couldn't close my eyes without seeing Alyssa's face staring at me through the lid of her coffin. In my mind's eye I'd see her eyes, liquid emerald saucers, pleading with me not to let her go. I'd roll myself off the sofa and walk to the refrigerator, open the door, and pray there would be enough beer or wine to give me safe passage into sleep.

A chorus of "Amens" reminded me that people who forfeited tickets to safe passages filled the room. I leaned back, lifted my head to face the ceiling, and hoped the tears would evaporate before Theresa volunteered me to lead the meeting.

The man at the table spoke. "Welcome, especially to our newcomers tonight. My name's Kevin, and I'm an alcoholic. By the grace of God and the fellowship of this group, I've been sober for eleven years."

The room answered, "Hello, Kevin."

Oh, no. For years I attended school board-sponsored meetings and spent more time engaged in silly icebreakers than in valuable ideas for . . . hello . . . teaching. I certainly wasn't prepared for this nonsense at an AA meeting. Did we end this holding hands and singing "Kumbaya"?

Kevin, who thankfully couldn't hear the conversation in my head, asked if first-timers wanted to introduce themselves. Before Theresa could even take her next breath, I grabbed her elbow and pulled her back against the squishy sofa cushions. "We're even," I whispered, but it sounded more like a hiss.

She looked at me, her eyes small round truth detectors scanning my face from forehead to chin. "Yeah, Miss Thing. We're even."

Thankfully, some brave soul spoke up. "My name's Todd."

"Hi, Todd." We were like a Greek chorus, only the tragedy was never over.

"I, well, this is my first time here." He locked his eyes on the open pack of cigarettes in front of him. His blond hair hung like a curtain in front of his face. "My wife, she said I need to be here." Heads nodded while ripples of affirmations floated through the room. He lifted his head, and I recognized what I saw in his eyes as two lighthouse beacons of panic and shame.

"Welcome, Todd. Thanks for sharing. You're in the right place," Kevin said, his consoling voice reminding me of my father's the months after Alyssa died. He had answered his cell phone every time I called, even when all I could do was stutter, "D-d-d-d . . ." He'd whisper, "Leah, my Leah. It's going to work out. Everything will work out." I believed him. When I was five and scared to sleep, he'd use his special spray under my bed and in my closet to make all the monsters disappear. I wanted to believe him again.

No one spoke, but it was an expectant rather than an uncomfortable silence. Kevin unbuttoned the collar of his pin-striped shirt. "If we don't have any more introductions, does anyone have any AA-related announcements?"

Coach Purse Woman raised her hand but didn't wait to be recognized. She pushed her glasses on top of her perfectly center-parted, high- and low-lighted, chin-length auburn hair. "Hi, I'm Rebecca, a grateful recovering alcoholic." She plowed through before the chorus's reply. "I'd just like to remind the regulars to pick up their coffee cups and ashtrays after the meetings. You know, your mother . . ."

The chorus finished for her: ". . . doesn't work here."

"Unless she's here with you," called out a springy-haired teen in the back who grinned and patted the knee of the woman next to her. Her mother smiled and shook her head gently from side-to-side with the experience of one who's spent years motioning no. If they were getting sober together, did they get drunk together? Interesting dynamics there.

Theresa picked up the Big Book from my lap, sighed, and thumbed through the pages. "Ain't that cute?" she said to the open book, but the question was delivered in an envelope of bitterness.

I assumed she was referring to the mother-daughter team since there didn't seem to be anything "cute" about a book full of stories about alcoholics. Surprisingly, Theresa's volume was lower than usual. I seemed to be the only person who heard her. Maybe she didn't even mean to be heard at all.

"Thanks for the reminder, Rebecca. And Jill—" he nodded in her direction "—is the only one with mother privileges, so the rest of you are on your own." Kevin pulled a worn blue book from the table. "This is a Big Book Study Meeting. If you need a book, we have extras around the room. We were in chapter five, page sixty-two. Could someone start reading?"

I opened my book. The chapter title was "How It Works." I know how alcohol works, so what's the "it"? I was on my way to finding out.

Jill's mother volunteered to read, her voice strong and resonate.

"So, our troubles, we think, are basically of our own making. They arrive out of ourselves, and the alcoholic is an extreme example of self-will run riot, though he usually doesn't think so. Above everything, we alcoholics must be rid of this selfishness. We must, or it kills us! God makes that possible."

She paused and looked at Kevin, who nodded, and she continued. "And there often seems no way of entirely getting rid of self without His aid. Many of us had moral and philosophical convictions galore, but we could not live up to them even though we would have liked to. Neither could we reduce our self-centeredness much by wishing or trying on our own power. We had to have God's help."

"Thanks, Shelia. Let's stop there," Kevin said.

Great. God's going to fix my alcoholism. Maybe Carl should've checked me into a church for treatment.

"Usually we cover a lot more ground, but it seems we have some first-timers here tonight. That little bit . . ."

I quickly diverted my attention to the book I'd snatched back from Theresa. No way was I going to risk being picked out of this group. Besides, what I just heard was definitely not about me. *As if I caused my own troubles. This God who's supposed to help? Isn't this God the one who took my baby?* How many times at Alyssa's funeral did I have to brace myself for yet another dunderhead's rendition of, "Honey, God missed Alyssa so much in heaven He took her back to be with Him"?

By the end of the afternoon, my raw hands were my red badges of tolerance, stung from the insistent patting of otherwise well-meaning people. My heart was enraged, subjected to hearing Alyssa's name cradled in the mouths of those who'd never kissed the dimple in her shoulder, who'd never felt the warm weight of her in their arms. I blasted a poodle-haired, tomato-faced little man who said God wanted Alyssa because she had finished her work on earth.

"Finished? Finished? You call forty-two days of life finished? So, why are the rest of us here? What are you saying?" I didn't care that with each question I pummeled him with, I grew louder. I didn't care that I sprayed his round, seedy face with gin-laced spit. I didn't care that the alcohol I'd gulped in the bathroom gurgled in my gut. I went for the kill. "So, what does that say about you? Why isn't God finished with you, old man? Maybe you're still here because God doesn't care about you. If God cared about you, you'd already be in heaven, right?"

Molly reached me before Carl's mother, Gloria, did. She steered me to the bathroom, locked the door, turned on the faucets full force, and let me scream every profanity I knew. Probably even some I invented that afternoon.

Molly saved my life then too. Molly was saving my life today in this room.

I missed Molly.

Why couldn't she be an alcoholic too? Then we could go through this together.

Some wisp of thought curled itself around me. "*Why can't you be sober? You could experience* that *with Molly.*"

Oh, my. Did I just have a mini-blackout, and I've been sputtering like an idiot? Did Theresa answer me? No.

Kevin had stopped talking. "Go, ahead." He pointed to a raised hand at the table.

"Hi, my name is Jesse, and I'm an alcoholic."

Here we go again. I couldn't bring myself to join the chorus, so I just mouthed, "Hi, Jesse." Too many people here for anyone to notice if I was playing by the rules.

Jesse closed his eyes as if what he wanted to say was written inside his lids. His mouth and his eyes opened at precisely the same moment like they were on the same switch. Both appeared wide and shockingly soft for a man who looked like he lifted trucks for a living. He picked his thumb with his forefinger as he spoke. He didn't lift his eyes from the book. "That part about being selfish. About how it could kill us."

A hush grabbed the room by its throat. We waited for the unspoken that would release us. Jesse glanced at Kevin and then as if tugged by the groaning of his heart, Jesse bowed his head. His words drifted up toward us. "I never really thought of myself as selfish. I'm in construction. I work hard. Gave my wife enough money to pay bills, take care of the kids. Figured, what's wrong with me going out drinking with a few of the men after work? I deserved it. I was the one sweating all day, every day."

Jesse paused.

I wiggled my toes inside my shoes. If they gave pedicures during these meetings, things would seem to move a whole lot faster. This guy's a bit too whacked out about having a few good old boy nights. Why should anyone apologize for wanting to hang out with their friends? I glanced at my nails. Hmm. Maybe manicures too.

Theresa shifted her cargo to the edge of the sofa, and I almost toppled over in the process. Her entire body focused on Jesse. I made an effort to pay attention.

"Well," he continued, but his soft voice had a jagged edge to it. I recognized that sound. "I told the guys I was passing up going to the bar this one night because I'd promised my little boy I'd take him to his baseball game. But you know one beer doesn't take too long. When I got home that night, nobody was there. It was almost eleven o'clock. Next thing I know, I'm on the floor, and the doorbell's ringing."

I plugged my ears with my fingers. *I don't want to hear this. I don't want to hear this.* But I did. Theresa and her musky perfume inched forward and left behind the smell of rotting carnations.

The man next to Jesse, whose skin looked like sand cracked and fissured by an unforgiving sun, put his hand on Jesse's shoulder. His fingers reminded me of gnarled tree roots.

"I'm mad 'cuz they woke me up," Jesse said. "I opened the door screaming, 'You got a key . . .' There's a man standing on my porch with the Sheriff's Department. He told me he'd get me to the hospital. That my son would be fine."

For a moment, I allowed myself to breathe. *See, his little boy's fine. He learned his lesson. Please stop there. Please make this be it.* But I already knew enough about AA to know we wouldn't all be sitting in this room if there were happy endings. And now, Jesse's heaving shoulders and the downcast eyes of everyone who sat near him made me want to fly out the front doors.

Jesse's voice strangled. "I didn't even ask about my wife. I was so relieved to hear about Ryan, I didn't even ask about Cindy. Sheriff told me when we got in his car. Told me the woman who ran the light hit the driver's side head-on. Cindy didn't have a chance."

No one moved. The sinners listening to the confession of a fellow sinner. No escape clauses here.

Jesse grabbed tissues from a box passed to him. "I was supposed to die. Not her. I'm the one broke my promise to my kid. Now I'm the one who killed his mother. You know, I thought drinking would kill me. But it killed Cindy."

He stopped to blow his nose. Mr. Gnarled Hands gave Jesse a one-armed hug.

"I've been sober almost a year. Only way I could stay that way was with God helping. And I'm gonna stay that way—one day at a time—'cuz Ryan deserves a dad who's sober."

Journal 7

Carl wanted a baby. He talked about having a son, about how much time they would spend together, about how he would teach his son to respect him. We'd been married only two years, as many years as I'd been teaching.

At first, Carl didn't mention the subject of babies very much. As two years turned into three, he became more insistent. He'd see a baby and ask me, "When? When is it going to be okay with you?"

All I could answer was, "I don't know." It wasn't that I didn't want children. I didn't know how to tell him that the thought of being a mother terrified me. I wasn't sure I could give up my life. I didn't know how to be a mother.

Months later, I discovered his mother doubted me too. Carl's parents were having dinner at our house. They were outside grilling steaks, and I went inside to finish setting the table. I was in the pantry looking for napkins when I heard Carl and his mother walk into the kitchen. I almost called out to tell them where I was when Carl's mother said, "I don't understand why you're so anxious for a baby right now."

I held on to the napkins and waited. Carl said, "Well, Mother, I'm surprised you're not ready to be a grandmother." Ice coughed out of the refrigerator dispenser.

"Carl, dear, for one thing, Leah already has, um, let's say, 'ample' hips for a woman her size. Having a child isn't going to help that any. And, another thing, she's just doesn't seem ready to give up that teaching thing of hers."

I quickly stepped into the bathroom behind the pantry. Flushed the toilet with the door open to make sure they'd hear and think I couldn't have heard them. I walked out, smiled, and played the good wife and daughter-in-law.

After all, it was my father-in-law's birthday. And I'd planned a surprise gift—for all of them.

I was pregnant.

19

The first time I called Carl from rehab, we sounded like a couple of robots. "How are you? Fine." "How are you? Fine." Mutual silence. I imagined him in the charcoal leather recliner, armed with the remote, channel surfing. He told me he'd called my dad, and my dad was going to call my brother. "Oh, and I told my parents where you are." His voice flat-lined.

I pressed my hand to my chest and tried to massage the pain away. "Everything else?" *Just please say yes. Don't rip me open.*

"Great. Everything's great." I knew he was lying. He knew that I knew.

"I don't have much time to talk. I can have visitors on Sunday. Are you coming?" A deep breath. Hold.

"Do you want me to visit?"

Exhale. "Do you want to visit?"

Silence. Wrong answer.

"Guess you still haven't learned how to answer a simple question with a simple answer. Guess that's next week, huh?"

Ignore that. Ignore that. Just say what he wants to hear.

"Sure. Sure. I'd like for you to visit."

"Then I'll see you on Sunday. Do you need anything?"

More than you know. "No. Not a thing."

⁂

"Why can't I have time off for good behavior?"

"Leah, if you'd get your head out of the freezer, I might be able to hear you." Matthew finished charting and was hanging out in the patient rec room waiting for Cathryn to relieve him. Everyone else vacated to settle their basketball competition. I wasn't all that interested. Besides, as usual, no one wanted me on the team. Some things about high school just never went away.

"Aha. Finally!" My search for the mini ice-cream sandwiches over, I held one out to Matthew. "Bribe?"

"Peace offering?" He took it and started unwrapping it.

"It's not a Christmas gift from Neiman's, Matthew. You can tear the paper. For someone who puts his hair in a ponytail every day, you're really precise about the silliest stuff." I'd almost finished mine, and he was still peeling paper.

"Maybe I can delay gratification," he smirked.

"Anyway. Speaking of bribes and delayed gratification. Do I have to have visitors? I'm willing to delay that."

Matthew finished off his ice cream sandwich in two quick bites. "Most people actually want visitors. You've been here almost a week now. Don't you want to see a civilian?"

Six days already. I'd survived a week of firsts, but I wasn't sure I was ready for first visiting day. I had rooted myself just enough to feel like I had something under me. Seeing those familiar faces would be like hurricane-force winds that could tear me right out of the ground. I needed more time. "Seeing them isn't so much the problem. It's talking to them," I said, wondering how long I'd have to leave my head in the freezer to get sent to the infirmary.

124

"Talk to who?" Cathryn walked up, tossed her purse on the sofa, and flopped her leggy self next to Matthew.

"*Whom.* Talk to *whom.*" I slapped my hand over my mouth. "Cathryn, I'm sorry. Habit."

She laughed. "Got it, Miss English Teacher. I guess you can fix us every now and then since we're working you over all the time."

"The *whom*," Matthew said, turning to Cathryn, "would be her husband and her friend who're scheduled to visit tomorrow." He stood up, patted Cathryn on the top of her head, "Good luck with that." He nodded his head in my direction.

"Thanks," I shot back. "See if I dig for ice cream sandwiches for you again."

"Nice try on the guilt trip, but I'm not buying a ticket," Matthew said, waving good-bye as he walked over to the counter, grabbed his backpack, and headed to the elevator.

"Is Matthew cutting his hair or does it just seem shorter now that I'm used to seeing it?"

"Why are you trying to change the subject?" Cathryn's mouth smiled, but her eyes were two blue bullets aimed in my direction.

"Since no one was answering me, I didn't think we had a subject."

"No, I don't think his hair's shorter." Cathryn tucked a rebel lock of hair behind her ear and looked at her watch. "Time to punch in."

I followed in her wake as she strolled over to the center station, her perfume drifting behind her.

White Linen. My mother wore it for years. After her funeral, their house overflowed with people Dad invited for lunch. We couldn't fill the emptiness in our hearts, but we were going to fill our stomachs. My brother told me to find Dad and tell him he'd better start praying he could turn water into wine because the bottles were emptying faster than the food trays. I was grateful for an excuse to de-hostess myself and escape from the swarming nests of conversations. I'd started self-medicating the pain with Robert Mondavi, one of Mom's favorite wines, in the limousine on the way to the funeral home earlier that morning. The constant drone of people's voices and the scent of apple pies and seafood gumbo had become suffocating.

Weaving through knots of aunts and uncles and vaguely familiar cousins to find my father, I passed someone wearing Mom's perfume. An explosion of memory. "Mom?" I thought I had whispered. *She had to be there someplace. Where?* "Mom?"

My Aunt Sheila materialized in front of me. She lifted my wine glass out of my hand, parted the sea of faces, and led me outside. For months after that, the scent of *White Linen* paralyzed me.

Now I trailed behind the scent, fully aware my mother would never appear. And not here, for sure, with meals on trays. I didn't learn until after Mom died the reason our family never ate at cafeterias. They didn't serve alcohol.

"Let's go to dinner early. The basketball crew's going straight there, so we'll just meet them," Cathryn said.

"I just had ice cream. For a change, I'm not all that hungry." By next week I wouldn't have to eat the ice cream—I could just apply it directly to my thighs. The three meals a day plus desserts were beginning to equal wiggles in new places on my body.

"So get a salad. We can talk about your new crisis. The new volunteer won't check in for an hour. I can't leave you here alone," she said.

"Right. I might impale myself on a sharpened pencil while you're gone."

"Or bash your brains out with that novel you thought you were going to read." She grinned and headed to the elevator.

Cathryn stirred her iced tea with her straw. She bowed her head to pray. After the first couple of days, I began to think praying over the food wasn't such a bad idea. She looked up, fanned her napkin out on her lap, and buttered her wheat roll. "Can you please explain to me, why, if you didn't want visitors, you asked your husband and friend to visit?"

"I liked the *idea* of visitors. And I didn't actually *invite* them. I just didn't tell them *not* to come." The omission defense theory. Rationalization worthy of a sixteen-year-old. Now I understand my students trying to explain to me that I didn't tell them they couldn't work together on their papers.

I pointed at Cathryn's dinner. "You know, I've never fried chicken at home. Carl said it made too much of a mess. And the fried smell stayed for days."

"Is that why you don't want to see him? Because of never having fried chicken?"

I dissected the veggies in my salad. They weren't very perky today. "Now that would be dumb. Of course not. Watching you eat reminded me of that. Does everything have to mean something?"

"It usually does. Look, let's . . ." the rest of her sentence fell off into the voices of the crew returning from basketball. Theresa pounded Vince's back and chanted, "Oh, yeah, we beat you. Oh, yeah, we beat you." I couldn't hear Vince's comeback, but whatever it was, both Theresa and Annie laughed.

"Annie laughing. Now that's not something you see everyday," I said.

Cathryn looked across the cafeteria at the group and grinned. "You're right. That is new," she said, slid her plate over, and looked at me. "Back to you. Bottom line. Visiting time is one hour. I think you can handle sixty minutes. In the rec room. Surrounded by other people. It's not the time for Dr. Phil-style confrontations."

I jabbed a grape tomato in my salad. *Stabbing tiny tomatoes with a salad fork was not conducive to releasing significant feelings of hostility.* "What are we supposed to talk about? And please don't ask me, 'What do you want to talk about?'"

She glanced out the window, probably wishing she was playing in the fountain. "It's awkward, I know. These first meetings always are. The time will pass faster than you think. Talk about your day, the food, or, in your case, the ice cream." Cathryn laughed and slid her chair back from the table. "And trust that God's going to help you through this too."

Enough with this God already. "Why, is He going to be there?"

"Well, He just might be." Cathryn smiled and walked away.

Everybody but Theresa and me would be checked out for overnights. After the group left, she and I were like two people on a blind date and about as comfortable as if we'd dressed for prom and found ourselves at a football game. Cathryn didn't even attempt to rescue either one of us. She'd blockaded herself behind the counter with charts, the telephone, and a stack of magazines.

"I know you're not the playing games kinda girl. You wanna watch TV?" Theresa aimed the remote, ready to fire away at channels.

So, this was my life. Saturday night in rehab. With another woman. A woman who collected bracelets like I collect pens.

We're both pathetic.

At least we have that in common.

Sunday morning. Two hours and counting.

One day at a time. Sometimes, one hour at a time.

Before that first AA meeting ended, Kevin told us, "This is a twenty-four hour program. Nobody's asking you to stay sober for the rest of your life. Just tell yourself, 'I won't take a drink *today*.' It's one day, one hour, one minute at a time." Then he had handed out what he called sobriety chips.

In the bus on the way back, I told Matthew when I first saw the box of chips, I thought Kevin might be tossing them out to the group. They looked like the doubloons that riders threw from parade floats during Mardi Gras.

"It was one of those rites of passage. Picking up a doubloon off the ground before somebody smashed your fingers trying to take it away. I've seen grown men lifted off their feet by puny grandma types."

Matthew looked perplexed. "Any why would anyone want these things?"

"I guess it's like catching money. Only we all knew it wasn't. But some people said they'd be valuable later. One year, I was standing on a ladder when one of the riders pitched a handful to the crowd. Hundreds of spinning gold coins, then the sound of all that aluminum hitting the street. Like rain on a tin roof. The crowd just folded in on itself, people slapping themselves on the ground to nab one. Watching from above, it was kind of silly and amazing at the same time."

"That's one problem you won't have when you get your sobriety chip at the end of a meeting. Alcoholics are actually more civilized than that." Matthew paused. "Well, at least the recovering ones."

One of the chips Kevin called the Desire Chip, for people who had the desire or who'd been sober for twenty-four hours. Theresa elbowed me, "Hey, Miss Thing, we can get us one of those." The thought of walking across that room made me want a drink, which I was sure was not what I would need to be thinking on my way to getting a sobriety chip. Seemed exactly the definition of irony. Alanis Moiresette should've written a song about it. I looked at Theresa. "No, thanks. I'll pass." She *tsk, tsk*-ed me, and Miss Bracelet jangled her way to Kevin while I sat on the sofa scratching my hand.

I regretted my dumb hesitation. If I had walked myself to the front that night, I'd at least have something to talk about this afternoon: my own little show and tell for company. I could tell Molly it was my prize for being a model patient for the first week. Carl would snicker and probably say something about how it didn't take much to make me happy. *And he'd be so right, but for all the wrong reasons.*

Theresa fell asleep in our room after lunch. I wandered into the hall looking for Jan. Pieces of sunlight jutted through the half-open blinds, a warm yellow pipeline for the dust particles floating lazily through before landing on whatever was in the room. Soft silence screamed and screeched in my brain, a tantrum of loneliness like the ones I used to drown with beer or gin or vodka or scotch.

Those first weeks after Alyssa died, earthquakes of silence shook the house. Rooms would have seizures, and I'd have to fling my arm on a wall to steady myself. Sometimes I collapsed on the floor, pushing the carpet with both hands to keep the ground from breaking.

We have to take her now, Mrs. Thornton. Please. We know how difficult this must be for you. It's time, Mrs. Thornton.

Time was all I had after they took her away from me that morning, carrying her out in her pink crocheted blanket. I refused to let them cover her face. *Please don't, I begged. Please, don't. She'll be afraid.* She looked like one of the Madame Alexander dolls Carl's mother bought her. Translucent and tranquil. Softly angelic. And still. Tragically still.

"Leah?" Jan's hand rested on my shoulder. She handed me a tissue. "Runny mascara."

"Thanks," I whispered.

"Your visitors are downstairs," she said.

20

I took advantage of Theresa's nap to snag some mirror time. Maybe that face I thought I'd seen all those years ago would finally appear.

When I was little, I'd play a game where I'd look in the mirror, but the face I'd see there wouldn't be mine. A wicked witch, insanely jealous of my be-yu-tee-full face, had put a spell on all the mirrors in the world. The only face I'd ever be able to see was oh so plain. A brown-eyed, nothing remarkable face.

I dusted powder on my face with the same vengeance I dusted the furniture. I hoped I could mash down the new roundness of my cheeks. Carl would notice the change. *Nah*. Other parts of my body were much rounder and much more obvious. I was sure he'd notice those first. He always noticed those first. Even when I was full-bellied pregnant with Alyssa, I'd scoop vanilla ice cream over my equally pregnant slice of apple pie, and he'd say, "Do you really think you need that? You know, you're just making it harder on yourself to lose the weight later." Of course, he'd never say I was fat. He didn't have to.

Theresa was snoring when I left our room. At least *she'd* be doing something constructive during visiting time. At lunch

Theresa told me she wouldn't be seeing her kids or her husband today. "My old man, he's working, so the kids don't have no way to get here." She shrugged, tugged on her bra underneath her striped tank top, and pulled a pack of cigarettes out of her shorts' pocket. "Going to find a light. See ya upstairs." By the time I saw her again, she was already asleep.

I slipped out and closed the door behind me in slow motion to avoid suffering whatever the consequence would be for waking Theresa. *Could they be worse than the one I'm about to deal with?* I should have worn something else. The denim skirt. Or the khaki pants. *I should have looked more L.L. Beanish.* The black shorts still didn't camouflage the food that had made regular deposits on my thighs. The yellow Polo shirt. *What was I thinking?* Great. I'm going to look like a midget bumblebee.

But there was no turning back. I was Odysseus stuck between two equally disturbing forces. Stuck between the rock of Theresa and the hard place of the elevator doors that just opened.

Carl and Molly arrived at the same time.

Maybe that God of Cathryn's *was* on special assignment this weekend.

The visit wasn't so bad in the way that shots aren't so bad. Once the swift, intense burning jab was over, the dull pain throbs only when you touch the bumpy spot where the needle punctured your skin.

Carl and I hugged as if someone had wrapped each one of us in cardboard from head to toe. He'd barely stepped back when Molly's long, tanned arms, almost as thin as the tennis racket she swings, wrapped around me. I didn't care that her silver butterfly pin smashed into my doughy right cheek. I didn't care that her left foot pressed itself on top of mine. I only cared that she was there.

If Molly was not my best friend, she'd be one of those women I'd wish would drag toilet tissue on her stilettos when she left a bathroom. When she walked into a room, even women noticed her. I used to joke that I was her friend so she'd never be accused of profiling or political incorrectness. I knew, though, what attracted people to Molly was not what they'd seen on her, but what they'd seen *in* her.

"You look great," she said after we disengaged. "Carl, don't you think so?" It sounded less like a question and more like a direct order.

I looked at Carl. He hesitated.

My cue. "Molly, you'd compliment me if I walked in here straight from a mud bath without rinsing off."

I led them to one of the sofas. "Not exactly *Southern Living*." I could see Carl and Molly scanning the room, but trying to look as if they weren't. "The idea was not to make the place too comfy or else we wouldn't want to leave," I said, relieving them of having to lie about the décor.

"Well," said Molly, reaching for my hand and pulling me next to her as she sat on the sofa. "You're not exactly here for the furniture. When you leave, we'll write letters to those Extreme Makeover people. That'd be a hoot." She grinned.

She was one of the only people I knew who could use the word hoot and not sound like she just arrived here in a time machine.

Before he sat, Carl brushed off the chair seat. He didn't exactly settle into the chair. He seemed to hover, holding onto the chair arms as if a flight attendant would come along and announce takeoff at any moment. His movements were wooden, but maybe it was the heavy starch in his white and navy plaid button-down collared shirt and solid navy chinos. *So, he does know how to pick up clothes from the cleaners.*

Carl sat across from me, looking, as my father would have said, "like a lost ball in high weeds." He stared at his barely scuffed brown deck shoes, then glanced at Annie's stack of outdated *People* magazines. He leaned back and entertained himself by removing ant-sized lint from his pants. Totally out of his element. A vulnerability had tiptoed out of his soul when he wasn't looking. It leaped the void between us, tripping the emotional siren I'd installed years ago. *No, go back. I can't trust you yet, but I want to. I really want to.*

Before the silence drowned us all, Molly threw out a lifeline. "Carl, tell Leah about your conversation with her dad." Had the words not been dressed in her party clothes voice, I would have panicked.

He cleared his throat, the noise like a closed mouth cough, and looked, not so much at me, but in the vicinity of my head. "Your dad called. He wanted to visit, so he's flying in on Wednesday. I'm not sure how long he'll stay in town."

I straightened and pulled threads from the sofa's cording with my fingernails. My inner child (Cathryn joked with me yesterday that I held mine hostage) bounced on both feet and clapped her hands deliriously, using my stomach as a trampoline. *It's going to be okay. It's all going to be okay.*

Carl grinned. *Had I spoken that out loud?* I shivered because what I saw in Carl's eyes was an approaching reprimand for that excited little girl who'd just made her appearance.

"Oh, I almost forgot. He's coming for family group," he said. He sat back and looked at me.

The clapping stopped. So, this was the new game. Words were the weapons. Information used as stealth destruction.

I scratched the top of my hand. Carl wanted this news to hurt me. Why? Because I had hurt him. This was still about him.

Journal 8

I was the blind date Carl met for dinner. Generally, Carl refused offers of blind dates. A year later he told me that he thought if a woman needed a blind date, then maybe her date needed to be blind. Besides, it wasn't as if he needed dates. But Nick and his wife, Brea, wouldn't stop nudging him about meeting one of Brea's teacher friends.

The first few times they asked, he always found a reason to refuse. Dates arranged by married couples were much more suspect than those arranged by single friends. He was suspicious of the hidden agenda—like the date interviewing for a spouse in the house. Brea reassured him I wasn't searching for happily ever after. So, Carl relented and made dinner reservations at Marsala's. Italian food would compensate for any dating disaster.

If I didn't have to see Brea every school day for the next four months, I would have refused this setup. And if she and Nick hadn't already spotted me at the entrance and waved me over to the table, I would have bolted out the leaded glass doors I had just walked through.

"I'm not ready," I had told Brea when she first suggested this date.

"This is a training wheels date. Nobody expects you to take off on your own yet," she said.

Fifteen minutes past reservation time. No Carl. Thirty minutes. No Carl. Nick had Carl's cell phone number on speed dial and left dozens of messages on voice mail. A bottle of wine and almost an hour later, Carl arrived.

Brea pointed him out to me. He stood at the bar, shaking hands with the badly toupeed man who had seated them. Carl's relaxed confidence annoyed and intrigued me as he smiled in our direction and maintained an unhurried conversation with the wildly gesturing gentleman. The Gundlach Bundschu merlot had long since soothed the tenseness that accompanied me to the restaurant. Carl and the man I'd come to know as Emil, the owner, ended their talk. Carl walked to their table—a man with the easy stride of someone comfortable in his own body.

"Leah," he said my name as if we'd been childhood friends. "I hope you'll give me a second chance at a first impression." *His grin poured itself out and warmed my bare shoulders.*

His ash grey sweater seemed dyed to match his eyes. He sat and looked only at me, as if Nick and Brea had disappeared.

"I would have been here on time but I was in the ER with my mother," *Carl said. He turned to the waiter at his elbow and ordered a dry martini and another bottle of merlot.*

Carl held up his hands to quiet the obligatory stirrings of the sympathy choir.

"She fell getting off the sailboat at the Yacht Club. She needs to be careful." *He paused and thanked the waiter for the bottle of wine and the drink he'd just delivered.* "I don't think we can get a handicapped boat slip." *He smiled to let us know laughter would be an appropriate response.*

Carl reached for the wine and said to me, "May I refill your glass?"

A sense of humor. Polite. And he cares about his mother. Perhaps he's worth a second chance.

21

The elevator doors closed.

Finally.

Carl and Molly had been transported to the universe beyond the locked doors, beyond the winding entrance, to the life I had plucked myself from, but from which my disappearance seemed only a speed bump. I'd expected more drama. Carl didn't look like a gaunt victim of emotional terrorism, pleading for my return. Molly's carbonated enthusiasm fizzed as though her energy compensated for Carl's indifference.

After Carl zapped me with the news of my dad arriving for family group night, Molly looked back and forth at us, like a Wimbledon spectator. She watched guilt and anger and disappointment volley between us.

I exited the elevator, clutching the gifts Molly had produced from the bowels of her purse to distract Carl and me from each other.

"Whatcha got there, girlie?" Theresa yawned her way into the rec room. Her zebra-striped slippers were on the wrong feet, but they navigated her to the sofa.

"Unfortunately, not candy." I handed her the two boxes. I paced.

"A book with nuthin' in it? What's up with that?" She opened the leather journal, lifted it to her face, and breathed in. "This smells rich." She closed it and gently massaged the embossed paisley designs on the cover with her pulpy little fingers. "Soft. What's in this other box?"

She handed me the journal.

"Your *friend* gave you a *Bible*?" Theresa eyed it like she was exercising some telekinetic power. She looked at me, the unspoken "Why?" captured in her eyes.

"Molly thinks the Bible's the only self-help book anyone ever needs. She and Jesus have some kind of hotline going on." I kicked off my white Crocs. Why do comfort and style have to be incompatible? My toenails and cracking heels screamed for a pedicure.

"It's kinda heavy." Theresa bench pressed it with one arm. "And you sure are stuck with it."

"Hmmm?" I'd been distracted flipping through the blank pages of the journal, wondering what pen I'd use to write in it.

I used to tell my students that writing was all about the pen. Like Goldilocks and the Three Bears. Everyone had to find a pen that was "just right." Not too slow that it couldn't keep pace with their thoughts and not too fast that it hurried thoughts and ink along, barely interacting with the paper. I'd show them one of my favorites, a stocky, lapis-colored, extra-fine point, marbled pen I'd ordered years ago from one of my favorite catalogs. Molly would always laugh and say she didn't have any *friends* except me who'd throw away the new Victoria Secrets catalog and immerse themselves in the latest from Levenger's. Finding a pen that fit my hand and writing style versus finding lace panties the size of dental floss that fit what I needed to sit on to write—no contest.

"I said you gotta keep the Bible." Theresa leaned over, her blouse pleading for mercy in the attempt, and shoved the Bible in my hands. "Look, she had your name put on it. See?"

Theresa pointed to *Leah Adair Thornton* inscribed on the burgundy leather cover. I opened it and found written on the first page: *"The grass withers and the flowers fade, but the word of our God stands forever"* (Isaiah 40:8 NLT). *Dearest Leah, this is God's journal. He'll be reading yours. Now you'll have some time to read His. I'm praying for you.—Molly*

Really? God should've watched Alyssa instead of reading people's journals. After all, if He's God, didn't He already know what I'd write on its blank pages?

Nobody knew about Alyssa, about nights I'd fall asleep on her bedroom floor clutching her soft baby powder-scented blankets, about how I'd slip my hand in my purse where I always carried her silver rattle so I could put my hands around something she had held.

Inside Edition's hostess filled the television screen. A man trapped underwater in a cylinder had thirty-three hours to escape before his oxygen ran out. "We'll let you know if he lives." She smiled. I'm struck by the fact that Alyssa had the same number of days with us as he had hours to live.

"Good luck," I told the screen.

22

While I reboxed my new, unasked for, and likely never-to-be read Bible, I was deposed as Queen Suburbia in Rehab. The Princess of Designer Drugs, accompanied by our very own Jan, teetered out of the elevator in Jimmy Choo teal patent leather sling backs.

A Prada dress splashed with blooming flowers in shades no flower would be caught dead in defined almost every inch of her body. I'd bet a Botox treatment that the purse Jan hijacked was also Prada. I couldn't wait to tell Carl's mother that her fashion training paid off and in the unlikeliest place.

The new client was a walking haute-couture advertisement, except for the blood-stained tissues she kept jamming into her surgically altered nose. Jan led her to the counter, steering her by the elbow as though she were an upright vacuum cleaner. Judging by the baseball-size roll of tissues she clutched, I'd say that nose of hers probably had sucked its share of white powder.

I looked around to make sure I wasn't so insensitive as to say that aloud. Even with crumbs of dried blood on her face and wobbling on knees about as sturdy as Play-Doh, she looked stunning—one of those women who wake up without morning mouth or helmet hair. Radiant. "Arm candy" my brother called them. This one would've sent most men into a diabetic coma.

Men like Carl.

And there it was—the putrid smell of insecurity.

She was everything I wasn't. Not that I envied her drug of choice (how noble of me). But without a dedicated team of plastic surgeons, a rack to stretch my body, blonde hair and extensions, and transplants, I'd be renting this body for always. Trapped in the same room with women like her, I felt like a piece of furniture—a piece Carl's mother desperately wanted to reupholster.

In my pre-recovery days, I'd have leveled the playing field with gin or vodka or wine or beer by now. I might not ever look like her, but I could pour in the security, composure, and assertiveness.

Owning these thoughts made sobriety feel like a horror movie unfolding one frame at a time. Any faster risked exposing the monster inside, and that would be entirely too frightening.

"Hey, now *she's* a girlie, *for sure.*" Theresa said to her fingernails as she chiseled off the red polish, the chips drifting to the floor like bloody snowflakes.

Empty urine specimen bottles lined the counter, patiently waiting to be claimed by their owners due back soon from their weekend passes.

Matthew looked up from labeling the last one. Strange sort of Welcome Wagon gift all in a row. Not something I imagined Mrs. Cleaver in her shirtwaist dress and pearls handed off to the Beav as he walked through the door after a date. *Hi, sweetie, so glad you're home. Now, be a good boy and go pee for me. And wash your hands. I have brownies waiting.*

In the alternate universe of rehab world, though, these babies had status. A rite of passage—like being assigned a parole officer meant being one step closer to civilian life.

"Play time's almost over." Theresa yawned, still attacking her nail polish and bypassing the social grace of covering her stretchy mouth with her hands. "Wait till they see . . ." She stood up and sent a flurry of red acrylic snowflakes to the floor. "Oops."

"See what? The mess you need to sweep off the floor?" I two-stepped around the red shavings and moved in the direction of my room to deposit my two gift boxes.

"Oh." The two letters rolled out of her mouth like they were on an amusement park ride. "You gonna pretend nobody's gonna pay attention to Glamour Girl? You jealous?"

Am not. Am not. My inner child pouted, stomped her feet, held her breath. My outer adult sent her to her room. "How ridiculous! Besides, do you even know how impossible it is to get blood out of designer clothes?"

I glanced at the door to Jan's office: closed. "Why would I be jealous of someone who has a bigger problem than I do?"

"I dunno. She come in here, and you doing elevator eyes up and down that girl. Like this." Theresa paused for a demonstration. "Then you get this weird look." She looked down and patted the pockets of her shorts, pulling a pack of cigarettes out of one and a stick of spearmint gum out of the other. "I'm getting me a light. Going outside for a smoke. You can come if you want."

An invitation to secondhand smoke leading to a slow, painful death, or I could stay and let my own thoughts keep me company. Both paths led to pain. "I'll put these away and find you outside," I said.

Theresa's eyebrows elevated a notch. Her expression reminded me of my students when I'd release them from morning detention two minutes after they arrived.

She walked over to Matthew, one of the keepers of the lighters. "I'll wait. Ain't like you going far."

How true. How true.

"Be right there," I alerted the back of her head as she leaned over to light her cigarette.

Journal 9

The tuxedoed waiter, with a deft and understated flair, snapped open my napkin and guided the fluttering white linen to my lap.

My last memory of fine dining was having a lobster bib tied around my neck the night of Senior Prom. "I'm not that impressed. They're just crawfish on steroids," I told my mother the next day and pretended the butter-drenched lobster jetting onto my ice-pink taffeta dress after I tried stabbing it with a fork didn't happen. I hadn't bothered to order lobster since then.

Tonight, though, was a covert operation leading me out of familiar territory and into Etienne's, where a reservation was as likely for someone outside the landed gentry as invitations to a debutante's coming-out party. Menus the size of a small infant and weighing almost as much were presented with a flourish as if recently composed by a Pulitzer Prize winner.

I scanned the pages searching for the translated version of the offerings. Even Shakespeare editions had user-friendly translations. But the only words not written in French were to comfort the diners that they'd be relieved of having to factor a twenty percent gratuity because it would be automatically added to the bill. How was I supposed to know that taking two years of Spanish to avoid the French teacher—because he looked like he'd stepped out of a totally off-off Broadway musical about bad hair days—would return to haunt me? Was there no Mexican dish at this restaurant? Surely there would have been something politically incorrect about translating chimichangas and flautas into French?

Dinner with Carl's parents: Carl's idea of announcing our engagement. I felt underdressed, over-menued, and outclassed. I prayed my internal squirming didn't pulse out of my body, sending waves of discomfort across the white sea of tablecloth.

Mrs. Thornton lowered her menu as if she'd been playing an adult version of hide-and-seek and spoke to me. "Dear, would you prefer the Poisson?"

How should I know? Frankly, I'd prefer your son's hand not making its way up my thigh while I'm sitting across from you.

23

Question: What comes after sobriety and before week two?
a) Week one.
b) Weak one.
c) Week won.
d) Weak won.
e) All of the above.

In seven days, God created the universe, and I followed along. Instead of His day and night, I had the inside of the second floor and outside AA meetings and the coming and going of the staff. Plus the cafeteria food and the ice-cream-stocked refrigerator.

I didn't mind the 6 a.m. wake-up calls. Most mornings they were a reprieve from Theresa's gargantuan snores. Breakfast was served thirty minutes later. I traded my normal face treatment time for sleep time.

After breakfast the group met to discuss urgent issues like who left magazines on the floor (Annie) or whose cigarette ashes continued to litter the floor and tables (Doug) or who kept hiding the remote control (the teenage duo).

No sign of Miss Nose Candy. The teens buzzed that they heard she hadn't been released from third-floor detox.

After our mandatory morning mauling, we were routed to occupational therapy or group therapy or meditation time or exercise time before lunch. Now that I'd identified protozoan blots, brain-cramped my way through number sequences, and reassured the white-jacketed psych staff I wasn't going to chain Stephen King to a bed anytime soon, I was cleared to start my occupational therapy sessions.

When I taught, occupational therapy meant I sipped wine in a bubble bath or released frustration by swiping my credit card. Was sobriety an occupation? If so, I was going to be painting my way to recovery with ceramic vases, ashtrays, and soap dishes.

After I splattered aggressive reds and calming blues all over my ceramic vase or whatever my object of the day might be, lunch followed. Always at noon. The predictability of that was comforting. And disturbing. I was disturbed by how comforted I was with routine. So much of what I thrived on as a teacher was wrapped up in the great unknown of each day. After losing Alyssa, my life's sameness smothered me. Every morning I opened the door to a steaming sauna, thick with grief and swollen with sadness.

Now, I welcomed the unsurprising complacency.

When lunch ended, we recycled the morning schedule offerings and ate dinner at six. Three or four weeknights of outside AA meetings, and weekends and other weeknights were in-house AA meetings. Ten o'clock lights out.

A schedule. A reliable robotic routine.

Then, in week two, the slithering snake of individual therapy sessions appeared in the form of Ron Palmisano.

At least the group therapy sessions were shared torture. Once Ron invaded my life all I could think about was that fire and brimstone sermon of Jonathan Edwards: spiders dangled over the fiery pit of hell by a God about as happy as a father who just found out his daughter's dating a convict.

Only my time with Ron makes the inferno seem like an enthusiastic sauna at a day spa. The first appointment was brutal—like labor pains. At first, I didn't know what to expect, so each new contraction was a frightful surprise. But as time passed, and the contractions grew stronger and more frequent, anticipating the pain only increased its intensity.

After the first session, I craved a cold six-pack or a small instrument of torture. Or both. Ron did not do nice. He did not want nice. And he thought I was nice.

"I've read Trey and Kevin's notes. You're the little housewife alcoholic." A verbal cocktail of two parts serious, one part sarcasm. Stirred slowly over a wedge of a smile.

My inner child stuck out her tongue.

Ron opened the manila file on his desk. "You are Leah, right?"

I knew a rhetorical question when I heard one. But what I didn't know was why I'd been auctioned off to this guy after I'd already faced off with Trey.

"I'm confused. I thought I was supposed to see Trey." Inner child just entered puberty.

"Sorry. I thought he or somebody—" he glanced down at my file and looked back at me "—explained the line-up. Trey's in charge of family sessions. You and I will meet for one-on-one sessions. Beginning today."

Obviously there was no limit to the number of people allowed access to my brain. At some point could I hang a neon "no vacancy" sign on my forehead? At least Carl might be placated knowing the insurance coverage provided generously.

"I already went over this with Trey." An all-too-familiar flush of self-consciousness bled out of my pores. I didn't need a mirror to know the blush would rise from my neck to my cheeks like mercury in a thermometer. How many times did I have to confess? How many times did I have to unfold the story from my memory, rolling it out like a beginner's crudely knitted scarf?

"I know. I don't want to read Trey's version of your version. I'd rather hear you tell me." He reached in the desk drawer, pulled out a paper clip, started it on tumblesets between his fingers, and stared at me.

"But I'm not a real alcoholic. I'm in mid-stage."

Ron's paper clip stilled.

"That's what the intake person told me." Oh, brilliant me.

"I see," said Ron, in a snarky way that said not only did he not see, but he saw I didn't see as well. He dropped the paper clip into a chipped mug on his desk that held two yellow pencils and a pair of scissors. "Not a real alcoholic. Hm. Tell me how you define this 'mid-stage'."

I didn't heed the cynicism that hitched a ride on Ron's voice. I pedaled right off into the land of eager-to-please and explained my mid-stagedness to him. How I didn't drink all day, how I waited until five o'clock, except on weekends when, really, drinking could start before noon or even at breakfast depending on the occasion, and I wouldn't get vomiting sick all the time, and I mostly drank beer, and wine—red wine, which is good for you—and sometimes vodka and gin, hardly ever rum, and I could stop drinking anytime I wanted to because I'd stopped for a few days and I was fine, but my husband and his family drank. And, of course, there were all these social events we had to attend, and it's rude to not drink when you're offered a drink, and I knew not to drive if I drank too much, and Carl always knew when I drank too much, so he'd be sure to take my keys, and I'd never had an accident from drinking—well, just that one time when I didn't see the mailbox, but that doesn't really count as an accident.

"You must be exhausted," he said. Sympathetic words dipped in battery acid. Ron leaned back in his ergonomically correct chair and pulsed gently. He scratched the side of his head with his pen. It didn't even disturb his close-cut hair the color of red clay I'd find in my backyard. Appraising eyes, like he was examining a diamond suspecting it was a fake.

I squirmed.

He rocked.

I knew this game. The waiting game.

Ron would lose this one. I was an expert at disconnect. On nights when Carl forced himself on me, I'd make grocery lists in my head or imagine myself in my closet wondering what I'd wear to our next social event. I pretended to examine Ron's navy- and white-striped tie while I mentally squirmed from underneath Carl.

"Where are you going, Leah?"

Ron lost, but I'm the six-year-old standing by the front door, clutching my Strawberry Shortcake suitcase, announcing to my parents I'm running away.

"Nowhere. At least until the end of this month." My voice pouted.

Rocking Ron stopped. "How difficult is it for you, being nice all the time? Must be mid-stage difficult, huh?"

He walked over to the window behind his desk and pulled up the shade. The sound reminded me of the backpack zipper symphony orchestrated by my students as they geared up to dart out of class the second after the bell rang.

"Predicting rain today." He jammed his hands into his pants pockets. "Shops don't look busy."

Since he spoke to the window, I guessed he meant the shopping plaza across the street with stucco store fronts shaded by wide forest-green awnings. Cafe Latte on the corner. Molly and I would meet there for lunch. Carl and Devin avoided the place.

149

Said it was too girlie. Like the salads wore lingerie. Two doors away was Babycakes, one of those stores that leveraged new parent angst into multiplying profits, full of cottony sherbet shades of baby-powder-scented everything. Lolly, the owner, sent us pink roses after Alyssa died. I'd plunged each one, bud first, into the garbage disposal. The stem didn't grind well, but for a few seconds, as it made its descent, it looked like a green straw spinning crazily out of control. I understood. The process and the bottle of Robert Mondavi next to the sink had entertained me until we were both empty.

I shoved my right thumbnail into the cuticle on each finger of my left hand, pushed the skin back, and wished I'd been blessed with my mother's smooth porcelain tapered fingers—hands that could've rested softly on piano keys instead of packs of cigarettes and cheap lighters.

"My mother drank." I worked back the skin on my ring finger. "Wine." I moved to my little finger. "Every day after work. Weekends, too." Finished.

Ron sat down. "Okay, we'll start there."

24

The white eyelet halter or the sleeveless red wrap?"

I stared at the dresses draped across my bed, tapped my foot on the floor, and pulled my robe tighter.

If I didn't start drying off better, my calves eventually would turn into popsicles from the air blowing out of the bedroom vents. That closet-sized bathroom invaded by steamy post-shower dankness suffocated me. I felt pin-pricks of anxiety about to give birth to panic, and I could hardly escape fast enough.

After several times of witnessing my desperate bolting out of the bathroom like my back was on fire, Theresa said she just stayed away from the door when she heard the water stop. Since after breakfast today, though, she stayed away from everything and everybody.

"Hey, you haven't moved in over an hour. And I know you're not sleeping because you'd be snoring by now. White or red? Come on. I need some help here."

Theresa looked like a life-sized rag doll. Her hair, roped and ribboned, fanned out over the pillow. Clasped across her stomach, her hands seemed puny and naked without her gallery of rings. The Pepto-pink velour pants encased her curves.

I couldn't tell if her too-small clothes were trademark or reminiscent of a Theresa past. Shame on me. I focused on the weight of her body and not the weight of her spirit. What was that line in Matthew about being judged by the same rules we use to judge others? God probably has a team of angelic architects designing a scale that would announce the weight of my sins to the universe.

"Girl, you can be one pain in the . . ." She slid the pillow over her face and smothered the rest of her sentence.

"Butt. Yes, I know. Just open one eye if that's all I can get from you right now and pick a dress. I promise not to bug you the rest of the day."

She shoved the pillow off her face, and it dropped on the floor. "I'll make that deal. Whatcha got over there so important I gotta wake up?"

"Carl's going to be here with my dad for our first family session. I don't want to look fat. Carl hates it when I look fat."

"Then he won't so much like me, huh?" She laughed and sat up on the side of her bed.

"I didn't mean it that way. He won't care how you look. He just cares how I look."

"Well, thanks again, girlie. Now, why I want to help you after you loud capping me and all?"

Clearly, sobriety was counterproductive to my diplomacy. I plopped on the bed next to Theresa and reached over for one of those one-arm hugs. "I'm an idiot."

She tilted her body away from me. "Yeah, you really right if you think we going to be huggy and all that." She pulled the red dress from my bed and handed it to me. "Wear this. You ain't got no business wearing a dress the same color you are. Besides, you still got a waist. No use wastin' it." She slapped her knee. "Funny. Wastin' it. Got it?"

I actually did laugh. For Theresa, a pun was bonus points on her humor grade. But if she noticed I was the shade of school glue, that couldn't be good. Then again, if I wanted a tan I should've found a seaside rehab facility.

"Who are you going to see today?" I unzipped the dress and pulled it over my head.

Theresa slid her back against the headboard and reached for her latest *People* magazine on the dresser. "That hoochie should be taking better care of her babies." She pointed to a recently crazed young singer on the cover and flipped through the pages. "Ain't nobody coming today."

Her voice dropped so low it could have met me under the bed from where I grabbed my white sandals.

I wiggled my feet into the sandals, then checked to make sure I'd shaved under my arms. Hair like that was only sexy on Brad Pitt's chin. "Nobody? Why not?"

"Noneya."

"What?"

"Noneya business."

Wolf words in sheep clothing. The universal "nothing" reply from a wife whose husband asked, "What's wrong?" Nothing meant everything. Nothing meant you should already know. Nothing meant ask me until I tell you.

A part of me wanted to agree with Theresa that it wasn't my business. I guess much like Carl wanted to believe "nothing" could really mean nothing. Those nights in bed when he scanned my face and asked what was wrong, did he know his actions always answered his question?

"You win. It's not my business. But I just asked because, well, I just didn't think it was that personal a question. But, apparently, it was because you're so defensive. So, if you don't want to tell me—" I tugged the dress over my hips. My hips tugged back.

"I don't wanna tell you. Know why?" Her voice was as tight as the magazine she'd rolled into a thick baton. Hoochie Mama's leering cover smile curled in on itself.

"Obviously not. If I knew the answer I wouldn't have asked the question." Weary sarcasm.

"Why you're here and not that husband of yours, I don't know. I could see him wanting to drink having to live with you and all. You think just because we're stuck in this room together we're gonna be sista-friends? You the kind of chick wouldn't pay no mind to me outside this place. I'm the woman who cleans your friends' houses or waits on you at one of them lady lunch places. You walk around here with your fancy clothes and get visits from your fancy friends and your Rolex husband—"

I opened my mouth to tell her it was his father's watch, but her words moved in before mine could move out.

"And, yeah, I know people like you wear 'em and I know a Rolex when I see one. In pawn shops when I bring my rings and bracelets there so I can feed my kids 'cuz I used the grocery money to feed my habit." She sighed and lowered her head.

I'm so stupid and so sorry. Shame smeared itself on my face like it did the afternoon Carl's mother whined about her half-completed pool cabana to her housekeeper who lived in a trailer with her sister and five children. How small was my world? I'd buried my mother, my sweet daughter. My losses were like globby scabs that would crust and heal and leave darkened remnants on my skin. Theresa's losses refused to die. Instead, everyday, they buried a part of her.

When she lifted her eyes to look at me, guilt and mourning tugged at the corners of her mouth. "Sometimes I done other stuff when I needed money. That's why my husband ain't coming to no family sessions." She clenched the magazine. "And my kids won't be, neither."

Sadness settled in my body and searched for familiar space. Only now, there'd be no floating along the river of alcohol to give it passage out. No way to drown itself in pools of forgetfulness. It crawled through the tender gaps in my heart and dragged wagons of memory behind.

"This is why I drank. To make life go away," I whispered to the pain that linked us. "What do people do with this? Where is it supposed to go?"

Theresa exhaled. "Guess if I knew I wouldn't be here."

I coaxed the door of my room closed so I wouldn't wake Theresa. She'd fallen asleep sometime after I'd lost the battle trying to blow dry my curls into submission, but before I slathered on lip gloss. I envied her temporary reprieve from untangling emotional knots, especially since I was on my way to a possible hanging with my own.

Some family members were already in the waiting room. Miss Designer Drugs held court with a tallish, smoky-grey haired man, attractive in your friend's father kind of way, and a freshly squeezed out of an Abercrombie catalog young couple. I walked by them feeling like a squatty tomato on legs.

Cathryn sat on the couch talking to Doug and a woman whose hand rested on his thigh. I'd expected Mrs. Doug to be a female replica of her husband, not an older version of Jan Brady wearing Birkenstocks.

I leaned against the wall facing the elevator doors, twisted my watch around my wrist, and waited.

Three twists, no Carl.

Four. Maybe he changed his mind.

Five. He would've called.

Six. Hadn't I wished he wouldn't come?

Seven. Maybe I changed my mind.

Eight. Cathryn announced group would start in five minutes.

Nine. The elevator shuddered its way up.

Ten. Trey trotted out of the elevator.

Alone.

Just like me.

Journal 10

The summer before college. Driving along the lakefront in Nina's new Cutlass convertible. Janie in the front seat. Me in the back. Humidity dragged its moist blanket through the night, the white leather seats of the car sweating underneath my bare thighs.

Somewhere along the serpentine road was Todd, Nina's almost fiancé, his fraternity brothers, and several kegs. On Friday nights, the park-like strip bordering the seawall that contained the smashing waves rippled with hives of bathing-suited bodies swarming around beer barrels.

Finding one worker bee even with the queen bee in control of the flight pattern was challenging. No Todd sightings. Nina's impatience escalated. Janie suggested one more swing around to Inspiration Park. The Cutlass coasted into the one vacant parking spot.

"I'm walking out to the pier. Maybe they're hanging out there. No way we'd see 'em from here," Nina said.

Janie opened her door. "I'm going with you. You coming?" she asked me.

"Nah, I'll wait here. You can come get me if you find him." The shroud of self-consciousness wove itself around me at the thought of walking up to a herd of frat boys. Let Janie and Nina part the sea of strangers with their lean bodies and long hair. I'd stay here, listen to the waves slosh against the walls, close my eyes, and imagine myself thin and cute.

I heard shouting and saw, in the distance, Nina and Janie running toward the car. At first I thought they were yelling for me. Too late, I realized they were yelling at me. "Start the car. Start the car, now!"

I started to fling myself over the front seat, but the back door opened, and hands slapped against my calves as they grabbed onto me and yanked my body onto the backseat. The hands moved up to my knees. Pulled me toward the now open back door. I grabbed the edge of the seat near the other door. I wanted to scream, but my face was mashed into the cushion. I turned my head to the side to breathe. My cheek burned as it skidded across the leather seat.

"Where ya think ya going, honey?" The wet voice was sticky and hot in my ear. The spoiled fruit smell of stale beer drenched my nose. The hands at my knees worked their way up my thighs. I twisted my body, but I flopped like a fish pinned to a pier. I heard myself grunt. I bit my lips and clenched my teeth.

Nina. Janie. Where were they?

One hand reached the hem of my shorts. The other fumbled its way up to my waist. I pushed my body against the seat to stop the fingers crawling over my bare skin. I let go of the seat with my hands and batted my arms behind me. I fought with air. I kicked. I felt him lean across my legs.

The door by my head creaked open and a new hand that reeked of cigarette smoke pushed my head into the seat. "Cool off, girl. You're not going anywhere," he laughed. A wave of warm beer splashed across my face, and my wet hair fell into my eyes.

The car started. Oh, dear God, please let that be Nina. Please let that be Nina.

"Janie, close the door. Close the door. Close it, now." Nina sounded like a siren wailing underwater.

"Let go of her," Janie screamed. I heard a solid thump. A male voice roared, spewed language as foul as the meaty hands that

held me. Hands that now slid down my body. The door by my feet slammed. My freed legs crawled up the seat.

The voice at my head yelled, "You crazy—" I reached up and dug my ragged fingernails into flesh, again and again, like raking wet sand to make trenches.

"It's gonna take more than that," the voice growled, but his grip loosened enough for me to pummel his hands while I scuttled away. When I could, I yanked away clumps of my hair not soaked with beer.

"Let her go 'cuz I'm backing up whether you do or not. Hold on, Leah," Nina screamed.

The stench of sweat and cigarettes released me. My jaw ached from the tightness.

I lunged for the door handle inches away from my hand.

"Wait, wait." Janie scrambled over the front seat, tumbled into the backseat, and fell over my now outstretched body. "The door's still open."

She reached over me. "Now, Nina." Janie's voice scratched against the dankness in the car, "Back up. Fast. Run over every disgusting one of them if you have to."

The door slammed closed. So did my heart.

25

That's why we hope you learn the Serenity Prayer early, you know. For times like this."

Cathryn leaned on the wall next to me. Handed me a stick of Wrigley's Spearmint gum. Whoosh of a memory. Rifling through my mother's purse. Bits of tobacco always dusted the bottom of the fabric liner and clung to the sticks of gum she'd tear in half and throw back into her purse.

"No, thanks. I saw a video of myself chewing gum. You would've thought my jaws were hinged with springs. Ugly. Haven't touched the stuff since."

"Hey, maybe I should suggest that to the intake counselors—videos of people drinking, using . . ." She elbowed me ever so slightly. Ha. Ha.

I contemplated my unpolished toenails and avoided eye contact with Cathryn. She'd see my naked sadness. "I guess Carl's not coming." The words dropped out of my mouth like pieces of dinners I'd thrown up after too many martinis.

"You stuck to this wall or can we sit down and talk?" I followed Cathryn as she walked in the rec room and sat on the sofa. "Like the dress, by the way. Red's your color."

When she reached over to stop my hand scratching, I smelled gardenias and vanilla. My stomach lurched.

"Did you really want him here? Or did you just not want to be the one left out?"

"Left out? Left out of what? Therapy torture? Who wouldn't want to miss that?"

"Exactly."

"Not what I meant." I inspected the warmish budding pink welts on the top of my hand. "Even if I didn't want him here, why didn't he want to be here? He didn't even call. What's up with that? Was this his way of punishing me? Making me look like—"

"Like what? You sound like you've just been stood up for prom. Whoa. That's it, isn't it?" She reached over and swatted my knee, a smile emerging like she'd just delivered a punch line.

"Hm." I folded my arms across my chest. "Well, since that never happened to me, I wouldn't know. Why, was that something you have personal experience with? Maybe you should tell me."

My meanness slapped the smile off Cathryn's face. Her mouth rippled into a smirk.

"Nice try, but you're not going to start a fire to take the heat off yourself. You need to own this one. Carl's not being here is about you, not him."

The roller coaster in my stomach chugged its way up my throat. I waved my hand in front of her. "Wait. Gotta . . ." I dashed for the bathroom, hoping the wheels would stop turning in my mouth before I retched them up.

Drunk vomiting had been welcomed. Cathartic, sober vomiting, not so much. The insides of my nose burned, and the sourness of the lasagna that recycled itself out of my stomach and into the toilet lingered on my tongue. Maybe I should have reconsidered that whole gum-chewing decision. I shuffled to the sink, latched onto the sides of it to steady myself, and dared look into the mirror.

The damp black, supposedly waterproof mascara puddled in the corners of my eyes. If only I could throw up the sadness and its emotional tug on my face. I searched for a fragment of long-ago Leah lurking in eyes shaded by doubt and confusion. *God, if you're really there, wherever there happens to be, now what? What do I do when I don't know what to do?*

No answer.

Where was that thundering God of the Old Testament? He's the one I needed. The God of the burning bush. Not the God of screaming silence.

I turned on the faucet, cupped my hands to catch the cold water, swished it around my mouth, and spit.

The lower half of my red wrap dress bunched up into itself. I smoothed it with the palms of my hands and wished I had another reason to stay in the bathroom. My guilt over my temper tantrum blocked my way to the door.

Can't hide in here all night. You need to apologize to Cathryn.

My lips didn't move, but the message could not have been any clearer had the face in the mirror actually spoken the words.

Maybe God's not mute.

Maybe I needed hearing aids.

"Leah?"

I opened the door and saw Cathryn's raised fist aimed at my forehead.

"I was going to apologize, really. No need for violence," I said.

"I was about to knock. *Really.*" She rolled her blue eyes in her best Leah imitation. "But more about that later." She twisted her ponytail on top of her head and secured it with a pencil she pulled out of her pocket. "You have company," she whispered and waved her left arm in the direction of the nurses' desk.

I took a few steps forward and heard Carl's voice before I spotted him leaning against the counter talking to Matthew and another man.

Carl bent down to tie the leather laces of his deck shoes—those things were always a problem—and I almost tripped over my own feet when I saw the broadly smiling, fast-talking, hand-gesturing man who stood next to him: my father.

26

Fashionably late arrivals work well for parties, not for family therapy sessions.

Even though Matthew practically oiled the hinge to slide the door open quietly, and Trey's eyebrows shifted less than a centimeter when the three of us coasted across the Berber carpet, our arrival shifted the group's emotional universe. Even a whisper can knock down a house of cards.

"Dad, this dude Paul said to the Romans not to get all eaten up with bad. He said—" A lip-pierced, gangly Doug of the future, stopped mid-sentence and scanned Carl, Dad, and me as we lowered ourselves into the only empty folding chairs in the room.

Definitely clueless as to group therapy protocol, Dad raised a hand and said, "Late plane. My son-in-law over there—" he reached around me and pointed to Carl "—had to drive like a bat to get us here. And in one piece too." He smiled at Carl who smiled back at him. At least I had one question answered.

"Oh, and the name's Bob. I'm Leah's father."

Random throat clearings and scattered "Hi, Bob" replies fell like dominoes falling around the circle.

Hello. And I'm his mortified daughter. I shrugged my shoulders, mouthed "I'm sorry" to future Doug, and checked out Trey to see if he was already popping a Pez. Not yet. The rest of the group played "pass a glance."

I didn't need to look at Carl to know he was brushing phantom lint off his pants. He used the technique to avoid eye contact when embarrassed, appalled, and/or inappropriately amused. Carl and Dad had been friends for years, so I doubt he was surprised by his introduction. If anything, Carl, who tended to be socially paralyzed, admired my dad's unabashed friendliness. I once teased that Tom Cruise's line, "You complete me," in the movie *Jerry McGuire* was meant for them. Though I'm sure Carl and my dad agreed with me, they were such self-proclaimed nerds, they wouldn't dare admit it publicly.

I leaned toward Dad and whispered, "This isn't an AA meeting."

Uh-oh. How had I forgotten? Peter and I learned early never to kick Dad under the table to forestall his reckless storytelling. For some people it might be a story-stopper move, but not my father. He stopped only to look around the table and ask, "Who kicked me?"

"Honey," he said and slid his arm around my shoulders and squeezed, "I know this isn't one of *those* meetings." I heard synchronized gasps. Designer Drug Princess crossed and recrossed her tanned and toned legs, a momentary entertainment for most of the males. Trey, however, captivated by his Blackberry, flicked his hand in one of those "Go on without me" gestures.

Dad loosened his grip around me, reclaimed his arm, and nodded in future Doug's direction. "Sorry to interrupt, son. You were saying?"

Mrs. Doug gently tugged on her son's shirtsleeve. "Go ahead, Danny. Finish what you were saying about Paul."

"Yeah, kid." Doug laughed, but it was Grand Canyon hollow. "Thump that Bible ya mother gave ya and give it to me straight." Doug slouched in the chair and waited.

⸺∞⸺

After that night, I truly understood the rationale behind scheduling our individual therapy appointments the day after family group.

We needed therapy to recover from therapy.

"Too bad you had to miss it. Maybe next week I can pass you off as my sister. You'd be hooting for days," I said to Molly. She'd picked up a few LSU tees from my house so I could simultaneously be comfortable and torture Jan, a graduate of Alabama. Nothing like an SEC rivalry to spice the gumbo of rehab life.

"All that energy planning your attire and look what you've been reduced to." Molly giggled as she handed me the shirts. "Promise me you won't ask me to bring over a purple and gold LSU bikini. If Ann Taylor found out I was transporting tacky, they'd cancel my shopping privileges."

"You're right, girl," I said. "It's a real opportunity they provided us, allowing us to dump bucks in their store. You're safe, though. Nobody's going to see this body in any kind of bathing suit, much less one that could fit in my pocket."

The atrium where we'd been sitting spared us the direct assault of the afternoon sun. July in Texas meant heat 24/7. Heat so dense it would mold itself to a body. Heat you could step in and out of like clothes. Heat that, by day's end, exhausted even the plants. Their leaves drooped in surrender like parched green tongues.

After spending so many days in climate-controlled interiors, I'd forgotten I was surrounded by a natural sauna. I'd also forgotten the joy of peeling myself off a wrought-iron chair that waffled the backs of my thighs. What I had not forgotten was the humiliation of wearing a bathing suit. Of overhearing Carl's mother, as she cooed and rocked Alyssa, tell her husband she hoped her granddaughter didn't inherit my thunder thighs. Of pretending to enjoy their lake house, the place Carl hoped to inherit one day. The place, Carl reminded me last night, my father missed out on because of what he called "my situation."

"How do you not want to dive into a pool in this heat?" Molly hooked a finger into the neck of her silk shell, stretched it out, and fluttered it against her body. "I'm sweating in places I didn't know people could sweat."

"Wow. Our friendship is crossing new boundaries." I grinned and clasped my hands over my heart. But I wondered if she understood the gratitude that washed over the walls she dared our friendship to climb. She refused to let me hide, she refused to let me disappear, and she refused to let me die inside myself. Molly heard a cry within me that I had made myself deaf to, and she didn't wait for a script to follow. She gave me the courage to take the next step. To go where I knew I needed to be.

"I'll see if there's any iced tea inside," I said.

"No, I'll go. It'll give me a chance at a shot of cold air," said Molly, and she walked off in the direction of the cafeteria.

Minutes later, she carried two tall glasses to the table. "Mango iced tea. And don't think you're going to get this service when you're out of here," she said, and smiled as she wrapped a napkin around a glass and handed it to me.

"Let's see." I held my hands palms up and moved them as if balancing a scale. "Rehab and being waited on," I said, pushing my left hand down, "or," pulling my right hand up, "sober and waiting on myself. No contest. In fact, I'll be happy to wait on you."

"Back to last night." Molly pushed her damp bangs off her forehead, sipped her tea, and waited.

I emptied a package of Sweet 'N Low into my tea and stirred with my straw. One month ago who would've figured my new drink of choice would be iced tea? Steamy days like this used to be beer days. I'd open the refrigerator, grab a can, and pop it open before the refrigerator door would swing closed. If only that first long sip had been enough.

"You look upset. You don't have to talk about last night if you're not ready."

"No, that's not it. I was just thinking about . . . " I pushed the straw aside and gulped tea; the end of the sentence tumbled down my throat with it. Maybe it was too soon to share this boundary. Romanticizing about drinking was something I needed to stop. AAers cautioned against it as a stumbling block on the way to sobriety. I wasn't sure Molly would understand I didn't dwell on these unexpected flashbacks. "I was thinking who else but you would enjoy the latest installment of the antics of the poster family of dysfunctionality?"

"Speaking of that, how's your dad?"

Molly and I knew the unabridged question was, "How's your dad coping since your mom died?" I shared his stages of grief with Molly. They ranged from isolating himself at home for days on end to leaving in the car and being gone for days on end.

"He actually seemed more like himself. You know, the heartwarming and totally humiliating-his-children self. Peter mentioned a few weeks ago that Dad said he's dating. We're not exactly sure what that means. We're not even sure we want to know what it means. But we didn't have time last night for any of those issues."

"Knowing your dad, I can't imagine how he managed to stay quiet."

"Exactly. He didn't. In fact, at one point, Trey had to remind him the session was only ninety minutes, and it was important for everyone to have a chance to participate. Then, when Trey asked him why he was there, he started rubbing my back and said, 'I just want my baby to be happy. If this is what she thinks she needs, I want her to do it.'"

Molly groaned, one of those sympathetic, you-poor-dear, I'm-so-glad-it's-you-and-not-me groans.

"Wait. There's more. He looked at Carl when he was finished and said, 'Right, Carl? Whatever Leah needs, don't we want her to have it?' There I am, sitting between the two of them. Trey was probably all over that seating arrangement with his therapist brain."

"You have to warn me about the funny parts before I start drinking and end up snorting iced tea out my nose," Molly said. "What did Carl say?"

"Not much. He couldn't disagree with Dad without coming off like a dirt bag."

"So Carl spent most of the session nodding yes? That's—"

"Unreal? Yes, but more like unrealistic because, of course, he politely wedged in a dig about having to be the one to 'fix the fiasco' of the July 4th plans and be the one left to make all the phone calls. Then Dad comes to his rescue. 'Carl's handled all this well. Stood up to the plate.' Yaddayaddayadda."

Molly finished her tea and dumped the ice in the plant next to the table. "You know, you might want to cut Carl some slack." She didn't rush the words. She just let them dissolve into meaning, melting like the ice in the plant. "I'm not saying Carl's actions were heroic. But his hand was forced. He had no choice in this decision. But he did what he had to do."

Maybe he's beginning to understand what it means to feel powerless.

Good.

27

How old were you when you lost your mother?"

I unwrapped my watermelon Jolly Rancher and popped it in my mouth instead of flinging it at Ron's forehead. "I didn't lose her, Ron. She died. That's a lifetime of being lost, don't ya think?" I ironed the wrapper with my finger. "Aren't we supposed to be past euphemisms by now?"

Dr. Ron and I verbally sparred on Wednesdays. Somewhere between the sarcasm and the silly, serious happened. He tolerated my not-always-so-wise-cracks, and I allowed him his psychobabble.

"That depends. Are you past needing your used candy wrappers to be wrinkle-free?" He grinned and handed me a small wicker basket off his desk. "Toss the trash in here."

"I'll hold on to it. I have a feeling I'll be overdosing on Jolly Ranchers this morning," I said. "Is there a twelve-step program for the sugar addicted?" I reached into the candy cache on his desk for two lemons and a sour apple.

"I think that would fall under the umbrella of Overeaters Anonymous. So, you're covered."

He moved from behind his desk and sat in the chair across from me. He set the digital timer for forty-five minutes, placed it on the lamp table next to his chair, and said, "The recommended time limit for therapy torture."

"If it wasn't so true, it would be funny."

"Well, I'd hoped for at least one of your pseudo-smiles. Guess you're picking flavors to match your disposition." He licked his thumb and flipped through pages of his legal pad. Yuck. Even doctors have gross habits. I did that thumb thing, too, when I looked for a number in the phonebook. Anytime I did it around Carl, he gave me the "that's a disgusting habit; please wash your hands before you touch anything else" lecture. One thumb lick, and Carl flipped right along with my pages.

Ron stretched his legs and propped his feet on the edge of the oversized padded leather ottoman between us. He glanced at the pad, uncapped his pen, and said, "Let's get started. I want you to pretend I'll be picking your mother up from the airport this afternoon—"

Eyebrow lift and a smirk. "Good luck with that one."

"Key word here is *pretend*. I want you to describe her to me in such a way that I'd be able to walk right up to her."

Maybe this session wasn't going to be an emotional jackhammer cracking through decades of petrified feelings. I allowed myself the luxury of a deep breath and began to sketch my mother using words as my watercolors. "Don't look for someone who looks like me. She's taller. Was taller? Anyway, maybe tall is relative because she was probably only five feet, five inches."

I closed my eyes and scanned my memories, a slideshow of collected images. Some throbbed in their vividness, others glimmered too briefly to capture. "She has brown eyes. Not coffee brown. Muted brown like a camel-colored suede coat. Her hair's almost the same shade. Straight, thin, left side part, cut in a sort-of bob." I opened my eyes. "This length." I ran my fingertips alongside the middle of my neck. "She had a mole right here." I pointed to the left side of my forehead. "She always said she wanted to have it removed, but then . . . well, cancer trumped mole. Otherwise, her skin was beautiful. Ivory with a sprinkle of freckles across the bridge of her nose and cheeks." I stopped to scoot myself back into my chair. Somehow I'd inched my way to the edge of the seat, caught up in recreating the woman who'd created me.

Ron flipped a page. "What would she be wearing? Tell me about her mannerisms, her personality."

I smiled remembering her monochromatic closet. "Definitely understated—her clothes and her personality. She'd be wearing, hmm, probably navy-blue linen pants. A blouse, I don't know, white? With buttons. I don't think she owned a turtleneck or sweaters. She despised pulling stuff over her head. Personality? Let's say she'd never have won a Miss Congeniality award."

"That fills some gaps in your profile." Ron's serious observation didn't match the laughter in his eyes. "Continue."

I told him about my mother's shyness, so perplexing at times because of her quiet ferocity when anyone, by omission or commission, hurt her son or daughter. Yet, she'd never initiate a confrontation. She fought by choosing not to participate.

Except for that one time. I knew *trouble* was about to get capitalized because Mom stayed home from work that day. After her morning tea and one slice of dry wheat toast, she blazed into the front office of my then eight-year-old brother's elementary school like she'd just been blown out of a welder's torch. Peter, who'd rather have every hair on his body plucked out one-by-one than go to school, had spent the day in the vice-principal's office. Mr. Eagen had taped Peter's mouth closed because his teacher said he talked too much in class. Two days later Peter started public school, and Peter's friend

Lance told him Mr. Eagen announced he would be retiring at the end of the school year.

That afternoon she told the two of us, "Always remember, God never sleeps." One day, she'd said, people were going to pay a price for their sins. "And don't worry. With God, it's pay now or pay later. Nobody gets out of paying. Nobody."

I kicked off my sandals and folded my legs under my butt. "So many stories died with her." Pinpricks of sadness found their way into my heart, but I did not want to do weepy. Weepy and therapy were toxic. I concentrated on the scuffed bottoms of Ron's shoes to distract myself.

"Your mother sounds like someone I wish I really could have picked up at the airport," Ron said softly. "Just a few more questions. This one's a shift: Did she and your father argue?"

"You know, I truly don't remember my parents engaged in verbal warfare with one another. But if she was mad I usually knew it. You'd think Mr. Eagen had taped her mouth shut. For days. When she would answer, it'd mostly be one-syllable words. My dad would warn Peter and me, 'It's hard to push a wet noodle, so don't upset your mother.'"

Ron tapped his pen on his chin and stared at his notes. "Wet noodle." He enunciated each word as if he'd just heard it for the first time. "So," Ron said, and turned another page, "your mother was passive-aggressive."

"Are you asking me or telling me?"

"Telling, but," he shrugged, "maybe not. Would you describe your mom as an affectionate woman?"

"Are you kidding?" This was a no-brainer. "Mom was the queen of the 'air hug.' You know, the stiff-armed hug where another person can almost fit in the middle between the two of you. When we'd kiss her, she'd give us a cheek."

"Back to our airport scenario for a minute," said Ron. "Let's say you, or your brother, or your dad will be meeting your mom's plane. Are we still talking air hugs and cheek kisses?"

"Oh, yeah. I remember my dad trying to be lovey in those dorky moves parents try around their kids. Sometimes she'd sputter around the kitchen, cooking supper, and he'd try to hug her. She'd lean back, look annoyed, and tell him, 'Not now, Bob.' My brother and I joked we could bank on their having had sex at least twice." I smiled, but what I'd just heard myself say didn't feel funny.

Ron swung his legs off the ottoman and sat forward in his chair, feet on the floor. "One more thing," he said, his voice settled like a silk scarf. "You never mentioned your mother's name."

"Lola. Her name was Lola. It means 'sorrow.'"

Another AA meeting. Another group session. Another AA meeting. Days like bumper-to-bumper traffic. Inches of time passed. Ever so often, a spurt of movement. Then, a minute later, nothing.

I decided since there was no way out of the jam, I might as well pay more attention to people on the road with me, and I started attaching faces and names at AA meetings. Hung around the coffee pot. Gushed AA mottos like "first things first," and "easy does it," and "live and let live" without looking over my shoulder to see if anyone heard me. Clapped when my fellow wounded walked to the front of the room to claim chips that marked their sobriety. One month. Two months. Six months.

At the end of one meeting, I grabbed Theresa's hand and asked her if she'd walk with me to pick up my Desire Chip.

The important one. The chip bought with humility, with the strength of admitting weakness, and with the promise of one day at a time. On the Theresa shock scale, my request registered a saucer-eyed O-shaped mouth and a high-five. Later, she hugged me, a warm, round squeeze, just Goldilocks right.

When Carl, Molly, and Devin visited the next day, I wanted them to understand what this chip meant to me. I wanted them to know that as frightening as the thought of staying sober was for me, it was the most important goal in my life. I wanted them, most of all, to see my baby step of faith in the Program, in myself, in God.

28

Less than ten minutes until visiting time.

I drummed my fingers on one of the game tables in the rec room. The vibrations sent the plastic red and black checkers scooting out of their squares. Annie and her stack of *O* magazines paused by the table on their way out of the room. "You know, you're messing up Benny and Vince's game with all that rattling. If I were you, I'd try to remember where those things were before they get back from lunch." She strolled out before my sarcasm pistol could fire off one of the five or so answers I had in mind.

My chip was on the table, Serenity Prayer up. Another slice of humble pie. Okay, God, I'm a work-in-progress and old habits are hard to break. "Grant me the serenity to accept the things I cannot change, courage to change the things I can, and wisdom to know the difference." Maybe I needed to bite the chip, not people, when I felt impatient and annoyed.

———

"If AA clubs had their own carnival groups, they could throw these as doubloons." Carl flipped my coin over before he passed it to Devin.

I was impatient for this? Once again, I'd written a script nobody bothered to read before rehearsal. I allowed myself one mental snapshot of Carl biting into the chip, set the Serenity Prayer on replay loop in my brain, and told God the rest was up to Him. Instead of answering Carl, I, well, tittered, which in itself was humiliating. My hand itched.

"Dude—" Devin elbowed Carl "—I don't think that's what Leah wanted to hear." He reached across the table to pat my arm. His fingers were thin, like bamboo stalks, and his hand almost as long as my forearm. "I'm proud of you. Big step you've taken, kiddo." He looked back at Carl as if to say, *"See, that's what you need to do."*

"Thanks, Devin. That means a lot to me," I said as he handed me the chip. "And thanks for coming to visit. Not exactly where we're used to meeting, but the ice cream's free."

Carl leaned back in his chair, surveyed the room, then stared at me and said, "Technically, not free. Right?"

Wisdom to know the difference. Wisdom to know the difference. Wisdom to know the difference. "Absolutely. Everything comes with a price. Right?" I said and hoped my saccharine smile would substitute for the real thing.

The deafening silence of Carl's ego deflating filled the space between us. He fiddled with the top button on his black Polo shirt.

Molly, ever the diplomat, pounced on the awkwardness and wrestled it into submission. "Devin, hand me Leah's chip." She read the Serenity Prayer aloud, and turned the chip over. "Leah, didn't you have this on a poster in your classroom?" She pointed to the inscription, "To Thine Own Self Be True," that encircled the triangle.

"Strange, isn't it? That banner stretched across the wall in my classroom for years. Guess I should have lived it instead of just read it," I said. "Who knew?"

"I don't get this." Molly twisted the chip in her hand. "Why are the letters H-O-W inside each angle on this triangle?"

"I just read about that in my *Reflection for the Day* book. It's Honesty, Open-Mindedness, and Willingness. Qualities we can use to help us see things differently. The Program's about remembering where we came from so we can really appreciate where we are." Teacher-voice had taken over. "Sorry, y'all. Didn't mean to shift into lecture mode."

"Don't apologize. It's cool to hear you talk about this," Devin said. He put his hand on my shoulder. "Molly and I want you to know we believe in you. And we want to help any way you need us."

I didn't have to look at Molly to know she'd melted right into him.

I should be so lucky.

"You're supposed to be excited about your first pass, unless squeezing the blood out of your hands is your way of showing how thrilled you are to be leaving." Jan looked up from the papers at the desk. "You look nice. Where's hubby taking you?"

I stopped pacing to explain to Jan why I wore a dress that cost more than my first car. And the hand-wringing was a form of prayer that it wouldn't meet the same fate: sandwiched between two cars in a four-car pile-up. Which, for the dress, would mean wearing whatever had been served at dinner and then, possibly, being rear-ended, so to speak, by a chocolate soufflé with raspberry sauce.

At the end of yesterday's visit, Carl had asked if he could speak to me alone. We sat in the empty office near the rec room.

"I want to apologize for showing my butt out there. I don't do well with so many people around, not knowing how to act, what to say." He reached for my hand. "But I want you to know I want you to be better. I promise I'm going to help you with whatever you need. We'll do this together."

It had been like a visit from the ghost of Carl past. The caring one. "That means so much to me. I know you're struggling too. Don't give up on me, please?"

"Never. You know you're the most important person in my life. I don't know what I'd do without you." He wrapped his arms around me and kissed the top of my head. He told me not to go anywhere—as if I could—and came back in with a large box.

The package was wrapped with white moiré silk. The red-and white-striped stitched silk ribbon was embellished with a script "NB." NB for Nan's Boutique where long ago I'd picked up a simple cotton tee, spotted the $125 price tag, and looked around to make sure I wasn't being "punked."

That was the first and last time I'd walked through Nan's antique doors, the ones with insets of leaded glass from England. Molly and I figured we could each afford one sleeve of the cotton T-shirt. And that was the end of that as far as my shopping budget was concerned. Carl's mother, however, shopped there so often I'm sure Nan sent monthly thank-you notes to Mr. Thornton.

"So, that's how this dress happened," Jan said as she walked around the counter for the full-length view.

"When Carl first handed me the box, I prayed that ridiculous white cotton tee wasn't in it. So, before I opened it, I asked him if the surprise was for our first date, thinking he'd planned something extraordinarily special." I sighed, re-adjusted the freshwater pearl necklace we bought in Maui on our honeymoon. Molly had dropped it off earlier.

"And the special is?" Jan twirled her finger in the air; the universal female sign for "turn around slowly so I can examine what you're wearing."

I circled in the rhinestone Valentino pumps Molly unearthed in my closet. "Anniversary party for his parents." The words were drenched in disappointment. "All this—" I looked down the length of the little black dress (what Nan referred to as "LBD") designed by Stella McCartney "—for them. It's decadent. I mean, who do I think I am? "

"Maybe it's more like who do *they* think you are," Jan said. She answered the phone. "You're about to find out, Cinderella. Prince Charming's on his way up."

⸻

Carl, as my grandmother would say, cleaned up nicely. I'd forgotten the transforming power of a man's suit, especially one tailored for him.

He walked over, stood in front of me, and, with unfamiliar gentleness, he reached out and cradled my elbows in his hands. "You look beautiful," he whispered and leaned in for a velvet soft kiss on my cheek. I captured the moment in the net of memory. He smelled like promise and comfort. My hands touched his chest and read the invitation of longing and belonging.

"So do you," I said.

He grinned. A genuine grin. An expression I'd not seen in a long time.

I signed the paperwork for my first night out, then Jan handed Carl my overnight bag.

"You two kids be good and enjoy yourselves." Jan gave me a quick hug. She tapped Carl on the shoulder. "Remember,

Cinderella needs to be back tomorrow by noon. Don't be late."

"No problem. She'll be here. I promise." He held out his hand. "Are you ready?"

I'm sucked back in time. Dr. Foret. Delivery room. "Ten centimeters, fully effaced. Let's rock and roll. It's baby time." He moved to the end of my bed. "Are you ready?"

I'm thinking, *"Wait, wait. Let me think about this. I'm not ready. My life will never be the same. Five more minutes, please."* But, of course, I don't say any of this. I take all the fears, roll them up, and mentally send them to my brain's trash icon.

I had looked at Carl and squeezed his hand.

I had told Dr. Foret, "You bet. Let's do this."

A lifetime later.

I looked at Carl. I squeezed his hand.

"You bet. Let's do this."

"I remembered you weren't allowed perfume. I brought your Hanae Mori. It's in the car."

"Thanks."

We stood side-by-side, not touching, except for the prickly current connecting my naked arm to his Armani suit. I channeled the electricity surging between us into my hands, tightening my grip on my Judith Leiber clutch. McCartney, Valentino, Leiber, and a perfume whose name was barely pronounceable. I'd spent almost two weeks in excruciating introspection, and tonight, in less than an hour, a blitzkrieg of designers annihilated my identity.

I handed Carl my clutch when the security guard at the door asked to see my identification. I pulled the hospital's white plastic bracelet out from under my silver and rhinestone cuff.

"Can she take that thing off just for tonight?" Carl's voice didn't suppress his irritation.

I knew the answer, but Carl didn't ask me.

"Sure, she can take that fancy jewelry off anytime." Mr. Jacobs rubbed his grizzly gray hair and man-giggled. He'd cracked himself up.

"Never mind. Was that all you need from her?" Carl handed Judith back to me. Without waiting for Mr. Jacobs's answer, Carl said, "Wait here. I'll get the car," and power-walked outside. After the doors sucked closed behind him, I turned to Mr. Jacobs. "Sorry. We're still looking for his sense of humor."

"Mrs. Thornton, right? I've heard worse and seen worse in all my years here. You don't need to apologize for him."

Why didn't I think of that?

Because if you would've thought of that on your own you probably wouldn't be here.

God, who belongs to that voice? And where's she been with all this insight?

You wouldn't believe me even if I told you. Not yet.

The headlights of Carl's car curled around the entry.

Part of me wished Mr. Jacobs would refuse to release me. Then, through no fault of my own, I'd be forced to stay. But, no, that's alcoholic Leah.

Recovering Leah knows fear stands for false expectations appearing real.

No fear. No fear. No fear.

Courage to change the things I can.

"Enjoy yourself. I'll see you tomorrow, Mrs. Thornton. Remember—one day at a time."

"Bye. Have a good night."

I gathered the parts of me and crossed the threshold.

One small victory.

One small victory at a time.

Carl held the car door open. I slipped into the seat and inhaled the familiar leather scent. A month before Alyssa was born, Carl surprised me with my first Lexus—a white RX SUV. He called it the mommy-mobile. I couldn't even drive it then. My bathtub-sized belly forced me to push the seat so far back, my short legs couldn't reach the pedals. Carl had teased me, and said he'd called Mark at the dealership and ordered extension blocks for the accelerator and brake.

It was the last laugh we had about the car. After Alyssa's funeral and a pitcher of martinis, I'd hurled the keys at Carl. Sober, I was a lousy pitcher. Drunk, I was dangerous. The keys had missed Carl, but not the armoire next to him. The mirror in the door shuddered, shattered, and crashed, littering the floor like puzzle pieces made of shiny glass.

Carl had screamed at me. His mouth moved up and down, up and down. He'd pointed at me, at the floor, at me again. Some words sloshed through the martini tunnel. Words like: do you know what that's worth blahblahblah crazy.

"Uh-oh," I'd replied and stumbled past him.

He'd grabbed my arm. His thumb and forefinger met at my bone. "Stop. Get away from here before you hurt yourself. You're barefooted. You can't walk on broken glass."

I yanked myself away and almost fell from the deliberateness. "Watch me."

The next morning, while I scrubbed dried blood off the floor, he traded in the SUV for a convertible.

29

Carl closed his door and pushed the button to start the car. "Want the top down?"

I weighed the hair damage risk against the pleasure of the wind in my face and a star-drenched sky for a roof. "How about up on the way to the party and down on the way home?"

"This is your night. Whatever you want." He leaned toward me, slid his hand under my hair, and massaged my neck. "I've missed you. Kiss me."

My hands moved toward him, cradled his face. My lips tingled against his. Soft. Trusting.

His hand moved from my neck to my shoulder. His lips parted mine. I tasted salt, a hint of desperation. His other hand cupped my breast.

I flinched. Pushed his hand away. I opened my eyes. Pushed myself into the seat.

"What's wrong?"

"I thought you wanted to kiss."

"I did. Wasn't that what we were doing?" His voice grew edgy. "I didn't know we had rules."

"Well, I mean, were we going to make out in front of the hospital?"

He smiled. Not a happy smile. A condescending smile saved for a four-year-old who would ask if she could drive to the moon. "Make—(he paused)—out? We're not in high school, Leah." He shifted into drive and headed toward the hospital exit. "I'm your husband. You've been gone for weeks. I'm not supposed to touch you? Never mind. Don't answer that. I don't want to fight with you. Especially tonight."

"I missed you too. I overreacted, I guess. I'm sorry."

Lie. Lie. Lie. Does AA offer confession? Accept the things I cannot change . . . wisdom to know the difference. When does the serenity happen?

"Being out feels strange after being in . . . and there's so much more going on . . . like I didn't expect to be going anywhere. Then you surprised me with this dress, going to your parents' anniversary party . . ."

"You'll be fine. We don't have to stay all night." He stroked my hair. "Besides, we only have this one night together before you have to go back."

I shivered. Carl grinned. "This is a big step for me, going to this party," I said. "I'm not sure if I'll know what to do with myself. What do sober people do at parties?"

"Guess you'll find out. You're not doing this alone. You've got me to run interference for you. I'll make sure you don't go anywhere near the bar tonight. I meant what I told you at the hospital. I want you to depend on me to help."

When Carl turned onto Oak Park Avenue, it was like turning into a festival of lights and noise. Harleys dodged around the snarls created by cars either too impatient or too oblivious to conform to lanes and traffic signals. Flashing business signs, the familiar bright arches, chicken buckets of chain restaurants, and the occasional exhaust of a city bus reminded me I'm gone and forgotten.

A few more miles. "I'm glad your parents will understand. That helps too. I'd hate having to explain to them why I'm not manning the blender for frozen daiquiris." I opened the glove compartment. "Is the perfume in here?"

"Oh, I need to talk to you about that." Carl switched lanes and waited for the turn signal.

"What? My perfume? I found it." I showed him the bottle of Butterfly. I first bought the perfume because I liked the top of the bottle. It was shaped like the folded wings of a butterfly. The perfume was equally delicate, a combination of flowers and almonds and berries. When the car stopped at a red light, I opened the bottle, applied dots of perfume behind my ears and knees, and returned it to the glove compartment. "So what did you want to tell me?"

"About my parents and the party."

"What about your parents?"

"Mom had asked me weeks ago if you'd want to be involved in all the details before she made the appointment with the party planner. I should've talked to you first, but I told her the end of school was a tough time for you. I figured you didn't need to be making decisions about catering, decorations, music. You know my mother. "

Another example of Carl saving me from myself, but this time I was relieved. It protected me from Gloria and her exasperating attention to minutiae. The woman could spend days deliberating between white-white and almost-white paint. And another week deciding if the painters should use flat or eggshell as a base. "I know your mother, so I'm eternally grateful you made that decision for me. Don't worry. I'll back you up if she mentions it. But I'm sure after you told her about rehab at Brookforest, she's equally as thankful I didn't help."

"Probably. But here's the thing." Carl pulled into the parking lot of the Starbucks around the corner from his parents' house. But he didn't ask if I wanted a venti or a grande.

"What are you doing? Why are we stopping here?" My chest hurt. "What *thing*?"

Carl turned off the car engine and stared out the front window. "Your decision to go to Brookforest was a shock. You were so determined to go in on the Fourth, even when you knew my parents already had planned the weekend."

I needed air. Too much perfume. "Please open the windows. Go on, continue." Whatever the "thing" was, I predicted it was my fault.

"I called your dad first and told him, you know, about why you thought you drank too much and what you'd decided to do. We talked for a long time." He ran his hands back and forth along the steering wheel.

I unlocked the seat belt. Everything felt tight. The car, the dress, the shoes, the necklace, the truth. If I could have reached the ropes knotting in my stomach I might have strangled him with them at that moment. "You told your parents. Please tell me you told your parents."

"Of course, I told my parents."

Noisy teens spilled out of the car parked next to us. Slammed car doors gave me a reason to raise my voice. "I know a 'but' when I don't hear one. But what?"

"It wasn't just me. Your dad agreed with me."

A foot stomped on my chest. "About what?" Loud didn't matter to me now.

He clutched the steering wheel and looked at me. "I didn't tell them about the alcohol thing—"

The other foot stomped.

"The alcohol THING? THING?" I heard blood vessels popping in my eyes.

"I told them you were having problems coping since Alyssa died. I told them you'd been in therapy, but you didn't want people to know. I told them the therapist thought this would help you, our marriage."

—————

The doors were bolted. I mashed the buzzer. No one.

Where did that man go? I buzzed again and slapped my hand against the door. The car behind me was reflected in the glass. I seemed to be slapping it too. *Good.*

"Hold your horses. I'm coming." A voice, then a shadow of a figure materialized and moved toward me. I didn't remember Mr. Jacobs having a rocking limp when I'd left. But it was Mr. Jacobs, and he showed only a ripple of surprise when he unlocked the door. "Come on in. Did you forget something?"

I shoved my suitcase into the entrance and saw the rear lights of the car dance on the walls until they disappeared. "I guess you could say that." I didn't turn around to watch Mr. Jacobs relock the door.

Betrayal was a rotting corpse: bloated and putrid. But that was more information than he really wanted. I kicked off my pumps and rubbed my feet against the cool terrazzo floors.

"I forgot the story my mother told me about tigers," I said.

Mr. Jacobs scratched his head. "Well, I might need you to explain that one."

"Tigers don't change their stripes," I said.

"Oh, she's right on there." He scratched his chin, stared out the front door for a minute, and grabbed his clipboard. "You're back for the night?"

We both understood it wasn't really a question.

I nodded.

"You have to sign back in. Policy."

I signed back in at 5:23 p.m.—fifty minutes after I left.

Mr. Jacobs waved me into the elevator. "You have a good night. And Mrs. Thornton . . ." His voice reflected the kindness I saw in his eyes. "God has a plan, I promise. Everything's going to work out."

"It's going to be better now that I'm—" I caught myself, about to say "home." "Now that I'm here."

If home was a place of safety and acceptance, maybe—for now—I was home. I just had to figure out how to make the one I'd left two weeks ago feel like the one I'd just come back to.

———— ∞ ————

"Stella's dress, Valentino's shoes, and Judith's purse, and I are all back. Where is everyone? Hello?" I dumped my shoes on top of my suitcase. Now that the elephant was off my chest, and I could breathe again, I headed to the refrigerator for an ice cream fix. I needed to check my Big Book for warnings about romanticizing about Blue Bell, Ben and Jerry's, and Nutty Buddies. In the meantime, I hoped Matthew remembered to restock. I found potential solace in a frozen Snickers candy bar and a Fudgesicle and headed to the rec room.

No people. No television. No music. I sat, leaned against the arm of the sofa, and stretched my legs out. In the last hour, I'd overdosed on emotions, and the hangover left me numb. But it was no different than waking up the day after drinking too much. Numb was only temporary. Like the quiet in here.

———— ∞ ————

Jan stopped dead in her tracks when she saw me. Clichéd, but I'd never seen anyone come to such a complete halt without walking into a wall.

I held up the Fudgesicle. "Care to join me?"

"You have to pee first. When you come back from an over-night, we have to take a urine sample."

"Jan, duh. If I'm here, I'm not overnight."

"Doesn't matter. You left. You came back. You pee." She walked off and came back with an empty specimen jar. "Here." She handed it to me. "Hurry up. I want to know what happened."

I handed her my ice cream. "Lucky for you, I happen to hold the world's record for fast peeing. But don't start timing me until I've ditched the pantyhose."

A few minutes later we traded again. Off she went with her specimen jar. I resumed my position, resumed eating, and resumed waiting.

Jan returned with a new supply of magazines. She stacked them on the table before she joined me on the sofa. "Are you hungry? It's not too late for me to get a plate sent up for you."

"Nah, I'm good, but thanks."

"You need to take care of yourself *nutritionally*, too. That body you're occupying has to last a lifetime. Would you take care of your car the way you take care of yourself?"

"Enough with the lectures," I snapped. I finished the ice cream, and tossed the paper and stick on the table. "You want to talk unhealthy? Let's talk about relationships. Unhealthy relationships. Like my marriage. How long does an unhealthy relationship last?"

I clenched and unclenched my hands. My fingernails dug into my palms. I wanted to go somewhere. Away. Far away. How far did I have to go to get away from myself? Anger surged down my arms, up my legs, flooded my chest. I wanted it to stop rising. Alcohol used to do that for me. Now what? Now what? Where did people go with this? I wanted this angry, rag-ing flood to go away. My grandmother used to make rain go away. *Rain, rain, go away. Come again another day.*

I stood. "I have to get out of here. I have to get out of here. I have to do something with all this." I waved my hands. The invisible *this* caught in the space between my hands and my body.

Jan put her arm around my shoulders. "It's okay. You're entitled to your anger. Let's go outside. We can walk on the trail behind the hospital, and you can tell me what happened."

She led me to where I'd dropped my suitcase. "But first you need to leave your designer friends behind." She pointed to my dress and my glitzy pumps.

"I have flip-flops and scrubs in my suitcase." I pulled them out, changed, and followed Jan outside.

30

Lesson of the Day: Sober = Pain

Not drinking meant I had to feel. But feeling meant I wanted to drink.

Sobriety was complicated.

Jan and I walked and walked and walked until I spewed and spilled the whole story of Carl's betrayal.

"We probably should have charged Starbucks. I think people hung around just to watch us," I said.

"Did you really think you'd walk back to the hospital?"

"Well, after I leaped out of the car and slammed the door, I had to go somewhere. But with my sense of direction, I would have ended up in Austin instead. All I knew was where I wasn't going. No way was I going to his parents' house. There I was, all designered-up, screaming like a banshee in the parking lot. 'Take me back to the hospital, right now!'"

"I'm surprised somebody didn't call a television station. How many people do you think demand to be driven *back* to rehab?"

"Good point. When Carl finally agreed to take me back, I wouldn't get in the car until he gave me his cell phone. I was afraid he'd go to his parents' house or who knew where. I told him if he didn't do what I asked him to do, I'd punch 9-1-1 in the cell and scream I'd been kidnapped."

"And you're the woman Carl told people didn't have common sense?" She shook her head. "I bet he's rethinking that one."

"Hmm, I don't know." I stopped at the water fountain, too thirsty to care about drinking lukewarm water. "Years ago, I heard a radio show with Dr. Laura. Some days I switched the show off because the callers were such goofballs. I don't even remember what the topic was that day. But I heard her say that at points in our lives, we have to choose the hills we're willing to die on. That stayed with me. And when Carl told me he'd sold me out, that was my hill."

"I hope you realize what this says about you, and your commitment to recovery," Jan said. "Honestly, I didn't think you should have gone to the party in the first place. That's a tough temptation for anyone whose sobriety is so fragile."

We'd reached the end of the blacktop trail. Jan pointed in the direction of the cafeteria. And air conditioning.

"I thought if I had Carl and his parents to support me it would be enough. Naïve, huh?"

"Step Two says, 'Came to believe that a Power greater than ourselves could restore us to sanity.' Carl and his parents aren't the 'greater' in that step."

"What if my marriage can't survive my sanity?"

"First, don't play the 'what if' game. Secondly, was your marriage going to survive your insanity?"

"Guess the fact that I'm here answers that question," I said. "I can't talk about this anymore. I'm hot. I'm hungry. Do you think there's anything left of dinner in the cafeteria?"

<hr />

Recovery reminded me of a clearance sale. Grabbing clothes helter-skelter, not knowing if the sizes fit, the colors coordinate, or the prices are palatable. You schlepped it all to the dressing room and refused to emerge until you tried and retried, matched and unmatched, added and subtracted.

For weeks I gathered AA Steps and Traditions, a Blue Book, collections of adages and mottos, theories, epiphanies, crazy quilt pieces of my life. At first, it all seemed random and disconnected. Then I'd find a missing link, or some days I'd throw a useless link away, and order overcame chaos.

The most frightening aspect of all this? It made perfect sense to me. Like strength in weakness. Freedom in structure. A bride in white who'd been living with the groom for three years.

My newest victory was that I'd survived Carl-gate. He lied. I called him on it. I woke up Sunday morning in a different bed than the one I'd expected to be in. I don't know how, but the idea that leaving here overnight included sharing a bed with Carl had failed to emerge on my radar screen. Sooner or later, I'd have to engage in sober sex. This morning, though, I was relieved it was later.

I'd forgotten Sunday mornings were generally quiet since check-in wasn't until noon. Jan told me last night Cathryn would be working, so I figured it'd just be us girls. I'd be lazy and sloppy until lunch. I didn't bother changing out of the camisole and plaid boxers I'd fallen asleep wearing.

I wandered to the front, so busy digging crud out of my eyes that I bumped smack into Designer Drugs woman in the hall. "Omph" met "Whoa. Oops." Followed by the "flump, flump, flump" of magazines meeting the floor.

"So sorry," I said.

"S'okay. I should know better than to read and walk at the same time." She bent to pick up the magazines.

"Wait, let me help." I handed her the last two. "Oh, these are the ones Jan brought in last night." *Vogue, Cosmo, Vanity Fair, Newsweek,* and *Psychology Today.* An eclectic collection. Had Designer Drugs asked for these?

"I didn't realize you were here. I thought you left on a pass," she said.

"I did leave. I came back. Long story. I didn't know you were here either." After my turkey sandwich, coleslaw, and chips dinner last night, I'd crashed in my room.

"Oh, um, I didn't have a pass this weekend. I could have, but my husband was out of town, so it didn't seem to matter." She passed her hand under her nose, a flutter of a movement.

I pretended not to notice. So generous of me as I stood there with morning mouth, clothes so wrinkled I looked like I rolled down a hill, red slipper socks, and eye gunk I'd wiped on my boxers. Meanwhile, she didn't stand, she posed, like a woman who felt comfortable in her skin. Her white linen nightshirt fell to her knees. She was prettier plain-faced than she was with make-up.

"I didn't realize you were married," I said. Oh, dumb me. Why would I realize that? I hadn't bothered to utter a syllable to her since she arrived. I didn't even know her name. Shame on me. Maybe there was a step for this I hadn't reached yet.

She shifted the magazines. "Do you mind walking with me so I can leave these in my room?"

"No problem." It wasn't until we'd walked past my room that I realized she shared a room with Annie. Why had I assumed she had a private room? "So, how's Annie for a roommate?"

"Great, really. We both love to read, so it works out." She opened the door. "I'll be right out."

Slug. I felt like a slug. She was not at all what I'd expected. No, what I'd assumed. I'd judged her with my puny self-esteem. If she'd judged me using her generous self-assurance . . .

Why did I struggle with friendships with other women? Molly and I met on the equal playing field of age and our husbands' shared jobs. We'd experienced, through the years, tragedies that bound us to one another. I never felt intimidated by her—and there it was. I'd heard at one of the AA meetings that in our recovery, God revealed truths slowly because we wouldn't be able to bear the weight of them all at once. Thank you, God, for sparing me the steamroller of guilt.

She popped out wearing khaki shorts, a sleeveless celery v-necked sweater, and white flip flops. Cute. Instead of the fitness trainer-toned body I assumed she'd have, her clothes had disguised legs and arms that were thin and knobby. *Everyone has a story to tell.* Another poster in my classroom. Time for the teacher to become the student?

"Want to see what we can find for breakfast? I'm starving," she said, and closed the door behind her.

"Sure. I'll need to change. Meet you at the desk," I said.

"You look fine. I looked like a ghost in that nightshirt. Besides," she lowered her voice, "my puny boobs and body are hard to hide in that thing."

"Fine? You didn't tell me you're almost blind. I look like—"

"—a recovering alcoholic who just woke up?"

For a swallow of time, I stared at her. Then we convulsed in laughter and headed downstairs.

Several waffles and three cups of coffee later, I learned her name was Gertrude and the silver-haired man from group was her husband, Adam. The woman was a bundle of surprises.

"I've never met anyone with the same name as Hamlet's mother. Please tell me they didn't know that Gertrude."

She smiled. A sad smile. "You know, in high school, I was that Gertrude. Shallow, promiscuous, manipulating men." She added more milk to her coffee. "But she drank poison, right?"

I nodded.

"I snorted mine. And I didn't die."

It sounded like an apology.

I squirmed. Over-sexed mothers who kill themselves didn't make for comfortable breakfast conversations. I steered in a different direction.

"Kids in school must have tortured you," I said.

Her face shed its veil, and she perked up. "They tried." A light clicked on in her eyes, and she smiled broadly. "When I was almost five, I beat up the kid next door. He called me Turd-trude. My father was so proud. Really. He bragged for years about that. Giving Cole that black eye saved me in kindergarten. In middle school, I added an "i" and told everyone my name was Trudie. And that's what I was until I met Adam." She looked past me. Her eyes dulled for a few blinks, then the lights turned on again, and she was back. "He called me Tru. Ironic. Considering the drugs and all."

I didn't say anything. I figured we'd talk about the "drugs and all" some other time. "I'm glad we bumped into each other." I hesitated. "I'm embarrassed I didn't try to talk to you sooner. I thought you'd be different. And you are different . . . in a good way."

"I get that a lot." She laughed as we walked away from depositing our trays. "Hey, it's not like I tried either. Those first few days were such a nightmare, I thought I'd come here to die. Maybe even hoped I would. Jan told me sometimes one day at a time's too unmanageable. So I started just trying to make it five minutes at a time." She pulled open a door outside the cafeteria.

"That's not a bathroom," I said.

"I know. Do you take the stairs too?"

"I do now."

We made it upstairs, but my stomach felt like it was headed another floor up.

"I'm going to lay down for awhile. Not sure breakfast is going to stay with me," I said.

"Too much exercise?"

Cathryn gazed up from her book. "Oh, hi, Trudie. I heard Leah, but didn't realize you were with her."

"We had breakfast together," Trudie announced like a five-year-old who'd just learned to tie her own shoes.

I pulled my hair away from my neck. "Is it hot in here?"

Trudi placed her hand on my forehead. The coolness felt good. "You do feel warm. Maybe you're coming down with something."

Cathryn stuck a pen in the book to mark her place. "Come sit down. I'll take your temperature. Lord knows, we already have enough diseases around here." She walked over to the chair where I waited.

"Joke alert, ladies." She smiled at us, then pointed the thermometer at my mouth.

"Here you go."

It beeped. 98 degrees.

"Maybe you'll feel better after you rest," said Trudie.

"We have antacid chewables. Want to try two of those to settle your stomach?"

"I'll try the rest first," I said, and headed to my room.

31

I woke up sad, but I couldn't remember why.

Sometimes I'd carry pieces of dreams back, and before I got out of bed, I'd arrange them on a table in my mind's eye. I hoped I could find a pattern to help me understand why I felt the way I did, why the feeling followed me from dream to reality.

Today the sadness clung to me. Whatever it was, I didn't want to face it today. Sunday was supposed to be a day of rest anyway. I could give myself permission to rest from my emotions.

The scritchy feeling that sent me to bed was gone after the two hours I slept. It was almost time for the overnighters to check in. Which meant Theresa would be back. Which meant if I wanted to shower until the hot water ran out, I needed to get moving.

I'd just finished blow-drying my hair and regretting I'd not thought to have it trimmed before I checked in—you'd think some piece of pre-admit literature would've mentioned that—when I heard Theresa.

"Hey, Miss Thing," she said and knocked on the bathroom door. "You best come outta there right now."

Since she followed her order with a laugh, I figured I was safe. With Theresa, I never knew what intestinal crisis might have befallen her on the way back.

I opened the door and almost backed into the bathtub from shock. It must have been some weekend.

"I surprised you, huh? I knew I would. Well? When you gonna tell me how fly I look?" She spun around for the full effect. A clunky spin since she was wearing, of all summer shoe choices, purple and black high-topped sneakers.

"I'm, I'm speechless," I replied, and I truly was. The trademark bracelets still jingled and clanged, but the hair she ran her hands through . . . oh, my. Theresa had returned as a blonde. With short hair. Very short hair. A boyish crop framed her face. Wow. I had to admire her bravery.

She grabbed my hands and pulled me away from the bathroom door. "Move over here so you can see me better," she said. Her eager smile and bright eyes signaled she anticipated more compliments about her new style.

"Theresa, it's such . . ." I reached over and gently touched the ends of her bangs. ". . . an amazingly different look for you. How did you ever decide on this cut and color?" Generic expressions, please don't fail me now, I prayed.

"Well, it was like this. I said to myself, 'Theresa, you been down this rehab road before, and you got on it again. You know you need to change.' So, then, I get this idea that maybe just changing inside ain't enough. I mean, most people, they can't see inside changes. Heck, most people don't ever look for inside changes anyway. Right?"

I nodded. She was making sense, in a Theresa sort of way. Maybe she was onto something. Or on something.

"I start thinking that maybe changing my outside would be how people would notice I was different than I was before. You see?"

"Yes. You're absolutely right."

She nodded vigorously. I had flashbacks of her formerly enthusiastic hair, springing out every which way, and her beads bouncing all over the place.

"For sure I am. My cousin, she's about to graduate from beauty school. So, we start talking, and I have this, this—what's that fancy word you got for when you figure something out?"

"Epiphany?"

She snapped her fingers. "That's it. I had one of those with my cousin."

"Uh-huh." Really. What else could I say?

"We got on it yesterday afternoon. I told her I wanted people to see me new."

I hugged her. "Well, sister, no doubt. You are a new woman. A brand new creation."

"Girl, I can't believe you just said that." She jumped back, covered her mouth with her hands, and her purple eyelids almost disappeared her eyes were so round.

"What did I say? Oh, my gosh. Did I say something wrong? What?" I floundered in my confusion and almost tripped over her suitcase.

"No, not wrong." She leaned her head back and spoke to the ceiling. "God, I knew you was with me. This was a sign." Then she threw her suitcase on her bed, unzipped it, and pulled out a Bible. "You ready for this?"

I didn't answer. I had no idea.

"My preacher in church this morning, look what he talked about. I underlined it right here. Second Corinthians 5:17. 'Therefore, if anyone is in Christ, he is a new creation; old things have passed away; behold, all things have become new.'"

I wanted to take another shower after Theresa left our room. I wanted a shower that would wash away my shallowness, my self-centeredness, and my selfishness down the drain where they belonged.

If faith had a school, I'd be in detention daily. God knew I'd be a slow learner, so He surrounded me with lessons on my level. The level of dumb and doubtful. He worked me over today. Trudie this morning, and now Theresa. The promise of old things passing away, and others becoming new. There's some hope. I'll be new. That's almost too good to hope for.

If Scrooge needed three ghosts to be brought to sanity, what did God have in mind for me?

"Carl called. Please call him back soon because those two words together are really tongue twisters," said Cathryn as she unlocked the door to the empty office. "I thought you might want some privacy after yesterday. Jan filled me in."

"Thanks. I appreciate that."

"And, Leah, you can't change the past, you can only change yourself."

I punched in the number with the hope he may have decided not to answer, and I could just leave a message. Nope. Second ring.

The crux of the conversation was he wanted to visit that afternoon, but not unless I approved. I'd asked him if his parents were coming with him. Of course not.

"So, just for kicks—they thought I'd be at their party. What did you tell them was the reason I didn't show up?"

"I told them the truth. That you were having a bad night, and you didn't want to leave the center," he said.

If truth can be counted in particles, then I'd say he'd told them not maybe "the" truth, but at least "a" truth. He said he couldn't tell them during their party, and today they were exhausted after the party, but he promised he'd talk to them this week.

I hung up and related the story to Cathryn.

"I told him to call me after he'd told them, and we'd visit during the week. He didn't sound too happy when he hung up. But since I'm not too happy with him . . ."

"How long are you going to hold on to that anger? Sounds like this might be a control issue. No truth, no visit. Is that it?"

"Shouldn't it be?" I said. "He lied about why I'm here. That's not a big deal?"

"Sure it is," she said. "But here's something I want you to process. Why does he have to tell them? He talked to your dad, which you'd asked him to do. Is there a reason you can't tell his parents yourself?"

"They're *his* parents, that's all. I just think they should hear it from him."

"Then why didn't you talk to your father? He's your parent. Did you call your brother?"

"No, Carl asked my dad to call Peter."

"So, besides Carl, did you have to tell anyone else?"

"Well, no. There isn't really anyone else." I tapped my foot on the floor, crossed my arms, and stifled my irritation with this barrage of questions.

"Exactly. You wanted Carl to do what you weren't willing to do. And now, since he didn't do it the way you told him to, you're angry."

"I'm angry because he lied to them. He didn't tell them the truth about why I'm here." I couldn't believe Cathryn wasn't getting this.

"Does it matter? The why, I mean. What difference does it make in terms of your recovery? And if it makes a difference, then you can call them. It seems to me you're holding Carl to a different standard."

"Yes, and the standard is the truth. That's the standard I'm holding him to," I hissed.

"If that works for you," She patted my back. "I have to work on a few charts. Let me know if you need anything."

Cathryn strolled to the office.

My indignation stepped up to the plate, but the pitcher disappeared. What team was I playing on?

Disappointed by Cathryn on Sunday, then ambushed by Matthew on Monday.

"Instead of group this week, you're scheduled for another session with Ron." He looked at the clock. "In fact, your session starts in ten minutes."

"Am I being punished because I disagreed with Cathryn?"

Matthew cleared his throat and leaned forward on the counter so we were just about on eye level. "Punishment isn't doled out here. Sick people who have enough courage to walk through those doors don't need us to dole out punishment. They've done it enough to themselves. Maybe just trust that session is where you need to be. We don't need to always understand something to accept it."

Maybe I've been here long enough. The AA blahblahblah was getting tiresome. "Do you have a catchy little aphorism for everything?"

"No, no, we don't," he said quietly.

I took the stairs to Ron's office.

The door was open. I didn't bother to knock. He knew I was coming. I strolled in.

"I'm here. The question is why am I here? I'm already scheduled to see you later this week."

"I'm wounded. You don't enjoy spending time with me?"

"Don't play around. I'm not in the mood. I've had enough of this place. I've had enough of these people. I get it now. Don't drink. Can I go home?"

"Have a seat. One issue at a time."

"I don't want a seat. I'm tired of sitting. I'm tired of everyone but me having control over my life. When do I get to decide?"

I didn't want to cry, but it was too late. I wiped my cheeks with the backs of my hands. Frustration gripped my chest. The tears came in spasms. I grabbed the box of tissue from Ron's desk and sat down.

"Rough weekend, huh? So I heard. You need a minute?"

I rubbed my fingers to sop up the wet under my eyes. Blew the nose.

"You were a voluntary admission. You were free to come. You're equally as free to go. You don't have to be in my office right now. After the staff talked about your weekend, I'm the one who suggested you have this time. I thought you might want to talk about it in here first. But, hey, take it to group. You decide."

"I'm so stupid. I was such a brat to Matthew when he told me about coming here. Probably worse than mean. I sounded like a ten-year-old having a temper tantrum. I'm sure I pouted."

"You can apologize when you see him. If it's any reassurance, you're right where we expect you to be. This is the tough time in treatment. One month seems long, especially to people waiting on the outside. But only thirty days to unravel a lifetime? Difficult even in the best of cases. Almost impossible in some. And then once we take it apart, people have to leave with tools to construct something out of the mess."

"Well enough to know I'm sick, but sick enough to think I'm well," I said.

"Yep. That's it. If you don't get it—that's trouble waiting to happen."

"I feel like my skin's been peeled off. And spare me the onion analogy. Shrek ruined that one for me. I'm raw. Stuff I thought I'd drowned years ago, it's all coming up for air."

"That's part of the seduction of alcohol. Or drugs, food, sex. Anything you use to feel numb. Your disease convinces you it took care of the pain while you were drinking, drugging, eating, having sex. But none of it dies a natural death. It's just suspended, like in cryogenics. So you stop drinking and things start thawing. You start feeling."

"Am I supposed to spend the rest of my life feeling every little thing that happens? How do people live like that?" Hysteria hijacked my voice.

"Addiction tricks us into thinking we can pick and choose what we feel. We can't. Real life means feeling. Life's supposed to have an edge. If it didn't, how would you know if you were falling off?"

I hung my snotty-nosed, runny-eyed head over the back of the chair. "I hate all this. I want recess. Is there ever recess? I knew I missed first grade."

"Let's get back to the feeling. When Carl lied to his parents about why you're here, now that felt like something, didn't it?"

"Betrayal. That's what it felt like. He sold me out for his parents."

"Is that the first time he's ever done that? Sold you out?"

"Well, yes. I guess. I mean it's never been an issue before. Carl's whole family operates in a universe I've never been a part of—socially or financially. Since we've been married there have been times I've been ticked because of their demands . . . go here, be there, dress like this . . . but I knew Carl wanted to make them happy. So if I had to go to an afternoon tea with blue-haired ladies, no biggie. Sometimes the vacations drove me crazy. Ski lodge, lake house. Under their roof 24/7. Carl's mom obsessing about lettuce. But they're his parents. He's all they have."

"Was your parents' relationship like yours?"

I snorted. "Not quite. My dad did whatever he could to keep my mom happy. At least it seemed that way to me growing up. They made sure I did what I was supposed to do and kept the whining to a minimum. If I complained, my father would give me the 'if you can't say anything nice, don't say anything at all' speech. The one about being grateful for what you have. Oh, and there was also 'God doesn't like ugly.' That one covered my sassy self."

"So, they must have been proud of the woman you became."

"I guess. Most of my life I just did what they wanted me to do. I'd get wild ideas about stuff—like wanting to be a cheerleader or learning how to play the piano—and we'd have these family meetings. Cheerleader was definitely out. They made me realize I had no chance. They gave in on the piano lessons. But I didn't always practice, and eventually I quit. Unfortunately, they'd remind me about that fiasco when I had some other bright idea." I stopped to blow my nose again.

"When I said I wanted to attend college, they freaked out. Asking me over and over if I was sure I wanted to do that and reassuring me I could change my mind."

We talked about my father, my relationship with him then and now. I wanted Ron to see my father as I did. "He'd help our neighbors build decks or donate money to every kid who came around selling junk for school. If I was out late, even in college and still living with them, I called home. He didn't want me to drive in the city at night because it wasn't safe. He still tries to protect me. He'll send me an airline ticket so I won't drive the six hours to his house alone.

"My dad's close to Carl. He likes that they can talk football, play golf, and fish. He told me Carl was a 'man's man.' But he'd joke around with Carl about how he'd take him out if he ever hurt me."

Ron unfolded his arms and picked up his legal pad. "I know this has been a tough session. We have a lot left to uncover, but I think I understand now why you married Carl."

I stood to stretch the numbness in my backside for using it so long. "Oh, I thought it was simple. I married him because I loved him."

"And you loved him because he reminded you of your father."

32

I left Ron's office with one thought: get to my room, lie on my bed, and prevent myself from thinking for as long as possible. I stared at the ceiling, afraid to close my eyes because movies I couldn't stop played in my head. With my eyes open, I could count the holes in the ceiling tiles. If I focused on mindless activity, I could put my brain on a continuous loop, like when the computer's hourglass stays and stays and stays.

But none of it worked for me. My brain wanted to hit "control-alt-delete." End the task. Start over. Maybe I could control the information. Let a few pieces out at a time. Process and move on. Process and move on. Next. Next. Next.

If I married Carl because he reminded me of my father, then who did I remind Carl of? That piece of information definitely had to go back and wait its turn. I mentally smashed it into the steel "waiting" bin in my brain.

Maybe I could sleep. At this point, sleep was as close as I was going to get to numbness. Unfortunately, it wasn't a strategy with much long-term usefulness like those "tools" Ron talked about. Voluntary narcolepsy was not going to help if I planned a vertical life.

Knock. Knock-knock-knock.

Something new to count.

Knock-knock-knock.

Was there a voice attached to this hand? Oh, maybe it thinks I'm asleep.

The doorknob turned. Slowly and squeakily. Like the one in horror movies. Maybe they're all the same doorknob. Like Carl was my father.

"Leah?" My name sounded like a question. My eyes were still closed, but I recognized Cathryn's voice. "Are you sleeping?"

Wasn't that question on the universal list of dumb questions? I'm postponing the inevitable. At some point, I won't be sleeping when she asks that question. It might as well be now. "Do you want me to be sleeping? I can be. I'd rather be." I opened my eyes. Ceiling hole number 1-2-3-4-5-6-7-8-9 . . .

"No, I don't want you to be sleeping right now. I want to talk to you before everyone comes back from group."

Oh, I'd forgotten. I'd traded one torture for another.

"I really need you to sit up," she said. "Look at me. This is important."

I massaged my temples. If I could just unknot my brain, I'd feel better. I pushed myself up to a semi-reclining position.

"Okay, I'm sitting up. This better be good." I scratched my bed-head hair.

She sat on the bed somewhere between my waist and feet. I'm so short, it's a small vicinity, but she's there somewhere. She wiped her palms on her uniform pants. She had my attention now because she was acting very un-Cathryn-like.

"First, I want you to know we all understand how much you've had to deal with, not just since you've been here, but in the past few days. And it's obvious to us how committed you are to your recovery and to staying here until you graduate."

"You're scaring me. What happened and to whom?" The brain knot relocated to my throat.

"Don't be scared. Your family's fine."

"Then what?"

"Usually one of the staff doctors handles medical issues with patients. But, since this is not a medical issue per se, I volunteered to talk to you."

I leaned forward, reached for Cathryn's hand, and squeezed. Gently. "If you don't get this out soon, I might have to squeeze until your fingernails pop off."

"You're pregnant."

A fifty-pound sack of surprise slammed into my reality.

"I'm . . . say that again."

"Pregnant."

In some movies, women fainted when they were told this. I very much wished to be one of those women right now. "This can't be. No. No. No. Oh, dear God. Why? Why now? How am I supposed to do this?" I mashed my pillow over my face. The pillow case smelled like lemons.

Cathryn tugged the pillow toward her. "What can we do to help you right now? Do you want to talk to Carl? I can call him for you."

"No. No. Don't tell Carl. It's early. It has to be. I can't be that far along. My periods have been weird all my life, so I don't usually panic when I'm late. But I know I just had one not so long ago. I remember because I'd run out of tampons. Carl had to buy them for me. He bought six boxes so he'd not have to buy them again for a long time. When was that? Did I write it down? Maybe I circled the date in my planner." I jumped out of bed. "Where's my purse? Here, here. I found it." I overturned it on the bed. "Planner, planner. I know it's here. Checkbooks. Wait. Aha." I pushed the lipsticks, pens, paper clips, coupons, and assorted purse trash aside and sat on the bed. "March, April, May, June. Maybe I missed it. May, April,

March." I counted months on my fingers. "It might be January or December. I'm not sure."

Cathryn watched me. Her head moved back and forth and up and down. She allowed my frenzy. "We can find out the due date. Are you sure you don't want to tell Carl?"

"He'll want me to leave. He won't let me finish. I have to stay. I have to. If I don't finish, I might drink again. I can't drink again. Ever. Ever. Ever."

She nodded. "Okay. No telling Carl. We want you to finish your program. And this baby wants you to finish too."

Alyssa. My sweet precious baby girl. Mommy is so, so sorry. Mommy didn't know. She didn't know. And now I do, and it's too late. I love you so much. I loved you so much. But I was too late. And you needed me. And I wasn't there. Alyssa, Mommy will never ever ever forget there's nothing worse than too late.

I smelled baby powder, felt the warm fuzzy softness of her round apple cheek pressed against mine, heard her cooing, and could not bear to take my eyes away from her when she nursed, and I would whisper, "I'm your mommy. And you are Alyssa. Jesus loved us so much he gave you to us. And Jesus loves Alyssa. I'm your mommy, and I will love you forever and ever."

And then I did what the ladies in the movie did.

Fainted.

33

We decided, the hospital staff and I, not to tell anyone.

I asked to attend AA smoke-free meetings. I told the group the smoking made me sick. I stayed back from some smokers meetings, and the smokers had to tap their feet through some of the clean air ones. Doug whined in group about my being too uppity, though he had a hard sell with that one around Trudie, who defended my right to breathe. The teens were, as Benny said, "a'ight with it" and told Doug not to "dis" me. Annie just shrugged, and Theresa liked that her pack of cigs lasted longer. One issue solved.

I didn't call Dr. Foret, even though he'd delivered Alyssa. Nothing about her death was his fault, but I couldn't help that seeing him made me think of her. Trey recommended Dr. Bethany Nolan, a friend from his med school days. They arranged for her to come to Brookforest for my first appointment. Her first words to me were, "Well, now this is a fine mess you've gotten yourself in," and then made me promise we'd never have to have another appointment at Brookforest. When she laughed, she shook her head, her braids swayed and remind me of Theresa. Oh, and she told me she didn't mind that I was white. She estimated the due date somewhere between December 24 and January 3.

Then there was the vomiting issue. Between using the cafeteria food and some "virus thing" as excuses, I managed to explain the morning sickness away. I also learned I was not the center of the rehab universe because apparently not as many people tracked my visits to the bathroom as I might have thought.

And then there was Carl. The family session after Carl-gate and my surprise news worked out for several reasons because: 1) my father wasn't there; 2) Carl arrived five minutes before and left five minutes after the session; and 3) Trudie, Adam, and Adam's daughter shared therapy spotlight with Theresa and her long-absent husband.

We started that night by saying the Serenity Prayer. Then, instead of just opening the floor for "check ups from the neck ups," Trey said he was conducting an informal survey. "I want everyone to participate. Be honest. I promise, you'll find out how much more we're all alike than we are different." He asked how many of us knew alcoholism was already in our families, not counting the person in the room they were visiting. Almost every hand shot up in the air. One by one, we just said the relationship of the alcoholic—fathers, mothers, aunts, uncles, siblings—and realized we were all parts of short or long family chains of drinkers.

"Remember these two words: genetic predisposition. We may not have control over the genes that are passed to us or that we pass on. But here's what you can control—the example you're going to be for your family."

When he asked how many of the people we just mentioned were in recovery, only two hands raised. "See the connection here? If you don't stop the chain right now, who will? That's why these groups are vital for families. So, good for you—for all of you—for making the decision to be here tonight."

And then it was "start your dysfunctional engines" time.

The couple with Trudie and her husband at the last family session was her sister and her husband. This week, Haley, Adam's *Mean Girls*-wannabe thirteen-year-old daughter decided to participate. When she didn't talk, Haley was a terrific kid. Mostly, she accused Trudie of marrying her father because he was rich enough to afford the drugs she needed.

"He's spending our money on this place. There's no guarantee this is going to work, right? How is that a good investment? And I have to consider my options for college." She alternately whined and sassed. Adam, literally and figuratively stuck between his wife and his daughter, kept asking what he could do to make everything better. On some level, I felt sorry for him because he was faced with a problem that couldn't be solved by throwing money at it. By the end of the night, though, I think he would have been happy to throw money at Haley—huge sacks of it.

Jules, Theresa's husband, sported wavy black hair, combed back, but not an oil slick. His eyes occupied most of his angular face. Before group started, he stroked Theresa's new hair and whispered something in her ear that made her giggle and then slap him on the arm. The kind of slap that invited him to repeat whatever he whispered. Theresa shared the "new creation" epiphany (she pronounced it *epeep-a-nee*) with the group. Then Jules told the group about "old creation" Theresa.

Carl and I didn't participate. We feigned politeness and rapt attention as the Tower of Babel resurrected in the room.

Trey earned his money that night.

I had one more weekend pass before I was scheduled to "graduate." So, in the "inmate" group later that week, Dr. Sanders asked me about my weekend plans.

"I really don't want to go home overnight, so I haven't made any plans," I said. Doug grunted something, and Annie looked up from biting the skin off her left thumb to ask why. The chick hardly ever opened her mouth, but today she had to ask the one question I didn't want to answer.

I looked at Dr. Sanders with my practiced blank-face stare and waited for him to rescue me with some therapy mumbo-jumbo, but he only tapped his pen against his notebook and stared back at me. The boys played air guitars. Trudie had introduced them to Queen and "Bohemian Rhapsody" a few days ago, and they became rabid fans.

"Do I have to have a reason?" I bit the inside of my mouth. I needed to make an appointment with my dentist. If I couldn't get happy gas, he wasn't going to touch the inside of my mouth with anything silver that made whirring sounds.

"Do you not have a reason or do you have one you don't want to talk about?" Dr. Sanders shifted to face me.

"That's a trick question. If I do go, I haven't made plans because I haven't discussed it with Carl."

"I've been meaning to ask you, ever since you shared with the group how Carl managed the money in your house, including giving you an allowance, because he said you can't balance a checkbook. He takes off work to drive you downtown because you get lost easily—"

"Wait," I sputtered. "You wrote all this down?"

"Yes, that's why I have a pen (he held it up) and a notebook (which he also held up) at every session. To write down what people share. He also—"

"Enough. What's your point?" I couldn't believe he'd mock me in front of everyone. I didn't have to look around the circle to know everyone else was looking back and forth between him and me, waiting for the strike.

He leaned back in his chair. "My point is that you're the epitome of a pampered little woman at home. I just don't understand how someone with your almost perfect life is here." He waved around the circle. "You're Miss Patty-Peace-at-any-Price, aren't you? Isn't that what you call yourself?"

What was with this man? Had anybody checked his urine samples lately? I looked around and could tell by the downcast eyes that no one was jumping in on this. I was on my own.

"Why are you being so mean to me? Carl cares where I go and how I get there. So what? That doesn't make him a bad person. I like and appreciate that he manages the money. He's good at it, and I don't have to putz with it. He works hard, and he takes care of me." I folded my arms across my chest in my best "how dare you dis me" posture.

"Well, we are all so glad you are taken care of. Aren't we?" He smiled, and a few faces in my traitorous circle actually grinned along with him. "But there's the problem. You don't get it, Leah. This isn't about Carl. This is about you."

He looked around the circle, in a way that was obviously for dramatic effect. Performance Art therapy. "I don't see Carl here. Do you?"

"No," I answered. I'm incredulous and confused.

"Me either. Maybe if you call him, he'll rescue you from all of us."

"What? You mean, call him on the phone? Why would I do that?" He'd baited me. I knew it, but I didn't get it.

"No, I mean call his name from right where you are."

"That's stupid. I'm not doing that."

"Yes, yes you are. You need him. And I want you to call him. Let's just see what happens."

He was never going to stop if I didn't just do want he wanted me to do. Arguing with him wasn't getting this over. "Carl," I mumbled. Already I felt truly dumb.

Dr. Sanders laughed. "He couldn't hear that if he'd been sitting next to you. Try a little louder."

"Carl."

"Louder."

"Carl!" I shouted.

"Well, he's still not here. Guess you're not loud enough. Maybe if you stretched your arms out while you called him. That way maybe he'll see how much he's needed."

I stared at him. A rolling heat traveled through my body. I felt anger and shame and confusion everywhere at once.

"Go on. We're waiting."

I reached out my arms into the empty space in front of me and shouted, "Carl!"

He made me call Carl three more times, each time louder and louder until, with the last scream, my throat burned. Tears streamed down my cheeks until my neck was wet.

Time four.

I stood. This time, my now shaking arms were straight against the sides of my body. I looked at Dr. Sanders. I channeled every ragged piece of rage and humiliation left in me into what I hoped he saw reflected in my eyes and face. Fueled by a current that surged through my soul, I told him, "I'm not doing this anymore. Carl's not coming no matter how loudly I scream. He's not coming. And I'm not going to do what you're asking me to do just because you think you have power over me. I'm not going to do it."

The room gasped.

Dr. Sanders walked over, gently placed his hands on my shoulders, and said, "I've been waiting for you to do exactly what you just did."

I shuddered and sucked in air.

Old things pass away. All things become new.

A new life. Not just a new life within me. A new creation.

"Don't compromise yourself. Don't ever, ever, ever compromise yourself. You're all you've got."

Journal 11

My life changed the instant Alyssa was placed in my arms. I gazed at my daughter through my mother's eyes and my grandmother's eyes and all the eyes before who held their children before me. Linked by the maternal cord of knowing how my mother felt holding me. The link of truly understanding how absolutely you had been loved.

Two days later we were home. A family.

Carl adored our daughter.

And he adored me for giving her to him.

I knew that for at least the first month, the doctor didn't want us to have sex. That freed me to be affectionate, to remember the times when every touch did not have to consummate itself in the bedroom.

Carl was patient.

Until he wasn't.

The last night of week four, Carl expected me in bed.

I was. So, when Alyssa awoke, I brought her into the bedroom.

At the end of week five, Carl expected me in bed every night. When Alyssa awoke, I'd stay in her room and nurse her. Some nights I told Carl I heard Alyssa, and Carl would find me asleep in the day bed of the nursery. Carl didn't understand and would ask me why he didn't hear our daughter cry. I'd tell him mothers are wired that way.

At the end of week six, when Carl expected me in bed, I expected to be just drunk enough to be there. When Alyssa awoke, I threw back the covers to get her.

"I didn't hear her cry," Carl said and wrapped his arm around my waist to pull me back into bed.

"Of course not," I said. "You're a man." I put my hands over his to move them, so my body could catch up with my heart, which was already walking to her room.

"If she was that upset, we would both hear her. She can cry for a little while. She'll be fine. You need to pay attention to me for a change."

Carl never heard Alyssa cry. I heard her cry from the first time she whimpered. Carl touched me until Carl finished. I was just enough drunk to fall asleep.

The next morning, Carl went to work. He thought I must have checked Alyssa during the night.

I woke up very late that morning. I thought Carl must have checked Alyssa before he left for work.

I opened the door to Alyssa's bedroom. Laura Ashley wallpaper. Handpainted murals. Pink and delicate and exquisite. Just like their daughter.

I tiptoed to the white spindled crib. "Good morning, princess." I picked up my daughter. Her body wasn't warm. Her face was blue. Her breath was gone.

Alyssa was dead.

My scream reached into hell, and the devil laughed.

My scream reached into heaven. God grieved.

I couldn't stand, or talk, or run. I stumbled and tripped and crawled like a rabid animal to the telephone.

Nothing would ever be the same.

I dialed 911. I couldn't speak.

I called Carl. He heard the gasping, heaving, groaning. He recognized my voice. He called the police. He thought some intruder might have hurt us.

I was alive. Alyssa was dead.

Where was the intruder?

When Carl got home I stared at him with eyes so full of hate I cried venom instead of tears. I beat his chest with my fists until they were bruised and swollen.

Later, the doctor said it wasn't our fault. He said Sudden Infant Death Syndrome is the leading cause of death for one-month-olds to one-year-olds.

I told the doctor I didn't need a leading cause of death. I needed my daughter.

We left.

I told Carl, "You killed her. You wanted to have sex more than you wanted me to take care of our child. I will never forgive you. You killed our daughter."

34

My exit from Brookforest would be two days early.

The staff allowed me to "trade" my weekend pass for the early out on the conditions that I leave with the name of someone from an AA meeting who would be my sponsor, commit to ninety meetings in ninety days, and have an extra session with Ron.

Carl had no problem with the early release. Neither did I, but I knew the real reason, and I waited for Ron so he'd know too.

I sat in the chair facing his desk, propped my feet on the edge, and rifled through the Jolly Ranchers basket picking out my flavors for the hour.

"Shouldn't you be eating a bowl of real fruit instead of those bullet-sized teeth breakers?"

Ron walked in and dropped his backpack on the sofa. He pulled his cell phone out of his jeans' pocket, pushed a few buttons, and set it on top of his desk pad. For a minute, he stood near his desk, head down, patting his pants pockets like he was waiting to be beamed up somewhere. "I think I'm ready now," he said.

"Are you talking to me or whoever's picking you up on that spaceship you're waiting for?" His face scrunched so that it truly looked like a question mark. "I thought you were about to take off for a minute. You meditate standing?"

"Oh, that. I guess nobody's usually in the office to watch me get ready for the day. It's my mental checklist pause—cell phone out, keys in, anything else I need to remember or want to forget—maybe it is a meditation."

I nodded. I remember school mornings. School keys here. Car keys there. Lunch. Coke Zero. Check. Check. Check. Check. Breathe in, Mrs. Thornton. Breathe out, Leah.

We volleyed the quiet between us until I was ready. Ron's invitation was obvious in his eyes. I trusted Ron, but even that didn't push the terror away, terror that enveloped me in suffocating thick darkness. It pressed itself on me, its oozing hot breath on my neck. I'd carried it inside for years. Learned, over time, I could gorge it with alcohol until it would drop its hold on my spirit. My spirit. Hollowed out and stuffed with grief and fear.

I had to summon it, confront it, and destroy it.

Sober.

The darkness stirred in me.

It was time.

Journal 12

I am Leah.

I was ten years old. I did not understand what happened that morning. I started bleeding. Watery red stains on the white towel. Bleeding between my legs. Something was wrong. Some place inside me twisted and cramped. I was scared I'd made this happen. Maybe I shouldn't tell. But what if all my blood came out? What if it wouldn't stop?

I opened the bathroom door. Stuck my head out. "Mom? Mom? Can you come here?" Nothing. "Mom. I need to show you something." My father hollered back. "Mom left for work. Hurry up in that bathroom. You and Peter are going to be late for school." Whatever this was, I knew I couldn't tell my father. Not about bleeding from there.

I folded a clean washcloth to fit between my legs. Wrapped it in toilet paper. I begged God not to let me die. And I dressed and went to school. My teacher let me go to the bathroom before lunch. I flushed the bloody toilet paper. Rewrapped my wash cloth. I became aware of an odor I didn't recognize. I walked back to my desk and wondered if the smell followed me. If Ben sitting next to me and Cathy behind me smelled it too. Musky like an animal smell. At lunch I stayed in the cafeteria. I read a book. I didn't want to walk outside with my friends for fear the washcloth would fall out.

Finally school ended, and I could go home. I waited hours for my mother. I didn't call her at work; I thought I might scare her if she knew I was bleeding. I stayed in my room. Closed the door. Finished my homework. I told Peter he could play next door.

She was finally home. I heard her car in the driveway. A battleship grey Rambler with no air conditioning. She was always so tired when she got home. I waited until she changed out of her dress and went to the kitchen to pour her glass of wine. Always red. Always in a bottle with a top that just unscrewed. She sat at the table with her wine and the newspaper. I told her I needed to talk to her.

"What's wrong? Did you get in trouble at school? What did you do?"

"Nothing, I promise. Something happened this morning. You weren't here. I'm . . . I'm . . . I'm bleeding . . ." I pointed between my legs. ". . . there." I still wore my navy blue pleated uniform skirt. Blood had stained the insides of my thighs. Half moons of red that I scrubbed off when I got home from school.

She looked so angry. "You're what? What did you do? You didn't touch yourself there, did you?"

"No. I swear." Why would she think I'd do that, touch myself there? Why would I make myself bleed? I didn't say anything because she now seemed angrier. I'd never seen her like this before.

"Did somebody else touch you there? Some boy at school? Is that it? You let a boy touch you there, didn't you?" Her voice was strange. It came from deep in her throat.

"NO, Mom. NO. I wouldn't do that. I wouldn't let a boy or anyone do that. I promise." Why would my mother think these things about me?

I remember backing away from her. So she couldn't reach me. Just in case. I searched all over her face with my eyes. I wanted to find something familiar there.

"Okay, okay. That's good." She calmed down, like something in her unwound. She picked up the glass, bent her head to make her neck straight. She finished her wine and poured another glass. "Good girl." She sipped again and raised her eyes to look at me over the top of the glass.

I waited. I didn't ask her if I might die. She wouldn't have been so mad at me if she thought I was going to die from the bleeding.

She slid her wine glass away from the edge of the table. "This usually happens when girls are older. You're starting young. Your menstrual cycle is going to come every month now. That's what it's called. This blood means you can have babies now. You have to be careful. Don't you let boys touch you or put things there. That's nasty and dirty. You understand me, don't you?"

I nodded. If boys didn't touch or put things there, I wouldn't have babies. Every month this would happen. I was not going to die from this.

"Now, I'm going to the store to buy you a box of Kotex. You'll need to start wearing them. Clean yourself good. And, Leah, you

don't need to go around telling people about this. Peter doesn't need to know about this. Not yet. And I'll tell your father."

She came home from the grocery, handed me the Kotex box, and said to keep it in the bathroom. "Well, Leah. You're a woman now."

We never talked about it again. "It" meaning what happened that day: periods, sex, pregnancy.

The night before Carl and I married, she told me, "It's going to hurt the first time. You might bleed a little. It doesn't hurt after that. Maybe sometimes. You won't always want to have sex, but men are different. They need sex. So you make sure he gets what he needs. That's part of being a good wife."

I stopped. Blinked. Where had I gone? I ran my fingertips along the braided edge of the chair's arms. I didn't know if five minutes or five hours had passed. I dropped my head forward, side, back, side. My neck muscles tightened, relaxed.

"When I was four, I had a tonsillectomy. I remember faces floating over me, somebody telling me to count, a black mask. Then I was gone. And then, I came back. Like seeing the world from a lens that opened wider and wider until the lens disappeared and only the view was left. That's how I feel now. Like I'm coming back," I said quietly, holding on to the leathery arms of the chair as if letting go meant floating away.

"You are coming back. The world's almost all in view," Ron said. "Only one more lens to open."

I didn't get it. Sex. Why it fascinated people. Why people risked their reputations, their families, their lives to have an affair. All that, for what? A few minutes?

225

I was a virgin when I met Carl. I think he was, too. I don't think he wanted to admit that. When we dated, I enjoyed kissing him and being touched by him. I know in today's world it sounds dorky, but I made him promise to wait until after we married.

At first, I managed sex with Carl. It wasn't awful. It was, I guess, like taking medicine. You know you need it. If you don't take it, you'll get worse. And if you hold your nose, it doesn't taste so bad. And sometimes, you'd get surprised by medicine that actually tasted pleasant. But you couldn't count on that every time.

He liked having sex. He liked telling me he liked having sex. He liked surprising me with sex. Telling me to meet him at his office because we needed to go over some paper about one thing or another. I'd meet him only to find out I was the paper he planned on going over. Or we'd be at the ski lodge with his parents. I'd be curled up reading a book, settled in with my coffee, the fireplace. His parents would be in the kitchen concocting some new drink or dinner recipe. Carl would go upstairs. Two minutes later, he'd shout he'd forgotten a towel or his cell phone or whatever. I'd trot up the stairs with whatever he said he wanted. He never wanted what he asked for. He wanted me.

He thought it was romantic. I felt ambushed. Eventually, I learned not to trust him. At first, he thought "no" was a flirtatious game, designed to make him want it more, a hard-to-get game. Eventually, he learned what it meant. He just chose not to hear it. Sometimes he did. Like when I'd have my period.

After a while, I didn't bother refusing him.

If I did, he'd pout. If I said no for a week, he'd be terribly unhappy. And then he'd be upset about the messy office, or the dirty floors, or the boring meals, or how much money I was spending. If I said no for more than a week, he'd be angry. He'd tell me I was selfish, frigid, dysfunctional. He'd throw the phone book into the bedroom and tell me to look up phone numbers of doctors.

It was easier to just do what had to be done.

Eventually, I learned a few strategies myself. Like my periods lasted longer. Like staying up late grading papers, reading. I'd force myself some nights to stay awake. If he fell asleep first, I won. I'd fall asleep on the sofa. I think he caught on because then he told me he didn't like finding me on the sofa in the morning. He wanted me to come to bed. I learned how to slide into bed as if I was water poured gently down the side of a tall glass. Some nights were better than others. It took practice. The secret was not moving. If I moved, the game was over. He'd know I was awake.

I knew he was right. Something had to be wrong with me. He knew I was smart; he'd tell people. But, he'd tell me, like many "book smart" people, I didn't have much common sense. Once, I told my parents and Carl that I considered going to law school. They didn't think it was a good idea. Law school was difficult, they told me, even for the most intelligent of people. When people would ask about my job, he'd tell them I was "just a teacher" in a public school where the trashy kids were. He'd say "those who can, do; those who can't, teach." He needed to be honest. It was for my own good, he'd say. He wanted me to see life realistically.

He gave me almost anything I asked for. He worked hard at Morgan Management. His father wanted him to have the experience of working for someone else. He wanted his father to be proud of him. And he loved my parents and was nice to Peter. We lived in a beautiful home, drove expensive cars, and traveled to fabulous places.

I loved his generosity and kindness and protectiveness. And I loved knowing alcohol could give Carl what I couldn't . . . my body. And I loved knowing I, Leah, did not have to be there.

We both had what we wanted.

35

It was the week of lasts.

Last breakfast, lunch, dinner at Brookforest.

Last painting of a ceramic thingy in outpatient therapy.

Last group therapy where I listened to Doug snore, Theresa pass gas, and the U2 boys' goofiness *de jour.*

Last family group therapy where I hoped Carl and I would not be the sacrificial family whose secrets would be spilled for the greater good. Last time I had to call my father two days before family group to reassure him his absence didn't impede my recovery. Last time I had to remind him he'd better send the staff the food he'd promised to cook them or they'd find a way to have him involuntarily admitted on the psych floor.

I decided to attend the Serenity group meeting before I checked out to talk to Rebecca about being my sponsor. I remembered her from the first AA meeting I'd ever attended in my little alcoholic life. She'd raised her hand to remind everyone not to be slobs. At other meetings there and as I got over myself, I made an effort to meet other women. Rebecca didn't hold back when she thought people were full of themselves or manure, as the case might be. She'd told one man whose self-pity party seemed to expand every meeting that if he wanted to be a martyr, he was in the wrong place. I liked that honesty and assertiveness. She was just as honest about her wrecked cars, buried wine bottles, and broken marriages.

Drinking coffee before one meeting, I told her I was afraid to leave Brookforest, afraid I wouldn't know how to function without the safety net.

"I've heard all the AA party lines about fear being false expectations. Let's face it, we're human and fear can paralyze us. You can't deny what you feel. You just don't have to act on it."

"So, I don't ignore it? What do I do with it?"

"Well, you do and you don't," she laughed. "Don't you love how AA brings clarity to your life! I guess what helped me figure it out was when I heard, 'feel the fear, and do it anyway.'"

"I don't know. Doing what terrifies me even as I know how terrified I am? That doesn't sound much better."

She tossed her coffee cup in the recycle container. "My father planned for almost a year to take me and the kids to Disney World. Only he died of lung cancer seven months after the diagnosis. At first, we decided to cancel the trip. But when my six-year-old asked if Granddad would be sad if he was waiting in heaven to see us on vacation, but we weren't there—that settled it. We went."

"Did I miss the fear part? I'm confused."

"Sorry. Long setup. The story should come with a warning." She pulled on the white knit headband she had wrapped around her wrist. "Fast forward. We're there. The kids are in line to ride Space Mountain, and they're wiggly, hopping excited. Me? I'm about to have a stroke. I hate even a plain vanilla roller coaster. This one's the Double Chocolate Brownie Overload of roller coasters. The whole ride is dark. Enclosed, roller coaster, dark. I didn't want to tell the kids what I said to their granddad at that point. We're next. I'm scared. Terrified. Then AA brain takes over. My dad died, and I'm afraid to get on a roller coaster? What's the worst thing that's going to happen? If I'm still afraid when I get off, I haven't lost anything. And what lesson am I teaching my kids? Be controlled by fear?"

"Well, how was it?"

"We screamed, screeched, and laughed the entire ride. When it ended, we ran back in line to go again."

"Leaving here is my roller coaster?"

"You got it. And it could be the ride of your life. Don't run away from it before you even run to it."

Being a sponsor means commitment to helping a newbie through the steps, holding the person accountable, and giving up phone numbers with the understanding that—short of abuse—you're willing to be called 24/7/365. Being sponsored has its own responsibilities, the most important being listening and, of course, staying sober. Matthew had suggested I ask Rebecca. He knew she'd been in the program for six years, and she'd sponsored women who'd maintained their sobriety.

After the meeting ended, I found Rebecca at her usual post, rinsing out coffee pots and setting them up for the next meeting. I tapped her shoulder to get her attention. "I hate to interrupt. I know cleaning is your life, but could I talk to you for a few minutes?"

She looked over her shoulder. "Sure, kiddo, give me a minute. Almost finished. Unless, wait, is the bus ready to go?"

"No, Matthew told everyone before we left that we'd leave late tonight. Take your time. I'll just sit at the back table," I said.

This was the last meeting of the night, so people tended to hang around. Fellowship. A word I'd learned when I'd started church shopping before Alyssa. We'd only attended four or five services between the time she was born and the time she died. After her funeral, I devoted as much attention to church and God as I thought had been devoted to us—none. Otherwise,

I'd still have my daughter and not have to visit her in the Little Innocents Cemetery.

Fellowship at AA meetings wasn't all that much different from the few I'd experienced in church, except we didn't bring covered dishes. Old-timers always said what happened before and after meetings mattered as much, maybe even more, than the meetings. At last week's meeting, Nolan B. said fellowship was how he knew AA wasn't a church. "If this was a church, we'd all be trying to leave early and kill each other getting out of the parking lot."

Someone had left a schedule of Al-Anon meetings on the table. As I folded it to shove in my purse, optimistic that Carl might be interested in going to at least one meeting, a man pulled out the chair next to me and sat. "You probably don't recognize me," he said, and pushed away from the table a bit to face me.

I hadn't looked at him when he first walked over. Just figured he needed a chair. I didn't think he'd sit. Didn't really want him to since I wanted to talk to Rebecca privately.

He recognized me. Great. It never occurred to me anyone would ever know me here. This was an unexpected embarrassment. Can't pretend I'm just here for the coffee. *No, dummy, but he can't either.* Thank you, voice of reason. I slipped the paper into my purse, pushed it aside, and turned.

Dark-brown hair parted on the side. John Lennon glasses. Stubble-faced. U-shaped jaw. I scrolled through the photo-file in my brain. Got it.

"You were in the Social Studies' department for a year, right?"

"I sure was. Wasn't sure you'd remember. Spring Creek has so many teachers. I'm an assistant principal at the new school, Woodville High. I'll start my third year there this August," he said. "Didn't you teach English?"

"On a good day, yes. I taught freshmen and juniors, but really, they were great," I said.

"Sometimes I miss the classroom. I don't miss grading papers, of course. Being on the other side now—" he shook his head "—I'm dealing with kids, teachers, parents, the school board. Some days I wonder if the pay increase was worth it." His cell phone shimmied across the table. "Sorry. Probably my son sending me a text." He picked up the phone and grinned. "Wants me to stop at Dairy Queen on the way home for Blizzards." He slipped it in his shirt pocket. "I am so rude. I just realized I didn't tell you my name. I'm Ethan."

"Leah." I checked Rebecca's progress at the sink. She was drying her hands, talking to Matthew. Out of the corner of my eye, I saw Ethan look in the direction I had.

"Hey, I'm sorry. I didn't mean to take up so much of your time. You were the first person I saw here that I actually knew." He paused. "I'm probably not supposed to be so excited about that, huh?"

We both laughed. "Well, you're my first too. I thought it'd be awkward meeting somebody here, but it's not like we have to ask each other what we're doing here," I said. "I'm leaving rehab in a few days, so I'm waiting to talk to someone about being my sponsor."

"Brookforest? I was there, too. I've been in recovery eleven months now. I know how important a sponsor is. Mine is awesome. I don't know if I'd be sober today without him. In fact," he stood when Matthew and Rebecca walked over, "here he comes now."

Myrtle pushed the speed limit, not too happy our extra time at the meeting meant she missed part of *Smallville*. "Clark's supposed to find out tonight that Lana's still alive, and now I gonna have to wait for the reruns."

"You need TiVo," Vince told her. "Then you could watch it without those dumb commercials."

"What I know about TiVo?" she grumped. While Benny and Vince tried to explain TiVo technology to Myrtle, I asked Matthew about his conversation with Rebecca. "Did you tell her I was going to ask her to be my sponsor? Is that why the two of you were talking?"

"I did tell her. I knew she'd probably ask me about you anyway. Look, she still agreed, even after I talked to her," he said.

"You're cracking me up, Matthew. If I could reach your head, I'd whop you." I was stretched out on the seat in front of him, wishing I had a pillow for my back, which bumped against the side every time Myrtle hit a pothole. "She already set up a time for the two of us to meet the first week I'm home. Lunch with my AA sponsor. Wouldn't have thought six weeks ago I'd be saying those words."

"By the way, I didn't tell her about the baby. Just thought that should come from you, in your time."

For a flash, I thought he meant Alyssa. "That's fine. I already told her. If it was going to make a difference in her decision, I figured we both needed to know tonight. New sober and new pregnant. She's got her work cut out for her."

"Don't underestimate Rebecca," he smiled. "Or yourself for that matter. Seems the two of you working together is one of those God-incidents. That first year of sobriety is tough, no lie. Most people who backslide do it before they pick up their one-year chip. But Rebecca's all over tough love sponsorship. And, since she's your sponsor, that means I might be seeing you more than I might have."

"Planning to check up on me, and I haven't even graduated," I said. I put my hand over my heart and pretended to be offended. Of course, we both knew I was anything but.

<hr>

My father called and wanted to fly in for my graduation. I explained it wasn't a cap and gown event—no awards, no scholarships, no pictures. "It's not that I don't want to see you," I said. "Carl and I need to spend some time alone this first weekend." I tried not to wince. Of course, I couldn't tell him the most important reason I needed to be alone with Carl. Once I broke the baby news, I might find hell broke open as well. "Peter isn't planning to come, is he?"

"I don't think so. But the last time I talked to him was when Carl called me about the news" . . . the new family euphemism for my rehab. "Haven't you talked to him?"

"Dad, you haven't talked to Peter in almost a month? You two live in the same city. What's going on?" I'd talked to Peter before "the news" long enough to know Dad was dating. Dad hadn't bothered to mention this to me at all. My father not telling us something said everything about the something. It was either a bad news something or a guilty something. He probably thought his dating was both.

"Now, you have enough on your plate." *Yes, if you only knew . . . and now I have a saucer.* "Peter and I will work this out. You don't worry about us. You just take care of yourself. Now, I don't want to talk anymore about this thing with Peter," he said. "Haven't you talked to him, honey? He should've called you by now."

"He sent me cards. I wrote him last week and told him I'd talk to him after I was home a few days." Peter was always much better at writing. Phone calls, he'd tell me, are ripe for misinterpretation. He blamed it on the disconnect between tone of voice and facial expression. Having received questionable voice mails from parents of my students, I understood exactly.

I guess God understood that because he left us the Bible instead of voice mail.

"You do understand Carl's expecting you to sleep in the same bed? He's also expecting you to have sex because he thinks, on some level, that you've been 'cured.' What's your plan?"

"I thought that's why I was here. That you'd give me a plan," I said. My last session with Ron, and it was as emotionally exhausting as the first one.

Ron flipped pages in my file. "I'm not the one who's going home to Carl. You are. You can't have it both ways. Recovery means gaining a sense of who you are. How you define yourself. Almost four weeks ago, you were asked, 'Who are you?' I want you to hear what you said: 'My name's Leah. Let's see. Who am I? I'm Carl's wife, I'm a teacher, I'm a sister, I'm a daughter and a daughter-in-law. I guess now I have to add alcoholic to the list.' Less than thirty days ago, you couldn't define yourself independent of any of your roles. You were whoever, whatever everyone needed you to be."

"I know. I know." I combed my hair back with my fingers. Closed my eyes. Tried to recapture that Leah for an instant. Stirrings of her like the scent of a candle just extinguished.

"I can't be independent and not be responsible for my own decisions. It was so much easier when I could be."

"Sure, so easy you ended up here to find that out," Ron smiled and closed my file. "So, back to the question. What are you going to do?"

"The opposite of what old Leah would have done?"

"You're stalling. Pretend I'm Carl, and I'm leading you into our bedroom, telling you how much I've missed you, how lonesome I've been for you in my bed, how I want to make love to you—"

"Stop. Stop. No. I can't. I won't. Not yet."

"That's good. Don't compromise yourself. If you forget everything else, remember that. Don't compromise yourself."

36

Leaving the staff was as difficult as watching some of my favorite students graduate. They march in, tassels swinging on their mortarboards, gowns swishing, and faces like fiery diamonds. In the instant they passed me, it was as if a balloon holding all my memories of them popped, and my heart exploded with hope. A hope that I'd given them the tools they needed, but knowing only they can be the carpenters. I prayed they fashioned a life from their dreams and desires.

The morning I left Brookforest every hug was a prayer. Theresa, Doug, Benny, Vince, Annie, Trudie, and I were a motley collection of people. A tradition, before leaving, was to pass around your Big Book, the AA Bible, so everyone could write a message. I'd read them in my room while I waited for Carl.

From Benny and Vince who, of course, wrote a combined message: *To our fav homegirl: We wish you could have been our teacher. But it's all good. Keep it real. And always remember, who's the champions. WE are the champions! (we hope we spelled it write!) Props . . . from ya boys.*

From Doug: *Leah, I know I wasn't too nice to you at first. I believe you now. That you really are an alcoholic. No. Make that*

WERE an alcoholic. I probably won't see you anywhere. But good luck. Big Dog Doug

From Theresa: Dear Roomie: Boo-yah! I'm glad I got to know ya 'cuz your not the stuck-up chick I thought you was. Don't be like me. Don't come back. Don't sell you're jewelry. If you see a fine woman at a meeting, probably me!!!!!! Remember, God made you a NEW CREATION. Amen to that, sister girl. I'm gonna miss you. I hope I get out of here B4 they get me a new roomie. Stay SOBER. Love. Theresa p.s. I know your an English teacher, I don't write too good, so don't grade this note!!

From Annie: Dear Leah: We didn't talk much, but that's all me because I mostly hide in my books. I really enjoyed your sense of humor and that you tried to be nice to everyone. I wish we had a chance to know one another better. Keep saying the Serenity Prayer and collecting chips at meetings. God bless you in recovery. Peace and blessings, Annie

From Trudie: Dear Leah: I'm so glad we actually bumped into each other that day. Who would have thought you and I would cross paths in rehab?! You reminded me not to take myself so seriously. I know I have a long stay ahead of me, so if you ever want to, stop by on visiting day. And you can take Haley with you! (LOL). Take care of yourself. I pray that everything works in your life for good. One day at a time. God be with you always. Love, Tru

When it was time to write my discharge statement, I didn't know what to write. Jan said it was supposed to be a reflection of what we learned, what the time there meant to us, how we changed, or whatever information we wanted the staff to know. The first attempt read like an essay for my National Boards portfolio. Crumpled that and tossed in the trash. The next one read like a list of things to do and not do in rehab.

Finally, I followed the advice I gave my students when they didn't know where to start or how to write. I asked Jan for a timer, opened my notebook, started the timer, put my pen on paper and wrote without stopping or thinking or correcting. I just let words flow out of my brain, down my arm, through my fingers, and into my pen. After the ten minutes, I read what presented itself. I revised and reshaped it, then turned it over to Jan. I felt like I'd lived another life in almost thirty days. So much I didn't know or I would have been more careful. I couldn't change my past. Maybe it could make a difference in the future for someone else who still had a chance in the present.

Carl turned the corner and pulled into our driveway. Seeing our house again reminded me of Carl's parents. They'd surprised us with it as a wedding present. No. Two untruths in that statement.

Lie #1: Use of the word "us." Carl had already known about the house and had approved the purchase.

Lie #2: Use of the word "surprise." See #1.

My surprise was that the house was mostly everything I never wanted in a house. Pretentious and impractical. Too-small kitchen, too-large master bedroom (especially since it was a room I didn't want to spend time in), detached garage, a formal living room I had no desire to decorate, and no other bedroom downstairs. As in no other bedroom to use as a nursery.

Not long after we knew I was pregnant with Alyssa, I had suggested we convert the living room into a nursery. I'd even sketched a plan for adjoining it to the master. Granted, the drawing was crude. It showed two adjoining rectangles with a one-inch erased section (the doorway) on the common wall. Seemed simple enough to me. Then, when we knew we were having a girl, and there was still no nursery downstairs, I went to Plan B. I told Carl we, really he, since the baby could not endure such gymnastics, needed to practice the up and down trips from our bedroom to the upstairs bedroom closest to the stairs. And I planned to start timing at midnight and two and four and every four hours thereafter. He relented. The architect and contractor appeared on our doorway in two days.

It was the first time Molly jeopardized our friendship. She happened to pop over the night after Carl approved baby land, so I happily explained the plan. With Carl in the kitchen with us, Molly said, "Gosh, you really wouldn't need to do all that. Your bedroom's so spacious, you could just move the occasional chairs into the living room and use that space for a crib." Trapped between the skull-drilling stare of my vexation and Carl's benevolent gaze of appreciation, Molly suddenly remembered she had a meeting. Onto Plan C, which involved a modicum of pouting, shouting, and foot-stomping, and the possibility of breath-holding. Alyssa's nursery was completed one month before my due date.

Now, if I hadn't been sober for almost a month, I would confess I'd heard the house dare me to enter. It never seemed welcoming, and I tried to convince myself the feeling had nothing to do with the oil painting of Carl's parents that I'd placed in the attic for safe-keeping.

We walked in through the back door. It didn't take much looking around to know Merry Maids had made merry while I was away. We could have used the house for surgical suites. It smelled sanitized, an odor as nose-burning as gasoline. Nothing that a few strategically placed vanilla diffusers wouldn't solve.

Carl stopped in the kitchen and set my suitcase by the table. I was about to ask why he wanted me to unpack there when he pulled out a pair of scissors from the infamous junk drawer.

"Is this the part where I'm supposed to scream?"

Carl laughed. "Not yet. I have something else planned for that." He reached for my right arm, gently lifted the hospital identification bracelet and snipped it off. After he returned the scissors to the drawer, he opened the cabinet above it and took out a small wrapped box about the size of a wallet. He handed me the gift. "Here. Now you can scream."

"I . . . I don't know what to say," I stammered. I know what I thought, and I was truly ashamed of myself for thinking it. *We hadn't been home ten minutes and already Carl planned to buy me back into bed.*

"You don't have to say anything yet. Open it first," he said softly, massaging the back of my neck.

I recognized the gift wrap as Southern Jewelers' signature. Whatever it was, it was overpriced and exquisite. I ripped off the paper. A smallish, ordinary white box. Hmm, maybe not what I thought. I glanced at Carl. His grin stretched across his face. It looked painful. I lifted the top, pushed aside the tissue, and sucked in so much air I almost had to beat my own chest to breathe. Nestled in the box was a woman's gold Rolex weighed down with an emerald and diamond bezel.

"I asked Scott to take the watch out of the Rolex box. I thought you'd be more surprised that way. Were you? Do you like it? If it doesn't fit, it can be adjusted to your wrist." I'd never heard Carl string together so many questions in so little time. He lifted the watch out. "I almost forgot. I had it engraved."

I turned the watch over and read the inscription aloud, "A new beginning. I love you. Carl." *Theresa's new beginning for a new creation.* "This is beyond beautiful," I said. "You were right, it was a bigger surprise finding it in such an unassuming white box. This is so generous and thoughtful, especially, considering . . . thank you. Thank you."

"Here, let me put it on your wrist. This can be your new bracelet," he said and snapped the Rolex closed. He held my hand and gazed down at my arm. "You didn't need that identification anymore. We know who you are."

37

Carl walked into the bedroom where I'd been unpacking, stood behind me, wrapped his arms around my waist, and nuzzled my neck. "It's been a long time since I've seen you in this room," he said. "I like this view so much better." He pressed his face into my hair. "You smell good."

"It's a new shampoo Gwen asked me to try the last time she cut my hair," I said, and concentrated on folding my dirty laundry. Anything to prevent me from having to turn around. "Have you made any dinner plans? I can't wait to eat somewhere that doesn't serve food in a divided tray."

He released his hold on my waist. "No, I didn't make any reservations if that's what you meant. I didn't know what you'd want to do on your first day home."

I walked into the bathroom with my makeup case to unload my "war paint" as my father referred to it and hair equipment. Carl trailed behind me. I shivered when I saw the shower reflected in the mirror.

"Are you okay?" He reached out and caressed my shoulders.

"Fine. I'm fine." I opened a drawer and started unloading. "We don't have to eat anywhere we need reservations. Mexican or Chinese would be yummy. Are you interested in either one of those?"

"We could do Chinese takeout and eat dinner here if you're not up for going out again. I'm sure this has been a tiring day for you."

"I haven't been out, as in real world out, in so long, I wouldn't mind going somewhere instead of ordering in. Besides, if we go out, then I can show off my new watch." I figured an appeal to his ego might swing the odds.

He massaged my shoulders. "If that's what you want, that's what we'll do."

We decided on Peking Garden. It was still early for dinner, so we were scored a window table overlooking the koi pond. The garden was styled with pine and mondo grasses and bamboo. Water burbled out of the fountain. I told Carl we needed to keep this landscaping in mind for the next time my father visited. Reproducing this in our backyard would keep him busy for months.

After hot and sour soup, a spring roll, fried rice, and moo shui pork, I told Carl I needed to be carted out in a wheelbarrow. "Maybe we could try to develop a taste for sushi?" I suggested.

"If I'm going to pay those prices for food, it's going to be cooked," Carl said, distracted by calculating the tip. "Ready?" As I'd expected, his change was stacked on the bills.

Since the restaurant was only a few blocks away, the ride home was short. Not much time for me to mentally rehearse what I knew I needed to discuss with Carl. *God, I'm counting on you here. I know you and I have had our differences, but AA's getting me back on track. Help me with this conversation. Open Carl's heart.*

Carl flipped on the den lights. "Did you want to watch television for a bit before we go to bed?"

I sat on the sofa, forgetting how much I enjoyed feeling the buttery leather on my bare legs. I'd already kicked off my sandals and curled my legs under me. "No television. I want to talk to you, though."

Carl lowered himself into a chair. He cleared his throat. "Sure. Sure."

"First, I want you to know that I'm committed to staying sober. I don't want to be the Leah who left here almost thirty days ago. I'm not saying I'm some entirely new person. But I am trying to get a handle on myself, and my life, and our lives together. And we can do this together, but it's not going to be easy and it's not going to happen right away."

The creases in his forehead ironed themselves out. He relaxed and leaned back into the chair. "I know this is going to be work. But like I promised, I'm going to help you every step of the way. I'm going to make sure you don't ever take another drink. You can be sure of that."

I wrapped my words in softness. "Carl, I want you to support me, and I'm grateful you're willing to do that. But you don't need to protect me from myself. It's not your responsibility to keep me away from alcohol. It's mine."

"I'm just trying to help you the best way I know how," he said, and the tint of defensiveness colored his voice.

He was right. Saving me from myself was the best way he knew how. In most cases, it was the only way. I remembered Trudie telling me sometimes she had to take things five minutes at a time. This was one of those times. "Really, I appreciate everything you've done and want to do. I didn't think we'd be able to settle everything tonight. But there are two important things I want to talk to you about before we go to sleep."

I watched his lips curl ever so slightly when he heard the word "sleep." He crossed his leg, put one hand on his knee. "Yes?"

"This is really difficult for me to say, but I don't want you to misunderstand or feel like I'm not being honest. I know I've been gone, and I know that's been tough for you, you know, as far as us, as far as sex. As far as sex is concerned."

"Got that right."

He wasn't making this easy. "It's going to take me some time to adjust."

"How much time are we talking about here?"

Anytime you want to jump in God, I'm ready. "Well, I don't know. I mean, that's part of what I, we need to work on. "

"Let me make sure I understand this. You're telling me that we're not going to have sex tonight. Correct?"

"Yes, that's what I'm telling you. Part of it anyway."

"And the other part is you don't know when you'll feel like having sex. Is that correct?"

"It's not so much a 'feel like.' It's more complicated than that. But as far as the when, you're right. I don't know exactly when. I'm not saying never. I'm asking . . . no, I'm telling you that I need time."

"Great. So what am I supposed to do? I've already waited a month. Now you're telling me you have no idea when you'll be ready to be my wife again. Nice. Well, let me have it. What's the other thing?"

"I'm pregnant."

Looking at Carl was like watching a space shuttle launch. Control, shaking, violent shaking, combustion, blast off. All I could do was wait for him to settle into his orbit.

"I'm speechless. Absolutely speechless."

Not a good time to point out that he obviously wasn't if he was speaking. I held onto my bare feet. They were clammy or maybe that was my hand.

"You're kidding," he said. "No. You're not kidding. This is crazy. Lunatic. What were you thinking?"

"Um, I didn't get pregnant by myself."

"Don't get smart with me right now. This is a shock, an absolute shock. Wait. When did you find out?"

"Last week. After I had to—"

"One week. So you knew about this before you left rehab. And you kept it a secret from me?"

Rage moved to sonic levels. "I was afraid you'd want me to sign out early. I didn't want to fight with you about it, and I wanted to finish the program. Get as much time working on me as I could. I didn't do it to hurt you. I'm sorry. I'm really sorry."

"Gee. I think I heard those words in this same room about a month ago. You're sorry. I'm sorry, too. I'm sorry you lied to me. How ironic. You had the nerve to jump all over me for not telling my parents, and then you turn around and lie. Do you really think you're in any shape to be a mother? You can't even take care of yourself yet. And now you're telling me you're going to take care of a child?"

I recoiled. "Hold on. Since when have I not been a good mother? Don't go there. We really don't want to have that fight now."

He calmed down. Radically. He scared me when he was this calm. That usually signaled he was going for the final emotional blow. "Well, since you did find out this news while you were in rehab, did all those counselors and doctors we paid all that money for help you in your research?"

"Research? What research?"

"Fetal alcohol syndrome. That research."

38

I slept in my own bed for the first time in a month.

Carl slept on the sofa.

In one way, a perfect end to a not-so-perfect day. In a million other ways, a perfect disaster.

After Carl's comment about Fetal Alcohol Syndrome, I calmly walked out of the den and into the bedroom and not so calmly slammed the door behind me. I flung the decorative round pillows, square pillows, and sausage-shaped pillows on the floor. Like so many nights before in this same bed, I climbed in and slid under the covers without bothering to change my clothes. A white eyelet sundress was close enough to sleepwear that night.

After a while of convulsing in tears, I forced myself out of bed. I washed my face, brushed my teeth, and changed into one of my long sleeveless nightgowns. Long, just in case Carl decided to leave the den and sleep in our bed. And then there was the ceremonial taking off of the watch. Years ago, I'd mentioned if anyone ever had a notion to buy me a Rolex, not to bother unless it had emeralds and diamonds in the bezel. I'm not sure at what point in which wine bottle I may have made that announcement. Kudos to Carl for remembering, but what

I thought was sarcasm, he took as a veiled request. Then again, I hadn't purged myself of all my shallowness because it was stunning, and I really did want to keep it.

I placed it back in the white box for tonight.

Good night, watch. Good night, closet. Good night, bathroom. Good night, my very own bed. Good night, Carl, sleeping in the den.

Morning tiptoed in so quietly, I didn't realize it arrived. Even the sun seemed less obnoxious. No Theresa snoring, burping, or gassing. A few twittering bluebirds, and I'd feel like I was on the set of a Disney movie.

Carl's pillow was as plumped up as it'd been last night. No tucked-in swaddling. I inched across the empty space to the other side of the bed to see if he'd left a note. No.

What time was it anyway?

My sassy new Rolex didn't have legs, so if I wanted the time, I had to walk into the bathroom to find it. I forced myself to roll out of bed. I passed the framed mirror and saw I had a crease from my right eyebrow to my chin. Lovely. Must have bunched up the sheets again. Where did the white box go? A sliver of panic sliced through me. I rubbed my eyes to clear the gunk and looked again. The whole length of the counter. Not there. I know it was there. I was sober. I clearly remembered this. I looked in the mirror. Well, Leah, there's one for you. Being sober meant clarity. Only this morning my clarity resulted in confusion. Uh-oh. Maybe Carl decided to return it.

I brushed my teeth. I found a clip, shoved it over a large clump of hair, and did something I hadn't been able to do in a long time. I opened my bedroom door and walked out in my nightgown. The blinds sliced the sun as it came into the den. From my bedroom door the room was awash in sun sliced into layers by the blinds. Those teeny particles floated by like they were on currents.

No Carl on the sofa. No evidence of Carl ever having been on the sofa.

I padded into the kitchen. The refrigerator hummed, the thermostat clicked on, the digital clocks on the microwave and oven blinked hello. All was well.

Still no Carl.

I looked around for Krups coffee maker. It was easier to find than my husband. It was exactly where it was supposed to be, in its appliance garage. We humans were bizarre. We bought things. Things we enjoyed. Things we needed. Then we decided that we didn't want to see the things, nor did we want other people to see the things. So we bought things to hide the things. I started the Krups, and heard my cell phone ring. I haven't heard it or seen it in a month. The "Celebrate" song, which I'd programmed in the last week of school, looped and relooped. If there's a surefire way to hate a song, download it as a ringtone. Naturally, the phone was exactly where it was supposed to be, in the electronics devices fueling station on top of the desk. The nifty little leather valet was home to my cell phone, Carl's Blackberry, two iPod Nanos, and their assorted chargers. Complete with a surge protector, thank you very much.

Missed call.

I just found Carl.

He and his father were on hole #3 at the club. I hated that one. A too-wide water hazard hole that held far too many of my cute pink Breast Cancer Awareness golf balls.

He didn't say hello because, of course, there are no secrets with cell phones. He used his "I'm upset with you, but I don't want my father to know" voice. The one that's too singsongy and too modulated.

Since I was alone, I could use any voice I chose. I chose perky.

"Good morning. I called to tell you I put your gift in the original box. It's in the safe." The generic nature of this led me to believe he didn't want his father and/or the other twosome of the foursome to know about the watch. Curious.

"Thanks," I lilted.

"Anything else?"

Was he kidding? But I ramped up the perk factor and answered, "No."

"I'll call you when I'm on the way home. Good-bye."

I'm not given an opportunity to say good-bye. But I said it anyway. For practice.

Then I realized I didn't ask if he'd changed the safe combination. I didn't call him back. It used to be the day of each of our birthdays. 070204.

Doesn't matter. In five months, there would be another Thornton. With a new birthday. We'll need a new combination anyway.

Golf was definitely a game invented by men, for men. It requires a gaggle of equipment, it is considered a legitimate place to conduct business all over the known universe, and it takes an extremely long time to play. Eighteen holes. Most people are usually ready to quit at hole #14. But an extra four holes is an extra hour.

I was one of those rare wives, the kind many married male golfers would sacrifice a new Ping driver to have. I encouraged my husband to play golf. I even endured lessons to learn how to play myself. But when I started to detect relief and not disappointment when I'd turn down his offers to play, I didn't push the issue. Now, I played every once in a while. Enough to justify buying myself a new golf shirt and skirt. Otherwise,

I made sure Carl was a happy golfer and bought him lessons as birthday and Christmas presents, greens fees to play other courses, a new club.

I figured his five hours parlayed into my five hours. I could read, have lunch with Molly, grade papers, shop, read, hang out at CC's, read more. With the exception of paper-grading and the coffeehouse, which I generally paired anyway, most of these had involved alcohol. Sobriety was going to require rethinking all of these activities.

I knew the watch was safe in the safe (lesson on redundancy), so I didn't mess with trying to figure out the combination. I calculated I had about four more hours before Carl would be home.

Rebecca had cautioned me about extremes, especially in early sobriety. Too much time could be just as dangerous as too little time. I needed to call Rebecca with my schedule for the day, which included the meetings I'd be attending. That was one of my post-Brookforest mandates from my new sponsor who told me, "I want to know what you're doing and what you're not doing. If I'm not home or I don't answer my cell, leave a message. If not, I will haunt you."

Five polite beeps. Coffee maker code for ready. Last week was my week of lasts at Brookforest. This would be my week of firsts. I was on my way to my first cup of coffee in my own kitchen. I found my usual coffee mug, a gift from my first Advanced Placement class. They'd pushed the envelope when they designed it, but they were so proud of themselves I had to laugh and, of course, accept. On one side, they'd written, "We survived this class," and, fortunately, on the side facing me, ". . . with AP-ness." My principal, who appreciated their cleverness, also told me he'd appreciate my not leaving it in the faculty lounge. I poured the coffee, but immediately experienced two sinking feelings. One was that I hadn't made decaf, and the other was that the reason I needed to make decaf was sending me to the bathroom for my first morning sickness at home.

Four hours seemed like a much bigger chunk of time last week. Over an hour had passed, and all I'd accomplished was waking up, throwing up, and dressing up. I found decaf, made a fresh pot of coffee, and sat at the kitchen table to write my first "TO DO" list as a sober person.

1. Don't drink.
2. Call Rebecca.
3. Don't drink.
4. Call Molly.
5. Read today's meditations in *The Promise of a New Day* and *Twenty-Four Hours a Day.*
6. Carl?????????
7. Make appointment with Dr. Nolan for 2nd OB visit
8. Find/buy journal for 12 Step work
9. GO TO MEETING AT SERENITY AT 6:30. (Al-Anon mtg. @ that time)
10. See #1 and #3

When Carl called to tell me he was on his way home, I'd finished #1-5. Rebecca and I had arranged the place, time, and date for our lunch. Molly said she was on her way to an appointment, but she was "grateful and ecstatic" I was home. She said she'd call back in a few days, but she knew Carl and I needed time together. I'd purposely waited on #7 because I wanted to include Carl in the appointment with Dr. Nolan or at least offer him the chance to be there.

I slipped on my canvas sneakers, cleaned the coffee pot, and brushed on enough powder and blush to not look scary white. I hadn't eaten breakfast, so I planned to ask Carl if he wanted to go out for lunch. We'd at least be forced to act civilly toward one another in a public environment. After last night, and especially with Carl having spent the night on the sofa, I had no idea which version of Carl would soon walk through the door.

My meditation today was, "I will accept my life and the paths it is taking, and trust that God is leading me where I need to be." When I read that I thought of Robert Frost and "The Road Not Taken" and it occurred to me that perhaps Robert struggled with his paths and decisions as well: "Two roads diverged in a wood, and I—I took the one less traveled by, And that has made all the difference."

God, if my path in life is a road not frequently traveled, I'm going to need a GPS or I'll be wandering around aimlessly. Hmm. GPS. God Protects Stupidity. That worked for me.

Or, Leah, God Provides Salvation.

That too, God. That too.

Pappasito's. A lively Mexican restaurant. Perfect. Background music loud enough to swallow conversations. Just sitting at a table is entertainment. Waitstaff carrying trays as round as manhole covers loaded with sizzling, "careful hot plate, don't touch" aromatic entrees. Why hasn't cilantro made its way into candles and aerosol sprays?

"Did you know cilantro is also called Chinese parsley?" I said to the menu across the table from me.

"Yes. I remember I heard that someplace. Maybe from you the last time we were here," it answered.

"Why do we look at the menu? We order the same thing every time. I'm not complaining. I love the shrimp fajitas. Crave them," I said, and felt the lumpy dough of the "crave" word drop between us.

"Shrimp fajitas. Extra guac, sour cream, and tortillas," Carl said to Andy, our waiter, a striking blonde in a surfer-dude way.

I dove in the pool of discontent headfirst. "I need to make an appointment with Dr. Nolan. She's the OB. I wanted to talk to you before I scheduled it. In case you'd want to go."

He pushed back in the chair, the one-shoulder-dropped look that radiated aggravation. "Now, when did you make this decision? What happened to Dr. Foret?"

I explained my decision had nothing to do with not liking Dr. Foret, but everything to do with not wanting to have everything about this pregnancy remind me of Alyssa. "Dr. Nolan was recommended by someone at Brookforest. I've already met her, and I really like her. I think you would too."

"It seems you've made a lot of important decisions without me. Is this part of how you changed? You stopped asking for my opinion?"

Serenity Prayer. Serenity Prayer.

"The doctor decision I made last week. If I'd talked to you about it, well, that would've been strange. Wouldn't you have wondered why I was asking you about an OB from rehab?"

"Whatever you want. If you want me to go with you, I'll make it happen."

Now I was on familiar turf. Artificial turf. In his veiled way, he told me he wanted me to be vulnerable first. He wanted me to say that I wanted him there, so his presence was a gift.

Is this the path, God? I step out first? This isn't seeming like the less traveled road.

You forgot about the trust already? GPS, not LPS. Got it.

"Yes, I would very much like for you to be at Dr. Nolan's with me." There, I told him what he wanted to hear.

Andy hovered with the tray, while Carl reorganized the table to accommodate the plates. "I'll go. Let me know the date, so I'll put it in my 'Berry." He nodded to Andy, and over the sizzling confusion of sliding plates onto the table, he said, "That'll be perfect. We can both talk to her about Fetal Alcohol Syndrome."

I mentally dumped the fajita plate in Carl's lap. I watched as Andy's eyes shifted to me and back to Carl in microseconds.

"Thanks," I said, and I meant it for more than just the food.

The day went, as my students were apt to say, from worse to worser.

At some point during lunch, Carl remarked that I wasn't wearing the Rolex. I told him about not being sure of the safe combination. He asked why I didn't bother to try.

The conversation crumbled like stale cookies. I was determined to not fall apart with it. Not anymore.

"This isn't about the watch, is it?"

He covered his plate with his napkin and pushed it to the side. "No, I guess not," he said, and wore the weariness of his voice in his eyes.

I asked the waiter, who probably now had a clue why we hadn't ordered wine, for a "to go" container.

"It's hard to pretend the last thirty days didn't happen. So much changed for me. But I don't even understand it all yet. Can you, at least now while we're hacking through this forest, give me the benefit of the doubt? Maybe not always presume I've done something intentionally or have an ulterior motive?" As soon as the words coasted out of my mouth, I had one of my *epeep-a-nees*. We disliked whatever we saw in others that reminded us of what we disliked in ourselves. Carl suspected

255

me of doing the very things he did himself. I didn't voice this. Not yet.

On the ride home, I told Carl about Rebecca, how I met her, and what it meant for her to be my sponsor. If I shared information in pieces, eventually the whole puzzle would come together. After all, who could assemble a 500-piece puzzle all at once?

Sure, God could, but He'd already assembled the entire universe. Bang or no Bang. Somebody had to make the parts ahead of time and know exactly where they'd fit when everything settled.

I dumped one too many pieces out of the box, but I wanted Carl to understand about the 90/90, especially since I'd be leaving the house that night to attend my first post-rehab meeting.

"Making ninety consecutive meetings in ninety days is committing to sobriety and to the program. It's important. Especially now that we're going to have a baby. Staying sober is more important than ever. The Serenity Club has Al-Anon meetings on some nights at the same time as AA meetings. We could go together."

"Let me think about the meetings. You're hitting me with a lot right now."

"Well, just think about Al-Anon meetings."

"Another nonnegotiable . . . this 90/90 thing?"

"Yes, but I'm already taking a sabbatical next school year. I'll be free to attend meetings during the day. They don't have to cut into our time."

"Fine, fine. Whatever works." He reminded me of movies where the sound track is off, and the actor's mouth isn't in sync with the words.

<hr>

Another first. Driving myself to an AA meeting. Big girl Leah. I did feel alone walking through the doors after weeks of being spilled in with the gang. I looked around for familiar Brookforest faces, but Rebecca told me they'd attended an earlier nonsmokers meeting.

"I thought that would end with my discharge. Guess Trudie's holding her own." I laughed imagining Doug when he heard they weren't stopping those.

Rebecca gave me a quick hug. "How's it going?"

"How much time do you have?" I wished I hadn't promised Carl I'd be home right after the meeting. Just being in the room provided emotional weight loss. Not that the problems disappeared, but I knew I was surrounded by people who understood.

"Based on the expression on your face, I don't have that much time," she grinned. "We're supposed to meet for lunch tomorrow. Let's meet thirty minutes earlier, and we can use that as dumping time. How's that sound?"

"Like a gift from God. Thank you," I said.

From the front of the room, Charles hit the gavel a few times. "Let's get started. My name is Charles, and I'm an alcoholic. By the grace of God and the fellowship of this program, I've been sober eight years, five months, and twenty-two days."

"Hi, Charles."

"Any newcomers here tonight who'd like to introduce themselves?"

"Hello. My name is Leah, and I'm an alcoholic."

39

Week One. Every day was like walking through a minefield. Help was always a prayer or phone call away, but the temptations were usually only inches away.

I expected to be challenged when I first went to the grocery. Not only was alcohol available, but in the drunk days, I carried a drink with me in a Styrofoam cup or one from any number of fast food places to hide the olives. Now, in recovery, I faced aisles of gin, vodka, rum, scotch, bourbon, whiskey, tequila, liqueurs, beer, and wine—just to name the biggies. Both sides of the aisle offered dozens of labels of each. In one store, I noticed aisles with the alcohol and wine weren't only a tad wider, their floors were highly polished wood, the shelves more substantial, and the bottles neatly displayed.

I wasn't even safe in the big box stores. They not only sold all of the above, they often had sampling stations that featured wine or liqueurs. Avoiding the aisles, obvious choice. I felt ambushed by the aproned sample ladies who were placed all over the store. Shaped like squeeze-doll grandmas, they'd croon, "Can I offer you something to drink? Would you like to taste our new ChococoMaraschinoChoclairFramboiseCrème deFraisesGrand Marnier?"

Then there was the dessert dilemma. Was there real Amaretto in the Amaretto Cheesecake or was that flavoring? Could I order the bread pudding with the rum sauce on the side? What about the rum balls? I wasn't going to a meeting to confess I backslid with three dozen rum balls and two bread puddings. As an active alcoholic I knew one drink was too many and a thousand weren't enough. I didn't care if the cook simply opened a bottle of Kahlua near the cheesecake so it would capture its aroma, I refused to eat it. Several servers reassured me about one dessert or another, "Don't worry, the alcohol burns off." Then what was the point? "The flaming dessert makes a wonderful presentation," one waiter explained. Wasn't it enough that my fireplace flamed? Hadn't one of those caused extensive damage to a French Quarter restaurant?

Carl's approach at restaurants required more diplomacy, "She's a recovering alcoholic. Is there any alcohol in that?" I'd asked him if, for the next few months, he minded replacing "a recovering alcoholic" with "pregnant" as the results would be the same.

Without alcohol, I was at the mercy of my feelings. After years of being numbed, they were coming after me with a vengeance. I empathized with Superman who had to struggle to control his super powers and not drill laser holes through unsuspecting people. Bushels and barrels of feelings demanded my attention. I flailed in them. Struggled to find balance.

Before my AA meeting yesterday, I had looked for a book I needed to return to Molly. I found it in my dresser between my socks and scarves—no clarity there—and when I picked it up, there was a photo of Alyssa. She wore a smocked Feldman dress, the cloud blue one, with lace around the neckline. Her fine, silky hair was too thin to hold her monogrammed silver barrette. It had landed just above her right eyebrow. One white crocheted bootie covered one foot. Her other foot was bare. I held the photo in one hand, the book in the other. I turned from one side to the other, holding her picture out like something passed between runners in a relay. If I could find someone to give it to, the feelings would go with it. Six weeks ago I would have carried her picture into the dining room, placed it on the table, and returned with a bottle of something. The blessing that day was that I had a place to take my body filled with the jagged bits of broken glass: The Program.

In some ways, I was an alien who'd landed with the wrong operating instructions. Someone added the words "without alcohol" to what had been familiar, and I didn't know the protocol. How does one celebrate without alcohol? How does one attend a party without alcohol? What do people talk about without alcohol? What do people drink at parties without alcohol? What do people remember the next day about the night before without alcohol? How do people act silly, sing, dance, and, most importantly, make love without alcohol?

Step Three: Made a decision to turn our will and our lives over to the care of God as we understood Him.

Maybe that was it. One day at a time. One step at a time.

I came home from my lunch with Rebecca with hope, challenges, and information. She said sober thinking takes time. "In the beginning of my sobriety, I just kept repeating to myself all those, what I thought at the time, were hokey AA-isms: One day at a time. Live and let live. Let go and let God. Easy Does It. There but for the grace of God. And the Serenity Prayer. I wrote them on index cards and taped them on my bathroom mirror, refrigerator, computer monitor, telephone. If my kids would have let me, I would have taped one on each of their foreheads. Take baby steps. AA isn't a program anyone finishes, so there's really no point in rushing."

She challenged me to find a church, a place to worship, where I could fellowship with other believers and find ways to serve the Lord. "I don't know what religion you were or are. It doesn't matter. If you have a church now, fantastic. If you don't, start looking for one. Visit. Keep visiting until you walk into one and you hear God whisper in your ear that you've found your place of rest."

Rebecca suggested Carl and I visit a counselor, together and separately. "Here's a card for a Christian counselor. I think she might be about thirty minutes away from where you live, but she's worth the drive. She's someone I've recommended to people for years. People in and out of recovery. I really think you'll like her."

"Melinda Mendoza. That's a lyrical name. What are the odds of that hook-up? How did you meet her?" I slipped the card in my purse.

"I met her through my mother. Known her for years," she laughed. "She's my older sister."

⸎

"It's finally going to happen." Carl rested his leather briefcase on the kitchen table.

My head popped up from my planner so quickly that I felt my neck muscle burn. I hadn't expected him home an hour early. I'd been lost in nerd-land setting up my new planner and color-coding entries. Birthdays in red, OB appointments in green, AA meetings in blue (the color of the Big Book), anniversaries in pink. Organization was one of my goals, and one I had control over. Courage to change the things I can control. I'd spent hours at bookstores and office supply stores looking for the right planner. The winner was a red leather-bound binder that I could pick just what I needed to fill it. Now what?

He had the one-finger tie-loosening going on while he looked out the window that overlooked what was now a weed-infested garden bed surrounding a giant pine tree. "It's a mess out there. I think you were right about the koi pond. Let's talk to your dad about working on it when he's in town this coming weekend."

"You're messing up my color system here." I looked at the calendar. "His coming as in three days? Why? What's going to happen?"

He pulled out a chair, sat on the edge, and reached over to hold my hands. "You know how long I've been at Morgan Management."

I nodded.

"And you know the only offer that would pull me away from there."

I nodded again, this time with less hesitancy.

"I knew about this three weeks ago. But there was Brookforest, then coming home, then the baby. I wanted to make sure it was definite before I told you."

I'm beyond nodding. "Tellmetellmetellme."

"My last day at Morgan is a week from Friday. I'm going to own forty-nine percent of Thornton Enterprises, and my first job is to open an office in Pine Knoll."

He stood. I hopped up and down. "Carl, this is incredible, wonderful, amazing, and every other synonym. This is big. This is BIG news."

He opened his arms and wrapped them around me. I pressed my hands against his chest, and laid my head between them, and felt the muffled beat of his heart. He rested his head on mine, and I felt warm and right. Safe. The way I used to feel and wanted to feel again. If I could just find a way. To stay sober, and to stay safe.

"It's what I've been waiting for ever since I graduated from college." He loosened his hug, but still held me, his hands clasped behind my back. I leaned against them so I could see his face. "I did what he asked. I went to Morgan to gain the experience he wanted. And now he's making good on his promise."

"I'm so proud of you. So proud you hung in. I know how important this was for you."

"And for us." He placed his hand on my tummy. "For almost the three of us."

I sent a prayer of gratitude to God for this extraordinary event in Carl's life—for his job and for his tenderness toward this baby.

Carl headed to the bedroom to change out of his suit. I set the table, then opened the refrigerator. For a whiff of time, I wondered where the champagne had hidden itself. Nights like this, for Leah of the past, justified celebration of the bottled variety. I reached for the pitcher of iced tea and wondered if there'd ever be a time I wouldn't think about drinking.

By the time Carl came back into the kitchen, I had everything ready for him to start the grill. He grabbed the platter with the steaks and stopped before he opened the back door. "I meant to tell you this earlier. I'd called your dad from the car on my way home to tell him the news. I wanted him to have a heads-up so he could plan his flights. Didn't want you to think I was one-upping him over telling you."

"Not a problem," I said, and I meant it. I finished slicing the plump creole tomatoes.

We barbecued steaks and ate steamed asparagus and a salad of tomatoes and feta cheese. I'd freed the leaves and pine needles from the antiqued wrought iron table and chairs, and we ate outside. We ignored the steamy August evening, so miserly there were no breezes, just shifts of warm air.

By the time the dampness settled on us like a second skin, we'd finished eating. I held the back door open for Carl who'd volunteered to carry in the wobbling stack of dirty plates, silverware, and glasses. He stepped over the threshold, paused, and turned to me. "This was nice. Our talking to one another."

My heart heard a whisper of trust in his words. "For me, too. It's been a long time since . . ." I stared at my hand on the doorknob. The unspoken floated between us like a bloated balloon that waited for the truth to explode it.

I looked at Carl. I whispered what I hoped his heart could hear, ". . . since I was sober enough to do this."

Later, I spooned my body inside Carl's, felt the length of him against me. His arm stretched down the side of my body. He lifted my hair, and covered the back of my neck in butterfly kisses. He reached over and patted our child, God's work-in-progress. "Good night, Leah. Good night, baby. I love you both." And we slept.

We'd been transformed by prayers answered, dreams lived, and promises fulfilled. We traveled the road of our shared lives, the markers along the way built by memory. I recalled that night whenever I thought of being held in the cleft of God's hand. Of the simple joy of a generous life.

Carl, my watch, and I waited for dad's plane to land at Fairway Airport. It was the smaller of the two airports in the city, but closer to the country club where we were meeting Carl's parents. Tonight was the dinner recognizing Carl's becoming a part of his father's business.

Somehow, I managed to squeeze myself into the black dress Carl had bought for the anniversary party. Thanks to the baby, I filled out the top of the dress. The horizontal pleats across the waistline left space for maybe half a slice of cheesecake for dessert. Carl's suit was also the same one he'd worn. A maddeningly unfair advantage men have, being able to not only recycle their suits, but to have anyone barely notice.

The days since Carl announced his news passed so smoothly they could have been lyrics in a richly mellow song. He didn't pressure me with expectations either inside or outside the bedroom. And his willingness to wait increased my willingness to take small, steady steps in the direction of trust. I continued my 90/90 AA meetings, and I called Rebecca every day. Molly and I talked again, but only briefly. She told me she was busy with doctor appointments. She and Devin were human boomerangs during the *in vitro* procedures and check-ups. We made a walk date for the next weekend. I told her if I didn't start exercising again, people wouldn't know which end of me carried the baby.

My brother Peter and I talked a few times. The attorneys had kept him busy preparing their trial notebooks for an upcoming asbestos suit. He had to finish before court, so he was going to the office early and leaving late, checking filings and evidence. Well compensated as a litigation paralegal, he rarely complained about his work schedule. The last time I'd spoken to Peter he asked if I'd check my calendar to see if I could squeeze in a weekend or longer in New Orleans. "I'll check on AA meetings close to my house. I wouldn't think we have a shortage of alcoholics in this city. Well, maybe of recovering ones," he'd said.

I hadn't mentioned the idea of marriage counseling to Carl yet. Whether he decided to go or not, I knew I needed to. Ron told me before I'd left Brookforest I had to start dealing with issues that came out during our sessions. "This is the scratch on the scratch. You know what that means, right? You've shared some intense situations. No way were we going to be able to process those in just a few days," he'd cautioned.

I asked Rebecca when I saw her at my next meeting, "Do I ask Carl now with the comings and the goings between Morgan and his dad's company? It might be better to wait until that settles down. Then he'll have out-of-town trips, setting up his new office." I looked at her. "I just answered my own question, didn't I?"

"Good for you," she said. "I bet you'll be talking to him real soon."

"After the dinner this weekend," I said. "I'll talk to him on the way home from dropping my father off at the airport. It's tough to ignore someone sitting in the seat next to you."

For now, Carl and I attempted to pick Dad up from the airport. The flight hadn't been delayed; we'd already checked. He had carry-on baggage, so we didn't have to swarm around the luggage carousel. But with my father, possibilities abounded. The most likely scenario was his having found someone he knew. For Bob Adair, "knew" was defined as sharing space with someone for five minutes. Peter and I used to play "name the state Dad's been to where he hasn't bumped into anyone he knew." We stumped ourselves.

"Don't forget. We're not telling him about the baby until we're all at dinner. I know how you are around my father. Secrets are not your forte," I said, attempting playful seriousness.

Carl spotted him first. Tall people have that advantage. "Bob! Bob! Over here." He waved his arm. I don't think Carl realized tall men's baldness alone equaled visibility in airport crowds.

Dad walked behind a petite woman, with a liquid honey complexion and a close-cropped Afro. She rolled a suitcase behind her with one hand, and with the other, she clutched the hand of a little boy, probably four or five, with the same smooth honey skin and close-cut hair. He twisted over his right shoulder like soft taffy, laughing at my dad who entertained him making smushy faces. The child tried to walk forward while he looked backward. His mom was as oblivious to what caused his slowness as my dad was to the fact that he caused it.

As the little boy plip-plopped past, Dad made one last fish mouth face and was rewarded with a snorting grin.

"Did you see that little boy? Cute one, huh? How are you two? Come here, honey. Give me a hug." He handed Carl his suitcase and wrapped his arms around my shoulders. "Let me look at you. You look terrific! Carl, she looks great, doesn't she? So, how have you been, my man?" My dad asked and answered his own questions so fluidly that we learned just to ride along until he stopped.

Dad grabbed Carl's hand and pulled him close so that he could reach around and pat him on the back. "Good to see you. Good to see you." He looked at the floor and swiveled his head. I could tell by the vacant expression on his face, he'd already forgotten where he'd put his suitcase.

"Carl has it," I said.

"Whew. Great. Let's go." We started walking in the direction of the car. "Where'd you park? Someplace close?" He patted his jacket pocket, pulled out a pair of glasses, and tapped me excitedly on the shoulder. "Look at his. Smart, huh?" He demonstrated the hinge action of his aluminum-framed glasses. "What'll they think of next?"

Carl and I shared an eye contact moment when Dad simultaneously shook his head in obvious admiration of the hinge inventor's cleverness and cleaned his lenses with a cotton handkerchief from his back pants' pocket.

"Honey, how are you? With the, you know, all that stuff in the hospital. It worked, baby? Feeling better?"

I slipped my arm through his as we walked to the parking garage. He was probably one of the last breed of men to slather Aqua Velvet lotion on after every shave.

"Yes, you know, I've been out over two weeks, going to meetings—"

"Hey, that's great. She's doing fine, huh, Carl? So good to hear that. Oh, look, is this your car? I'd forgotten you had this one."

"So, I was telling you about the meetings, I go—"

"Bob, why don't you sit up front. Leah doesn't mind. I can catch you up on the business news. And, hey, what's happening with the Saints?"

"Oh, let me tell you this . . . Is this the seatbelt buckle? Leah, honey, you see the buckle back there?"

"Here, Dad."

"Oh, thanks. You know, they've gotta do something in that running back position. You agree?"

Carl nodded and drove down three levels of the concrete corkscrew, stopped at the parking booth, and we were on our way.

I looked out the side window. My dad and Carl hit words between them like a friendly game of air hockey. After every four or five words from my father, Carl slipped in a few of his own. Sentence completion rarely occurred in conversation with him.

Ron's words, "You loved him because he reminded you of your father," didn't ring true tonight. How was Carl anything like my father? I didn't remember this dismissive side of my father. The token attention to an uncomfortable topic, like my rehab. Once I told him I was fine, he didn't want details. Not that there's anything wrong with his not wanting me to drone on and on about AA when he just landed. And I didn't mind sitting in the backseat. It's miles more comfy. Besides, when Mom was alive, we'd always sit women in the back and men in the front.

Don't compromise yourself, Leah, you're all you've got.

Now where did that come from?

40

Carl was Landon and Gloria Thornton's only son when I met him. Their only living son.

Vic, Carl's brother, died in a car accident at the age of eighteen. He and his new Mustang convertible left home one Monday evening so he could start college at Louisiana State University's Baton Rouge campus. Neither one of them made it. The details, over the years, have faded as has the mention of his name. For whatever reason, the song on the radio, the sun in his eyes, Vic didn't know two lanes had been narrowed to one as he exited the Atchafalaya Bridge. By the time he realized he'd run out of a lane, he'd run out of a life. His Mustang careened into the boggy ditch. They found his body, a crumpled mess, several feet away.

If the subject of Vic or the accident broke hallowed ground, there were two taboos.

Never to be discussed in the Thornton house:

1. That Vic was not wearing a seatbelt at the time of the accident.

2. Empty cans of Amber Beer covered the floor of the car.

Carl was eight years old when he became an only child. His parents, for almost ten years after Vic's death, built their business with a vengeance. By the time Carl was Vic's age, his parents had accumulated lots of stuff purchased by lots of money.

When I first met Carl he told me his parents were in sales. There's in sales and then there's IN SALES. His parents were the second. They appeared entirely too squeamish to be making major drug or weapons runs. I knew people with oodles of money who built Amway businesses, but their products were all over their homes, their faces, their bodies, their cars. I didn't understand what pipeline the Thorntons had located, and I still don't. But it worked, and I don't have to understand how. Now that I'm in AA, I can wrap my brain around that a little better.

Landon sold things to people who needed things—sort of a one-man offline eBay, moving larger commodities. Let's say you have ten thousand whatevers and you need to sell them. Landon found someone who wanted ten thousand whatevers or two people who wanted five thousand each, and he hooked them up. He earned a commission. He never had to touch the products. Personally, I thought it was brilliant. Landon and Gloria did, too; if you asked them, they'd tell you.

Carl graduated from college (not LSU) and thought he would work in his father's business. The machine hummed along, and Carl figured he'd play a tune or two. Landon and Gloria thought Carl needed to serve time in the "real world of work." I guess for the truly wealthy, that's a sort of prison.

So Carl served his time, and tonight we'd finally be able to celebrate his initiation into his family's business. At least that was the plan.

As usual, the country club dining room was bountifully decorated with candles and brimming with bow-tied waiters. The Thorntons had a table center stage. Landon and Gloria were truly gracious to Dad. Since Mom died, I'd seen a glimmer of something in them that might be called compassion.

The Thorntons had already ordered appetizers and a bottle of wine, something with *Beernauslese* in the name, and the waiter started pouring. I turned my glass over before he reached me. Gloria, always quick on the uptake, looked at the glass, then at me, and said, "Leah, dear, don't you like this wine? If not, we can certainly order another bottle of whatever you want." She looked over her shoulder at the waiter, "Gary, would you mind bringing the wine list out again for us when you finish pouring? I think Leah might like to look it over." She turned to me. "Unless you want something else entirely. A mixed drink?"

I bit my tongue. Hard. "No, thank you, Mrs. Thornton," I said. "Gary, I don't need a wine list. I'll have a glass of water with lemon. Thank you." I glared at Carl. He looked like I imagined he would at the Second Coming. Terrified. He opened his mouth, but words came of his mother's mouth instead.

"Aren't you feeling well since your—" she paused "—rest? Did they advise you not to drink?"

"No, Mrs. Thornton," I said, softly gracious, like I imagined Melanie in *Gone with the Wind* would speak. I placed my hand on top of Carl's clammy and shivering one.

He cleared his throat with a wet cough. The sound attracted the attention of Landon and my father who'd almost solved all the social, financial, and political issues of post-Katrina.

I summoned my inner Southern-magnolia and said to my Benedict Arnold husband, "Carl, honey, I thought you explained to your parents why I'm not drinking. Do you need me to tell them?"

"No, no. I'll tell them," he said. His spinal fluid had probably leaked out and drenched his shirt. "The reason Leah's not drinking—" He cleared his throat.

My father glanced over at him and reached for the bread basket.

What followed was a disaster of cosmic voiceover synchronicity. I watched my father's mouth open just as Carl choked out his own words. In that scope of time, each one speaking over the other:

Carl: "She's going to have a baby."

Bob: "Because of her alcoholism, right?"

———— ∞ ————

Gary brought my water to the table.

He must have sensed the impending explosion, like sensing the almost imperceptible shudders of the earth before it screamed open, swallowed what fell in its mouth, and settled into a gaping yawn. Gary placed the glass and a small crystal bowl of wedged lemons down, tipped his head, and, with a small Fred Astaire move, he disappeared.

Landon and Gloria, much to their credit, didn't collapse on the tiled floor or leap out of their chairs. Landon straightened his array of silverware, aligning the squared ends of the utensils on each side of his dinner plate. In the meantime, Gloria lightly rubbed the front of her neck with one hand, and held the stem of her Waterford crystal wineglass with the other. She focused on it so intently, she could have been attempting to levitate the glass. Landon folded his napkin into a perfect square and placed it in the middle of his plate. He stood. "Son," he placed his hand on the top of Gloria's chair, "your mother and I would like to speak to you, privately, in the Grill."

He pulled out Gloria's chair. "Please excuse us."

Carl didn't protest. He looked in my direction, not really at me, and said, "I won't be long." He touched the top of my shoulder, then trailed into the Grill after his parents.

I refused to sit in the middle of the country club dining room to wait for Landon and Gloria to finish their grown-up time out with my husband. "No problem. Take as long as you need. Dad and I are going home, so if you'll hand me the car keys."

"You and your father don't have to leave," said Landon, and he truly sounded kind.

"I know we don't have to. I just think it's best."

Dad still held the bread basket like he'd float off somewhere if he let go. "Don't you want to wait for Carl?"

"I'm sure his parents wouldn't mind driving him home," I said, as I took the keys from my husband. "Dad, let's go." For a minute, I thought the bread basket might be going home with us. I was so hungry, I almost hoped it would. Dad set it on the table, then stood and shook hands with Landon and Carl and gave Gloria a brush-by kiss on her cheek.

"Well, good to see you, um, thanks. Maybe we'll get together before I leave," Dad said.

I slid my chair out. "Yes, Mr. and Mrs. Thornton, thank you for everything."

We waited quietly until the valet brought the car. Dad buckled in, reached over, and patted my back, "So, you and Carl are going to have a baby. That's great. That's great."

I ordered pizza after we got home, then Dad and I watched a golf tournament Carl had TiVoed a few weeks ago.

At nine o'clock, I kissed Dad good night.

"I didn't know Carl hadn't told them yet, honey."

"It's not your fault, Dad," I told him and went to bed. I fell asleep before Carl arrived home.

41

On Saturday morning I had two legitimate reasons to leave Carl and my father alone. First, after the previous night, they deserved one another, and second, I was on my way to meet Molly for our Saturday walk.

With Molly and Devin focused on *in vitro* again, I'd hoped to postpone our baby news. But with Carl's job, AA, and his parents knowing, I wanted Molly to hear it from me before the gossip grapevine strangled her with the news.

"My thighs wiggled with anticipation all the way from the house," I told Molly and hugged her, willing every ounce of gratitude I felt to seep through my skin and into hers. After a lifetime of struggling to define emotions, I hoped God created a way to give them physical forms in heaven. We could have guided tours: gratitude and joy on your right, peace and thanksgiving on your left. I've spent more time contemplating heaven now that I've included God in my contact list. Even before AA, I knew it was important to know where I was going; otherwise, how would I know if I'd arrived? In my meditation last week, I read a passage from Corinthians where Paul said that when Jesus returns, we'll all have new bodies for heaven. What a spectacular going-away gift.

"I'm glad we're doing this again," she said. "I feel like we haven't spent time together in years instead of weeks."

"Crazy, huh? Summer's almost over. At least I'm not manic trying to get ready for school again. A one-year sabbatical was a brilliant idea." I'd bent over to grab my ankles to stretch out when the baby reminded my digestive system s/he didn't care for that position. I straightened my body and settled for side stretches instead.

"And whose idea was that?" Molly teased. She'd thought to mention it to Carl and me the first week of rehab.

Of course, being the consummate overachiever, I bristled. "I can handle sobriety and students," I'd told her.

"Not the point. You have the time coming to you, take it. Why set yourself up for failure?" She bristled herself on that one.

I relented when I'd thought about using the time to take classes . . . not at the university, but yoga and cooking and spin. On this side of rehab, I couldn't imagine preparing for school. Not to mention my extra cargo. And Carl's new job. I didn't know it then, but now I realized God had spoken to me through Molly. I could just hear Him telling Mom, "She wouldn't listen to me. No, of course not. What do I know? But Molly, she'd listen to. What's a God to do?"

I was glad we had the tree-shaded trail to escape the sweltering outdoor oven. No one joked about frying eggs on streets and sidewalks in the heat of a Texas August. We'd bring along bacon too. During the brain-boring summers when we were still too young to be double digits, Peter and I would dare one another to walk down the driveway. Barefooted. The prize for the one who reached the edge of the driveway first or at all was an extra Popsicle. We'd race to pull off our Keds, and "eech and ouch" and "I-yia-yia-yia" down the cement fire. Peter lost almost every time. I reveled in my victories, too dumb to consider he was the smart one.

"Tell me about dinner last night. How'd it go?"

"Honestly, it made me acutely aware of how sober I was, and how dangerous it could've been if I'd been drinking," I said.

"You're kidding? Were Carl's parents that obnoxious? You'd think with your dad there . . . and they knew you hadn't been home long. I'm surprised." She shook her head. "I gave them more credit than that."

I stepped up my pace, so I wouldn't be talking to the back of Molly's head. I told her, "You're going to pass out when you hear this, but I can't hang this one on them. They were the innocents last night."

She didn't stop on that, but she slowed down enough to give me a friendly push, "Get out!" In Molly-speak that translated to, "You've GOT to be kidding."

I spent almost the next mile relating the airport to dinner table timeline of the previous night, up to the Carl/Bob chorus. I stopped and tugged her off to the side of the trail.

"What's wrong?" She tucked her hair behind her ears and pressed her hands together.

"Nothing, nothing." I pulled up the neck of my T-shirt and bent my head so I could wipe the sweat off the sides of my nose. "I need to tell you the good news, so you'll understand why the other news is so bad." I paused, braced myself for the aching happiness that would fall like a veil across her face. "I'm pregnant."

She hesitated, then wrapped me in her arms. "That's so wonderful. Oh, my gosh. I'm so happy for you. That's great. That's great." She let go and ran her fingers underneath her eyes. "I'm about to have raccoon eyes. These are happy tears. I promise."

I believed her, but I saw the brief shadow in her eyes, and I hated I was so helpless. "I know, and I so love you for that. It didn't make sense that we were surprised with a baby, while you and Devin are investing everything to have one. But I'm learning, sometimes the hard way, to trust God. This baby, this baby . . . is such a gift."

"It is a gift. And God's going to take care of Devin and me. I know that. This is almost too much news at once. I don't know what to ask about next. You have to finish the dinner story, then we'll do the baby story."

We started back down the trail, and I told her about Carl and Dad's double-barreled announcements. She had a five-second gasp, then laughter contractions.

"Molly, it's not funny. Once again, Carl lied to me about telling his parents."

"I'm sorry. I'm cracking up thinking about Landon and Gloria just sitting there, with their wine glasses frozen between their mouths and the table. I wish you could've taken a picture. Priceless. Priceless." She shook her head.

"Maybe I've lost my sense of humor, but the whole night is still a nightmare. We were going to tell them about the baby. *That* was supposed to be the surprise. Was Carl thinking he'd never have to tell his parents? I don't get it. With my dad there, did he really think the subject wasn't going to come up? He should know by now my dad's missing that little person who's supposed to sit on your shoulder and warn you not to say things."

"Wait. What did Carl say?"

"No idea. I was asleep by the time his parents dropped him off. He must have slept in one of the bedrooms upstairs because he didn't come to bed, and he wasn't on the sofa when I left this morning." I shrugged.

"It's a shame this all had to happen at what was supposed to be a celebration, but now everybody knows everything. It's going to get better."

"I'm counting on it," I said. "If it doesn't, I'm moving in with you and Devin."

Molly had a giggle about that one. The last laugh might be on her because I wasn't kidding.

The sizzling steam of frying bacon met me at the back door to our house. If I hadn't heard Dad's voice, I might have thought someone else had moved in.

"Come on in. Serving breakfast now," Dad called from the kitchen as I pulled off my walking shoes.

"Did you get permission to—" Carl was drinking coffee and reading the newspaper, so he had to know bacon was splattering demon grease everywhere.

"How was your walk?" Carl closed the paper and folded it in half.

"Nice. Hot. But it was good to talk to Molly." I asked Dad to fix me two eggs over easy. "So what time did you come home?"

"Probably right after you left for your walk," he said.

"What? This morning?"

"We were at the club later than I thought we'd be. Didn't want to wake you up, so I just went home with my parents. My father dropped me off on the way to his game."

"Here they are, honey. Eat while they're hot," Dad said, and slid the plate with two fried eggs and wheat bread in front of me.

"That's so considerate of you, caring about not waking me up." I broke the white tops and dipped my bread in the eggs.

"Don't be like that. You know how I feel about your sarcasm," he said, lowering his voice.

"And you know how I feel about you lying to your parents and to me, but you did that . . . twice."

"Do you have to be so loud? We can talk about this later." He looked at my dad and back at me.

We didn't talk about it later, and I was the one who regretted it. I didn't get too many answers from Carl because Dad had his own agenda. He heard us, of course, and told me I was "overreacting."

"How did I do that? I'm not the one who sold me out."

"Carl, she's right. You should have been honest with your parents, especially your dad, talked to him man to man. He could have told your mother. Heck, you could have just talked to her, if you didn't want to talk to both of them. One could have told the other."

Carl nodded. "I know. I know."

"And Leah, all I'm saying is maybe, you know, you're better now. Maybe you could have a drink every once in a while now that you know what to do. Moderation, isn't that what they say?"

"It doesn't work like that. Alcoholism isn't cured. I'll always be an alcoholic."

Dad looked wounded. "Now, honey, don't say that. You don't know . . . "

"No, Dad. I do know. I can't drink like other people. I never did, I never will. But I'm a recovering alcoholic now. That's what matters. If I was suicidal, would you say I could shoot myself every now and then?"

"Now, baby, we both know that would be just stupid."

"Exactly. It would be just as stupid for me to drink. It can kill me too. I just take it one day at a time."

"I'm glad it's working for you. I'm glad. Besides, you have to take care of yourself. You've got that baby to think about. How about you, Carl? Awfully quiet, there."

"Great, Bob. I'm great." He put his coffee cup in the sink and walked outside.

42

As I had promised Rebecca, on the way home from taking my father to the airport, I brought up the idea of marriage counseling. The good that came out of the Great Dinner Disaster was that I used it as an opportunity to guilt Carl into agreeing to an appointment. Carl used counseling as an opportunity for penance. We were even.

Our first session with Melinda was the getting to know one another, let's make sure we're comfortable introduction. After we'd arrived at her office, an unassuming cotton candy pink wood-framed house in an older section of the city, Bonnie, her receptionist, handed a blue clipboard to Carl and a pink one to me. "I know, sexist. Please fill these forms out, and no cheating, kids." She smiled and sat back at her desk.

A few pages of the usual medical information requests, but other pages asked about our dreams and goals, strengths and weaknesses of ourselves, our spouse, our relationship, our opinions about money, education, sex, families, children. We finished within a few minutes of one another and handed them over to Bonnie. She took them into Melinda's office.

Carl and I sat next to one another like strangers on a bus. Carl picked up a *Sports Illustrated*. So reminiscent of Annie, who I'd not seen in weeks. I said a quick prayer for her and for everyone at Brookforest that I'd probably never see again. All those weeks our lives were intertwined by our shared weaknesses, and once we became strong, we unraveled from the group. God's way of binding us somewhere else?

Melinda walked out holding our clipboards. "Hi, you two. Come in." I wouldn't have known she was Rebecca's sister because they shared little in terms of their physical appearance. Only a few inches taller than I, Melinda had curly, dark brown hair past her shoulders. Her generous curves contrasted Rebecca's tall, sleek frame. But once she started talking, I had no doubt they were siblings. They shared an assertive sassiness and a warm, honest compassion.

Carl and I sat in separate chairs facing her desk while she talked about how she envisioned couples' therapy, what she expected from us, and what we should expect from her. Carl asked about her experience with couples in therapy because of alcoholism.

"I've been working with couple and individuals for almost eight years now. Are they all alcoholics in recovery? No. Sometimes the addictions are food, drugs, sex, gambling. Some of my clients are the children of the others or the adult children of the others. We all have something that brings us here."

She told us that, after today, the three of us wouldn't meet until she'd met with Carl and me individually. Carl squirmed. I saw her eyes made note, but she kept talking. "When the three of us come together again, I'll share what each of you want as the three most important areas to talk about here. After today, your chairs will face one another, not me. I'm not the one you're here to build a relationship with. I have my own I need to work on." She rolled her eyes, laughed, and pointed to a picture of a handsome, shiny-haired, black cocker spaniel.

"People tell me Sigmund and I have an amazing resemblance. More than Becca and I, wouldn't you say, Leah?"

We scheduled our next appointments, and she gave each of us a set of Scripture passages she wanted us to read before our next couple time together. "You need to congratulate yourselves for being here. The first year in recovery is tough. Most marriages don't survive the first year, and the majority of those who relapse are going to do it the first year. Think there's a connection? Oh, yeah. If you had kept drinking, Leah, you could've shortened your life by as many as fifteen years. Now that's sobering, don't you think, Carl?"

I didn't have to tell her how Carl felt. His body language and monotone, clipped responses conveyed it all. She focused most of her eye contact his way, and when he responded to something she said, she rewarded him with a smile or nod.

Melinda sold me. Now if Carl could just buy in.

I expected my days as a sober person would be excruciatingly long ones involving teeth-gnashing, wailing, hand-wringing, and gazing with naked longing into liquor store windows. Time and circumstances controlled my drinking life. Like many with alcohol-crazed brains, I had my routine, my standards, my inflexible self-imposed tyranny.

WEEKDAY VS. WEEKEND RULES

1. No drinking earlier than five in the evening on weekdays.
2. No drinking earlier than ten in the mornings on weekends.
3. If the weekday was a holiday, then it fell under the weekend rule.

VACATION RULES

1. Weekdays and weekends shared the ten in the mornings rule.

2. *If* the vacation involved morning brunch, drinking before ten o'clock was acceptable (by definition, a morning brunch was breakfast where the following were available: a milk punch, Screwdriver, or Bloody Mary. If attending a Jazz Brunch, champagne was acceptable.)

OTHER RULES

1. NEVER, NEVER, NEVER drink at school.
2. No drinking before church services of any kind. (Since we generally didn't attend, the ten o'clock rule applied.)
3. No drinking while driving. Unless in Louisiana, where this rule was suspended since "to go" cups were available when exiting a bar, and Drive-Thru Daiquiris provided acceptable locations for getting a drink "for the road" on the way to a party. (Rule amended to take into consideration new driving laws requiring covered drinks for drivers and passengers.)
4. After three consecutive days of raging hangovers or worrisome blackouts, there would be a three-day rule of ABSOLUTELY NO ALCOHOL. By the second day of the three-day rule, if no alcohol had been consumed, then it was assumed that no alcohol would have been consumed on the third day. In which case, a drink at five on the afternoon of the second day was acceptable since no drinking on the third day was assumed.

CONTAINER RULE:

CONTENT DETERMINES CONTAINER

1. Anything Not Clear: This is the preferred container. Required to disguise gin or vodka drinks requiring an olive as pure drinking water.
2. Clear Container: Use with caution.
   a) If the gin or vodka drink necessitated a lemon, orange, or lime slice, a clear container was acceptable, because lemons, oranges, and limes are acceptable water fruits.

b) May be used any time drinking is acceptable under conditions outlined above under Weekday vs. Weekend Rules.

DISPOSAL RULE:

ABOVE VS. BELOW NEWSPAPER

(PRIOR TO CARL'S ARRIVAL HOME)

1. Drinking alone on a weekday (see above), fewer empty cans (two or three) could be viewed in the garbage can.
2. If drinking on a weekend (see above), more cans were acceptable. Any cans above acceptable had to be placed under the newspaper.

In the name of everything holy, how did I ever find time to drink?

43

Well, look who it is," said Dr. Nolan, who entered the exam room and looked at my file at the same time. "The little princess sprung from the big house. Life on the outside must be good."

Carl sat across from the exam table. With her back to him, it wasn't until I said, "Carl, this is Dr. Nolan," that she realized he was there.

"Oh, I am very sorry, Mr. Thornton. I was so busy reading about Miss Leah here, I didn't look where I was going," she said. "Glad to meet you."

"Thanks. Nice to meet you," he said. "I have a few questions, Dr. Nolan."

"Good. I like dads with questions. Let me just bother your wife a minute, then we can talk. You know how grouchy these moms can be," she said, shaking her head. "Leah, you didn't tell me you were married to Jean Luc Picard." She talked and prodded and prodded. "That man is one fine-looking white man. Um-mm-mm." She said to Carl, "My husband said I have a thing for bald men. So this is why Momma over here and I liked each other so much, I guess."

Dr. Nolan helped me to sit. I felt like a giant fly squirming off sticky flypaper. I skipped the torture of subjecting my bare feet to frostbite-inducing stainless steel stirrups. The solution in most offices? Athletic socks. Is that the best we can do?

She checked my ankles and feet for fluid. Asked about the vomiting, my food and fluids, and sleep. I told her I'd started walking again. "Only once a week, so far. But we walk two miles."

"Any exercise is better than no exercise. Build up one day at a time. Now that should be an idea you can relate to," she smiled and patted the top of my knee. "Okay, Jean Luc, your turn."

His face did that eyebrow and mouth twitch like his muscles forgot what to do for an instant. One of those perplexing expressions of his when I don't know if he's suppressing a grin or a grimace. "I'm sure you knew this pregnancy was an accident. Leah being an alcoholic at the time. I calculated she'd probably been drinking for at least four to five weeks. My concern, of course, is for the baby. What I want to know is how her drinking may have affected our baby."

Hello? Guilt Trip Planners? Ticket for one, please.

Dr. Nolan, who looked at the floor for most of Carl's oration and nodded every ten seconds, waited before she looked at him and answered.

"Mr. Thornton, Leah's first appointment was at Brookforest, so we've been quite honest with one another from the beginning. For the record, I usually don't refer to a pregnancy as an 'accident' as most people do understand that most intercourse is not 'accidental' and one of its natural consequences is pregnancy. The reason I mention this to you, and the reason I feel so strongly about using the word 'accident' is for some parents, and I'm certainly not suggesting that you would be one, the 'accidental' pregnancy is born and becomes the 'accidental' child. I've had adults sit in this office telling me they were accidents. It makes me sad to hear. Imagine carrying that burden for life. But in God's eyes, not one of us is an accident. Now that's something I wish people would carry around with them."

Carl picked up a striped cotton teddy bear perched on the desk and examined it during Dr. Nolan's reply. "Now about Fetal Alcohol Syndrome," he said and returned the little bright bear to the desk.

Dr. Nolan explained Fetal Alcohol Syndrome, or FAS, is at the most severe end of an entire spectrum of disorders known as Fetal Affective Spectrum Disorders. "One out of 750 babies is born with FAS. Another 40,000 have some fetal alcohol effects at birth," she said. "Sometimes there are effects going back to the first four to six weeks, the time when most women aren't even aware they're pregnant, like Leah." She explained the effects ranged on one end to a low birth weight to FAS babies born with central nervous system disorders and a host of other complications.

"Can I guarantee that this baby has absolutely no effects? No. But I wouldn't expect there to be from the history I've taken from Leah. And we're going to turn that baby's life over to God."

Carl's expression buckled on that one. "We've been down that road, Dr. Nolan, I . . ."

"I know about Alyssa. We're trusting God with this baby, and this baby's road."

Later, when Carl opened the car door for me, he said, "Did you say anything to Dr. Nolan about my parents when you first met her?"

"No. She didn't even ask. Why?"

"Just curious.

Dr. Nolan was God's mouthpiece today. I knew Carl's parents were fond of referring to him as "their little accident."

"You were right. I do like her, but next visit I'm calling her Whoopi Goldberg."

"I think she'd get a kick out of that," I laughed.

Thank you, God. Thank you.

———⌘———

Another Saturday walk with Molly, but my steps outpaced hers today. Something was wrong.

"I know I've been exercising more, but even on one of your slow days, you're ten steps ahead of me. What's up?" I shifted down to her shopping mall speed.

"Devin and I decided to postpone *in vitro*." She soccer-kicked a pine cone in her path. "It's the money. Our finances just can't bear it anymore."

Their finances can't bear their wanting to bear a child. Interesting verb choice, especially for a diction discussion. Two things I couldn't control—alcohol and teacher brain. Teacher Leah corrected errors on restaurant menus and berated television reporters who said, "Between you and I . . ." or "irregardless." You can take the teacher out of the classroom, but you can't take the teacher out of the teacher. Friend Leah understood Molly was learning lessons, gut-wrenching ones.

"But you two have spent weeks getting ready. Why now?"

"We calculated what we've spent and what we will be spending. It's tens of thousands of dollars. Our insurance doesn't cover it. It's our savings, our retirement, the second mortgage on our house. We want to be able to afford the baby after it's born. Great parents we'd be. What do we say, 'It's like this kid, we spent all our money trying to have you, and now that we have you, we can't afford you'?"

"Maybe Carl and I could help. We could set up a *baby in vitro* fund. We can do that, really. Carl loves you and Devin. He'd want to do this too. I'm sure of it. Of course, I'd talk to him first, but God blessed us for a reason. Why can't we use our money to help someone who needs it?" *Wow, did I just look like my father because I so sounded like him.*

Molly's eyes widened into the agitated look I felt the night I heard Dad and Carl's duet. She veered around a fallen tree branch and accelerated to her usual pace. I trotted to stay with her.

"No, Leah. Absolutely not. This is our decision. Thank you, really, but no."

⸺∽∞∾⸺

Four steps forward.

I've not missed one AA meeting since I left Brookforest. Rebecca and I have met every week, I've steadily worked on my Steps, and I spend time reading the Bible, my Big Book, my daily meditations.

Six steps back.

Just when I rejoiced about some progress in our marriage, the wheels not only stopped turning, they peeled out in reverse.

We both had appointments with Melinda the next day, one after the other. Our couple meeting had been scheduled for Friday, and we had reading homework I hadn't started. Carl hadn't bothered to share his assignment, even though I was sure we wouldn't be cheating if we knew. My passages were *The Virtuous Wife* of Proverbs 31, and something from *Song of Solomon*. I started with the outstanding wife of the Bible universe, but about six lines in, I felt sick. Not pregnant sick. The "how am I ever going to measure up to this woman" kind of sick. I wanted a nap just reading about what this woman accomplished. Had I leaped too quickly? Maybe Melinda wasn't the match for us. I closed my Bible and opted for the nap. Maybe after rest—which, hey, AA said we needed to take care of ourselves—I'd be more open to Mrs. Goody Twenty Shoes.

"Amazing Grace," my new ringtone, woke me. Carl told me Friday's appointment might be a problem because his father scheduled meetings with contractors.

"What came first on the appointment schedule? Melinda or the contractor?" Since dinner disaster night, Carl and I have seen his parents on only two occasions: once for a weekend breakfast and the other time we stopped by their house so Carl could sign paperwork for an insurance policy. They were adequately attentive, but with the emotional enthusiasm of people forced to watch home movies of your cats or the four-hundred-ninety-two photos of your vacation in the Smokies. They were pleased about the baby, but probably not so much about the baby's mother.

"Why?" he asked. "You think there's a conspiracy? There isn't."

"Couldn't you reschedule the appointment with the contractor?" I turned on my back and contemplated the dust edging the fan blades. How long had that been there? Good reason to keep a fan on, especially if company's here . . . like the in-laws.

Just because you choose to hide it or not see it, that doesn't mean it isn't there.

It's dust on a fan blade, God.

Have you forgotten, "The Lord formed man of the dust of the ground?"

"Leah, did you hear a word I said?"

Yes, God.

"No, I'm sorry. What did you say?"

"I'd asked if you could reschedule with Melinda. Call me back later, and let me know."

"For dust you are, and to dust you shall return."

—∞∞—

"I rescheduled a business meeting so we could be here," Carl said as he tapped the arm of the barrel chair. "That means we have to leave here exactly at one o'clock."

He faced me, but he swiveled his conversation to both Melinda and me. I looked at her.

She sat, impassive, and twirled a yellow highlighter between her hands. "Fine. Who's going to be the timekeeper?"

"Me," Carl said. "I'll do it. That way I can be sure we won't go over."

"What are you suggesting?" I asked.

After several more volleys across this net of hostility between us, Melinda said, "To your corners. Remind me, why did the two of you come here? Leah, you start. Tell Carl the first issue on your list. Then, Carl, you tell her the first issue on your list. Let's start there."

"My first one is I want to talk about being sober and staying sober and who I'm trying to be."

"That's three. Right, Melinda?" Carl definitely wanted to tattle.

"No, Carl, that's just it. If we'd talk about number one, you'd see why it's not one, two, and three. Right, Melinda?"

"Go, Carl," Melinda said. "And would you two just stick to the plan."

"My first one is sex," he said. "I don't understand why you've been home so long, and the most we do is make out like we're in, what, high school? And then there's your obsession with these AA meetings."

I wanted to focus on sobriety. He wanted to focus on sex.

At least we shared this truth:

The more we had of one, the less we wanted of the other.

———— ⊙∞⊙ ————

Carl was leaving the next day to open the Pine Knoll office, six hours away from our house. His parents rented a nearby apartment, so he planned to live there during the week and come home weekends. They'd told Carl I could stay there with him, but after our contentious sessions, Melinda suggested we give one another a two-week "timeout." In my last one-on-one, Melinda explained I needed to allow Carl time to "catch up" in the way I'd had time. "And don't think I'm saying you're at the finish line," she reminded me.

I'd decided to use part of the two weeks to visit my father and Peter, who lately seemed to be involved in their own emotional-tug-of-war. Carl dropped me off at the airport on his way to Pine Knoll. The awkward quiet settled on us much like the dust on the fan: layers of it, months, years of bits of life, accumulated. We didn't realize how much had built up on the fan until it stopped and forced us to see what was there. Melinda handed us the tools, but the business of cleaning hurt. After every session, she'd pray with us, and I'd want to reach for Carl's hand. I wanted my desire for him to find God and for us to find a church home to burn through to him. On Sundays, I'd visit a church, he'd visit the golf course, and we'd both visit a restaurant. So far, I hadn't found a place to worship God, and Carl hadn't found a God to worship.

This, too, will pass.

Carl pulled into the line for airline drop-offs. "Did you remember to bring cash?"

"Got the debit card," I said. "I'm good. Oh, I decided to rent a car while I'm there, so I won't have to depend on Dad or Peter to taxi me around."

"When did you decide to do that? Why didn't you tell me?"

"I called yesterday for the reservation. With trying to pack for both of us, arrange Merry Maids, postpone the newspaper and the mail, and leave a check for the lawn-care service, I honestly didn't think about it until we drove past the rental car sign. It's not like I'd keep it a secret; it's on the credit card."

I shoved my sunglasses up as a headband and looked at Carl. I wanted him to see my eyes, to see the new Leah, who had made the responsible decision and thought ahead to make reservations. Not the old Leah whose entire month's check would hang in her closet, with the price tags cut off. He'd ask, "Is that new?" That Leah would answer, "No, silly. I've had this. You just don't remember seeing it on me."

"I would have appreciated if you would have mentioned it to me first. You know I hate surprises on the credit card. Did you ask Dr. Nolan about driving? You're not driving in the city, are you? Since Katrina, you know it's not safe."

We coasted to the Southwest Airlines zone. He parked and hopped out to roll my baggage to the Sky Cap. I waited for him at the curb. "I didn't ask Dr. Nolan because I still have four months to go. I'm not going to drive in the city alone. I promise."

He lifted the sunglasses off my head and handed them to me. He moved my floppy bangs aside; his hands dusted my forehead with tenderness. Carl's eyes traced the outline of my face like he was searching for something he could recognize. He placed a hand against my cheek and said, "You know I love you, don't you?" I nodded.

"I just worry about you when you're not with me. I don't want anything to happen to you. That's why I ask and say the things I do. I care about you." He kissed me on my forehead and hurried to the car.

Carl bathed his words in sincerity, and I wanted to honor what he'd expressed as love. But as I pulled my bags up and handed my tickets over, I felt as if the gift he'd tried to give me was one size too small.

44

I'm relaxed now," I said to Peter. "Go ahead. Hit me with it. I know that's why I'm here. Spill."

Four hours after Carl dropped me off at the airport, I sat in my brother's den with my feet propped on his ottoman to keep the rest of my body from disappearing into his sofa. He walked in from the kitchen, handed me a water bottle, and sat in a deep-chocolate leather armchair.

"Sorry. I'm rude," I apologized. "Love the house, love the furniture. Did you pick one of everything in Pottery Barn or did they have a special on buying an entire house of furniture?"

"That's not very nice," he said. "I thought you'd feel right at home. I forgot. You're a decorator snob now."

We both laughed, and I remembered the luxury of being with someone who knew your history, someone who didn't need a map of your bumps and bruises, someone who could climb up into memories with you.

Peter and Dad had stayed with Carl and me while Hurricane Katrina "remodeled" New Orleans. Dad wanted to return home ten minutes after the last winds died down. Almost two weeks later, they left. Dad lived on the Northshore of the city, over one hundred feet above sea level. Two shutters were in the front garden, four of his neighbor's trees had leveled his wood fence, and every tree in a ten-mile area had wept needles and branches into his yard. Peter, on the other hand, found a stray car in his kitchen, an assortment of dead animals, and everything else ruined. He salvaged his sanity, sold the remnants, and started over. He moved to the same area as Dad, far enough away that Dad couldn't wander over, but close enough to breed contempt.

"I can't believe Dad spent all that time with you and didn't tell you about Dani."

I tucked one of the throw pillows behind my lower back. Pregnancy back aches already. "Dani? I thought you said he was dating? He's . . . wait a minute. He's dating a man?"

"D-a-n-i. That kind of Dani."

"We didn't exactly have the world's best weekend. I'm sure Dad drowned in all the drama. You know how he adores being involved in any confrontation," I said. "Are we eating real food anytime soon? This baby and I will pour gravy over that media suite soon and serve it with rice."

"Come on," he sighed, but playfully. "I now have to take care of big baby and little baby."

"Don't be a martyr. Red is not a color you wear well." I poked him as we headed out the front door. "Take me anywhere I can feast on a fried shrimp po-boy."

Peter drove along the lake front where the serpentine seawall edged the expanse of Lake Pontchartrain. On the right the street split a wide expanse of grass and oaks in varying stages of regrowth and the edges of neighborhoods on the left. The stores facing the lake were like the end-cap displays of a grocery: seafood restaurants from formal to frumpy, coffeehouses, bistros, and an assortment of buildings between their before and after photos.

Peter parked near Sissy's, a newish seafood restaurant, meaning the owners hang out and still care what the customers think. Since it was early evening and the old-fashioned fans on stands on the deck stirred the warm air, we ate outside. I had a "drunk moment" passing the long, shining brass-topped bar, dozens of glasses like so many empty mouths to be fed, hanging over it. I made myself not think of that first sip of beer and followed Peter to our table.

The issue for my brother wasn't that our father dated; it was the woman he'd chosen to date. Dani met Dad three months ago. Dani's good friend waitressed at the restaurant where my parents and a group of friends ate dinner every month. After Mom died, Dad continued to eat with his friends. On one of those nights Dani "suddenly" happened to show up.

"What can I get y'all to drink?" Our server, Nick, placed two sets of silverware rolled in napkins on the table. "Our evening specials are Apple Martinis—"

Peter interrupted. "Just two unsweet iced teas. Heavy on the lemons."

Was it my imagination that the servers seemed disappointed when no one ordered a drink? Or was that alcoholic thinking?

I thought everyone paid attention to how many times they drank or when everyone postponed tasks because what was the point, really, to make the bed when it would just get messed up later?

One of the advantages of hanging around other alcoholics was the "aha" moments when you'd hear someone's story and know being afraid to check the mailbox is alcoholic brain. My brain had to dry out to realize it was wet.

I doubt Nick or Peter thought about iced tea as much as I did.

"So, there was Dani. You know, Dad," Peter said. "He'd talk to a lawn chair, and that's when he's sober. I'm sure he'd had a drink or four by the time he met her. She was probably flattered he was so attentive. She had two ears. That was enough for him."

"I don't get why the two of you aren't talking," I said, temporarily distracted by the two seafood platters topped off with fried softshell crabs delivered to the next table.

"We'll order appetizers. Are you listening?" Peter continued. "Dad called and asked me to help move one of his friends. When he said the place was his and the friend was Dani, I decided it was time to visit."

Peter said he saw an American Express bill on the coffee table, and he "happened" to see over five hundred dollars of it was from four restaurants. Peter confronted Dad, who said where he ate, with whom, and how much money he spent was none of Peter's business.

"Basically, that was the end of that. We haven't spoken since then. And she's moving in this week."

The waiter set my plate down. I was in boiled shrimp heaven.

"And you want me to play peacemaker?" I asked between peeling, dipping, and eating.

"If you could play sense-maker that would be enough. I'm not happy that Dad and I aren't talking. But I know this woman is bad news. This is going to end badly. If he could just see that and be smart about it, then I'd be able to live with not talking to him. At least then I'd know he's fine, and he's doing what he needs to do to protect himself."

"How is this supposed to happen? Plan an intervention? We go to his house, tie him to a chair, stuff a handkerchief in his mouth? There's always an involuntary admission to the psych floor."

"How about something simple—like lunch? Did you already forget it's all about the food?"

I looked at the shrimp po-boy Nick just dropped off. "Nope. Haven't forgotten."

"When I heard you were pregnant, I was excited—for myself. I loved being Alyssa's uncle. Selfish, but I didn't remember if I'd ever told you that. She changed my life too. I think she was the first newborn baby I'd ever held for 6.2 minutes that day." Peter knew I would laugh about the timed baby-holding. The first grandchild and everyone jockeyed for arm rights. We had a button made for Mom, "I'm the Grandmother. Back off. I'm always next."

"I don't remember either. If you did, I needed to hear it again. Some days I'm so afraid, and I almost can't stop the Alyssa tape. I repeat the Serenity Prayer until I fall asleep. I know this baby is a gift, especially because of the circumstances. God gave me another reason to stay sober, another reason to stay strong, to fight. He knew I might not do it for me. But I'll stay sober and fight for this baby with every ounce of strength I have."

⸻ ∞ ⸻

"How about a celebratory snowball for your new sobriety?" Peter asked and headed in the direction of the best snowballs in the universe. Papa Sam's. Summer. Snowballs. Sam's.

When we were kids, we waited for the summer day when we could stand in the long, long line in the hot, hot sun for the first snowball of the season. Younger and shorter, stretched on tiptoes, my fingers would curl over the windowsill, my nose almost dented by the aluminum window ledge so I could watch the magic: the SnoBall Wizard ice machine blew shaved snow crystals of ice into cups. An ice-packed funnel, mashed on the top, formed a white mountain. The best tippytoed part was watching the glistening rivers of syrup as they drenched the ice and the mountain became yellow or red or green or, in my case, chocolate.

We ate our snowballs sitting under the striped-umbrella-shaded picnic tables—Peter with his usual traffic-signal green spearmint, and me with my thick, dark chocolate. I couldn't remember how long it had been since Peter and I shared this ritual. Years, probably. Years I spent polishing off bottles of wine or fruit-flavored martinis, and didn't make time for my brother. And if I did spend time with Peter, I would hardly remember the next day. This, I realized, would not be a memory drowned in alcohol.

I reached across the table and carved out a spoonful of Peter's snowball and mixed it with my chocolate. "I have an idea," I said. "Did you know if you mix these two flavors it tastes like that chocolate candy with the green in the middle?"

"If that's your idea, I made a mistake asking you to come here to help."

"You're the one asking a pregnancy-surprised, marriage-impaired, newly recovering alcoholic for help. I called Dad before I left and told him we'd work something out for tomorrow. Why don't I invite Dad and Dani to lunch? Since he knows I'm staying with you, he'll definitely want me to meet her, so he can prove to me how wrong you were about her."

Peter tossed his empty cup into the clown-mouth of the trash barrel. "And the fun begins . . ."

———— ∞ ————

"You want me to swing by and get you? I'm not so sure you should be driving right now," he said.

"Dad, if the doctor didn't think it was safe, I wouldn't be driving. I'll be fine. I'm on my way out the door," I said. The doctor defense usually quieted him. He'd argue with me, but not with the doctor. I only came to know that, unfortunately, because he never questioned Mom's doctors. "They know what's best for her, honey. Now don't argue. We don't want your mom upset," was his standard answer. I'd asked if he'd discussed it with Mom. That's when he told me a doctor said it might be best if she didn't know her cancer was stage 4, which meant the lung cancer, when they found it, had metastasized to her brain. That's when I booked a flight home.

And, once again, I'm home because, when it came to women, my father sometimes malfunctioned.

Dad and Dani didn't see me walk into Moran's Deli. They were looking at the daily specials posted on the front chalk-board. Not much to tell from the back, except her red hair had to be salon-induced, and the vertical purple and gold striped knit pullover over black stretch pants was not her best ward-robe decision. She had her arm around Dad's waist, which, besides being overkill affection for deli lunches, tugged at my memories of Mom.

Wisdom to know the difference. Okay, God, we're on.

I smoothed my sleeveless cowl-neck sweater over my baby bump, brushed off my linen skirt, and stepped over to the other side of Dad. Looking at the same board, I leaned his way and said, "Excuse me, do you know what's good here?"

His laughing surprise made the corny entrance worth-while. I hugged him and felt more than saw Dani taking out her woman-to-woman ruler. He introduced her as his "good friend, Dani" and me as "my daughter, Leah, the one I told you about, remember?"

I smiled. She smiled. We all smiled.

Dani was either a deceptively young fifty-year-old or a prematurely aged thirty-year-old. She fit the definition of a handsome woman. Not beautiful, not delicate, not cute, but not unattractive. Milky blue eyes were outlined by a too-heavy hand with blue eyeliner. She definitely didn't have my mother's graceful hands. Her long strawberry red acrylic fingernails looked misplaced on her chiseled and rough hands.

"You ready to order, honey?" Dad asked.

Dani and I both said, "Sure."

We found a booth because "Dani has back problems." She and Dad shared a side, but Dad scooted to the wall seat because "Dani has claustrophobia."

Peter was right. Dani had a hold on Dad.

"Leah, can you believe Dani has two sons? She looks great, doesn't she? How old are Cash and Sam? Oh, wait, seventeen and twenty. That's something, huh? She's been raising those boys by herself for years, and they're terrific kids. She's done a fine job being a single mother."

Her beatific smile after hearing his praise wasn't lost on my Dad, who glowed. "I'm just blessed to have such fine young men who listen to their mother. You know, Leah, some boys make bad decisions when they don't have a father figure around. Not Cash and Sam. Those boys knew we had to work as a family, even though their father didn't want to be part of their lives. Like I said, the Lord just blessed me." She said this against the backdrop of my father's woebegone expression punctuated by a "tsk, tsk" at the abandonment part of the plot.

"Can you believe a father would leave like that?" Dad asked. "What'd he do, honey, oh, just not come home one night? It's a shame, that's what it is. A shame."

She nodded, then patted his hand. "Have you told Leah about your fishing trips with the boys and the deck they're planning for your backyard?"

A smart woman, indeed. She knew that to brag on her own sons would've been cloying. Dad bragging on them let me know how much time they've all spent together and how proud he was to have done so.

He smiled. She smiled. They both smiled.

Right again, Peter.

Dad and Dani split a large fried oyster po-boy and a basket of sweet potato fries because "Dani's system can't tolerate too much fried food." Dad insisted we try the bread pudding, and Dani graciously allowed him to scoot out of the booth to order it. She did, though, smile sweetly and tell him she wouldn't mind at all "taking care of dessert," which gave him an opportunity to, once again, crow about her generosity and kindness.

She eyed Dad as he excused himself through a mixed bag of construction workers, suits, and soccer dads, then she turned and made dead-on eye contact. "Your father is won-der-ful. One of the nicest men in the world (which sounded like "whirled"). Of course, you know that already."

Her cell phone jingled, and I was treated to a mother-son bonding moment. "Hi, sweetie. No, I'm not at work. Remember I asked for the day off so I could meet Mr. Bob's daughter? (smile) No, no, I've been working so many hours, they were happy to let me go for a day. (eye roll) Um. No. I don't think we're going to be long. (eyebrows raise questioningly) Well, okay, but you know you don't have to do that. (unabashed pride) Sure, sweetie, I'll tell Mr. Bob you said you can't wait to go fishing. Bye, Sam-Sam. Talk to you later."

Dani snapped her phone closed. "Sam called to ask if he could go to Home Depot and buy a book of deck plans. Those boys just adore your father. They've been such company for him. You know how lonely he must be, poor man. I'm so glad he's had some time to enjoy himself. He certainly deserves it."

She must have spotted Dad headed back to the table because she leaned my way, and said, "Sometimes it's just hard for men to do what they need for themselves. Your dad deserves to be happy, and he seems to be really happy since we met."

I sat back and waited for the credits to roll.

⸺◦⊗◦⸺

"Dani made Gloria Thornton's performances look like Scout Finch's ham acting in the county play."

Peter and I shared his backyard swing. Since my feet couldn't reach the ground, Peter pushed us back and forth.

"Can you stop with the literary references already?" He looked up, then back at me, "Wait. I've got this one. *To Kill a Mockingbird.* Atticus Finch. He was a lawyer I remember."

"You *did* read in school," I teased.

The sultry quiet erupted. A trio of white-faced squirrels on a feeding frenzy, pecans clutched between their tiny paws, chased one another up, down, and around the trees. The neighbor's orange cat watched in bemusement from its perch on top of the fence post. It had jumped down once already, sending the squirrels into a manic run to the tree's top branches. I watched their crazed but amusing behavior, and knew I'd felt that same frenetic lunacy. I knew, too, that wasn't the life I wanted.

"I forgot to mention Dani figured out Dad's hot spot—"

"Yuck, Leah, what—"

"I meant she's all over the 'I love to garden and plant flowers and play in the dirt thing.'"

"Didn't I tell you?"

"Stop. You're almost sounding like him. Do you want to be the cat or the squirrel?" I pointed to the nature drama in front of us. "I've been watching them, thinking how I've been like

306

those squirrels, running all over the place trying to get what I need. Sometimes I do. But I'm always at the mercy of that thing hanging over my head or scaring me away from what I need to do. You can't let his problem become your problem."

"Might be too late for that."

"I hope not," I said, and hopped off the swing to call our father.

Knowing Dani would be working Sunday, I called Dad and asked him to come to Peter's house so we could talk. I told him and later, Peter, if they didn't agree to meet with me, I'd stop talking to both of them. Sometimes, guilt is an effective motivator.

The next morning, the three of us sat at Peter's pedestal table, and I held court. "You're both going to listen, and I'm going to talk. I'm leaving here tomorrow knowing my family is not like those goofy squirrels outside."

"What squirrels? What is she talking about?"

"Dad, no talking, remember? I'll start with you. I know you're lonely. You have to give Peter and me some credit. When's the last time you dated? Almost thirty years ago? You have every right to spend time with someone who makes you happy. And don't think this is about your kids not wanting Mom replaced. You're a successful man, generous, and kind. Not many men like you are left, and sometimes you're the ones taken advantage of. Why would you want to live with someone you're not ready to have a permanent relationship with? You've known her three months. Just be careful."

Dad opened his mouth, then looked at Peter and closed it again.

"I'm almost finished," I told him. He resettled himself in the chair, "harrumphed," and waved his hand for me to continue. "Once she moves in, especially with her sons, your life is going to change. It concerns us that she's hurrying this along with the 'have to renew the lease, don't have enough money, where are we going to live' story. What would she have done if she hadn't met you? Where would she have gone? And if this doesn't work out between the two of you in a month or a year, then what? If you're going to do this, you need to protect yourself financially. By the way, if you don't want people up in your business, don't leave credit card bills hanging around. Peter may have looked too closely, but he was right. Did you win a lottery you didn't tell us about? A daughter who's a recovering alcoholic, and you're spending more money on drinks than dinner. Dad, really."

Then I turned to Peter. Dad seemed almost amused.

I told Peter we didn't have to like Dani. "It would make life easier if we did, but this is Dad's choice, not ours. If there's one thing AA is teaching me, it's that people have to be responsible for themselves—not just their decisions, but the consequences of them."

"I want the two of you to agree to be honest with one another. For me, right now, agree to allow one another a life. One day at a time, guys."

"Leah, before you and Dad leave, if we're going to be all about honesty, I need you to hear this."

If Dad hadn't looked as confused as I did, I might have suspected they'd planned their disagreement to suck me in.

Peter apologized for being invisible, for not making time to spend with me, especially after we lost Alyssa. "I used school and my job as excuses, but the truth is you know I don't like Carl. I know what you mean about Dani, because I wasn't all that fond of Carl, but you loved him."

"Carl's a good man. He's given Leah a nice life. He works hard," Dad said.

"Dad, you don't have to defend Carl," I said. "I've known for a long time how Peter feels about him. I don't think you ever understood because, well, you've had more of a relationship with Carl than with Peter."

"Leah, your turn not to talk. Dad, you know she's right. You and I don't have the same things in common that you have with Carl. I don't blame either one of you. Sometimes it's like he's your son, not me. But that's something we need to work out between the two of us. Later."

Dad said nothing, but I could tell by the way he stared at the table, running his fingers along the thick edges, he was beginning to own some of what Peter had said.

Peter continued. "When you first married, Leah, you seemed happy. As time passed, you seemed less like the sister I knew. Then, when Alyssa died, something died in you. Whatever and whenever Carl and his family wanted you to do something, you did it. Did you think you owed them something for getting to live the lifestyle you have? Carl degraded you, made jokes at your expense, and you'd just take it. Carl's parents had control over him, so he had to have it over you?"

"I know, Peter," I said. "I've been dealing with some of this for the past two months. I guess I don't understand why you're telling me all this now."

"Truth? You wouldn't have believed me before or even listened. Truth? I think Carl's the one who should have been admitted, not you. Final truth? You need time to yourself—time to focus on being sober, on being Leah again. I want you to think about that. You can stay here for as long as you need.

You and the baby. Carl's controlled your life a lot longer than you have. You had to go to Brookforest to get sober. I think you need to consider being on your own to stay sober."

Dad shook his head, his voice low. "You know your mother and I were never big churchgoers. Felt like we could live as good, honest people without the hoopla. We probably should've done a better job with the two of you. I don't claim to know much about the Bible, but I'm pretty sure that walking out of your marriage isn't something God would want. I'm kind of glad your mother's not here. Break her heart to know you were telling your sister to leave her husband." He looked at me. "Break her heart if you did it too."

"Leah, I didn't mean you should divorce Carl. I am saying you can't have it both ways. You can't preach being responsible for yourself and your decisions to other people and not follow your own advice."

Peter's bluntness didn't shock me. What shocked me was that his words found safe passage through my defense mechanisms to connect to feelings I couldn't yet speak myself.

I knew you could stay in a marriage and really not be there at all. I didn't know you could leave a marriage to try to stay in it.

45

Melinda suggested I use Carl's session time plus my own while he was away. After the weekend with my brother and father, I regretted I couldn't have given our sessions to both of them.

"Analogy woman that I am, I'm so enamored with myself for this brilliant squirrel/cat connection to our lives, I shared it with Peter. Then after my brother, Dad, and I talked, I realized we weren't either one of those. We're the nuts."

"It's important to discover who you are, don't you think?" Melinda's attempt at a granite-face only made both of us laugh more.

"Let's talk about Peter's concern," she said. "He's right about your needing to focus on sobriety. From what you've told me, you've made a meeting everyday since you were discharged. What about when you went home?"

"Peter had already checked out meeting times and places. Who knew you could Google AA meetings? I just made it work. A weird feeling at first, going to an out-of-town meeting. Regulars think you're new, and then you have to convince them you're not. Makes for a fun beginning."

"Planning ahead. What a concept. If it works for out-of-town, it works for everything else. It appears you and Carl have a number of social events to attend because of business. Have you thought about how you'll handle those?"

"Yes. I'm staying home with the baby. Honestly, I was never a barfly kind of drinker, so that's not the problem. Happy drinking, wahoo party drinking, that's a tough one for me. Rebecca suggested holding a glass of water, club soda, or ginger ale because people usually don't ask if you want a drink if you're holding one. For right now, a virgin version of an alcoholic drink is still too close. I've told myself to stay away from those because it feeds into stupid brain and the whole 'romanticizing' about the glory days."

"Good strategies. Those could make the difference between Drunk Leah and New Leah. Sobriety's your focus, and you don't need to carry any other emotional baggage during your first year. That's why we tell new people in the program not to make any drastic, life-changing decisions for the whole first year of sobriety. Like Peter, I'm not saying stay or go. I'm not sure you're at a place in your relationship to decide yet. But a year's a good rule of thumb."

Melinda had read notes from Ron's sessions with me at Brookforest and wanted me to consider how some of my feelings about sex may have been seeded. "I know you love your mother. We're not placing blame, but if we don't say, 'I see where this started,' we pass on behaviors. Here's what I think you need to consider giving back to the past: How did you know when your mother was angry?"

"She wouldn't talk much."

"What if she was very angry?"

"She'd talk even less."

"Would you say your parents had fights often?"

"No. In fact, only one that I can remember. She threw one of her shoes at him one night. It might have been a spiked heel. I don't even know how it started."

"Not *showing* anger can be a form of being angry for people who shove it all inside. Your mother may have grown up thinking anger is wrong. Maybe she was told to be nice on the outside, even though you may be seething inside. How much anger can one body hold? Not much, and it gets handled in some unhealthy ways . . . like addictions, like your mother's afternoon drinking."

"Well, she must have stuffed more than anger. Can you stuff affection in there too?" I crossed my arms and hoped this would soon end.

"You already know the answer to that one. She had a difficult time expressing emotion, not feeling emotion. She emotionally detached, and I think that's what you've been afraid of as a mother yourself. You don't want to emotionally detach from this baby because of Alyssa. Your mom did the best she could with what she had. You need to remember that. Because your mother's dead, you may never know what precipitated these behaviors for her. The good news is you don't need to know to heal."

Listening to Melinda, I began to see my mother not as her "mom" label but as a young woman like myself: hesitant, uncertain, a woman told to deny her feelings. I wanted her to know that I understood.

Mom didn't give it back.

She never had the chance.

I'm your chance, Mom.

My cell phone rang just as I fastened my seat belt. I dug it out of my purse, flipped it open, and started the car. Carl called to tell me that he wouldn't be home in a few days like we'd both expected.

"Another two weeks?"

"Unexpected delays. Had to rebid some of the jobs. Construction costs increased. We're reviewing the building plans for the retail and office spaces. I thought I'd be able to make it home this weekend, but I don't think I'd be able to leave until late Friday night. My Monday meeting starts at 7:30, so I'd need to leave home Sunday." The fatigue in Carl's voice surprised me. I expected him to be energized in this effort to prove himself worthy of the business.

"Do you want me to drive there for a few days?"

Please say no. Please say no.

"I'd love for you to be here, but I'm so busy right now we'd barely see each other. Besides, you have your own stuff to do . . . your meetings, sessions . . ."

When I asked him if he wanted me to reschedule the appointment with Dr. Nolan next week where we'd, hopefully, find out if we should buy blue or pink, his response lapsed into an irritation I hadn't heard for a while.

"When did we decide we wanted to know this?"

"I don't think we talked about it specifically. It's just what happens next."

"Well, do we have to do this? I thought we wanted to be surprised like we were for Alyssa."

I hesitated.

The truth will set you free.

"Honestly, I didn't press the issue then because you're the one who didn't want to know. Not me. If you don't want to know the sex of this baby, Dr. Nolan and I won't tell you."

"Anything else you haven't mentioned?"

"I made an appointment with a contractor. I had some ideas about expanding the nursery to make—"

"Why aren't you talking to me about this before you go off and make plans?"

"Carl, it's an appointment to talk. I haven't signed papers. I thought I needed to not wait until a month before the baby's due to make changes."

"You seem to be doing a lot of thinking while I'm gone."

"Yes, I guess I am."

Isn't it great?

I closed the cell phone, rested my forehead on the steering wheel, and gave myself time to decompress. I didn't want to drive under the influence of disappointment. Not even to an AA meeting.

Melinda started my session where we ended the last. "A mother afraid to show affection doesn't provide a healthy climate for showing any kind of physical tenderness," she said.

"My mother never discussed sex, didn't see herself as a sexual being, and certainly didn't want to see me that way," I said. "She warned me so often about being touched and how it could lead to pregnancy, I thought feeling good had to be bad."

"You talked about connecting the dots with Carl, sex, and alcohol. Other dots needed to be connected. Like the ones we talked about last week," Melinda propped a small white board on her desk. She drew circles with a marker as she talked. "Like this dot. Your mother's inability to feel good about being sexual and intimate."

A few inches away, she made another circle. "Then, that experience in high school. God watched over all three of you girls that night. Maybe you haven't even thought about that, but I hope you thank Him. You were assaulted by drunks, who threw beer on you, degraded you, and one put his hands between your legs. Just because his hand never reached his intended target didn't make the whole incident any less invasive or repugnant."

Those hands, from all those years ago, crawled on my skin. I looked out the window. "Well, he didn't rape me."

Melinda closed the marker. "Listen to me. Sexual assault is rape without penetration, but the stress disorders are the same. Clearly, this incident didn't 'go away.' And it's the source of some of your avoidance or withdrawal behaviors."

"I've tried to bury that night for over ten years," I said. "The only people who knew were in the car with me. For certain, I wasn't going to tell my parents. I shouldn't have been there at all. I already knew how my Mom felt."

"You didn't cause this by being there, Leah. This was done to you. I want you to understand this connection of that experience not being your fault because the sexual abuse in your marriage isn't your fault either."

Confusion. A disconnect in my brain signaled an alarm. "I don't think you understood Ron's file. Carl didn't abuse me." I shifted in my chair. Why didn't she have candy on her desk? My hand itched.

Melinda moved to the chair across from me and crossed her legs, still holding her two-dot board and marker. "You weren't sexually abused in your marriage?" She drew another dot. A small silver cross swung away from the hollow in her neck when she leaned toward me. "Really? So explain to me what I may have wrong."

I stood and edged my hands into the pockets of my skirt. I rocked heel to toe, heel to toe.

Melinda sat back, her hair a black curly pillow pressed against the chair. "What's this all about?"

"It's uncomfortable, sitting so long. I need to stretch." My trembling voice couldn't make the lie sound like the truth.

"No problem. You can still explain to me what happened between you and Carl. Help me understand."

"Do we have to do this? You obviously don't believe me. What do you want me to say?" *Isn't living it enough? Do I have to talk about it too?* I paced in front of the desk.

"Just tell me whatever you need to." Melinda's soft voice spread itself like a blanket on my cold fear.

I sat again and kneaded the back of my neck, pushed my fingertips into my muscles.

"Abuse is different. It's not like he hit me. He didn't."

"No, of course not. Do you think that's all abuse is? "

I shrugged. "Well, I guess I did, but I'm sure you're about to tell me that's not true."

"You were sexually abused in your marriage. No is no is no."

"But what's that submit to your husband passage in the Bible? Not that we spent much time in church or in God's word, but Carl remembered that one. He'd tell me wives were supposed to please their husbands."

Melinda reached for the Bible on her desk. "Listen to this passage from Ephesians 5:22-25: 'Wives, submit to your own husbands, as to the Lord. For the husband is head of the wife, as also Christ is head of the church; and He is savior of the body. Therefore, just as the church is subject to Christ, so let the wives be to their own husbands in everything. Husbands, love your wives, just as Christ also loved the church and gave Himself for it . . .'" She left the Bible open to the passage and placed it back on her desk.

"Does that sound like God said husbands should force their wives to have sex? Was there anything about ignoring your wife when she tells you to stop? No. We serve an equal opportunity God. Husbands and wives have different roles, but one is no less a person in God's eyes than the other. Submission isn't slavery. It's not about allowing someone to rule you with abusive control. Would Christ love the church as Carl loved you? Being under someone's protection means feeling safe, honored, respected. Is that how you feel?"

I didn't answer. I curled my hands into fists. I wanted to curl my entire body into one.

"It wasn't your fault. Do you hear me? Just like that incident at the lake wasn't your fault. It's not unusual for victims to feel responsible and take the blame for what happened to them. That's exactly what their abusers want them to think. If you feel guilty, then you're going to continue in the cycle of abuse because you think you've done something to cause it. You've blamed yourself. It's time to stop."

I collapsed inside myself like a fluttering parachute at descent, covering broken images. My soul clenched, hands tugged at silk sheets, breaths pushed against pleading. Biting my lips until they bled. When I tasted the iron sweetness of blood, it was almost over. I could close another curtain.

But the curtains of memory wouldn't stay closed, they were shoved opened by something unexpected. A word, the short click of a locked door, a certain touch. I'd carried Alyssa to our bedroom to nurse her. Carl was eating breakfast. I drank in Alyssa's softness. Her urgency and persistence in feeding delighted and amazed me. Propped in bed, my back to the door, I didn't know Carl walked in. I didn't know he had undressed until I felt him slide next to me.

"Alyssa's nursing," I said.

"I know," he said, "but you have more than one breast, don't you?"

I wasn't sure when I'd started crying. I wasn't sure when I'd stop.

Ironic. Carl and I both are so needy for attention. What I wanted from my mother, he wanted from his own parents. After losing Vic, they discarded their emotions and replaced them with control. Melinda said Carl sought in me the affection he craved from them. And in the same way his parents controlled him, he controlled me. Powerlessness bred control.

"The Carl you fell in love with was the Carl more like your father. You recognized what Carl felt for you as love because it's what you felt from your father. Taking care of someone and letting someone take care of you, that's what you defined as love. But, ultimately, you can't marry your father."

Melinda waited quietly as the sobbing gave way to uneven shuddering breaths. She held my hands in hers and prayed.

Then she asked me, "What was in all this for you?"

I wanted to slap her. Manipulation. When had it acquired a zip code here? "I can't believe you're saying this to me," I said, my words strangled with anger. "What are you talking about? You already told me it wasn't my fault. You changed your mind? I don't get it."

"Sexual abuse—no abuse—is never the victim's fault. That's not what I'm talking about—being victimized. I'm asking you about this role you have as a victim. What's the payoff?"

"I don't understand. Payoff? Are you saying I got something out of being controlled? Sure, I was . . . what . . . being paid by Carl to stay powerless?"

I opened another curtain. Memory flashed.

I remembered the day at Brookforest when Matthew told me about the other session with Ron. I'd pouted and said I was being punished, no one gave me choices, allowed me decisions. Why did everyone pick on me?

"Your being a victim of sexual assault, the subtle manipulations, that's something else entirely, do you hear me?" Melinda said. "This 'Leah as victim' is the Leah your brother Peter saw overtaking his sister. You need to own this Leah too. When you wrote checks that bounced, what did you do?"

How many curtains, God? How many?

You can do all things I ask you to do. Christ gives you strength and power.

"When you overspent on the credit cards, what did you do? When you backed into the mailbox? When you got drunk at company dinners? How did you make it all go away?"

"I chose to not make decisions. I asked Carl what he wanted me to do. Should I buy this or that? If this didn't work, then it certainly wasn't my fault. I didn't make the decision," I said.

Deciding not to decide is a decision.

I learned, through my years with Carl, how to maneuver my way through his world. To get what I wanted, I'd give him what he wanted. Alcohol was my key. It opened the door to falseness that could buy me peace.

I didn't have to like having sex to understand and know what it could do for me when I was sober.

46

After my marathon session with Melinda I told Molly that my drive home was sobering. Neither one of us laughed.

As close as I felt to Molly, I couldn't share any more than that. I didn't even know how I would share it with Carl. The delay in his finishing the project proved to be a blessing. It bought me time.

Carl couldn't come with me to Dr. Nolan's, so I asked Molly if she'd go with me. I didn't want to be alone when Dr. Nolan told me pink or blue. As thrilled as I was about this baby, I'd already spent weeks and months collecting passport stamps out of "what if?" land. I tried to reconcile my joy and my pain. My excitement about the baby felt like betrayal when I thought of Alyssa. But yet I couldn't deny the happiness I felt carrying this child. I prayed not to be consumed with worry. Some days I did better than others. Some days the questions stung like bees. What if the baby's a girl? What if she looks like Alyssa? What if she doesn't? What if she's not as cute as Alyssa? What if she's cuter? What if . . . ?

This pregnancy was different, not just emotionally, but physically. Dr. Nolan mentioned toxemia and the issue of pregnancy-related diabetes. I didn't remember gaining weight like this when I was pregnant with Alyssa. Not that I'd stopped to calculate the gallons of ice cream I'd consumed since the beginning of July. I trusted Dr. Nolan to figure it all out.

I changed into my fashionable, crinkled paper, baby chicken yellow exam wear and waited for Dr. Nolan. Molly amused herself with the assortment of dolls, bears, and toys around the exam room.

"You'd think she was a pediatrician," Molly remarked, opening a quilted cotton ark filled with finger puppets of Noah, his family, and a few animals. "This is too cute." Molly giggled as she slipped Noah on her finger. She started to slip on more of the ark, when Dr. Nolan stepped in.

"Hey, isn't that a clever thing? Watch this." Dr. Nolan showed Molly how the ark became a carrying pouch, handed it to her, and said, "All the way from Peru."

"Are we on *Jeopardy*?" Molly looked at me with eye-rolling confusion.

"That ark was made in Peru," Dr. Nolan said. "From all over the world—Africa, India, Kenya, Vietnam, Bangladesh—handcrafted. God blessed me when I opened my practice here. I wanted to bless mothers who didn't have the advantages we have. I found A Greater Gift, and I've been gifting ever since."

Molly was entranced. She traded Noah for a parrot flute.

"Don't even think about it, girlfriend. This baby's already wiggling all over the place," I only half-jokingly warned her.

"Speaking of advantages," Dr. Nolan laughed, "how's Princess Leah? And where's Jean Luc?"

Molly's eyebrows met in the middle when she heard Dr. Nolan's name for Carl.

"He's on a mission in Pine Knoll, sent by the Federation Thorntons. They're opening a new enterprise there. Lowercase 'e' enterprise."

Dr. Nolan gooped up my growing belly with gel. "This stuff wasn't always heated, you know. Now everything's supposed to be some kind of spa experience. How are we doing, Princess?"

Molly picked up a little drum. "No, you can't play with that either," I said.

"She's no fun," said Molly.

"I hope that's a pretend pout or no Snickers Blizzard for you on the way home. And, to answer your question, Dr. Nolan, I don't know. I'm not feeling like I did with Alyssa. Maybe I don't remember feeling swollen. "

"Um-hm. Hm. Yes." Dr. Nolan scanned and looked at the ultrasound screen. The probe glided through the gel like a rollerball.

She scanned the screen. "What do you think, Molly?"

Molly squinted, tilted her head from right to left, poked the screen, and then leaned in. "Well, I'm not really sure." She reached for my hand. "I think I'd have to say, based on the equipment, a girl?"

I closed my eyes as I felt the sting of bittersweet joy. God, I don't want to cry in this room with my very best friend who is desperately trying to have a baby. I opened my eyes wide and hoped nothing would drip out.

"Can you do this?" Molly knew. I didn't have to pretend to be brave.

I tapped Dr. Nolan's arm. "My turn."

"Now, wait a minute." She turned the monitor toward me. "Tell me what you think." The probe skated across my tummy again.

"Molly, you either need glasses or biology class. That looks like a boy," I said.

"Well, well," Dr. Nolan said, and gently squeezed my arm. "God is quite the character. When He tells you all things are

323

possible, you'd better listen, sister." She set the probe down, stripped off her gloves, and grabbed one of my hands and one of Molly's. "You're both right. Twins."

———— ✺ ————

Somehow between the hysterical teary-eyed blubbering and the spontaneous open-mouthed giggling, we made it to my car.

Dr. Nolan practically had to kick us out of her office. "No more baby viewing. Buy your own ultrasound machine. I hear tell some of those Hollywood types have. The Thorntons could buy one for every room in their house. Now take these pictures." She handed them all to Molly. "Leah, you make an appointment for when Mr. Man's in town. Having two babies is a new game."

In the car we called Carl, Devin, my dad, Peter, my in-laws. They all had the same reaction: stunned silence followed by questions, screeches of excitement, and more questions. I also called the staff at Brookforest and Rebecca with the same results. Carl wanted to drive home that afternoon. I reassured him I could email the pictures. Otherwise, I looked the same.

"Gloria's probably already calling Ivy League schools to find out if they can get a discount," said Molly. She volunteered to drive my car home, so I could start multiplying by two.

"Glad I had that brilliant idea to get in touch with the contractor," I said. "Now we have to figure out where these babies are . . . Babies." My heart pounded with grateful disbelief. "Babies, Molly. I'm having ba-bies. Can you believe it?"

"It's so incredible. God is good, isn't He?"

Her eyes were fixed on the Post Oak Road traffic, but I knew that hard stare was not simply concentration. "Molly, you're so right. God is good. He put you in my life, and you've saved me over and over again. I feel like I can never repay you. I pray for you and Devin all the time. Your blessing will come, too, I know it. Little Molly and Devin babies . . ."

She held up her hand, "Stop. No little babies."

"But, Molly, you and Devin will go back to *in vitro* or you could adopt. A private adoption."

Her fingers tightened on the steering wheel. "Leah," her voice was raspy, "we postponed *in vitro* because . . . because I have breast cancer."

"Believe me, this isn't what I had in mind for telling you. It was too much to hide, especially when you'd go for broke talking about babies." She said, "But you're my crazy best friend, and I expect that from you."

We stopped about forty-two seconds after Molly dropped the news because I threatened to throw up if she didn't. We still sat in the car in the parking lot of a nail salon, a dry cleaners, and a bakery. A perfect setting to discuss your best friend's almost accident-inducing announcement of cancer.

My best friend has cancer.

Sky-high joy followed by plummeting pain.

Molly explained she'd gone for a routine mammography because of her family history. "The Breast Center called after the first mammogram and asked me to come back. That's happened before, so I didn't think it was anything to be concerned about. But after that appointment, they said I needed a needle biopsy."

"Why didn't you tell me? Call me?"

Molly smiled at the question. "Your dance card was full, sister. Besides, the biopsy could've come back clean."

"But it didn't. And you still didn't call. Now I'm sad, and I'm puzzled."

"Devin and I needed to sort things out. We wanted to know what we'd be up against before we started telling everyone. We figured it'd be easier that way."

She told me the oncologist reported it was stage 1, which meant it hadn't gone to the lymph nodes. "If there aren't any cancerous cells around it, and Dr. Warriner said she doesn't suspect there will be, the survival rate's usually one hundred percent."

"When are you getting it removed? Isn't there something you can do now?"

"The lumpectomy is scheduled for next week, and the game plan is five to seven weeks of radiation therapy, five days a week. Pray. You can pray now."

—∞∞∞—

Instead of driving home right away, Molly and I went to the bakery shop we saw when we'd pulled into the parking lot.

We ordered croissants with chicken salad and a large slab of carrot cake. I could've skipped the chicken salad, but Molly said eating for three required some protein.

I squeezed a lemon in my water. "Molly, I'm so sorry. For weeks now, you've focused on me. Heck, for weeks, I've focused on me. And now, here you're facing this awful news, and I feel like a slug."

"How could you know? Don't be upset with yourself. Before we got the report, Devin and I thought about important stuff we had to do. Like turning the sprinklers on, changing the air conditioner filters, and dropping clothes off at the cleaners."

"You're kidding." It wasn't a question.

"Well, sort of. We decided to not think about it until we knew for sure. We just went on with the day to day stuff. And we prayed. I mostly prayed not to look like Carl if I had to lose my hair."

I almost choked on my sandwich. "Now that would be a fright. He could loan you one of those toupees he never wears. They're in boxes in our attic. I made sure to label them because opening one of those boxes can be scary. His mother bought those things, she said, for his self-esteem. I think she didn't like his baldness because she thought it made her seem older."

"Thanks, but I think I'll pass on the hair rugs. Devin said I'd make a lovely bald woman," she laughed. Molly's voice slid into serious when she said, "I couldn't do this without him. He's my first best friend."

Whatever twinge of silly jealousy vibrated in my heart, I hushed it just looking at Molly when she talked about her husband. Something inside her illuminated her face, her eyes, her body.

She scraped the cream cheese icing off her carrot cake and spread it on my slice. This dessert thing always seemed to work out in my favor.

"I'm not glad this happened. But it's made me realize what Devin means to me in ways I never expected. He sees in me what I can't see in myself. Like he can reach into my soul, put it in my hand, and tell me, 'Here's your gift. It's you.' I don't know how he manages to make me feel so special." She wiped away tears and, when I saw the unabashed love in her eyes, I had to turn away for a moment. The brightness burned.

I stopped eating. I wanted to say something, something meaningful and important, but I couldn't. I was in unfamiliar territory.

She ate the last bite of cake from the plate, and said, "You know what I love most about Devin? We can be alone in a closet and make one another laugh."

That night, as I chopped mushrooms, onions, and green peppers for my omelet, I pictured Molly's intensity this afternoon when she talked about Devin. I'd carried it with me since she'd said "alone in a closet."

I pushed the knife through the onion. The knife thwacked against the maple cutting board. Thwack. Another cut. Thwack. Thwack. *Carl and I struggled alone in this oversized house.* I moved the knife slowly through the layers as the pungent odor burned the inside of my nose. I sniffled and wiped my stinging eyes with the back of my hand.

I finished chopping, but tears plopped on the cutting board. I'm a well of emptiness. The truth rumbled in the hollowness like an earthquake. It cracked open the walls of my heart, and sand poured through like trying to fill a sieve.

Carl and I weren't going to make it through this together. We had too many spaces in ourselves and in our marriage.

We shared painful closet experiences.

Molly and Devin shared intimacy.

It wasn't about the sex.

It was about the intimacy.

47

So, how was your day?

Fine, thank you.

I'm having twins, and my friend's having cancer.

I told Rebecca after the AA meeting that if I hadn't been in recovery, I don't know how I would've made it through that day. As usual, no-frills Rebecca reminded me pronto, "You wouldn't have made it. You would have been drunk."

We talked about Step 4: Make a searching and fearless moral inventory of ourselves. Rebecca told me to think of it as cataloging the closet of our souls. Another closet. I told her the inventory might be searching, but I couldn't promise fearless, at least not without a drink or two or ten. The 12 Steps are clever though. The first three suck you right in, and then they slam you with this one. Right about the time you've got a grip on this sobriety business, they send you to a step that makes you want to dip your Big Book in a barrel of beer. Here's the deal breaker as I saw it. No Step 4. Then no Steps 5-12. Step 4 was the gatekeeper step. Without it you couldn't climb the rest.

A sufficient explanation for me. I wouldn't sacrifice eight steps because I balked at spilling out my guts on paper.

I'd spilled them out for years in toilets and yards all over the country.

———✖———

I called Molly and asked if she wanted to go shopping while she still had hair. "My maternity clothes won't make it through twindom. Besides, it's not healthy for you to stay inside and think about your boob all day," I said. Before I left, I dumped everything out of my "go to AA purse," a large hobo, which held my Big Book, a steno pad for notes, pens, a few pieces of chocolate, and the usual wallet, lipstick, keys. Retail therapy required a smaller option, which I'd bought not long before my addiction therapy. I tossed a few essentials into my snazzy Coach metallic crossover purse, then went to my closet to find my credit card wallet. It looked more pregnant than I did. I opened it and flipped through dozens of my little plastic tickets to happiness. A euphoria I now realized I paid for some nights with my body.

I looked at my Big Book, dumped on my bed with my other purse paraphernalia, looked at the wad of credit cards, and headed to Carl's office. I fed the credit cards to the paper shredder one by one as the steel cutters grinded their satisfaction. And with each one, I whispered a prayer for the strength to avoid temptation.

I walked out of the house, my purse and my soul leaner.

Carl called my cell as I turned into Molly's driveway. He said he'd left the site and would be home by dinner. He told me he needed to talk to me—one of those generic, ambiguous statements that created macramé with my internal body parts. His responses to my questions sounded clipped and abrupt, like the gardener had sheared them with hedge trimmers. I wondered if he had arrived at the same realization about our marriage. Or our lack of one.

I didn't tell Molly about the plastic card slaughter or Carl's news. I didn't tell her I struggled with when and how and where to tell Carl that I wanted to leave. She needed relief from drama more than I did right now.

We spent two hours flinging clothes around in the maternity boutique. Finally, I decided I'd burned so many calories pulling clothes on and off that I could eat an ice cream sundae at Cold Stone. Twice.

"The mountain of outfits by the register is taller than I am. That means I'm done," I announced when Molly walked into the dressing room. She didn't answer me, and her face looked like it had been cast in concrete.

I regretted thinking this would be a pleasant distraction for Molly. But before I said anything, her expression cracked a bit, and I spotted a twinge of a smile. I looked her over. Something seemed curiously skewed. "Isn't that one of the tops I tried on?"

"Yes, so what do you think?" She straightened the shoulders on the white sleeveless smocked shirt she wore, then she slowly turned around.

"Oh, you didn't," I said, Theresa-like, with attitude, and cracked up.

"Oh, yes I did," she said, and her laugh filled the dressing room.

She'd turned the fake baby bump around so that it rested right above her fanny. We laughed all the way to the register where I paid for everything in cash.

Molly wanted to stop in the shoe store, and I welcomed the chance to sit.

"I wonder if it's possible to have a shoe addiction," I mused as I ogled Christian Louboutin pumps and Stuart Weitzman flats. "Why do I love shoes? Is it something Freudian?"

"People think making love starts in the bedroom, but it really doesn't. It starts in the kitchen," said Molly, ever-so-casually, as she walked around in a pair of knee-high natural suede boots while she held a pair of black vintage leather ones.

"When did we start talking about this? And are you supposed to be that loud when you're being so freaky?"

"I heard 'love' and 'Freud.' Made an assumption. Oops." She sat next to me and held out her feet so I could pull off the boots.

"The kitchen? Really?" I didn't know if I might have treaded on sacred ground. But Molly and I had traveled so far, maybe we found new boundaries to cross.

She alternately grunted and yanked the other pair of boots on her feet. "I don't mean location. Well, maybe. But Devin and I realized if we couldn't be friends and enjoy one another's company in the kitchen, then why would we think the bedroom's going to work? I think too many couples try to start a relationship in the bedroom, then get to the kitchen and realize they don't have anything to say to one another. That's all I meant."

No, Molly, that's everything.

While I waited for Carl that evening, I bombarded God with prayer. Stalker prayer. I even called Rebecca with one of those "unspoken" prayer requests. Loops of "what if" and "maybe" careened around my brain. I asked God to give me serenity. I didn't know what or how to pray, but I trusted God knew.

I ordered Chinese for dinner so we wouldn't have to go out in public. I even set the dining room table, with plates you couldn't throw away and silverware, not plastic ware. The take-out boxes decorated the table like little gifts. Fragrant presents of ginger, peppercorns, and garlic.

When I saw the headlights of Carl's convertible through the silk taffeta drapes in the dining room, I pushed aside the uneasiness that threatened to come between us and sat in the living room to wait for him. He opened the door, and fearsome pain and sadness walked in with him and left their footprints on every feature of his face.

I raised my face to him. He leaned in my direction, but looked over my shoulder as I kissed his cheek. "Welcome home," I said, and tried to decipher the worry etched in his forehead.

"Thanks. It was a long ride," he said and draped his suit jacket on the winged-back chair, unknotted and pulled off his tie, then folded it in half, and set it on top of his jacket. "What's for dinner?"

"I ordered Chinese. Everything's in the dining room."

"Great. I'm going to wash my hands, throw some water on my face," he informed me as he headed to our bedroom.

Whatever distracted him rendered me invisible. He didn't look at me; he looked through me. I filled two glasses with water, set them down by our plates, and opened the containers of ginger salmon, lemon pepper shrimp, lettuce wraps, and fried rice. My stomach growled its impatience, so I spooned some of everything in my plate. I'd just started to serve his food when he returned.

"You don't have to do that," he said and reached across the table so I could hand him his plate. His voice wasn't at all boorish; in fact, it sounded like he buried a "thank you" in his words.

We both sat, I nodded "grace" at God, and Carl adjusted his napkin.

I plunged into the ocean of confusion. "So, you said there was something we needed to talk about."

He set his fork on his plate. I realized at that moment that he hadn't cleaned his fork before he ate.

"I wanted to wait until after dinner—"

Maybe I should've worn a life jacket before I jumped.

"I'm sorry. I—"

He raised his hand. "No, don't apologize. I didn't expect to get home so late. We can talk now."

"Can we eat and talk?"

He almost smiled. "Sure. But I need you to just listen. As in try not to ask questions right away."

Fried rice occupied most of the space in my mouth. I nodded. Whatever this was, it wasn't about us. I sensed a weariness in him unconnected to me.

"My parents, specifically my father, informed me that they've been in discussion with a major industrial supply chain for several months. About selling their business. Last week, the corporation made my parents an offer they said they couldn't refuse, and they didn't. They sold the business."

I swallowed my dumbfoundedness. But I could almost feel my eyelids leap to my eyebrows. My eyes felt like flashbulbs.

"Apparently, they were about to sign an agreement to purchase, and that's when my parents invited me into the business." He paused and looked at me. "Here's the killer part. My parents knew that even if I stayed at Morgan Management, because it's privately owned, Morgan would never offer me a percentage of their business. So Mom and Dad figured forty-nine percent of the family business was better than zero percent working somewhere else. If my parents had me on board before they made the sale, then I went as part of the agreement."

"Wait, I know I'm not supposed to talk, but I'm really confused."

He pushed his plate away. A plate he didn't have to cover because most of his food was still on it. "Go ahead. I know it's confusing. It gets worse, so ask now."

Dread just tapped on my shoulder. "They pulled you away from Morgan to do this? Why didn't they talk to you first? They've told you since before college that the business was yours to inherit."

"My father said he figured I'd never leave Morgan unless another company gave me an over-the-top offer or unless they offered me part of their business. Well, they couldn't control an over-the-top offer, but they could lure me away with their percentage. I couldn't buy-in, my father said, if I stayed at Morgan. So, they gave me forty-nine percent."

He slumped in the chair and stared at the table. "All those years my father joked that he buys and sells and doesn't even need merchandise. And now I'm the merchandise."

Not once had rage crept into his voice. But quiet resignation and defeat crawled all over him.

"They said they didn't include me in the buy-out discussion because they didn't want my hesitation ruining the deal for them."

"But that doesn't make sense. They could've sold a hundred percent without you."

"Yes, but in their minds, that meant I might never own a business. He pushed his palms into the table. "Do you mind if we sit outside? I'm not hungry, and . . ."

I carried my plate and glass outside to the patio table. Carl lit citronella candles to discourage the mosquitoes. He pulled out a chair for me, then sat in the one next to mine. The thick night air closed in around us.

He unbuttoned his shirt sleeves and folded the cuffs up—equal widths of course. "I devoted my life to them, to being the son they wanted." Carl sounded broken. "I went to the college they wanted me to attend. I wasn't given a chance in their business when I graduated. I didn't question their decision. Then they sell me out. Manipulated the entire chain of events. Orchestrated it all."

A coil of anger wound itself around the solid brick of resentment in my gut, and I wanted to fling the entire contraption at Carl's parents. But a familiar breeze stirred in my consciousness. I leaned back as Carl continued.

"In fact, that night at the club when they found out you'd been at Brookforest for drinking, they wanted to talk to me because they knew this deal was in the works. Hate to say it, but they didn't care about you. They were afraid of any scandal. That's what they told me that night. They wanted to know if very many people knew." At this point in the telling, Carl's demeanor shifted. His indignation resurrected his betrayal.

"That depends if you count the AA people," I said, "but we don't share last names. Lucky for your parents."

I pushed a chair over and propped my feet up. We never did install that fountain we talked about. It would have made for a much more soothing backdrop than the neighbor's kids jumping like human popcorn on their trampoline in the yard behind us. In a few years, there might be payback from this backyard. I consoled myself with that.

"What really infuriates me is they told me they did this for me," he said. "To help me. To give me a chance at a life like theirs. They were saving me from myself. And what they were really saying is that I was too dumb to make my own decisions. They don't understand what I'm so upset about. My mother suggested I was ungrateful."

That breeze of recognition I felt earlier gathered wind. I understood more than he realized.

"After Vic's accident, they threw themselves into their business to kill the pain. They'd planned to turn it over to him. I knew that. But after he died, I was all they had. And I was never going to measure up." He looked at me with genuine confusion in his eyes. "Did they think I was so stupid that I didn't connect the beer they talked about in Vic's car to the crash?" He shook his head. "The home of the 'no-talk' rule. We all know Vic died because he drove drunk, but we're not ever going to talk about it. I spent my whole life trying to be the good son. And look what it got me—betrayal. What was the point?"

He'd been talking to the cedar decking under his feet and didn't look at me when he asked the question. The unspoken answer bored a hole through the family façade. Carl knew if he could see through the veneer that it meant everyone else could now see in. I reached for my glass and wished the water could dilute the swell of regret rising in my throat.

"When you went into Brookforest," he said, "I felt like I do tonight. Betrayed, angry, resentful. Probably said some of the same things. Then you came out, and I expected the Leah who went in, but without a drink in your hand. But it hasn't worked like that. Now my parents aren't the people I thought they were. Or maybe they never were. Maybe they were like this the whole time, and I couldn't see it. Where does that leave me?"

That leaves you where I began months ago.

I gathered his hands in mine. If trust could begin with this touch, with knowing our brokenness bound us to each other, it might be a place to begin. If not, it would be a place to end.

"I know you're in pain," I said, "and maybe this isn't the ideal time to share this. But sometimes you can't write a script for grace."

He looked at me, a shade drawn over whatever expression might have been there.

I told him about Molly's breast cancer and what I learned was possible in a relationship. How friendship can sometimes take you places love is afraid to go.

I told him about the last two sessions with Melinda, what I had learned about myself, and how the seeds of fear that my mother planted grew in my relationship with him.

Serenity. Courage. Wisdom.

He didn't say anything. The glare of street lights blocked the view of the stars. I felt surrounded by scowling white eyes.

"I blamed you for Alyssa's death," I said. "I blamed you for not letting me go to her that night." I let go of his hands and wiped the tears wetting my cheeks. "If I blamed her death on you, then it didn't have to be my fault. I had the power to say no. Anytime. All those years, I could have said no. I just couldn't see it then."

He looked confused instead of relieved. "What does this have to do with my parents?"

Where are you, God?

"Nothing." Confusion must be contagious. I wanted to be angry with him. I'd ripped my heart out and handed it to him, and he'd tossed it away like a child who plays with the wrappings instead of the gifts. Maybe I spoke too early, but it was too late to be careful with my words now. I tried again. "This is about us. Before tonight, I didn't think we could save this relationship. Maybe this is a chance."

"I don't know anymore," he said. "I feel like I don't know you, my parents, myself. I feel like you've expected me to change along with you. Not like you've given me a list, but I almost wished you had. I thought if you fell in love with me back then, you could fall in love with me now. I thought you'd still love the Carl you married."

The clarity of seeing myself in Carl broke me open, just like God's grace had intended. It struck the fault lines in my life. But I didn't shatter. God used my weakness for His strength. Perhaps those shattered pieces could begin to fill the spaces between us.

"The Carl I married and the Leah you married no longer exist—at least not in the ways we expected. That doesn't mean love is impossible," I said.

Silence.

Carl stared at me as he did that day at the airport, curious, knowing, and yet not. "I don't know. I'm overwhelmed. I don't know myself or what I want. For so long, my parents steered my life, and I trusted them. Now the people I love aren't who I expected them to be. I don't know if I can be the husband you need. I don't know if I can love the person you're becoming."

I hadn't been able to predict that his parents were going to betray him because I couldn't see past my own hurt—past how they felt about me. The winds carried me back to a grocery store. Apple juice. A sense of being outside of myself to see above the fog.

"If I'd known who I was, I wouldn't have needed the time away to get well. You gave that to me." Carl shifted in the chair. "Okay, maybe not so willingly. But you were still here when I came home, so you didn't give up on me—on us. We don't need to solve everything tonight."

He covered my hands with his own. "I've always loved your intensity. At times I admired it. Sometimes it frightened me." He sighed. "But there's just so much pain between us."

"What are you saying?" The tug in my heart suspected the answer, but I needed to hear it from him.

He stood up and walked around the table, lowered himself on his heels, and placed his hands on my knees.

"I need to spend another month on the job I started. Or, I guess I should say the one my parents started. So, that's what I'll do—stay one more month. By then, their part of the sale should be finalized. The office should be finished."

He stood and drew me up toward him. "I need time, Leah. Time to catch up with you. Time to learn who I am. Time to learn who I can be."

I had memorized his face so many times in anger; I couldn't remember the last time I looked at him with love. I cradled his face in my hands. My fingertips brushed his forehead. What would become of us? Could forgiveness be enough?

"One month. You waited for me. Now it's my turn to wait for you."

Discussion Questions

1. Molly puts her friendship with Leah on the line when she confronts her about drinking, and though Molly didn't know it until later, Leah was ready to hear the truth. If you have friends involved in behaviors, either addictive or questionable, are you hesitant to approach them? What prevents you from having this discussion with them? If you've had a discussion with a friend, like Molly with Leah, how did that turn out? What difference did it make, if any, in your friendship?

2. Sometimes, like Leah, we believe we're keeping our image under control. And sometimes, like Leah, we discover we aren't. What perception did Leah want people to have of her? Her marriage? Why? Was the "emotional cost" paid by Leah for managing her image more than she thought?

3. What preconceived notions about people does Leah have that surface in rehab and AA meetings? Did this discovery influence your perception of Leah? Explain.

4. The author included Leah's personal journal entries. What were your feelings as you read those? How did the journals contribute to the novel?

5. Why do you think the author chose to reveal Leah's thoughts by interspersing the journals throughout the novel? How does writing about something affect your perceptions of the people involved and/or the situation?

6. Why do you think Leah married Carl? Would that be the same reason(s) Leah thinks she married him?

7. What are your thoughts about Carl? Does your opinion of him change during the novel? Explain.

8. Discuss the influence of family dynamics in both Carl's and Leah's family.

9. How important is Leah's relationship with God as she faces recovery?

10. Leah finds her physical relationship with Carl difficult, if not impossible. Do you believe Carl was as demanding as she portrayed him? In other words, is she a reliable narrator when it comes to their physical relationship?

11. What advice would you give couples who face intimacy issues in the bedroom like Carl and Leah?

12. Carl and Leah blame one another for what happened to Alyssa. Why?

13. Glass is a recurring motif in the novel. Discuss what it represents to Leah.

14. Does Leah use her humor as a shield or a weapon? Explain.

15. How is this a "story of unscripted grace"?

16. What does Molly really mean when she says that she and Devon can have fun in the closet?

17. How important does Leah's relationship with God become when she decides not to return to a *Southern Living* life?

18. Titles are always important. Why do you think the author chose *Walking on Broken Glass*?

Want to learn more about author
Christa Allan and check out other great
fiction from Abingdon Press?

Sign up for our fiction newsletter at
www.AbingdonPress.com
to read interviews with your favorite authors, find tips
for starting a reading group, and stay posted on what
new titles are on the horizon. It's a place to connect
with other fiction readers or post a
comment about this book.

Be sure to visit Christa online!

www.christaallan.com

What they're saying about...

Gone to Green, by Judy Christie
"...Refreshingly realistic religious fiction, this novel is unafraid to address the injustices of sexism, racism, and corruption as well as the spiritual devastation that often accompanies the loss of loved ones. Yet these darker narrative tones beautifully highlight the novel's message of friendship, community, and God's reassuring and transformative love." —*Publishers Weekly* **starred review**

The Call of Zulina, by Kay Marshall Strom
"This compelling drama will challenge readers to remember slavery's brutal history, and its heroic characters will inspire them. Highly recommended."
—*Library Journal* **starred review**

Surrender the Wind, by Rita Gerlach
"I am purely a romance reader, and yet you hooked me in with a war scene, of all things! I would have never believed it. You set the mood beautifully and have a clean, strong, lyrical way with words. You have done your research well enough to transport me back to the war-torn period of colonial times."
—Julie Lessman, author of *The Daughters of Boston* series

One Imperfect Christmas, by Myra Johnson
"Debut novelist Myra Johnson ushers us into the Christmas season with a fresh and exciting story that will give you a chuckle and a special warmth."
—DiAnn Mills, author of *Awaken My Heart* and *Breach of Trust*

The Prayers of Agnes Sparrow, by Joyce Magnin
"Beware of *The Prayers of Agnes Sparrow*. Just when you have become fully enchanted by its marvelous quirky zaniness, you will suddenly be taken to your knees by its poignant truth-telling about what it means to be divinely human. I'm convinced that 'on our knees' is exactly where Joyce Magnin planned for us to land all along." —Nancy Rue, co-author of *Healing Waters* (*Sullivan Crisp* Series)
2009 Novel of the Year

The Fence My Father Built, by Linda S. Clare
"...Linda Clare reminds us with her writing that is wise, funny, and heartbreaking, that what matters most in life are the people we love and the One who gave them to us."—Gina Ochsner, Dark Horse Literary, winner of the Oregon Book Award and the Flannery O'Connor Award for Short Fiction

eye of the god, by Ariel Allison
"Filled with action on three continents, *eye of the god* is a riveting fast-paced thriller, but it is Abby—who, in spite of another letdown by a man, remains filled with hope—who makes Ariel Allison's tale a super read."—Harriet Klausner